THE PALACE

A SIMON RISKE NOVEL

CHRISTOPHER REICH

MULHOLLAND
BOOKS

Little, Brown and Company
New York   Boston   London

Copyright © 2020 by Christopher Reich

Hachette Book Group supports the right to free expression and the value of copyright. The purpose of copyright is to encourage writers and artists to produce the creative works that enrich our culture.

The scanning, uploading, and distribution of this book without permission is a theft of the author's intellectual property. If you would like permission to use material from the book (other than for review purposes), please contact permissions@hbgusa.com. Thank you for your support of the author's rights.

Mulholland Books / Little, Brown and Company
Hachette Book Group
1290 Avenue of the Americas, New York, NY 10104
mulhollandbooks.com

First Edition: August 2020

Mulholland Books is an imprint of Little, Brown and Company, a division of Hachette Book Group, Inc. The Mulholland Books name and logo are trademarks of Hachette Book Group, Inc.

The publisher is not responsible for websites (or their content) that are not owned by the publisher.

The Hachette Speakers Bureau provides a wide range of authors for speaking events. To find out more, go to hachettespeakersbureau.com or call (866) 376-6591.

ISBN 978-0-316-45601-2
LCCN 2019955205

10 9 8 7 6 5 4 3 2 1

LSC-C

Printed in the United States of America

THE PALACE

To my daughters, Katja and Noelle,
and my mother, Mildred "Babs" Reich,
with love

THE PALACE

CHAPTER 1

Cannes
Côte d'Azur, France

Set the timer," said Simon Riske.

"How long?" asked Lucy Brown.

"Four minutes." Simon moved across the spacious bedroom, eyes fixed on the painting.

"Why four?"

"The security system monitors activate all locks every two minutes. I figure we have another two on top of that in case they decide to send someone to check. I don't want to be here to find out if I'm right."

"In case? I thought you stole the key. Why would they check?"

Simon looked at Lucy. Enough questions. "Set it. Now. And make it three minutes thirty seconds."

Simon took the phone from his pocket and approached the painting. Activating the camera, he stepped back to ensure the entire canvas was in the frame and snapped a photograph. He examined the result. Satisfied that it was in focus and that the artist's signature was visible, he sent it to an office on the eleventh floor of a modern steel-and-glass skyscraper in the heart of the City, the one-square-mile section of London that was home to many of the world's financial juggernauts. The reply came back like a bullet.

Confirmed. Proceed.

Simon lifted the painting off the wall and set it on an onyx coffee table in the center of the bedroom. The canvas measured forty-two inches by thirty. It showed the façade of Rouen Cathedral at sunset and had been painted by Claude Monet in 1894. Estimates of its value ranged from thirty to fifty million dollars. Twenty-five years ago, it had been stolen from the famed Rijksmuseum of art in Amsterdam.

Simon Riske had come to steal it back.

"May I?" He extended his hand. Lucy placed a tube of lipstick in his palm. Simon removed the cover and spun the bottom, releasing a razor-sharp blade. "Time?"

"Three minutes." Lucy bounced up and down on her toes, not an easy feat given her four-inch heels. She was dressed in a black designer cocktail dress with a plunging neckline and high heels with fire-engine-red soles. Simon didn't care much about fashion. Prior to this assignment he'd thought "mules" were animals, not shoes. He'd accompanied Lucy to Harvey Nichols to buy her outfit and was still in shock at the price of feminine couture. He'd been sure to keep the receipt for his expense report.

During daylight hours, Lucy worked as an apprentice mechanic in his automotive repair shop in southwest London, a stone's throw from Wimbledon, better known as the All England Lawn and Tennis Club. Instead of a three-thousand-dollar dress and fancy high heels, she wore a gray coverall and work boots, and kept her blond hair tucked beneath a baseball cap. Simon's relationship with her was strictly platonic, somewhere between friend and father. In a sense, she was his own restoration project. But that was another story.

As for Simon, he was dressed befitting the occasion, a black-tie dinner dance and auction to benefit an international charity held on the first night of the Cannes Film Festival. He was a compact man, markedly fit in a peaked-lapel dinner jacket, his bow tie hardly perfect, but his own doing. His hair was dark and thick, receding violently at the temples and cut to a nub with a number two razor. He had his father's dark complexion and brooding good looks and his mother's beryl-green eyes. People mistook him for a European—Italian, Slavic, something Mediterranean. His nose was too bold, too chiseled. His chin, too strong. Take off the tux, add a day's stubble, and he'd fit in hooking bales of Egyptian cotton across a dock in Naples.

Simon had a second profession besides restoring old cars. It involved remedying thorny, often unorthodox problems for an array of clientele: corporations, governments, wealthy individuals. Or, in this case, an insurance company—Lloyd's of London—and, by extension, the Rijksmuseum of Amsterdam.

Back to work.

With care, he punctured the canvas at the uppermost corner and drew the blade firmly and steadily along its perimeter—down, across, up, across—wincing at the rip of tearing linen twill. Removing the canvas from the frame in this manner would reduce its size by only an inch on its borders, or so he'd been told. Still, it was hard not to feel as if he were desecrating something sacred.

From the floor below came the sound of applause and laughter, followed by a burst of music. The auction was over.

"Time?"

"Stop asking," said Lucy. "You're making me nervous."

"Don't be," said Simon, giving her a smile to calm her down. "We're almost out of here."

A sharp knock on the door erased the smile.

"Mr. Sun? It's Pierrot from security." English with a strong French accent.

Lucy shot Simon an angry glance. "I thought you said four minutes."

"You locked it, right?"

"I know how to follow instructions."

"Stall."

"How?"

"Talk to him."

"And say what?"

"You're a woman in a billionaire's bedroom. Think of something."

The billionaire in question was named Samson Sun, the nephew of the Indonesian minister of finance and brother-in-law of a Malaysian king. To the world, he was known as a businessman and philanthropist, and, more recently, a movie producer.

Simon had met him a month earlier at an automobile auction held

5

at the Villa d'Este on Lake Como. It was a setup to begin with, the Monet having been spotted in a photograph in a piece on Sun appearing in the French edition of *Architectural Digest*. When Sun purchased a Ferrari at auction the final day (a 1966 275 GTB Berlinetta for fifteen million euros), Simon introduced himself as the man who'd overseen its restoration and offered his services should Sun have any other automobiles so in need. A conversation ensued, then later a lunch and a dinner, after which Sun insisted that Simon attend his fundraiser the following month in Cannes.

"I'm sorry," called Lucy, cheek pressed to the door. "Mr. Sun is in the bathroom."

"Please open up, madame. It is necessary."

"I can't," she said. "I don't have any clothes on."

"Is Mr. Sun with you?"

Lucy looked to Simon, who nodded. The security system would show it was Sun's key that had opened the door. "Of course he is. Who else do you think I'm with?"

"Please ask him to come to the door."

"Oh, all right," said Lucy, aggravated. "Don't get in a tizzy. I'll tell him."

Simon returned his attention to the job at hand. One by one, he sliced the last stubborn threads and freed the canvas from the frame. "Give it to me," he said. "Quick."

Lucy reached into her purse and took out a plastic packet the size of a neatly folded handkerchief. Simon tore open the packet and shook loose a black polyurethane cylindrical tube. Handing it to Lucy, he rolled up the painting as tightly as possible and, with her help, slipped it inside. A drawstring drew the cylinder snug, hardly more than an inch round. Lucy removed another item from her purse—a red bow—and affixed it to the carrier.

"A present from our host," said Simon.

The knocking recommenced, louder this time.

"Madame, please. Open the door."

Simon heard the guard trying the lock, finding it secured from the inside. He imagined Pierrot had just learned that Samson Sun was not, in fact, in his bedroom about to enjoy intimate relations with one of his guests, but downstairs presiding over his auction.

The pounding increased in intensity.

Simon placed a call. Somewhere circling above them in the sky there was a helicopter waiting to pick them up. "We're ready to skip town. How far out are you?"

"No go. Mechanical issues. We're still on the ground."

"What do you mean? We need to get out of here yesterday."

"Nothing I can do. I'm grounded until a mechanic gets here. Good luck."

Simon muttered an appropriate expletive and hung up. "We're on our own."

"I guess it's too late to put it back," said Lucy.

"Just a little."

"Your move, boss."

"Open the door," said Simon. "Let him in."

"And then?"

"I tell him a bedtime story and give him a kiss good night. Ready?"

Lucy nodded, but he could read the fear in her eyes. It was not the first time he'd brought her along on a job, but it was the first time he'd enlisted her active participation.

He extinguished the lights and took up position beside the door, back against the wall.

Lucy swallowed hard, then opened the door. "Yes? Can I help you?"

Pierrot the security guard looked at Lucy, then shouldered his way past her into the bedroom. Simon stepped forward and punched him in the kidney, as painful a spot as there was, then placed him in a headlock, arm drawn savagely across the neck to impede the carotid artery and cut off the flow of blood to the brain. Pierrot struggled but was no match for surprise and superior strength. His body went limp. Simon lowered him to the floor, removing his earpiece and lapel microphone.

"*Pierrot, ça va?*" asked a rough voice. "*Qu'est-ce qui se passe?*"

"*Tout va bien,*" answered Simon, his French that of a native.

"C'est toi, Pierrot?"

Simon frowned, dropping the microphone and earpiece onto the floor. That was a fail. "Time to move."

Carrier in hand, he guided Lucy into the corridor, turning left and advancing down the narrow hall before descending a flight of stairs. The music grew louder. The din of excited voices reached them as the dance floor came into view. A man in a dark suit identical to Pierrot's pushed his way toward the stairwell. Simon stopped. Options for escape were dwindling rapidly. Turning, he told Lucy to retrace her steps, placing a hand in the lee of her back. "Faster."

Lucy ran up the stairs, pausing at the top to remove her shoes.

"To your right," said Simon, praying that his memory of the location's layout held up.

A glance over his shoulder proved the security guard was following. Ten feet away a door blocked their progress. Lucy struggled to open the latch.

"Let me." Simon threw the lock, sliding the door open. A stiff breeze rushed over them. A spray of water. The sharp scent of salt, brine, and rain. "After you."

Lucy stepped onto the fourth deck of the ship, seventy feet above the Mediterranean Sea. Two miles distant, across an expanse of sea, the lights of Juan-les-Pins and Cannes glimmered like diamonds. "Which way?"

"Aft." Simon noted Lucy's puzzled gaze and pointed to the rear of the vessel. "That way."

The vessel was the *Yasmina*, a 503-foot mega-yacht built by Blohm+ Voss shipyards of Hamburg, Germany, with a crew of seventy, including two full-time skippers and room for thirty guests, powered by a triple-screw diesel engine with a maximum speed of thirty knots and a range of three thousand miles.

Lucy jogged across the deck, stopping alongside the elevated helipad. Simon stared into the night sky, hope over reason. A gust knocked him back a step. He saw no flashing lights, only a bank of clouds approaching from the Maritime Alps. There would be no miracles tonight.

Behind them, the security guard emerged onto the deck, pistol drawn and held to his thigh. "Excuse me, monsieur. Would you mind stopping for a moment?"

Simon deftly handed Lucy the carrier. "Oh, hello. Is there something the matter?"

The guard spoke a few words into his lapel mike, then holstered his weapon inside his jacket. "Can you both accompany me?"

"We were just enjoying the night air," said Simon, as a drop of rain struck him in the eye.

"Of course you were. I'm sure it won't take more than a minute."

Simon looked toward Lucy. "Honey, can you come here? This gentleman would like to have a word with us."

"Really? What for?" A look of confusion for Simon. A smile for the security guard. She took Simon's hand and leaned her head against his shoulder.

Not bad, thought Simon. Not quite ready for the BBC production of *Romeo and Juliet,* but well done, all the same.

"Happy to," he said to the guard. "We just left the auction. I never knew dinner and a boat ride could cost so much."

"I'm sure Mr. Sun will be grateful."

"I certainly hope so." As Simon spoke, he stepped toward the guard, placing one foot inside his stance, then attacking—as nimble as a cat, as fast as a cobra—taking hold of the man's lapels, pivoting sharply, launching him over his hip and shoulder, and out over the railing of the boat. The guard's cry and subsequent splash was drowned out by the pounding music emanating from the open-air dance floor. The *Yasmina* was underway, making 10 knots. In moments, the man had disappeared in the roiling sea.

"Will he be all right?" asked Lucy.

"A mile to shore," said Simon. "Give or take. He'll be fine." But he wasn't sure. A mile at night was an eternity. *With the storm . . .*

"We need to get off the boat. Pronto."

He directed her to the far side of the helipad and down a flight of exterior stairs, calculating the time until the painting was discovered missing, if it had not already been. At the bottom of the stairs, guests spilled onto the main deck. Most were dressed similarly to him and Lucy. Men in dinner jackets, women in cocktail dresses. Inside, the grand salon had been transformed into a mock-up of Studio 54, the fabled New York discotheque. A raised dance floor lit from below, DJ booth, mirror ball, go-go dancers on pedestals. Earth, Wind, and Fire blasted from the speakers. The only thing missing was Bianca Jagger riding a white stallion and Andy Warhol huddled in a booth with Halston and Elizabeth Taylor.

Simon led the way across the salon, happy for the anonymity afforded him by the throng of revelers. He stole a flute of champagne from a passing waiter and downed it. There was no reason to believe anyone would be looking for them. One guard had seen the two of them in Samson Sun's bedroom, and that had been but briefly and in the dark. He'd been left unconscious, but for how much longer? The only other person to suspect them was currently swimming to shore.

A British actor famous for his blue eyes, tousled hair, and beguiling stutter placed a hand on Lucy's arm, nuzzling her with far too much familiarity. Simon couldn't hear what he said to her. It didn't matter. The actor was older than her by three decades. Simon whispered a few words of his own into the actor's ear and the man dropped his hand as if he'd been shocked.

"But that was—" Lucy said.

"Yes, it was."

"And he wanted to—"

"I'm sure he did."

"Mr. Riske! There you are!"

Simon turned and found himself face-to-face with a short, pudgy, bald Asian man of indeterminate age. Thirty? Fifty? It was impossible to tell. "Samson, hello. And please, call me Simon."

"I missed you at the auction." Indonesian accent by way of Oxford. At least, that's what he'd told Simon.

"Too rich for my blood, I'm afraid."

"You? I doubt that." Samson Sun was dressed entirely in white—suit, shirt, tie, even his shoes—his one contrasting feature the round, black-framed eyeglasses that were his trademark. Sun turned to Lucy, the top of his head reaching her chin. "And who's this lovely creature?"

"My friend, Lucy Brown. Lucy, say hello to Samson."

"A pleasure, I'm sure."

Behind the pebble lenses, Sun's eyes stayed on Lucy a beat too long. "What's this, then, Miss Brown? A present for your host?"

Lucy's mouth worked, but no words came out.

"Actually, you gave it to her," said Simon.

"Me?"

"A door prize."

Sun returned his attention to Lucy. "Please join me," he said, gesturing to a table at the back of the room. "You may find some new clients."

"Thank you, but we wouldn't want to interrupt." Simon placed a hand on Lucy's elbow as his eyes scanned the room for trouble.

"Not at all. Perhaps Miss Brown would like to meet the cast of my movie." He took Lucy's hand. "Are you an actress by any chance?"

"An actress? Me? Course not."

Sun had come to Cannes as the producer of a movie called *The Raft of the Medusa*. The film was based on a true story of a group of African refugees whose boat had sunk as they made the crossing from Libya to Italy and had spent three hellish weeks adrift on a makeshift raft, nearly all of them perishing. Several of the survivors played themselves in the movie. Simon spotted them seated at Sun's table.

"Next time," said Simon. Then: "You'll be in Cannes the entire festival?"

"Naturally," said Sun. "Our film is to be shown closing night. A prestigious honor."

"Congratulations. We'll see you on the Croisette. And thank you for the invitation. Great party."

"Good night, Mr. Riske. And good night, Miss Brown. I hope to see you again."

Simon guided Lucy across the floor, past a vodka bar carved

entirely from ice and tended by pretty blondes clad in string bikinis and faux-fur *shapki*. Out of the corner of his eye, he saw that Sun had returned to his table, taking his place at the center of his entourage. A moment later, a commotion as two security guards arrived at his table. One was Pierrot, no longer unconscious nor on the floor of Sun's bedroom.

Time's up.

Simon ducked out a side door, Lucy in tow, and onto the fantail. He glanced over the rear safety railing. Two RIB tenders—twenty feet long, rigid inflatable hull, dual Mercury outboards—sat moored to the floating dock, crew in white tunics and navy-blue shorts at the ready. Somewhere belowdecks there was a miniature submarine as well (for pleasure? escape?), but Simon was no Captain Nemo. He was, however, a good Marseille boy who'd spent enough hours making trouble on the docks of the Vieux-Port to know the difference between a half hitch and a reef knot, and how to drive anything with a motor, on land or sea.

"This way," he said, setting off to the crew's ladder, which descended to the floating deck. "If anyone asks, you're sick. You need to get to a hospital straightaway."

"I am?" said Lucy. "I mean, *yes, I am.*"

"Quick learner."

Simon reached the bottom of the ladder, offering Lucy a hand. "The lady needs to get to shore," he said to the mate. "She's ill."

"The boat will dock in forty minutes. We're returning to port due to the weather."

"Too long," said Simon, palming the mate a wad of one hundred euro bills—he didn't know how many.

The mate glanced at the money. The film festival. Movie people. Rogues. Rule breakers. He answered without hesitation. "Come aboard."

Simon helped Lucy onto the nearer tender. A high-pitched whistle sounded as he placed his foot onto the gunnel. Pierrot was leaning over the railing above their heads, hand pointed at them. "Keep them here," he shouted as he made his way to the ladder.

Simon jumped into the cockpit, tearing off his bow tie and throwing it into the sea. The engine was idling. The mate stood onboard, mooring rope in hand, looking confusedly between Pierrot and Simon. The tender's skipper—eighteen, crew cut, yet to have his first shave—confronted Simon. "Sir, I can't—"

"Get off," said Simon.

"Yes, sir." The skipper and the mate both stepped around him and boarded the *Yasmina*.

Simon put the tender into reverse, spinning the wheel to port, then sliding the throttle forward. The nose rose. Wake spread behind the boat. Pierrot and another guard clambered aboard the second tender. Simon increased his speed. The sea was rising, wind from the Maritime Alps scudding across the surface, stirring up whitecaps, sending spirals of spume into the air.

Simon killed the running lights. The speedometer read 25 knots, and he was astonished to see the markings went to 80. "Hold on," he called over his shoulder. "This is going to get bumpy."

He shoved the throttle forward. The twin outboards roared. The hull slapped the water with force. Instead of heading toward shore and safety, however, he steered in a straight line, retracing the *Yasmina*'s path.

"Where are you going?" shouted Lucy.

Simon ignored her. He looked over his shoulder. A quarter of a mile separated them from their pursuers. He searched the water to either side of the boat, looking for a head, an arm, any sign of the man he'd thrown overboard. *There.* He spotted him, the man no longer wearing a jacket, his white shirt visible. He was on his back, struggling.

Simon cut the engines and made a tight circle. "Give me a hand."

Leaning over the gunnel, he grabbed the guard's collar and, with Lucy's help, hauled him aboard.

The guard lay at Lucy's feet, coughing seawater, exhausted. *"Merci,"* he managed, weakly.

Simon freed the man's pistol from his shoulder holster and threw it into the water. "Stay," he said to his face. Then to Lucy: "Watch him. If he moves a muscle, shout."

Simon removed his own jacket and tossed it to the guard, telling him in French to cover up.

He retook the wheel. A hundred yards separated him from his pursuers. Rain began to fall in earnest, wind freshening by the minute. He turned the boat toward shore and hit the throttle for all it was worth. The nose jumped precipitously, knocking him to his knees. It wasn't a tender, it was a Cigarette in drag.

Across the bay, boats were making for port. On shore, dock lights blinked red. Danger. Storm conditions.

Simon scanned the coastline. He couldn't go to Cannes or Antibes. Sun's security team would have radioed ahead to arrange a welcoming committee. He fumbled in his pocket for his phone. Under *M* he dialed a number he'd sworn never to call again. A familiar voice answered.

"Ledoux. What now?"

"Where are you, Jojo?"

"It's nine o'clock on a Wednesday night. Where do you think I am? In the middle of ten plates of *moules-frites*."

Jojo Matta was a lousy hood and a gifted cook. Once, a very long time ago, they'd worked together committing all manner of illegal acts. Last year Jojo had helped Simon with a small problem in Monaco. As payment, Simon had helped Jojo open a restaurant in Juan-les-Pins, a leafy hamlet adjacent to Antibes.

A spit of land extended into the bay to his right, the peninsula that separated the Bay of Cannes and the Bay of Nice. At its very tip, barely visible, two lights burned red. *Maybe,* he thought.

"Jojo, how long to get to Eden-Roc?"

"People like me don't go to the Du Cap unless we're lifting something."

"Du Cap" for the Hôtel du Cap, built in 1870, long home to wealthy Europeans, cosmopolites, and their hangers-on.

"Tonight you do."

"I'm in the middle of a shift."

"You own the place. Your sous-chef can fill in. Be there in twelve minutes."

"Get lost. I'm not your errand boy."

"Who paid for your restaurant? I'll yank it. Watch me." There was only one way to talk to a gangster.

"That's not fair."

"Twelve minutes, Jojo."

Without warning, the windscreen shattered. Something struck one of his engines. The men were firing at him.

"Lie down," he called over his shoulder. Lucy didn't need telling. She was already flat on her belly.

The other tender had shortened the distance between them. Visibility was deteriorating. Rain fell in sheets, the wind a pernicious force, howling like a banshee. Lightning flashed nearby, a bolt running from heaven to sea. For a moment, the bay was illuminated, vessels of all kinds frozen in place by the burst of white light.

Simon saw his path.

Directly ahead, another mega-yacht, the *Eclipse*—five hundred feet, shark's snout, a radar globe like a Christmas ornament—Abramovich's before he sold it to an Emirati prince. A small armada had grouped off its port side, five motor yachts, give or take. He steered toward the immense vessel, speed 40 knots despite the wild bucking. He hugged the giant boat, starboard side, aware of its crew gesturing madly at him…then he was past it, spinning the wheel to port, cutting across its bow, perilously close, a 180-degree turn. He straightened out the tender, coming back along the *Eclipse*'s port side, darting in and among the smaller vessels. He cut his speed. The only sound, rain pummeling the vessel, as loud as a corps of drummers. They were a shadow bobbing on the waves, black on black.

He caught the other tender's lights rounding the *Eclipse*'s bow, turning toward them, slowing, confused, its prey lost.

Suddenly, the rescued guard was on his feet, arms waving. "Pierrot! Over here! Pierrot!"

Simon turned to see Lucy on her feet, driving her shoulder into the man, sending him toppling into the sea. "And this time you can stay there!" she called.

Simon hit the throttle and the tender sped away, the man lost among the whitecaps.

The guard shouted for help. A spotlight from another boat searched the water and found him.

By then, Simon and Lucy were far away, headed in the opposite direction, out to sea.

The second tender picked up their colleague. A moment later, it headed away, returning to the *Yasmina*.

Simon guided the boat to the dock by the Eden-Roc. A man dressed in a chef's smock, soaked to the bone, caught the mooring rope.

"I thought you were in trouble," he said as Simon cut the motor.

"I was. Now I'm not."

Jojo offered Lucy a hand. She stood unsteadily on the dock, shivering. Simon followed, taking the mooring rope and fastening it to a cleat. They climbed the stairs and walked along a gravel path beneath the pines. Jojo had parked in a lot at the base of the hotel's driveway. It was the same beat-up Peugeot he'd driven last year.

"Keys are in the ignition," he said.

Simon opened the door for Lucy. She fell into the passenger seat, wet and exhausted. He closed her door and went around to the driver's side. "I'll leave it at the airport," he said to Jojo. "Keys in the fender."

"First place anyone will look."

"Get there early."

"Tomorrow's my day off."

"Then I guess you'll have to take your chances."

"Hey," said Jojo, looking back toward the Eden-Roc. "How much do you think I can get for the tender?"

D'Artagnan Moore called as they left the hotel lot and drove along Boulevard J. F. Kennedy toward Antibes. "Get it?"

Simon handed Lucy the phone. "Tell him—"

He saw the car for a second, maybe less. Far too short a time to react. It was a Citroën panel van, the driver intoxicated, blowing through the red light, striking Simon's car on the passenger side at a speed of 70 kilometers per hour. Simon's last thought was for Lucy. She had not put on her safety belt.

He felt the blow, heard the sickening crash of metal colliding with metal, saw the lights of the van inside his car, the world suddenly a terrible blinding white.

Then darkness.

Chapter 2

Six thousand miles away, overlooking another fabled beach, this one situated on an island off the southwestern coast of Thailand, Rafael de Bourbon was suffering his third nervous breakdown of the day.

The first had come shortly after he arrived at the hotel, a few minutes past seven, and involved a malfunctioning septic tank. The second was brought on by a faulty air-conditioning unit. The third had as its cause a loose gasket that had cut all water pressure in the kitchen and was the most serious, for this was the first thing the inspectors would check upon their arrival. Hotel inspectors always started in the kitchen. Should he be unable to bring back the pressure, any chance of receiving a permit to operate the Villa Delphine in time for its first guests' arrival would go out the window.

"How long?" shouted Rafael from beneath the industrial sink.

"Thirty minutes," responded his wife, as calm as a Sunday morning.

"You're sure?"

"It's only a pipe. No one keeps a hotel from opening because of a gasket."

Rafael finished tightening the gasket and slid from beneath the sink. "I'm not taking any chances. This time we're going to do things the right way."

"By the book," said his wife, as if reciting a family rule. Her name was Delphine—a French name for an English rose, he liked to say. Delphine was thirty-four years old, lean and blond, an intelligent beauty, and holder of a First in economics from Cambridge.

"By the book," said Rafael, sealing his declaration with a kiss to his wife's lips.

Rafael Andrés Henrique de Bourbon—"Rafa" to anyone who'd known him long enough to share a beer—was six years his wife's senior, a tall, rangy Spaniard with cropped black hair, eyes that glittered like obsidian, and a trimmed beard he'd borrowed from Satan himself. In fact, "devilish" was an adjective often connected with his name, for better or worse. Stretching, he toweled the sweat from a torso covered with tattoos. There was a Madonna and child he'd gotten after a night of carousing in Rome. A Maori war band around his left arm he'd gotten in Christchurch. And a Russian Orthodox crucifix on his back he couldn't remember where he'd gotten, or why. There were sixteen in all, and he was eager to find a reason to add another.

"Watch out, darling," he said as he freed the cleaning nozzle. A torrent of pressurized water shot into the sink, spraying them both. Rafa shouted with joy. "Strong enough to strip a barnacle from a ship's hull. The Villa Delphine will have the cleanest plates on the island."

He switched off the water and replaced the nozzle in its holder. "Time to shower. A filthy hotel owner does not make a good impression."

"Stop," said Delphine, taking his hands in her own. "I want to tell you something."

"Can't it wait?"

"No," she said, giving his hands a tug. "It cannot."

Rafa stepped closer, looking into her clear blue eyes, amazed as always that a woman as beautiful, educated, kind, and selfless had decided to marry a man like him. A man far from beautiful, hardly educated, kind when it suited him, and selfless never. *"Sí, mi amor."*

"I want you to know how proud I am of you."

"For screwing up so many times?"

"For never giving up."

Sincerity. Was anything more painful to a Castilian? "Please."

Another tug to remind him who was boss. "I know things haven't gone as smoothly as we would have liked since we left Geneva."

"Smoothly? No, they have not gone smoothly."

"I want you to know, it's all right," said Delphine. "I never expected you to be perfect. What I love about you…maybe the reason I married you…is because you never give up. Never. I don't know that I've ever seen you not get back on your feet. It's who you are. These past years, sure we've made a few mistakes."

"I've made a few—"

"*We've made a few*. But look at what you've built here. It's magnificent. None of that matters anymore. Right now, right here, I'm the happiest I've been in a long, long while." She put his hands to her lips. "Thank you for not giving up."

Rafa took his wife in his arms and held her to him. After a moment, he put his mouth to her ear and whispered, "Sweetheart, may I ask you something?"

"Of course, my darling," she said, head to his chest. "Anything."

"How long until they get here?"

The Villa Delphine was indeed magnificent. Built on the last open plot of land atop the hill separating the island's two beaches, the hotel was a masterpiece of whitewashed concrete and limestone offering thirty guest suites, a dining room overseen by a Michelin-starred chef, a spa, two swimming pools, and the island's only tennis court.

It was Rafa's first foray as a hotelier, but not as an entrepreneur. Since fleeing Europe, he had opened a Mexican restaurant in Kuala Lumpur, a chain of tanning salons in Singapore, and a spin studio in Jakarta. Each had launched amid a flurry of great expectation and high hopes only to quickly and spectacularly crash. If his current maxim was "By the book," formerly it was "Cut every corner" and "Don't sweat the small stuff." Time, experience, and the demise of his personal finances had dictated a change in ethos. The Villa Delphine was Rafael de Bourbon's last stand.

And so it was that Rafa did not hurry straight to the shower as he'd told his wife but stopped first in his private study. There, after locking the door, he sat at his desk and logged on to his email. It was not his regular email, but a secret address used for the most sensitive matters accessed through an encrypted website on the dark web.

A single message from "PM" waited in the inbox. *P* for Paul. *M* for Malloy.

Rafa's finger hovered above the trackpad.

Once, in better times, he had worked with Paul Malloy in the Swiss city of Geneva. Their business had been finance—more specifically, capital: the raising thereof. In those days, they'd communicated via shared company servers using standard email addresses. No longer. The closest of friends had become what might politely be called "estranged colleagues." Depending on the contents of the message blinking on Rafa's laptop the nature of their relationship would change once again. For better. Or worse.

Rafa opened the message.

Go to hell.

Three words. Impossible to misunderstand.

Rafa felt his guts twist. It was not the answer he'd wanted. Regardless, he must now embark upon a threatened course of action. It was not a matter of a wounded ego. It was a question of justice. Of right and wrong. Of keeping one's word and honoring one's promises. As in all business affairs, it dealt with money. A severance payment of five million Swiss francs, already several years late.

For worse, then.

He double-clicked on an icon titled PETROSAUD. A list of spreadsheets appeared. They had names like: "Emirates Lease 7.14," "Indo Drill 1.15," "Saud Refine 3.16." And others named: "Commissions."

He'd always been good with other people's money: asking for it, investing it, spending it, losing it. But this…this in front of him was different. A crime. Not a single instance, but many. Over and over again. With malice aforethought. Rafa had objected. He was many things, but not a criminal.

An offer had been made. Join them. Not just Malloy, but all the big boys at the company, PetroSaud SA. It was easy money, Malloy had argued, over white wine and Dover sole at the Lion d'Or. Victimless. No one would find out. Billions for the picking.

Rafa knew better. There were always victims.

He hadn't participated, but to his lasting shame, he hadn't done anything to stop it. He was making too much money working the clean side of the business. He was in love. He planned on getting married. This was his chance to build up a stake. After a while, those justifications had worn thin. Silence amounted to complicity, sure enough. He had resigned, asking only for the bonus owed him. Five million Swiss francs.

Before him on the screen was a compendious record of Malloy's acts: names, dates, banks, accounts, monies taken in, monies invested…*or not.* Commissions paid. And more commissions. The sums were staggering. Millions. Tens of millions. Hundreds of millions. It was all there in its fantastically illegal glory.

A flash of blue caught his eye. A spray of red. Rafa looked out the window to see a procession of automobiles enter the hotel forecourt and stop in front of the fountain. He'd been expecting one inspector, maybe two. Not the entire Thai Hotel Association.

The doors of the cars opened as if synchronized. Men in tan uniforms, peaked martial caps, and mirrored sunglasses poured from the vehicles. All carried sidearms. Not hotel inspectors. Police. The "men in brown," as they were known and reviled.

Rafa understood everything at once. He'd waited too long to make good on his threat. He'd given Malloy and his friends too much time to agree. Another mistake added to the litany before it.

He had a minute to act.

Quickly, then. A new email address. A last hope. He chose several files, not all the material, but for the right set of eyes, enough. A trail.

His index finger pressed the SEND key. He waited a second, then typed in a four-digit code ordering the hard drive to destroy itself.

"Cry 'Havoc,'" he whispered, "and let slip the dogs of war."

Rafa left his office, hurrying down the stairs to the lobby. Delphine was speaking to one of the officers, the tallest one, and, by his demeanor, the leader of the group. Never one to rest on her laurels, she spoke fluent Thai to Rafa's colonialist minimum. He attempted to smile, as if he were accustomed to receiving unannounced visits from the police.

"Good morning, officer," he began in Thai, placing his palms together and bowing his head in welcome. "I am Mr. De Bourbon. What seems to be the problem?"

The policeman's answer was delivered with actions, not words. He nodded to his colleagues. They threw Rafa to the floor, hauling his long arms behind him and snapping handcuffs onto his wrists. It was a violent act, leaving Rafa stunned, bleeding from his mouth.

"Stop this," Delphine cried out. "What are you doing to my husband?"

Rafa struggled to free himself, shouting for an explanation. A baton landed on his ribs. A boot dug into his neck. From the corner of his eye, he observed the officers running upstairs to the executive floor. Delphine stood alone, hand covering her mouth. He met her gaze and read only despair and resignation. This was no accident, no case of police malfeasance or random error. The police were here because of him.

"What do you want?" Rafa managed, his mouth filled with blood. "Tell me."

Rough hands dragged him to his feet. "You are under arrest," said the tall policeman, spitting the words into his face. "You will come with us."

"What for? I've done nothing."

"Rafa, please tell them." Delphine's eyes pleaded with him. "Whatever it is they want, give it to them."

"It's nothing, Dee. I swear it."

Delphine grasped the policeman's tunic. "What has he done? Please."

The policeman shoved her violently. She fell to the ground. The other policemen returned to the lobby, one carrying Rafa's laptop, another hoisting a box of documents. In seconds, they were outside, loading their vehicles.

Rafa followed, propelled by a stiff arm to his back. At the car, he put up a fight, refusing to lower his head and climb in. The leader hit him in the solar plexus and, when Rafa doubled over, took hold of his hair and folded him into the back seat. The last words Rafael de Bourbon heard as the door slammed and the cars raced out of the forecourt were his wife's.

"Rafa...what did you do?"

CHAPTER 3

London

"**H**ow is she?" D'Artagnan Moore stood at the entry to his office on the eleventh floor of the Lloyd's of London building.

"Not good," said Simon, brushing past.

"Any improvement?"

"We'll know more in forty-eight hours."

"It's not your fault."

"Whose is it? I should never have brought her with me."

Three days had passed since the accident. Simon's shoulder ached from a partial dislocation and he'd gotten a nasty bump on the head. Otherwise he was fine. He'd handed the painting over to a representative of Lloyd's in France. He'd come to get paid.

"Sit down," said Moore. "Have a drink. I might have a bottle of that Tennessee cough syrup you seem to favor."

"You purchased a bottle of Jack Daniel's?" D'Artagnan Moore would sooner drink an ice-cold German Gewürztraminer than American sour mash whiskey.

D'Art hesitated. "Not me personally. I asked my assistant. Can't be seen to be lowering my standards."

"God forbid."

"Testy, aren't we?"

"Watch it, D'Art. Today isn't the day."

D'Artagnan Moore walked to his drinks trolley and opened the bottle of Jack. He poured two fingers into a glass, saw Simon motioning for more, and added another two. For himself, he chose a crystal decanter, single-malt scotch with an unpronounceable name, and matched Simon drop for drop.

"Health," said Moore, raising his glass. He was a big man by any standard, six feet five inches tall, three hundred pounds, a huntsman's untamed beard touching his chest, dressed as always in a three-piece suit of Harris Tweed, a calico pocket square waving from his jacket.

"Health," said Simon, finishing half the glass. He dropped into a quilted club chair, wincing only a little. "Well…does the Monet check out?"

"Ninety-nine percent. Looks very bonny."

"What does that mean?"

"It means we were right to recognize the work as the Rouen façade stolen from Amsterdam's Rijksmuseum. The first experts are inclined to confirm that it is the original."

"How many experts are there?"

"The museum received fifteen million dollars as compensation when it was stolen. Before they hand back the money, they want to be damned sure it's the real thing. The answer to your question, I imagine, is 'as many as necessary.'"

"Any word in the press?"

Moore shook his head. "A bit difficult to report the theft of a theft."

"And my fee?" asked Simon.

Moore cleared his throat. He might as well have sent up a distress flare. "Pending."

"Pending?"

"Forensics in progress. Testing the paint and canvas to confirm that they date from the era and match the artist's other works."

"If you sent me to steal a forgery, I will wrap my hands around your neck and strangle every last drop of life from your body."

"You'll do nothing of the kind," said Moore. "Since when is there anything like a sure thing? The watch you stole from Boris Blatt a while back could have been a counterfeit. We had no way of knowing beforehand. I know you're worried about Lucy, and I'd move heaven and earth to change things. But I can't. Neither can I change the nature of our work."

Simon stared out the window, down the Thames, to Tower Bridge, the HMS *Belfast,* the river coursing with maritime traffic. The world went on.

Earlier in the day he'd paid a deposit of two hundred thousand pounds for Lucy's care and rehabilitation, enough to cover a thirty-day stay. He wasn't a greedy man, far from it, but he didn't care to go bankrupt while Lloyd's took their own sweet time authenticating the painting. His fee was six percent of the paid claim, nearly a million dollars. As far as he was concerned, the money was Lucy's.

"Twenty-four years old," he said wearily. "What am I going to tell her family?"

"They don't know?"

"Lucy doesn't speak with them. I only found out where they live this morning."

"Tell them the truth, or a modified version thereof. She was injured while working." D'Art stretched a long arm for a dossier on his desk and deposited it on the table in front of Simon. "What do you Yanks say? If you get kicked off, it's best to get right back on."

Simon looked at the dossier. "I wasn't kicked off. I brought back the painting. There were just…complications."

"Ready to tell me what happened?"

"The thing was we had it. We were done." Simon ran a hand across his mouth, seeing the events of the evening play out in his mind. He'd given Moore the briefest of explanations from the hospital in Nice. Now he related in detail all that had happened, from the moment they'd boarded the *Yasmina* to the seconds before the car crash.

"Who is Samson Sun anyway?" he demanded when he'd finished. "Run-of-the-mill billionaires don't employ the Waffen-SS as security."

"No idea beyond what he says he is. Investor. Film producer. Does it matter?"

"He's no investor. I don't know what he is. All I can say is that he didn't earn the money himself to buy that yacht."

Moore pointed to the dossier. "Which brings us to your next assignment."

Simon lifted the cover, then, thinking better of it, let it fall. "Pass."

"It's right up your alley. Executive defrauding his employer. You can work from your home on this one. I don't foresee any automobiles or boats on the horizon."

"Pass," said Simon.

Moore raised a finger, a magician with one last trick. "The fee is—"

"I said, I'm done."

"Of course," said D'Art, all apologies and deference. "Forgive me for being callous. Take some time. A week. A month, even. A holiday will do you good."

"I'm *done* done," said Simon. "Tendering my resignation."

"You're not serious. You suffered a mishap. It was an accident. It can happen to anyone. Come now, Simon. I won't hear of it."

"Do you ever wonder if it's worth it? I mean all this running around to return items to their rightful owners. Watches, cars, paintings. Tracking down a million pounds pilfered here, two million there. Who really cares if a Monet stays on the wall of a boat for another twenty years? How does that measure against Lucy's life?"

Moore's expression indicated he thought this was as selfish an argument as one could make. He was a man defined by his profession. Insurance was as essential to civilized society as the rule of law. "It's not a question of the painting or of a watch or of a few million pounds pilfered here or there. It's a question of maintaining order. Of doing the right thing and punishing those who don't believe they have to. I can't think of many things more important."

"I don't do abstract. I'll leave that to you."

"You're upset."

Simon stood and went to the drinks trolley, pouring himself another. "There's a young woman I happen to care for very much lying in a hospital bed with her brain so swollen they had to cut out a piece of her skull to relieve the pressure. There's a good chance she won't live, and if she does, it's a lock she'll never be the same person she was before. If she can talk again, it will be a miracle." He finished the drink and set the glass down. "D'Art, if I don't restore one of my cars as well as I'm able, it might not win a gold medal at a Concours. Maybe it won't drive as fast as it possibly could, but that's where it ends. No one gets hurt, except for maybe a bruised ego. No one shoots at me. And I'm happy that way. I've had enough of maintaining order, as you say. Order can maintain itself without me."

Moore took a step toward him as he passed. "Please, Simon. This isn't you."

Simon stopped at the door. "You know something, D'Art? This feels like the best decision I've made in a long time."

CHAPTER 4

Tel Aviv

The chartered Gulfstream jet landed at Ben Gurion Airport at one minute past nine o'clock in the morning. It had been an eight-hour flight, two hours faster than commercial. The pilot had his instructions. Deliver the package as quickly as possible. He'd chosen the most direct route, a straight shot from Bangkok over the Bay of Bengal and across Central Asia, clipping the no-fly zones of Iraq and Iran, altitude 45,000 feet, speed 590 knots with a rare 60-knot tailwind.

A panel van waited on the tarmac. Its driver stood alongside a customs official and a member of IDF airport security, Uzi submachine gun hanging from one shoulder. They had received word, too. Formalities were to be carried out without delay.

The plane came to a halt, the fore passenger door opening before the engines spooled down. The driver climbed the stairs the moment they touched the asphalt. He disappeared inside the aircraft. When he reappeared, he carried a sealed pouch beneath one arm. As per international regulations, he handed the flight manifest over for inspection. A nod of the head and he was free to go. A longtime member of the Israeli Defense Forces and veteran of Unit 8200, the country's top-secret intelligence-gathering organization, he fired off a salute before hurrying back to the van.

He took Route 1 west, leaving the main highway at Ganot and turning north to skirt the easternmost suburbs of Tel Aviv past Ramat Gan and into the Shama Hills. His destination was a nondescript two-story office building, gray, windowless, a staple of industrial parks around the globe. There was no marking above the door, no corporate sign or logo, nothing to indicate the identity of the building's tenant. The only evidence that it was occupied at all were the numerous satellite dishes arrayed on the rooftop and the intimidating antenna that looked like the mast of an interstellar spacecraft.

"She's waiting," said a bleached-blond receptionist whom office lore claimed held the IDF women's marksmanship record. The driver ran upstairs and entered his superior's office, setting the pouch on the desk. Mission completed, he turned about-face and left the room. He knew better than to expect a thank you, or any acknowledgment at all.

The woman seated at the desk slid the pouch toward her. From her drawer, she took her paratrooper's KA-BAR knife, blooded in the line of duty, and with care sliced open the pouch. She was forty-two years of age, raven-haired with hard, unflinching blue eyes, her once considerable beauty eroded by the rigors of twenty years' toil in the service of her country. She was dressed in a tailored navy-blue suit and white T-shirt, a Star of David hanging from her neck. It was a nicer uniform than the one she'd once worn but a uniform all the same. Her name was Danielle Pine, but she was known to anyone who mattered in the business as Danni. No last name needed. She replaced the knife in its sheath and returned it to her drawer before continuing.

After completing her obligatory military service, Danni had earned a degree in applied mathematics before returning to the army as a signals intelligence officer, a code breaker. She possessed other talents and before long was snapped up by the darker side of the game, the Mossad, Israel's spy service. At some point she'd disappeared entirely, gone "deep black," working as a covert operative on missions so secret few others knew about them even today. And then, after six years, she was back, spat out the other end of the tunnel. "Blown," she'd said, on the rare occasion she discussed her work.

Today, her job title, if she had one, would be president of the SON Group, a cyber-intelligence firm founded by her father, retired general Zev Franck, himself a former spy and pioneering member of Unit 8200.

The SON Group's technology wasn't just cutting-edge. It was past that. Way past.

Danni drew the pouch toward her, already uneasy about the job, and removed the two items inside. First, a late model iPhone. No protective case. Scratched all to hell. She turned it on. A picture of an attractive blond woman filled the screen. There was no prompt for a numeric passcode. The owner preferred facial recognition. Fair enough.

Danni set the phone to one side and examined the second item: a MacBook laptop. This pleased her. The SON Group specialized in iOS and macOS operating systems—specifically, how to hack them and breach their every security measure. There was a rumor going around that the SON Group had inserted one of its engineers into the Apple software development team in Cupertino to "help" develop the latest iteration. If asked, Danni would answer with a smile to rival the Sphinx. The less said, the better.

Two men appeared in the doorway. Dov and Isaac, her two best engineers. One was short and fat. So was the other. Both had shaved heads and three days' growth of stubble. Neither had spent so much as a minute beneath the Mediterranean sun these last years.

They approached Danni's desk and without bidding scooped up the phone and the laptop. "The usual?" said Dov.

"Drain them," said Danni. "Not one drop left."

"Who's it for?" asked Isaac. "Langley? London? Hey, the phone has a little sand in it." He laughed snippily. "Don't tell me the Saudis again."

Danni shot him an angry look. The Saudis were a sore point and the reason she had barely slept these past weeks. The SON Group's clients were limited by strict company policy to governmental organizations: intelligence agencies, defense entities, security forces, and the national police of countries deemed friendly to the cause—the "cause" being democracy and the advancement of Western ideals. SON's technology had been developed with a singular purpose: to combat terror and crime. They were the good guys, even if they did charge top dollar. Danni had no problem with that.

She did have a problem with her company's technology falling into the wrong hands. Word had gotten back to her that the recent murder of a journalist critical of the Saudi ruling family (and attributed to a Saudi prince) had been abetted by SON software secretly installed on the journalist's phone, thus allowing the prince to track the journalist and lure him to his death. Needless to say, the Saudis were not a client.

"Don't ask," she snapped. "Just get it done. And fast. By yesterday."

The men left the office with the offending articles.

Danni checked her watch before placing a phone call. The time in Italy was one hour earlier. If her client wasn't out of bed, he ought to be.

"Pronto," said Luca Borgia in his rumbling baritone.

"Your package arrived from Thailand. I've assigned my best men to it."

"Danni, I cannot thank you enough," said Borgia, all charm as always. "What would I do without you? A serious matter. I'm concerned."

His unctuous manner did little to lessen her anxieties. In no way did Borgia fit the description of a SON Group client. He was as far from a governmental entity as could be imagined. Luca Borgia was a businessman. A billionaire industrialist who controlled one of Italy's largest holding companies with interests in everything from silk to steel. One of those interests happened to be a twenty percent stake in the SON Group. Borgia had been one of her father's initial investors. He was family. Company policy or not, Danni had no choice but to assist him in solving what he'd claimed was a case of industrial espionage.

It helped that she in no way countenanced the theft of company secrets. Someone had gotten their hands on her own company's closely guarded software and gifted it to the Saudis. Now a journalist was dead.

"Give me a day," said Danni.

"A day. But no longer," said Borgia. "Some matters cannot go unpunished."

CHAPTER 5

The Warwick Arms was a grand name for a block of council flats in Stepney, East London. Four grim twenty-story buildings huddled in a cruciform around an unloved park with rusting swing sets and neglected picnic tables. Simon found a parking space nearby, guiding his car through a maze of broken bottles, beer cans, and assorted trash. A group of sullen-eyed teenagers monitored his approach. Somewhere a hound was baying. He'd arrived at Gin Lane, two hundred some years later. Hogarth would feel right at home.

The Brown family occupied a flat on the sixteenth floor. Simon had called ahead. A corpulent, weathered woman in a flowered housedress, cigarette dangling from the corner of her mouth, greeted him.

"You're him," she said. "Riske. I don't suppose you have good news, seeing as how my Lucy isn't with you."

Simon nodded. "May I come in?"

"I'm Dora. Lucy's mother. But you know that." The woman swept him inside with a wave of her cigarette. "What's she done now? Go ahead. I don't shock easy."

They walked down a short hallway to the living room, just big enough for a couch, a recliner, a coffee table, and a television. All had seen better days except the television, a brand-new seventy-inch flat-screen broadcasting football highlights. Before Simon could sit, a tall, rail-thin teenage boy with a bad complexion and tousled blond hair the color of Lucy's ambled in. "Who's this, then?"

"I'm Simon Riske. Lucy works in my shop."

"This is Brian," said Dora Brown.

Simon shook their hands and said he was pleased to meet them. He noticed Brian absently scratching his upper arm and remembered that Lucy had said he was an addict. Heroin, meth, opioids, all of the above. An older brother had overdosed years before while Lucy was still at home.

"Lucy's been in an accident," he said after they'd all sat down and Dora Brown had decided not to offer him anything to eat or drink. "She's in the hospital."

His words were met with dead glances all around. No gasps of distress. Just a grudging acknowledgment of the news, as if she'd finally gotten what was coming to her.

Simon kept his explanation to the essentials. Lucy had been helping with a job in France. On the way home, they'd gotten into an automobile accident. A car had run a red light and struck the passenger side of their vehicle. Lucy had suffered a broken leg, fractured ribs, and a fractured skull. As soon as she was stable, he'd arranged for an airlift to bring Lucy to a private clinic in Surrey, where she would receive the finest treatment.

"So she's all right?" said Brian, shaking loose a cigarette. "Having a bit of a kip?"

Simon stared at the young man. "She's been placed in a medically induced coma to help relieve the brain swelling. The good news is that she's breathing on her own. The doctors are hopeful."

"She's a vegetable, then?" said Brian. "Going to be one of those drooling out the corner of her mouth, stares at you like a zombie."

"That's enough," said Simon, a bat of an eye away from dusting the kid.

A tear ran down Dora Brown's cheek as her jaw began to quiver.

"Who are you, then?" asked Brian, all outrage and bravado. "She's my sister. I can say what I please."

"Shut up," said Dora, lashing out at her son. "It's Lucy we're talking about."

"Just joking, Ma."

"Get out," she said. "Go. Leave us be."

"But—"

"Now!" Dora was out of her chair, hand pointing to the hall. Brian stormed from the room, but not before making more mocking noises.

"I'm sorry, Mr. Riske. We do what we can. Please go on. How is Lucy really?"

"As I said, she's in critical condition. We just have to wait and see."

"See what?"

"If she recovers and how well."

Dora's face clouded, and she regarded him with suspicion. "But you...you're fine. Doesn't look like you have a scratch."

Simon nodded. "I was lucky."

Dora dismissed this with a roll of the eyes. "And now? What am I supposed to do? I suppose you've come for money. Look around you. We can't afford a fancy clinic. The NHS barely pays for my diabetes medicines as it is."

"I'm seeing to her care."

Dora Brown's gaze shifted. She appraised Simon in a different vein. "You and her...you aren't?"

"Lucy is my best apprentice. Our relationship is strictly professional."

From the recesses of the flat came the sound of a baby crying. Dora didn't appear to hear. Simon rose from the sofa. "Well, then," he said, taking a step toward the hall.

"She was in France, eh?" Dora looked past Simon and out the window to a world she'd never have. "I always wanted to go to Paris."

"When Lucy's better, I'm sure the two of you can both go." Simon smiled. "Together."

Dora Brown shot him a dark glance; she'd have none of it. "Just because she's ill doesn't mean she's going to come home when she's better. Or that I'd welcome her." She leveled an accusing finger at him. "It's your kind's fault. Everything was fine until he left. He was a chartered accountant, my Reg was. Making good money. We were in Fulham then. Edward, my oldest, won a scholarship to the church school. Lucy was just a sprout. I'd just had Brian. He was difficult even then."

Simon clasped his hands, giving Lucy's mother his attention. He could see that she needed to unburden herself, as if Lucy's accident was as much her fault as Simon's.

"Are you in touch with your husband?" he asked.

"With Reg? He's gone. Twenty years now. Fell off a curb stone drunk and caved in his head. Lucy needed a father. We all did."

"I'm sorry." Lucy had told him only that her father had deserted the family, not that he was dead.

"In our blood, it seems. Reg liked his pints. My Edward used drugs. Brian, too. I like the occasional drop, don't I?"

"I have a card from the clinic where Lucy is recovering. The phone and address are right there. If you'd like to visit, I can send a car."

Dora took the card without looking at it. "Of course, we will. I work tomorrow, but maybe the weekend."

"I'm sure Lucy would like that."

The baby was still crying, louder now, and Simon wondered if anyone at all was looking after it. Dora lit a cigarette, her eyes once again hazy. "France, you say?"

Simon backed out of the room, stating that he would show himself out.

He saw the man as he exited the cracked glass doors of the Warwick Arms. A stocky figure in a black T-shirt stretched across the hood of Simon's car, for all appearances removing the wiper blades and having no qualms about doing so in full view of all passersby.

"Hey," Simon shouted, breaking into a trot. "Get off my car!"

The car was a Volkswagen Golf R, pearl-gray, polished and waxed, Momo rims, a coat of Armor All lending the low-profile tires a rich sheen. It was a stylish automobile, nothing flashy. Simon thought of it as a wolf in sheep's clothing. The 2-liter 4-cylinder turbo-charged engine put out 300 horsepower with 288 pounds of torque and was capable of propelling the vehicle from zero to 100 kilometers per hour in 4.3 seconds. He had no need to drive that fast and, with traffic as it was in London, rarely had the opportunity. For the record, he considered himself a conservative driver, almost law-abiding. Once a month, however, he drove into the countryside and put the car through its paces up and down the hills and valleys of Devon. It was his speed fix. Simon liked fast cars. It was that simple. The French had a term for this condition. *"Déformation professionnelle."*

And he had a particular affection for his windshield wipers, which were custom order from Wolfsburg.

Simon shouted again. This time the man glanced over his shoulder and returned the greeting. "Sod off," he shouted back.

The picnic tables had filled up with a dozen locals, mostly scruffy young men furiously engaged in their late-morning workout of guzzling beer and smoking cigarettes. Lift, gulp, smoke. Repeat. Simon knew the type. Once he'd been like them. Probably meaner, he decided. Definitely crazier.

One by one they abandoned their seats and moved into Simon's path.

"Leave our mate be," said one, maybe twenty years old, broad in the shoulder with muscular arms, a crew cut, and a lazy scowl. He wore a Mötley Crüe T-shirt. Simon hated Mötley Crüe.

He stopped, face-to-face with the man. He wasn't frightened. He was exhilarated. He'd been wanting to hit something since leaving Lucy in the clinic. The JD he'd had with D'Art encouraged the notion.

"He's your friend?" Simon asked.

"That's right."

"What's he doing to my car?"

The hooligan turned, addressing his crew with amusement. "This one here's a Yank." He returned his attention to Simon, giving him his best American accent. "Excuse me, sir, but you must have taken the wrong bus. I'm afraid you're in a very dodgy part of town. Bad element, if you know what I mean."

Laughter and jeers.

"I asked you a question," said Simon, matter-of-factly.

"So?" spat the hooligan. "Think I care?"

The hooligan's friends closed ranks behind Simon. There were six in all, two in tracksuits, the others in ripped jeans and T-shirts. Veterans of three-month stays in prison. Small-time drug dealers. Loan sharks, provided they could do their math. Dangerous enough.

"It would be impolite not to answer," said Simon.

"Are you saying I'm rude?"

Simon considered this. "Uncommunicative."

"This one here's got some big words. *Un-com-mun-ic-a-tive*."

The wiper thief had managed to free one of the blades and was starting on the other. The blades cost thirty pounds apiece. Simon would have to special-order them or get some of lesser quality from the dealership in Hounslow. It wasn't the cost that bothered him so much as the inconvenience.

A hand shoved Simon in the back. "Am I being uncommunicative, too, boss?"

Simon turned. The man was the biggest of the group, heavier by forty pounds, a head taller, beady eyes, arms as thick as an oak.

"No," said Simon. "You're being an asshole." He threw a jab, knuckles extended, and struck the man squarely beneath the jaw. It was a lightning strike, delivered with half of what Simon had. Half was enough. As the man collapsed, Simon spun and grabbed the hooligan, Mötley Crüe T-shirt gathered in his fists, and brought his forehead down on the bridge of the man's nose. The crunch of collapsing cartilage was audible. Still clutching his shirt, Simon chucked him to one side, if only to avoid the blood spouting from the man's ruined nose. That one was full strength, thought Simon. He didn't want to show any disrespect.

"Leave," said Simon. "Scram. It's how we Yanks say 'Get lost.'"

The remaining four turned tail. Two backed away cautiously. The smarter two ran.

Simon reached his car before the wiper thief could react. The purloined blade lay on the hood. Simon dragged the man off the car by his waistband. The thief threw an elbow. Simon grabbed the offending limb and twisted it behind the man's back, ignoring his own discomfort, giving it a powerful upward thrust, dislocating the man's shoulder, tearing a tendon or two.

The scream brought a smile to Simon's face. It wasn't a humorous smile, and part of him had an urge to use the wiper blade for an entirely different purpose than what the manufacturer had intended. Reason prevailed. Simon kicked the man in the ass as he fled.

He needed a minute to replace the blades on his wipers.

A minute after that he was driving west toward his shop.

CHAPTER 6

Singapore

In the Lion City of Singapore, it was seven o'clock in the evening, and London Li was beginning to think she'd been stood up. Seated in the Renku Lounge of the Marina Bay Sands hotel, London scanned the lobby using her well-honed instincts to select who her contact might be. Dozens of people walked past in every direction. To the casino, to the luxury shopping mall, to their hotel rooms. Was it the crooked, balding man in the gray suit or the muscular bearded man with the bowling-ball belly? The Indian with the shaggy gray hair or the elderly Chinese man who looked as if a strong wind might blow him clear across the Straits of Malacca.

The problem was twofold. First, the lobby was enormous, a hundred meters at least, running the length of the hotel's twenty-three-story atrium. And second, she didn't know who she was looking for. The email she'd received had simply instructed her to be seated at the rear corner of the lounge adjacent to the piano bar at six p.m. It had been signed "R." For all she knew, R could be a woman.

London Li was not anxiously awaiting the arrival of a date. She was here on business. Thirty-one years old, staunchly single, London Li worked as a reporter for the *Financial Times,* the newspaper printed on pink paper. Her beat was white-collar crime: fraud, corporate malfeasance, insider trading. And not your garden variety either. The big stuff only. Front page, above the fold. She'd exposed an African dictator who'd emptied his national treasury, a Scottish banker who'd manipulated the LIBOR to the tune of twenty billion dollars, and a Colombian drug lord who'd purchased a chain of U.S. banks. If half of what R claimed was true, she might be on to her biggest scoop yet. The files he'd sent painted a picture of theft on a monumental scale. Scratch that. A gargantuan scale.

Or, in the journalist's vernacular, a "Pulitzer."

London Li was ambitious. Like a shark is hungry.

An attractive Western man approached. Well-dressed, black hair, wolfish good looks. She perked up, sitting taller. He looked the type. I-banker, trader, salesman for a hedge fund. Dark suit. Open collar. AP Royal Oak. Definitely something to do with money. The man stopped at her table, appraising her a little too frankly. For a year she'd had a column in a local paper with a dreadful picture of her. Maybe he'd seen it.

"Hello," she said.

The man stood a few feet from her table, sizing her up.

"Looking for someone?" she asked.

"I think I've found her."

Maybe too "wolfish." Alarm bells sounded. "Pardon me?"

"I'll bet we could have some fun. I'm a generous guy. I'm in town for a few days. What do you say?"

French. Of course.

With a sly smile, London beckoned him closer. He placed a hand on her arm. *"Oui?"*

She dug the pointed heel of her shoe onto the man's toe and ground it as hard as she could. The man's eyes watered. His cheeks flushed. "Please. I'm sorry. I thought…"

"Va t'en foutre, con." No translation necessary.

She lifted her foot and the man limped away.

London checked her attire. Cream-colored blouse, black slacks, low heels. She wore no makeup except for eyeliner. Her hair hung to her shoulders, parted on the right and combed to one side. She was wearing her horn-rimmed glasses. How dare he think she was a hooker!

The fact was, her looks had always been a problem. Born in London (of course) to a Swedish mother and a Chinese father, she was the perfect mix of both. Hair the color of teak streaked with caramel. Eyes more Western than Asian, green in one light, hazel in the other. Sharp cheekbones and lips that were a little too suggestive. God had made a mistake. She was a serious person stuck with a seductive face.

The pianist arrived and started with Debussy. "Clair de lune." He wasn't bad. A little forced. Too much pedal.

There but for the grace of God go I, she thought, looking at the young Asian man at the piano. For the first sixteen years of her life, London's only goal had been to be a classical pianist. The next Hélène Grimaud. Maybe even Martha Argerich. She was gifted. Very good. Almost something more. With work, maybe. Ten hours a day. Six days a week. Practice, practice, practice.

And then, life…

Leaving a recital, an accident. She had reached her hand into the car for a score as the valet slammed the door. Four fingers broken. Twelve pins. Multiple surgeries. Months in a cast. And after, the inevitable. Arthritis. Fifteen years later, she couldn't entirely close her left hand. It was hard to pick up a plate; napkins were impossible.

She would never play the Salle Pleyel.

But a person like London required attention, and if not adulation, then at least appreciation. Recognition. She had always been a reader. A fan of nonfiction. True crime. She liked to write. She was driven, not especially friendly, congenitally cynical. Journalism was a perfect fit. Her professor had said she was a born muckraker. But where to look these days? The same place as always. Business. The bigger, the better. Behind every great fortune lies a great crime. It was true in Balzac's time. It was true today.

By now the time had gotten to 7:30. The seat across from her remained empty. London was a realist. R was not coming. She ordered a cold sake and a plate of dim sum, then dug her laptop out of her shoulder bag and opened R's email. She reread the letter and examined the attached spreadsheets. Was such a brazen act of larceny possible? Who would have the audacity to think of such a plan, let alone to execute it? And how had it gone unnoticed all this time?

She stared at the open seat, seized by a surge of rage at R, *whoever he or she was.* How dare he whet her appetite and not show up? If half the information he'd sent was true—and he would have to provide verification—he had an obligation to meet with her. Not to London, but to the wronged parties—in this case, millions of men and women. An entire country.

London took a sip of her drink.

Fence or ladder.

She smiled wistfully. One of daddy's sayings. Daddy, who'd abandoned them for another woman when London was just ten. How terribly un-Chinese. And then, even worse, had the audacity to go and die at the age of forty, leaving them utterly broke.

Maybe she wasn't congenitally cynical. Maybe life had made her that way. But really, what did it matter one way or the other?

Fence or ladder.

A problem, a disappointment, a failure, could be either a help or a hindrance. It could stop you cold or carry you over an insurmountable obstacle. Up to you to decide.

Without corroboration, the information R had sent her was worthless. No different than a note received from an anonymous party saying they'd seen who shot President Kennedy and it was Fidel Castro. The *FT* did not print innuendo. London needed hard proof to write an article. Without R's help there was no point in going on.

Fence.

Or…

The material was true, all of it. It was a beacon pointing her in the direction of the biggest story she'd come across in her career. She didn't need R to go on. She'd been a reporter for ten years. She had all the skills necessary. If the material was true—and her every instinct told her it was—there would be a great many people upset to see it revealed. More than upset. R could be in danger. Or worse.

A chill rattled her spine.

London stood, throwing her laptop into her bag. Forget the drink. Forget the food. She dropped fifty dollars on the table and stormed from the lounge. She wasn't afraid. She was inspired. It was her story now.

Ladder.

CHAPTER 7

London

Simon slammed his foot on the brake pedal as he passed the entrance to his shop. Parked out front was a silver Rolls-Royce Phantom: no two alike, three hundred fifty thousand pounds apiece if you could get one. Vanity plates. He knew who the car belonged to. Everyone in London did. They called him the "Sultan of Stratford," and he'd recently purchased one of the city's football clubs, returning it to English ownership after a decade of Middle Eastern control. Simon knew him for a different, less celebratory reason.

He drove around the block, turning into the alley that led to a fenced-in security lot at the rear of the shop. A sign above the work entrance read, EUROPEAN AUTOMOTIVE REPAIR AND RESTORATION. Inside, he crossed the shop floor as if on a mission, not slowing to inspect any of the dozen Ferraris currently being restored.

"He's in your office," said Harry Mason, standing in the reception, looking awestruck. Harry was pushing seventy, Irish, too feisty for his own good, and ran the shop's day-to-day operations. He loved football the way a wino loves his red. The Sultan of Stratford was the closest thing to English royalty he'd ever see. "He said he knew you, that you two went way back. Why didn't you say so?"

"Don't ever let anyone into my office again unless I say so." Simon spoke the words with more venom than he would have liked.

"But it's the Sultan—"

"Ever!"

Harry promised and withdrew, though not before muttering what he thought of his employer.

Simon drew a breath to gather himself, seized by an instinct to stand taller, puff out his chest, hating himself for it. He opened the door with authority. "Make yourself at home, Dickie," he said, striding into his office. "Or is it Sir Dickie? Or Sir Richard? I suppose congratulations are in order."

"Piss off, Riske. Just a bloody ribbon with a slug of lead on one end."

"I hope you didn't say that to the queen."

"Course not," said Sir Richard Blackmon. "Asked her if she knew the one about the three priests who walked into a pub—Anglican, Lutheran, and Protestant."

Neither man made a motion to shake the other's hand.

Richard "Dickie" Blackmon was a towering presence all the way around: size, personality, and influence. He stood six feet two inches tall, two hundred fifty pounds easy, muscle gone to fat long ago. He wore a navy-blue pin-striped suit, white shirt, and pink silk necktie with a Windsor knot as big as Simon's fist. He was not a handsome man. Watery blue eyes, a bloodhound's jowls, a nose that stuck out like a thumb and was decorated by a road map of broken blood vessels. He wore his thinning reddish hair swept off his forehead and long in the back. Several prominent rings made his enormous hands appear even bigger, great sparkling mitts that swung through the air to underscore his words. When Dickie Blackmon entered a room, people took notice. He liked it that way.

"Why the long face?" asked Dickie when Simon failed to smile. "You could give aspirin a headache."

"Probably the sight of your Roller out front. We service real automobiles here. Not half-million-pound monuments to your ego."

"I didn't know a man could bear a grudge for ten years. I'm impressed."

"Not easy," said Simon. "I'll grant you that. But against a real bastard, it can be done."

"Present and accounted for," said Dickie Blackmon, expansively. Then with an earnest aside: "The Simon Riske I knew would never have uttered an expletive."

That Simon Riske had been a private banker employed by one of the City's most prestigious institutions. Back then, Dickie Blackmon had been among his biggest clients. In a sense, Simon knew him better than most, certainly better than Blackmon would like others to. Dickie Blackmon had earned his money in commodities—silver, gold, unobtainium—and, later, real estate and property development. His code of conduct lay somewhere between the gilded side of crime and the tarnished side of business.

"What do you want, Dickie? You've got your CBE and your soccer team. I can't imagine what brings you to my neck of the woods. Don't you turn to stone if you get too far from Belgravia?"

"How about a drink to start?"

"Look around you. This is an auto shop, not *Claridge's*."

"You're telling me. I know a good cleaning service. Have this place sorted out in a day. Happy to foot the bill."

"I like it the way it is," said Simon. "If you want a drink, I'm sure there's one in your car. Doesn't your Roller run on single malt instead of gasoline?"

"I'm a gin man, as you know. Boodles, if you'd like to make a note for my next visit."

"I'd forgotten, Dickie. You can bet that I didn't forget everything else."

"May I sit?"

Simon took a seat behind his desk and motioned his unannounced guest toward the couch. With distaste, Dickie Blackmon moved the files and magazines and bric-a-brac until he had space to sit. The two men looked at each other. It was a duel. The weaker man spoke first. Finally, Dickie Blackmon cleared his throat. "I've heard around town that you're some kind of problem solver. Find people. Find money. Root out a crook here, a thief there. Bottom line: you're a man who gets things done. And discreetly. Quiet as a church mouse."

Simon tapped his armrest, noticing that his knuckles were bloodied. So much for discretion. "I'm sure you know plenty of people like me," he said, taking care to keep his hand out of sight.

"Like you, yes, but not you. You're family. Well, almost."

Simon couldn't help but smile. Dickie Blackmon must be up some kind of creek to suggest he was family. Not after all he'd done to prevent Simon from being just that.

"Spill, Dickie. I'm as wet and ready as I'll ever be."

"I see the time away from the bank has done wonders for your social skills."

"Just you wait."

Dickie leaned forward, his blue eyes like lasers. "Listen here, Riske. Serious business. It's about my daughter, Delphine."

Ten years after the fact, the mention of her name made Simon forget about everything else. "Is she in trouble?"

"In a manner of speaking. It's her husband."

"Rafa?"

"Señor Rafael Andrés Henrique de Bourbon. One and the same. Seems my son-in-law has been arrested by the Thai police and thrown into the klink on charges of blackmail, extortion, and theft, with assault and attempted injury to a police officer thrown in for good measure."

Dickie Blackmon went on to explain about Rafa's latest venture, a boutique hotel on Ko Phi Phi that was slated to open this weekend. The Villa Delphine, and yes, Dickie had put a few dollars into the thing himself. After a string of failures, Rafa looked like he'd managed to turn things around. The hotel was booked for six months. It had received a glorious write-up in the international press. All he had to do was open the doors for business. Then the police arrived. "They're talking a twenty-year sentence."

"Blackmail and extortion? Against who? Why?"

"Details are sealed in the complaint. Seems it has to do with his old shop in Switzerland. Geneva, I think. PetroSaud. Know it?"

Simon shook his head. He'd lost touch with Rafa when he'd left the bank, though, of course, that wasn't the real reason. "Blackmail? The Rafa I knew didn't have a dishonest bone in his body."

"People change," said Blackmon. "Look at you."

Was that a compliment? Simon didn't think so. "And Delphine?"

"She's beside herself. I have her tucked away at the Oriental in

Bangkok. The police dragged Rafael to the most notorious jail in the city."

Simon set his elbows on his desk, fingers steepled. Dickie Blackmon hadn't driven all the way from his home north of the river to give him news about a woman Simon hadn't spoken to in ten years and the man who'd once been his closest friend, no matter what kind of trouble they were in.

"So how can I help?"

"Can't put one past you, can I?" Blackmon stood, rolling his shoulders. "I'm working a deal to get him out. If I can secure his release—and believe me, that's a big 'if'—I need you there…*on site*…to be my eyes and ears."

"A deal?"

"Just a question of getting to the right man. It's Thailand. Rule of law written in pencil, not ink. Short of murder, everything's negotiable. Maybe that too."

"I've never been to the Far East. I don't know anything about Thailand."

"I don't need you to do the talking. Already have a lawyer to do that. I want you there as my proxy and to bring him home."

Simon weighed all he'd heard. Something was missing. He wasn't interested in finding out what. "Bad timing," he said with a pained smile. "I'd like to help, but I can't. There's someone here I need to look after. I'm sure you can find another person better suited to the task. Someone who speaks the language, to begin with."

"Kidding me? Everyone speaks English over there."

"A former government official. Someone the Thais respect. I fix cars for a living. I'm sorry, Dickie."

Shaking his head, Dickie Blackmon approached the desk, staring down at Simon with all his fury. Hammurabi standing tall to deliver his code. "You don't get it, do you?"

"Get what, Dickie?"

"'Sir Richard' to you, pip-squeak. You think it's me wants you to go? I made my opinion of you known loud and clear ten years ago. You're a guttersnipe. A pissant. Sure, you clean up nicely, but you and I both know what you really are. A thug. One more punk from the wrong side of the tracks trying to put one over on the rest of us. A convict, no less. Did you really think I'd sit still and let you marry my daughter…after all that I'd found out about you?"

Simon remembered the day, one of his worst. The threat from Dickie, still a long way from being knighted but one of London's wealthiest businessmen. Stop seeing his daughter or he'd go to the bank and give them everything he'd dug up: the truth about a felon named Simon Ledoux who'd done four years' hard time in a French penitentiary for armed robbery and attempted murder. At Les Baumettes, no less, home to the worst of the worst.

Simon rocketed to his feet. "Time to go, Dickie."

"Not quite yet." Sir Richard Blackmon drew a fat envelope from his jacket and dropped it on the desk. "Travel documents. Flights. Hotel. Even a map of the city. I'm old school. Prefer things printed out. Don't trust all that digital mumbo jumbo."

Simon looked at the envelope. "I told you, no."

"You did indeed. But, you see, I'm not the one asking. It's your friend Rafa. He isn't cooperating. He says no deal until he speaks with you."

"He asked for me?"

"Hard to believe, isn't it?" Dickie chuckled, a connoisseur of humiliation. "I thought so too."

"Well?"

"He told me to give you a message. Something about needing the monsignor if he was going to get out of this."

Simon kept his eyes locked on Dickie, hoping his surprise didn't show. "'The monsignor.' He said that?"

"Oh, for fuck's sake. Do I have to read it to you verbatim?" Dickie Blackmon shoved a hand into his pants pocket and, after a pained search, pulled out a rumpled paper. He made a face as he read the words aloud: "'Tell Simon Riske that only the monsignor can get me out of this. I need his blessing.' There, happy? Mean anything to you?"

Simon nodded. Only those closest to him knew about the monsignor: who he was, where Simon had met him, and how he'd saved Simon's life.

It was a call for help. The only words Rafa knew that would impress upon Simon the gravity of his situation. There was more, though it remained unsaid. A debt in the Spaniard's favor, but Rafa was too much the gentleman to bring it up even under the direst of circumstances. "The monsignor" was enough.

Dickie Blackmon tossed the paper onto Simon's desk. "He said that you would understand. Old times, best friends. The usual horseshit. Oh, and, of course, that he was sorry about everything."

Simon stared through Dickie, past the fleshy cheeks, the watery blue eyes, the too-white teeth. He was looking into the past, seeing himself as a newly minted banker, barely a year on the job, and seeing Rafael de Bourbon, too, his fellow trainee. It had been the beginning of an important friendship, kindred souls, latching on to each other for the difficult ride ahead. Brothers, really.

Until...

"So?" barked Dickie.

Simon slid the envelope toward himself. "When do I leave?"

CHAPTER 8

London

You, sir, are a liar."

Dickie Blackmon was gone. Simon sat alone in his office, the words echoing in his ears as if Rafa had just spoken them. In fact, it had been eleven years earlier. Half past six on a Friday night. The Blackfriar pub at the foot of Blackfriars Bridge. As was their custom, they'd met after work at the bank to trade war stories of the week past and to get the weekend started on the right foot. A minimum of three pints was obligatory to achieve what Rafa called "the proper perspective." Guinness for Simon and Stella for Rafa.

"Where is this coming from?" asked Simon, setting his pint on the counter.

Rafael de Bourbon stood next to him, nearly half a foot taller, tie loosened, glaring down at him like the devil himself. "I like to know who I can trust."

"And you can't trust me?"

"Difficult when I'm not even sure who I'm talking to."

Simon looked into his friend's eyes. Usually, they sparkled with mischief and good humor. At the moment, they were dull and steadfast.

The pub was packed to overflowing, mostly youngish men and women from the myriad financial institutions that made their home in the City. The air was warm and fuggy, the din loud enough to make conversation a chore.

When Simon said nothing, Rafa slapped a fat envelope against Simon's chest.

"For me?"

"Not *for you*," said Rafa. "*About you*. Addressed to no less than Sherlock herself."

Simon took the envelope, noting its girth and heft. "Sherlock" was the nickname given to the bank's head of human resources, or HR, a rail-thin, intense, and feared woman named Edwina Calloway who wielded absolute power over the trajectory of one's career.

"I nicked it," Rafa went on. "Go ahead. Take a look. Nothing you don't know. A chronicle of your life, or maybe I should say your secret life... *Monsieur Ledoux*."

At the sound of his former name, Simon's stomach dropped. Rafa was right. He was a liar. In a way, his entire life—or the part of it he'd fashioned with careful planning, dedication, and unremitting toil since he'd left France—was a lie. A hard-won lie, but a lie nonetheless.

Simon studied the institutional envelope, the words "Ministère de la Justice" stamped on the upper-left-hand corner, an address in Paris beneath it. The envelope had been opened and not much care given to conceal the fact.

"My first job every morning is to open Sherlock's mail and sort it according to priority," said Rafa. "Hope you don't mind that I gave it a read. Decided that Sherlock didn't really need to see it."

Simon looked through the papers. He needed five minutes to revisit the worst episode of his life. It was all there. His criminal record courtesy of the Marseille police, the highlight saved for the final page: felony armed robbery and attempted murder of a police officer. There were copies of court transcripts, the order for his delivery into the French penal system at Les Baumettes, a maximum-security prison located on the outskirts of Marseille.

"Is Ledoux your real name?" asked Rafa. "I've always thought Riske sounded rather too clever."

"My mother's married name, second time around. Sorry, I really am Simon Riske."

He replaced the papers and handed Rafa the envelope back.

"Yours to keep," said Rafa. "We sure as hell can't let Sherlock find them."

"But how…?" Simon narrowed his eyes, shaken by the turn of events.

"You're a rock star. You're being put up to work as an assistant to the vice chairman. Sherlock decided to do a little more digging to make sure they had the right man and requested your transcript from Sciences Po. Somewhere there was mention of both names, Riske and Ledoux. Her curiosity was piqued."

"And now? She'll be expecting something."

"Relax. No one has ever accused the French government of being efficient. We'll have some fun. Copy the stationery, write our own reply. 'Nothing found. All a clerical error.' She won't look any further."

Simon tried to share in his friend's jocularity. He couldn't. He felt as if he'd stepped off the curb while looking in the wrong direction and only narrowly avoided being run over by a city bus. Had Rafa not been assigned to HR, had he not broken every rule imaginable and risked his own job to steal the envelope, Simon would have been summarily dismissed from the bank. There would have been no question of a letter of recommendation. His career in finance would have been over before it started.

"Thank you." Simon could think of no other words.

"De nada," said Rafa, gifting him with a pat on the shoulder.

"I owe you."

"You would have done the same," said Rafa. "Cheers, then. To both of us." Then after they'd taken a swig: "I have a confession to make, too. I'm a liar, just like you. No jail. We called it *el reformatorio*."

"You?"

"Don't tell me you thought I was a saint. I'm insulted."

"You don't have to worry on that account," said Simon, feeling a little better already.

"When I was sixteen I was sent to *el reformatorio*. Half boarding school, half prison. For teenage boys who'd gotten into trouble with the law one too many times and whose parents couldn't or wouldn't buy them out. I wasn't really bad, I just liked to get into a little trouble. Pinch a bottle of beer. Break a window. Borrow a Vespa. Finally they got sick of my nonsense and sent me to the *reformatorio*. When I left two years later, I took two things with me." Rafa rolled up his sleeve, revealing a colorful tattoo. "This lovely piece of artwork and a vow never to set foot in that place again. I got a job as a runner at a bank in Madrid paying spit and a little change. I never looked back." Rafa pointed at a sliver of blue ink extending from beneath Simon's sleeve. "You too, I see. What's that one?"

"Nothing."

"Come on, let Rafa see."

Simon rolled up his left sleeve, revealing a larger, more intricate, and colorful tattoo of a grinning skeleton with its arms around an anchor, surrounded by crashing waves.

" 'La Brise de Mer,' " said Rafa, reading the words scrolled across the anchor.

"It means 'sea breeze.' Corsican mafia."

"You? Riske…the teacher's pet? You were in the mafia?"

"Made man at eighteen. Youngest ever. Guess that's something to be proud of."

"Now it all makes sense," said Rafa. "So how did you get here…from there?"

"Long story."

"I'm from the land of Cervantes. We love long stories."

"This is one you can't tell anyone."

"We're brothers, no?"

Simon rolled down his sleeve and buttoned the cuff. "Give me a cigarette."

"You don't smoke."

"I don't. Ledoux did."

Rafa shook loose a cigarette and offered the pack to Simon. He rolled it between his fingers but refused the lighter. Holding it was enough to trigger the memories. And so Simon told him.

How after his father's death—Simon never said "suicide"—he was sent to live with his mother in the South of France. He was the sixth child and eighth body in a house built for four. His stepfather viewed the new arrival strictly as another mouth to feed, one that didn't speak French and looked nothing like him. Marseille was a violent city, especially the northern districts. Simon, always a quick learner, adapted. By fourteen, he had forsaken homework for a job acting as a lookout for the small-time crime bosses who ruled the government housing blocks that sprung from the steep hillside behind his home. By sixteen, he was no longer a watcher but a participant. His specialty was boosting automobiles. No one could break into a car and have it running and on the road faster than Simon Ledoux.

At eighteen, after taking part in a series of audacious heists targeting jewelry stores, banks, and armored cars, he came to the attention of Il Padrone, a fifty-year-old Corsican who ruled organized crime in Marseille with an iron fist. Il Padrone gave Simon his own crew, and Simon delivered in spades, turning over hundreds of thousands of euros to his boss in short order. He learned how to use an AK-47. He also learned how to drink and abuse drugs on a daily basis. Life was good and getting better.

At nineteen, he planned his most daring heist yet, taking down a government payroll delivery to the French navy. Unbeknownst to him an informer had alerted the police. When it was over, four of his men were dead. Simon took three bullets before laying down his weapon. His sentence was six years. He spent the first two in solitary confinement, imprisoned in an underground cell measuring ten feet by six without a window and lit by a weak incandescent bulb twenty-four hours a day. A fellow prisoner saved him from insanity. He was an elderly man, a fallen Jesuit priest sentenced to life imprisonment, for what, he never would say. Simon called him "the monsignor."

The priest gave Simon the education he had so assiduously avoided yet secretly yearned for. Classes were taught through a tunnel the width of his fist, which he and the monsignor had bored in the rotting concrete and plaster that divided their cells. Math, history, philosophy, art, Latin, modern languages. No fee was extracted, save Simon's promise that one day he would leave his old life behind. The monsignor eventually told

Simon he had only one thing of value to his name. A treasure held inside a safe-deposit box at a prominent bank in London. The monsignor had no key, no proof that it belonged to him. He couldn't remember the number, just the name and branch of the bank. To gain access to it, Simon took the only route he could. He earned a university degree, then obtained employment at the bank. One day he would find out what was inside.

All this he'd told Rafa.

Slowly, Simon returned to the present. An urgent energy ran through him. He looked at the envelope Dickie Blackmon had left him.

Long ago a debt had been incurred, and damn the Spaniard, despite his desperate circumstances, for not reminding Simon of it, for not shouting that he was owed and that it was Simon's obligation to repay him. A man incarcerated in a foreign prison thousands of miles from his home, facing a sentence that would surely kill him, had taught Simon the ultimate lesson. How to behave as a gentleman.

The monsignor would approve. Cervantes, as well.

CHAPTER 9

Umbria, Italy

Luca Borgia stood on the terrace of Castello dell'Aquila, one leather boot on the stone retaining wall, as he overlooked the rugged, densely forested hills of the Nera Valley. It was old country, dark, imposing, essentially untouched since man had come to the Apennine Peninsula millennia before. It was a land of myth and folklore, of legend and superstition.

The Borgia family had owned most of the valley and adjoining countryside for five hundred years. He could recite the names of the ten oldest families in the region, most of whom had lived here as long as his own. Many worked for the Borgias, on farms growing olives and hunting truffles, on ranches breeding cattle and sheep, in towns and cities toiling in factories owned by the Borgias. He knew everyone, and everyone knew him. It was a land of long tradition and prized heritage. Proud country for proud Italians.

As the sun edged above the horizon, mist shrouded the treetops, snaking through ravines and rising up the steep mountainsides. Borgia turned his head, catching the far-off growl of an approaching vehicle. Flashes of silver and black blinked from beneath the canopy. He checked his wristwatch, his father's Omega worn strapped atop his cuff. His visitors were on time. One would expect no less from the German military.

Borgia slipped his sterling-silver cigarette case from the pocket of his riding jacket and, using a manicured thumbnail, flipped the catch. He favored English cigarettes, Silk Cuts, a reminder of his time at

Cambridge, limiting himself to ten a day. As he lit the cigarette, his phone rang.

"*Guten Morgen, Herr General,*" he answered in perfect High German.

"*Guten Morgen,*" answered the German. "We will be there in ten minutes."

"You'll be the first to arrive," said Borgia. It was ever so. First, the Germans, and last, his own Italians. "The coffee is hot, and Mariella has prepared a plate of your favorite pastries."

"Thank you, Luca. Prato Bornum."

"Prato Bornum."

Borgia ended the call. By now he'd spotted the convoy of vehicles climbing the switchbacks leading to the town of Castelluccio, and he set off across the terrace. He was a tall man, fifty years old, wiry black hair swept off his forehead and kept in place by a generous handful of pomade. He walked with an aristocrat's bearing, shoulders back, jaw raised, and had an aristocrat's features, too: prominent cheekbones, a Roman nose, steadfast mouth, cleft chin adorning an indomitable jaw. His skin was tan and weathered, his forehead carved with deep lines. One eye was blue, the other brown. This never failed to provoke a moment of discomfort when first meeting someone. His profile belonged on a valuable coin. A gold aureus, if he had his choice. He was not a handsome man, thank God, but there was no mistaking his vigor. So when he smiled and broke into a spontaneous laugh, which he did often, it came as a surprise. One didn't expect such warmth from so fierce and commanding a figure.

Borgia walked through the stable, stopping at the ties where a groom curried his horse, Charlie, and instructing him to add an extra measure of alfalfa to the animal's breakfast. Charlie, short for Charlemagne, a fitting name for a Hanoverian gelding that stood eighteen hands and thought himself a king. Borgia ran a hand along the horse's muzzle and kissed his nose. After a last pat, he left the stable, walking briskly through the rose garden. In the cool morning air, his breath was visible, his boots raising puffs of dust from the gravel path.

Inside the mudroom, he pulled off his boots and threw them in the corner to be cleaned and polished. A servant waited with his espresso. He drank it and replaced it on her tray before running upstairs to his living quarters. He showered and dressed, a bespoke midnight-blue suit of Vitale Barberis Canonico wool, white shirt, no necktie. He took care with his grooming and appearance. A splash of cologne…

His phone rang. A familiar name on the screen. He put the call on speaker.

"Danni," he said, impressed. "A woman who keeps to a schedule. You may be the first."

"Your boy is a smooth operator. He knew we'd come looking."

"How so?"

"He fragmented his hard drive. It's like throwing a hand grenade into a china store."

"Has that stopped you before?"

"Nothing stops us. It has, however, slowed us down."

"I thought I'd made the urgency of the situation clear. Perhaps I'm speaking with the wrong person."

"You have my father's number."

"Please excuse me, Danni. I didn't mean to insult you."

"Ah, Luca, you never have to worry about that."

Borgia fought down a bolt of anger. The woman was impudence itself. "Am I permitted to inquire about the length of the delay?"

"Twenty-four hours."

"That long?"

"I can tell you one thing we've learned. I don't think you will find it good news. The last action Mr. De Bourbon performed before destroying his computer was to send an email from his personal address. It appears he'd opened a message from a Mr. Paul Malloy approximately ninety seconds before. Does the name mean anything?"

"Go on."

"There was a packet attached."

"A packet?"

"Files. We have no idea what they contained. However, if you were worried about the theft of corporate materials—"

"How many?"

"Impossible to say."

"Can you at least tell me who he sent the files to?"

"For the moment, no, but soon."

The sound of footsteps congregating in the welcome hall drifted into the bedroom. The Germans had arrived. General Hugo Voss, chief of the country's elite counterterrorism force, GSG 9, along with his deputy, and Renata König, the leader of the New Germany party, a potent voice from the Right.

"Give me a name, Danni. I want to know to whom De Bourbon sent that message and what exactly was in that packet."

Borgia ended the call before she could respond. *Take that.* He walked to the door and peered downstairs, glimpsing several dark uniforms. More guests would be arriving at any moment. It was imperative none found out about De Bourbon and the threat he posed. He closed the door and placed another call.

"Any change?"

"Stubborn as ever," said Colonel Albert Tan. "Let me arrange for an accident. A fight in the cell. An unstable prisoner. These things happen."

"And then? It's urgent we recover the information De Bourbon stole."

"I can be quite convincing."

"I have no doubt of that, but I prefer a lighter hand. At least for now."

It wasn't just a question of recovering the information De Bourbon had stolen. Borgia needed to know the actions he'd taken to carry out his threat against Malloy. First and foremost, if he'd sent sensitive information to a journalist.

"I beg you to reconsider."

Borgia could hear the disappointment in Tan's voice. The man was a thug. Like a carpenter, give him a hammer, and, well…easy enough to guess the results. Better to go the other way. The carrot, not the stick.

"For now, we play the game by De Bourbon's rules. Let him believe we are cooperating. There will be more than enough time to deal with him after we get back what's ours."

Borgia ended the call. He reconsidered his words to Colonel Tan. If anyone were to take care of De Bourbon, it would not be the Thais. They were impetuous, undisciplined, and messy. God forbid De Bourbon's name appeared in the newspaper beneath the headline FORMER EUROPEAN BUSINESSMAN MURDERED IN THAI JAIL CELL. Borgia might not know much about computers, but he knew more than enough about the Internet and the word "viral."

A steadier hand was needed.

Still, it was time to start cleaning things up before they got any messier. A last call.

The man answered on the first ring. Sometimes Borgia felt certain he possessed a sixth sense.

"Kruger."

"Hello, my friend," said Borgia. "Ready for a short trip? I hear Switzerland is beautiful in the spring."

CHAPTER 10

Bangkok

The heat.

Half conscious, knees buckling, Rafael de Bourbon slumped against the wall. Sweat streamed from his forehead. His mouth was parched, thirst so severe it blurred his vision. Only the weight of the other prisoners packed around him and the certainty of punishment, immediate and brutal, kept him standing.

He was one of a hundred, maybe more, made to live inside the cell. There were no beds, no chairs, no toilets, only concrete. Concrete walls. Concrete floor. A faucet dribbled brown water, and, in the center of the cell, a hole. Light came from a narrow opening cut high into the wall. The air was still and heavy. After two days, the stench still sickened him.

Rafa wiped the sweat from his brow, growing fainter still, unable to stop himself from sliding down the wall. An elbow to the ribs. A harsh admonition. A head taller than the rest, a Westerner, or *farang,* he was a target. Somehow he found the strength to stand. He wore the clothes he was arrested in. His shirt was torn, his shorts soiled with sweat and grime. He looked at his bare feet, filthy, bloody, a nail torn off. Three days before, he'd been walking on a white-sand beach, the warm sea washing between his toes.

The first meeting was already hazy, a fever dream. A hint of sanity amid madness.

The lawyer was named Adamson, an American from one of the big multinational firms. A killer—you could see it. Dressed to the nines. Enough navy-blue and starch to captain a Yankee clipper. Not a drop of sweat dampening his forehead. Adamson had come to help, to end this nightmare. The Thai government wanted the matter resolved expeditiously. Surely Rafa wanted the same thing. It was a question of cooperation. He had sounded like the soundtrack from a bad courtroom drama.

The accused, Mr. De Bourbon, was to admit to the crimes of blackmail, extortion, theft, on and on, and agree to turn over the fruits of his larceny, namely confidential financial information and emails belonging to one PetroSaud SA, 16 Rue du Rhône, Geneva, Switzerland. In exchange for said admission and transfer of property, the accused would receive a suspended sentence of twenty-one years and be declared persona non grata in the Kingdom of Thailand, to be shipped out of the country at the earliest possible moment.

All well and good.

Please sign here.

But when Rafa asked to have an attorney of his own review the papers, his request was denied. Adamson was his attorney, paid for by his wife's family. He needed no other. And when Rafa asked to speak to a representative from the Spanish embassy, his request was again denied.

And so Rafa suspected the papers were a ruse. He would admit to being naive. He'd believed that Paul Malloy would honor his word. Maybe Malloy needed a push, a reminder, but after all, they'd had an agreement. A handshake between gentlemen. Honor ran deep in the De Bourbon blood. Did it not in all men?

But Rafa was not that naive.

He knew.

Others knew that he knew.

And so he'd made a last request. He would not sign any papers until he spoke with a person he could trust. Only one name came to mind. A ghost from the past, hovering on the far side of another of the bridges he'd burned. No longer a friend, but a man whose honor ran as deep as his own.

That had been twenty-four hours ago.

Three blows against the steel door signaled mealtime. The cell came to life. Torpor turned to motion. A path was cleared. Policemen hauled a barrel inside. It contained rice and scraps of fish. A third policeman entered carrying a tray piled high with fried meatballs and satay. One by one the prisoners received their allotment.

One of four Europeans, Rafa was made to wait until all others had been fed. A guard ladled a portion of rice into his hand. A fish tail poked through the surface. Rafa was lucky. He knew better than to wait for a second spoonful. As he moved away, a shadow filled the doorway. A Westerner in a business suit. Adamson the lawyer. And, behind him, a familiar face even without his mirrored sunglasses: Colonel Tan.

"Bourbon," said Colonel Tan. "Rafael de Bourbon."

Inside the interrogation room: air-conditioning, a can of Coca-Cola, a glass of ice, a sandwich. Rafa's reward.

But not yet.

"How are you, Mr. De Bourbon?" asked Colonel Tan, sunnily.

"Fine, thank you," said Rafa. "How are you today, sir?"

The Thai's smile flickered like a candle in a breeze. His eyes shifted toward Adamson. A dossier was placed on the table. The lawyer guided it across the table. Rafa opened the cover. A court document. The same one as the day before? But, look here, something new. Attached to it, a check drawn on the Krung Thai Bank in the amount of one million U.S. dollars and made out in his name.

"As you can see," said Colonel Tan, "we're reasonable men." He had traded his brown uniform and peaked cap for sky-blue slacks, a white short-sleeved shirt, and open-toed sandals. A poorly dressed tourist in his own country. This was a new Colonel Tan, but more dangerous than ever. He was likeable. "We have no interest in seeing this matter go to court. Trials are expensive. A poor use of government resources. There is no need to adjudicate this matter. We have abundant proof of your guilt. Emails to Mr. Malloy. Texts. At this moment, a cybersecurity firm is gathering evidence of your theft. Case closed. Really, Mr. De Bourbon—may I call you Rafa?—let's shake hands and put this behind us. Take the money. Give us what we want. Be gone. So much easier for all involved."

One million dollars.

Rafa drew the papers closer. There was no point trying to read them. He could hardly say his own name let alone make sense of so much legalese. What did it matter? There was a check for one million dollars attached. He must take the money. After all, as Tan had stated, he was guilty. The evidence was incontrovertible. A trial really would be a waste of government resources. It wasn't all he was owed, but it was enough.

Adamson handed him a pen. Gold. Expensive. A pleasure to hold.

"One last question," said Tan.

Rafa nodded. Anything at all to get out of there.

"Where did you send the stolen information?"

Rafa shook his head. They were mistaken. He hadn't sent anything.

"You threatened Mr. Malloy that you would send the papers to a certain reporter. Someone who liked to 'dig,' to use your words. A name, please."

Rafa put down the pen. No more use in lying. But how could they know?

"Is there something wrong?" asked Colonel Tan. "We only want a name. In case such a person is foolish enough to take you seriously."

Adamson said nothing. He was a seasoned attorney. He knew the smell of defeat.

Rafa looked at the can of Coca-Cola, the glass of ice, the club sandwich.

"Not until I see Simon Riske," he said.

CHAPTER 11

Saas-Grund, Switzerland

The sky was as blue as a sapphire.

Paul Malloy drew in a breath of the crystalline air and stared up at the wall of ice. Before him stood the Weissmies, a 13,000-foot peak in the canton of Valais, straddling the Swiss-Italian border. He gathered his climbing gear from the rear of his Range Rover and crossed the lot to the cable car. His guide, Rolf Brunner, waited at the *Mittelstation*. They enjoyed an espresso and a *Gipfeli*, then left the warmth and comfort of the station.

Outside, Malloy checked his watch: 7:00 a.m.; 2 degrees Celsius, or 35 degrees Fahrenheit; 10,800 feet. He could feel the altitude already and knew he wasn't in as good a shape as he should be. He had a four-hour climb ahead. It would be taxing, but nothing he couldn't handle. He needed the exertion. No better way to clear his mind. He zipped up his jacket and pulled on his mittens.

"Shall we?" said Brunner, a compact, bearded man who'd spent his life in the Alps, as experienced a climber as ever there was.

Malloy set out, leading the way. The first hour was a hike, more or less, as they approached the north face, a concave vertical wall towering nearly three thousand feet above them. The trail grew steeper, then disappeared into a pile of scree and rubble. The men stopped and roped up.

"I'll take the first pitch," said Malloy, ice axes in both hands, glacier glasses in place, a red cap pulled down over his ears.

"Up, up, up," said Rolf. Legend was he was born with crampons on his feet.

Malloy dug his axes into the ice and began to climb, kicking the spikes on the toes of his boots into the snow. The north face of the Weissmies was more a question of conditioning than technical skill. One step after the next, setting ice screws every thirty feet. Already he felt better, lighter, shedding the emotional burden of the past weeks. *Damn that Spaniard!* It was all because of Rafa and his relentless campaign to recover the bonus money owed him. Four years Malloy had kept him at bay, offering excuses and explanations. The man simply would not give up. And now it had come to this. Blackmail. Extortion. A threat to reveal PetroSaud's deepest, darkest secrets. He'd tried to warn Rafa, but the Spaniard was too proud, too stubborn, too arrogant. Now he knew, didn't he? Maybe a stint in a Thai hellhole would finally drive some sense into him.

Malloy stopped, fatigued, his breath labored, and waited for Brunner to catch up. Their climbs followed a strict regimen. Move for an hour. Stop. Hydrate. Snack. Check equipment. Continue.

"Next pitch is yours," he said, forcing a smile. God, he was weaker than he'd expected.

Brunner gave him a pat on the back and moved up the face. Malloy waited until the first screw was set, then followed. Below him the cable car station looked like a speck. He kicked a chunk of ice free and watched it fall, bouncing off the wall once, twice, three times before disintegrating on the rocks below. He gripped the axes tightly, the muscles in his hands aching as the face grew steeper still.

Whether Rafa was owed the money or not, Malloy could not pay him. He'd transferred the money to his own account the day Rafa resigned. Five million Swiss francs didn't go far in today's world, at least not the world Malloy inhabited. There was the house, the car, private schools for his daughters, an apartment for his mistress, his wife's passion for horses, *la vie équestre.*

"*Lo siento, amigo,*" Malloy said under his breath. "That boat sailed long ago. *No màs dinero.*"

He remembered hiring Rafa. Tall, handsome, debonair, Rafael de Bourbon, the bright, shining face of the firm. PetroSaud sold oil leases in yet undeveloped lands deep inside the Kingdom of Saudi Arabia. A billion-dollar investment promised a ten percent yield in perpetuity.

There was another side to the business. Malloy's side. And it was even more lucrative. To the investor…and to Malloy. It was that side Rafa had foolishly threatened to expose. The Spaniard had no idea of the hornet's nest he was disturbing.

Malloy put Rafa out of his mind and concentrated on the climb. He caught up to Brunner and, over the next hour, led several pitches, a "pitch" being one length of rope, or approximately one hundred fifty feet. The wind had picked up, snow and rime skidding across the face, making visibility difficult. Squinting, he could just make out the summit, another five hundred feet. *Thank God.* He didn't think he could make it any farther. He looked down, signaling to Brunner that they were almost there.

It was then he saw the flash of red below them. A solo climber, no visible ropes, and moving fast. Malloy took off his gloves and dug in his pocket for a protein bar, one last shot of energy. When he looked back, the solo climber was nearly level with Rolf Brunner. The kids these days. It was all about speed, setting records. They took no time to enjoy themselves, to revel in nature and appreciate their surroundings.

He felt a tug on the rope. A second, sharper still. And then, hidden in the howling wind, a scream.

That kind of scream.

Malloy pulled the glasses from his face and looked down. Rolf Brunner was no longer there. The rope whipped wildly back and forth. It had been cut. And in Rolf's place, the climber in red.

Malloy was tired and confused. Precious seconds passed before he was able to grasp the fact that, yes, it was the climber in red who had cut Brunner's rope and pushed him off the face. And then, with terror, to register that the climber was following directly in his own path.

Malloy looked up. Five hundred feet. Less even. He struggled to put on his gloves, then freed his axes and began to climb. He didn't bother with the rope or screws. There was no time. The climber was gaining rapidly, moving more quickly than Malloy had ever seen.

Axe. Kick. Step. Axe. Kick. Step.

His muscles screamed. His lungs burned. *Why?* he asked himself, knowing full well who had sent the climber. Malloy had not only betrayed Rafa. Far worse, he had betrayed the firm. His larceny had jeopardized everything.

Malloy could go no farther. Panting, he dug his crampons into the wall and cleared one of his axes, turning to meet the climber. The man drew closer. He wore no hat and, frighteningly, no gloves. Blond hair as thick as a whisk broom. Broad shoulders. Complexion the color of milk coffee. A last step. He came even, blue eyes as flat as ice, a hard face. Malloy swung his axe. The climber avoided it easily. Despite his terrific pace, his breath was even. Malloy swung again, his left foot losing its purchase. The climber caught his axe and wrenched it from his hand, tossing it into the void.

"Why?" shouted Malloy, crying now. "Dammit. I'm loyal."

"Sorry, brother. Just the way it is."

The climber showed no emotion. Not anger. Not exertion. Nothing. He grabbed Malloy's parka in one hand and yanked him off the face. For a moment, he seemed to hold Malloy, all of him, as if he were as light as a doll, then he opened his fingers and Malloy fell.

Kruger did not watch the body fall. There was only one possible outcome and he was not a cruel man. A professional, one might say, though he knew of no others he might measure himself against.

He gazed up. Two hundred feet to the top. Malloy had almost made it. Not that the outcome would have been any different. Kruger was not a man who permitted another to get the better of him.

Immediately, he commenced his descent. He realized that he could no longer feel his fingers, or his hands, for that matter. He didn't care. Where he was going, it was much warmer.

He'd always wanted to visit Thailand.

CHAPTER 12

London

The next day, Simon arrived at the entrance to Scotland Yard as retired commander Ben Sterling passed through the security gates.

"Riske, that you?" he called, by way of introduction. "Looks like you had a rough night."

Sterling was sixty-something, a ruddy-faced bantamweight with steely gray hair, china-blue eyes, and a handshake that would crush a walnut. Hence his nickname, "Iron Ben."

"Tough week," said Simon. "But I'll get by. Good to see you."

"So," said Sterling when he'd relinquished his grip. "Headed east, eh? Got any space in your suitcase for an old man?"

"Not sure if I can fit you into my suitcase, but there's probably room in the overhead bin. Dickie Blackmon's flying me out first class."

"Of course he is, our Sir Dickie. Good to see you, too. What's it been? A year?"

"Two. The ivory smuggling case at Heathrow."

The case had involved a team of Chinese immigrants illegally importing ivory from Tanzania under false bills of lading. Simon didn't know what had angered him more. The fact that the men had been doing it for fifteen years or that they'd managed to smuggle over ten thousand pounds of the banned material before being caught. The court delivered a sentence of five years in prison and a hundred-thousand-pound fine.

"They'll be in jail a while longer yet," said Sterling, setting off at a brisk pace. "Cold comfort."

Simon had a different punishment in mind. It involved a tree stump

71

and an angry elephant. Let justice be served. "I appreciate you making time on such short notice."

Sterling waved away the thanks. "This talk of Thailand made me hungry. Decent curry shop just up the road. Fancy a bite?"

"Sure," said Simon, hurrying to keep up. "I could eat."

The decent curry shop turned out to be Gymkhana, one of the city's finest. At a few minutes past twelve, they were the first to arrive. The maître d' showed them to a table by the window. Sterling sat down with a contented sigh. He was a small man of big gestures.

The son of a tea plantation manager, Ben Sterling had grown up in Sri Lanka and Burma. In 1972, he'd joined the Royal Hong Kong Police force and stayed until Great Britain ceded the crown colony back to the People's Republic of China twenty-five years later, on June 30, 1997. He left the force a superintendent, his career spent combatting drug trafficking, primarily the flow of heroin from the Golden Triangle—the northern provinces of Thailand, Burma, and Laos—to Hong Kong. He spoke Cantonese like a native, and fluent Mandarin, Thai, and Tamil. If there were such a thing as a "Far East Hand," it was Ben Sterling. Scotland Yard scooped him up in a heartbeat, and he'd been in London ever since.

"Ceylon curry's decent," he said, studying the menu. "But mild. Pablum. Me, I like the hot stuff. Five alarm. Ten thousand on the Scoville scale. Like to challenge the chef to see if he can make me cry. Care to join me?"

Simon was nursing a sore hand in addition to his bruised shoulder. He didn't care to add a scalded tongue. "Ceylon curry," he said the moment the server arrived.

"Traitor," barked Sterling.

"I'd like to be able to taste the food when I get to Thailand."

"So," said Sterling, rolling up his shirtsleeves and placing his elbows on the table, leaning in. "Dickie Blackmon's got you going to Bangkok to pick up his son-in-law. Rum, you ask me."

"Dickie's working a deal with a Colonel Albert Tan, head of the national police. There are a few road bumps. I'm supposed to smooth them out."

The waiter brought a basket of naan and papadum. Sterling grabbed a naan and tore it in half. "Know anything about the place?" he asked, taking a ravenous bite.

"I've never been."

"Wonderful country, don't get me wrong. Lovely people. Beautiful beaches. Fascinating history. 'Land of Smiles.' And the king will tan your hide if you say otherwise." Sterling laughed, a riotous thunderclap. "In name, Thailand is still a monarchy. The Thais love their king. Not allowed to say a bad thing about him. Something called lèse-majesté. Few years back, an Australian newshound sent his friends a pic he'd gotten ahold of showing the king cavorting in a swimming pool with a karaoke girl, both of them naked, of course. Having a frolic. Pic was twenty years old. No big deal. That's what the Aussie thought. Twenty-four hours later, he found himself on an airplane, declared persona non grata. Never allowed to return. He got off easy. King sent his wife to an 'attitude adjustment' camp for two years. Kids, too."

"Sounds harsh."

"The king is still new to the throne. He's a fighter pilot. Smart as a whip but has a bit of an inferiority complex. His father was the most popular monarch in the country's history. On the throne for seventy years. New one needs to make his mark."

"But does he have real power?"

"To an extent. By law, the country is a parliamentary democracy with a constitution and everything. Problem is they keep electing one party more corrupt than the next. Every ten years the military stages a coup to set things right. Of course, they're as bent as the day is long, too. Somehow the whole thing works. Country's prosperous. Bangkok's a boomtown. Two million residents when I first visited in '75. Nearly eleven million today and growing like gangbusters. But nothing, I repeat, *nothing*, gets done without a tip of your hat and a wave of your hand. Grease makes the wheels go round."

"Money."

"Graft, honest or otherwise. There isn't anything that can't be bought…including, apparently, the freedom of your friend, Rafael de

Bourbon. I made some calls after we spoke last night. I still have friends over there."

"And?"

"Den of vipers."

"Pardon me?"

"That's what you're stepping into. I don't know what your chum did, whether it really was blackmail, extortion, or corporate theft, but he's managed to make a lot of people upset. Word to the wise. Do not mess with Colonel Tan."

"I looked him up. Career army. Paratrooper. Served as defense attaché to the Thai embassy in Rome and Istanbul. Currently, head of the Royal Thai Police."

"You're not going to find what you need to know about Albert Tan on the Internet. Tan is the ultimate inside man. Married to the daughter of the biggest sugar baron in the country. Worth billions. Brother's head of the ruling party. More billions. Cousin owns Mekong Distillery, largest spirits producer in Thailand, Laos, and Vietnam. Lots more billions. Pounds, not baht. Tan is the man you go to when you want to get things done at the highest level. Whatever De Bourbon did, it must be bloody important if Tan himself flew to Ko Phi Phi to make the arrest."

Simon took this in. "My friend worked for a company named Petro-Saud. You can guess by the name it's in the oil business, representing the Kingdom of Saudi Arabia. Offices in Geneva, Singapore, and Jeddah. But, Ben, why did the Thai police arrest him for stealing information from a Saudi company?"

"Simple. On behalf of one of the countries where the company has offices."

"Long arms," said Simon.

"With very sharp claws," said Ben Sterling. "Careful, Simon. Den of vipers."

A waiter arrived with their curries.

"Ah," said Sterling as his plate was set before him. "Heaven."

Chapter 13

London

It was more than an hour's drive west to Southall. Simon passed the gurdwara temple and turned onto a quiet side street. By a miracle, he located a vacant space that was almost legal. He entered a gate at number 34 Carrington Mews and continued to the back of the house, where he knocked at the rear door. He was never sure why Dr. Vikram Singh insisted he go to the back. He'd been doing business with the electrical engineer for years, and frankly, he was beginning to have a complex about it.

A tall young man wearing a Caltech hoodie answered the door. "Hey."

"Is that you, Arjit?"

"Back early for summer holiday."

"You grew a foot."

"Two inches. I'm officially six feet tall. Dad thinks I'm taking steroids."

"To get taller?"

"Otherwise he can't explain it. He's five eight. Mom's barely five feet. He said there were stories about a distant uncle who was over six feet tall. Supposedly, he was some kind of tiger hunter. Stupid family lore. He looks at me like I'm not his son. He's weirding me out, Simon. Talk to him."

"Will do," said Simon. "What are you studying out there in California?"

"Quantum mechanics."

"So you do like cars after all? If you need a summer job, let me know."

"Quantum mechanics has nothing to do with automobiles," said a distraught Arjit.

"That right? My bad." Simon made a face. "Do they still say that? Anyway, from now on I'm going to call you 'Tiger.'"

"I don't have to play golf, do I?"

"Just keep studying. You'll make more than the other Tiger ever will. Maybe you can solve the Higgs boson quandary. Win a Fields Medal. That would be something." Simon pointed a finger at Arjit "Tiger" Singh, as if to say he wasn't as dumb as he looked. "Tiger" was not amused.

"Dad's in his lab. He's been up all night. He's not happy about it."

"Some things never change."

"Knock, knock," said Simon, rapping on the wall as he descended the stairs to Vikram Singh's basement lab. "Anyone home?"

Vikram Singh stood at his waist-high worktable, a halogen lamp attached to his forehead, its beam directed at a small, shiny object in his hands. A Sikh, he wore a flaming orange turban and kept his long salt-and-pepper beard tied neatly under his chin. His eyes darted to Simon, then returned to his work. "Sit. Silence. Patience."

Simon dropped into a chair in the corner. Vikram Singh had every right to be angry. It seemed that every time Simon needed his services, it was on a rush-delivery basis. Simon would feel the same way if a client demanded he renovate a car faster than he would like or was capable. Hurrying was not only an inconvenience; it threatened one's reputation for quality.

Simon eyed the various and sundry items scattered across the table, mostly metallic black boxes with nobs and toggles that he identified as StingRays, devices designed to mimic cellphone transmission towers and capture cellular communications. Either with a warrant or without.

A graduate of the Indian Institutes of Technology, India's most prestigious academy of higher education, Vikram Singh had immigrated to the United Kingdom with a PhD in electrical engineering at the age of twenty-two and went straight to work for MI5, known colloquially as "Box," Britain's domestic security service, where he spent twenty years using his skills to outfit officers for undercover work. Seeing greener pastures in the private sector, he left to offer his services to a higher paying clientele. The spotless BMW 750iL saloon parked in front of his home testified to the wisdom of his decision. His son, Arjit, only fifteen, attended Caltech. His daughter, Vandita, was reportedly even sharper, the subject of a recent article in *The Times* after she aced five O-level examinations at the age of eleven.

"Still there?" asked Vikram Singh.

"Sitting and silent. Definitely not patient."

Singh extinguished the halogen beam and removed the lamp from his head. "I have good news and bad news."

"Good news first," said Simon.

"Against all odds, I've managed to fulfill your requests."

"That is good news."

"You may stand now." Singh circled the table and slid a rectangular tray toward Simon. The tray was bare except for two pea-sized pods the color of flesh and a black square-shaped strip of metal. "Try one. Goes in the ear. Your choice. Right or left."

Simon placed one of the pods in his ear.

"Make sure it is on."

Several months earlier Singh had built Simon a device capable of detecting the presence of a digital camera. The first time he used it, Simon had forgotten to turn it on, to near disastrous effect.

"My iPods turn on automatically," he said.

"Do I look like Tim Cook?"

Simon plucked the pod from his ear and flicked a pale nub on one side. A green light appeared and he replaced it.

"Hello, hello," said Singh.

"Hello, hello," said a voice in Simon's ear. It was a female voice with a seductive English accent.

"I think I'd rather have HAL," said Simon.

"Over Helen Mirren?"

"That's Helen Mirren?"

"A voice print compilation."

"Never mind. I'll take Helen Mirren."

Singh walked to the far side of the room and spoke a few words in his native Punjabi.

As he spoke, the woman's voice translated the words into English. "Smart man, Riske. I'd take her over HAL any day. Did you know that HAL is a play on IBM? The letters *H, A, L* are each one earlier in the alphabet than IBM. Kubrick was quite a clever fellow." Singh then asked in English: "Get that?"

"I didn't know you were a film buff."

"I'll take that as a yes."

"Yes," said Simon.

"This device is capable of simultaneously translating most Indo-Asian languages, including Thai, Isan, and Khmer, into English. A Bluetooth transmitter inside the pod sends the audio to software housed on a cellphone, or if the cellphone is unavailable, via a booster to the cloud, provided you are within five kilometers of a transmission tower."

Simon picked up the square-shaped black slab. "The booster?"

"It can run for three hours on a full charge. Not enough, I know, but you wanted something concealable."

"It'll do." *Den of vipers.* Even before meeting with Ben Sterling, Simon suspected he might be walking into a loaded environment. Dickie Blackmon's business dealings didn't inspire confidence in his partners, no matter where in the world they were. "And the other part of my order?"

Singh picked up a signet ring from the tray and flipped it to Simon. "The ring contains a miniature parabolic antenna capable of picking up voices up to fifty meters away. I programmed a frequency differentiation algorithm that allows you to select the voices you wish to listen to. There's a small button on the underside of the ring. Each time you press it, it will cycle through the voice patterns the antenna is picking up."

Simon slipped the ring on his third finger and aimed it at the ceiling. Immediately, he heard Arjit telling his sister Taylor Swift was awful and demanding that she shut the door to her room. "Works through walls?"

"Intermittently. This is an old house with wooden floors. You'll have less luck with concrete. None with steel."

"Nifty. Is there a way to program more languages?"

"The fewer we upload the better the result. Second-generation software. Bugs galore. Besides, the number of dialects in that part of the world makes precision impossible. No one speaks textbook Thai. Remember that if Miss Mirren misspeaks herself now and again."

"Why do you know so much about Thailand?"

"My cousin owns a tailoring shop in Bangkok. His name is Bobby Gulati. The store is called Raja's. Look him up if you need a new suit."

"This isn't that kind of a trip." Simon slipped the ring off his finger and replaced it on the tray. "You were saying something about 'bad news.'"

"While small in size, these toys were quite expensive to procure and program at such short notice."

"Don't tell me," said Simon.

Vikram Singh said a figure in Punjabi. Helen Mirren spoke the sum in Simon's ear. "Bastard," he muttered.

Singh smiled archly. "Someone's got to pay for Arjit's education. University in the States is damned expensive. Oh, and one more thing."

"I'm all ears."

"Cash only."

CHAPTER 14

Singapore

Years of daily practice in hopes of one day walking onto a stage in Vienna or Berlin or New York and sitting down at a concert Steinway, nodding to the conductor, her posture immaculate, slowly raising her hands above the ivory keys, had made London Li a creature of habit. She rose every morning at 5:30, made herself a cup of coffee, drank exactly half, laced up her running shoes, fed her cat, and left her apartment on Fort Road for a jog around Katong Park—2.3 miles, 4,700 steps, give or take. After her run, meditation, a shower, and only then, breakfast. Two pieces of dry toast, a banana, and the second half of her coffee.

She adhered to the schedule every day of the year. Rain or shine. Sick or well. On the road or at home. No excuses.

But not today.

This morning London rose earlier than usual, at five a.m. on the dot. Still in her pajamas (Hello Kitty—yes, she was a fan), she went straight to her desk, sat down, and opened her laptop. No run. No meditation. No shower.

Something better.

A story.

An email was open on the screen.

High-ranking executives at the Geneva-based advisory firm Petro-Saud conspired with managers of an Asian sovereign wealth fund to defraud investors of billions of dollars. Instead of placing the fund's assets in listed investments, PetroSaud funneled billions to accounts in offshore banks controlled by the fund's managers (including government ministers) while charging excessive commissions.

Signed,
R

"R," her unreliable man of mystery, last reported MIA.

Why had he missed their meeting? A change of heart? An unseen inconvenience? Or something else? Something sinister.

Attached to his email were three files.

The first was a copy of a bank transfer to PetroSaud's account at one of the big Swiss banks in the amount of seven hundred million dollars. The sender's name was partially blacked out, or redacted. Only the words "D. ███, Director of Investment Corporation of ███" were visible. In the section marked "Comments," it read, "Purchase of Parcel 254A-D, Ras-al-Aliya, Saudi Arabia, Royal Saudi Oil Authority. Oil and Mineral Rights Exclusive."

The second file showed the copy of another bank transfer, this one from the same PetroSaud account at the big Swiss bank, also in the amount of seven hundred million dollars, made that same day to a numbered account at the Bank of Liechtenstein.

The third file was a copy of the account documents for said numbered account at the Bank of Liechtenstein naming the account holder as the Private International Investment Holdings Corp., domiciled in the Netherlands Antilles and listing among its directors "███, director of the Investment Corporation of ███" and "███, finance minister of ███." The missing words or names, again, redacted.

London didn't need a road map. The money transferred to PetroSaud from the Investment Corporation of [country unknown] had not been used to purchase the oil lease in Saudi Arabia but instead had been sent to an account controlled by the person or persons who ran the Investment Corporation of [country unknown], one of whom was also the finance minister of that country.

As R had stated in his letter, executives at PetroSaud had worked with the managers of a sovereign wealth fund to defraud it of seven hundred million dollars.

London printed the files and laid them on her desk. Her head began to throb, demanding its daily dose of caffeine. She rose and walked to the kitchen—ten steps—and put a pod in her Keurig. Her apartment was small, but it was her own. Nine hundred square feet. One bedroom, one and a half baths, the "half" so tiny it made a coffin feel spacious, and an alcove she used as an office. The price was two million Singapore dollars. She would be paying off her mortgage until her grandchildren graduated from high school. On the plus side, she did have a view of the sea, if, that is, she walked to the far end of her terrace, stood on her tiptoes, and craned her neck.

The *FT* had suffered the same fate as newspapers everywhere. Readership had declined drastically over the past ten years. Bankruptcy was knocking at the door. To stay alive, management was making a push into the digital arena, publishing an online lifestyle magazine, producing short films, and posting stories on social media outlets the world over. Anything to generate revenue.

London's style of investigative reporting was perilously out of date. She took too much time to produce a story, filled in too many rows on her expense reports. Often months passed without a byline. Her publisher had grown tired of paying her while he waited.

She'd had offers to work in television, but that was even worse. Quicker turnarounds, less fact-checking, and one producer's advice to keep the top three buttons of her shirt undone and get a spray tan. And, oh, she might want to consider a push-up bra…

Last week her publisher had drawn a line in the sand. A story—and a good one, at that—or she was out. One more Fleet Street casualty. It was with a fervor born of survival that she attacked the story of R's anonymous leak.

London drank her coffee, then returned to her desk. Her cat, Freddy—for Frédéric Chopin—rubbed himself against her leg, and she placed him on her lap, stroking his back as she reread the printouts. It was like a game. R had given her a few clues to get started, not many, but with her expertise, enough to deduce who he was talking about. She just had to dig.

She logged on to the *FT*'s proprietary database and searched for a list of Asian sovereign wealth funds. There were twelve funds with assets over five billion dollars, the biggest owned by Japan, with a value over one trillion dollars. She ruled out Japan. Too many eyes. Too many cooks in the kitchen. Similarly, she ruled out China. This was the work of a smaller fund, one overseen by a precious few. A monarchy, maybe. Probably not a liberal democracy. Then again…

She decided on Singapore, Thailand, Malaysia, Indonesia, Taiwan (as cunning a people as she'd come across), Brunei, and Vietnam.

Sovereign wealth funds were simply investment funds where the money in play came from the populace—either via government surpluses, taxes, or monies underwritten for just this purpose. Most sovereign wealth funds, or SWFs, were required to file quarterly reports that included a comprehensive list of their investments. But not all. Many got away with listing investments by sector—energy, manufacturing, gaming—and providing a few financial highlights, primarily the announcement of important new investments and/or the successful liquidation of profitable positions. Everybody liked a winner.

R had provided London with two paths to follow. Find a fund that had invested seven hundred million dollars in a Saudi Arabian oil venture (on or around the date listed on the transfer) and/or identify those funds managed by that country's minister of finance.

She shooed Freddy off her lap, then double-checked the dates listed on the bank transfers. Next, she downloaded PDFs of the quarterly reports issued by each of the seven countries' sovereign wealth funds for that time period. Reporting was detective work, a slog through facts and figures, your magnifying glass ever at the ready.

Two hours later, the first cull. Out went Thailand and Vietnam. Neither had reported any investments in Saudi Arabia. Which left Singapore, Brunei, Indonesia, Malaysia, and Taiwan. All five listed investments in Saudi Arabian entities for the dates mentioned on the transfers.

More digging. More quarterly reports, these from the periods immediately preceding the transfer date. No joy. All five countries had made investments in Saudi Arabia going back years. None gave specifics about amounts invested.

London told the countries what she thought of them in no uncertain terms and stood from her desk, stretching her arms over her head. She didn't know if she loved this part of her work or hated it. A tour of the apartment. Five minutes straightening up the bathroom. Another five in front of the television, channel surfing.

She needed reinforcements. Coffee wasn't enough. Time for her secret weapon. From the back of the fridge, an ice-cold Snickers bar. This was war.

Back at her desk, she picked up her phone and scrolled through her contacts, stopping at the letter *C. Chow, Benson. Singapore National Bank.* An irritated voice answered. "Yeah?"

A small favor, London told him. Could he possibly ask around and see if any Asian SWFs had dropped nearly a billion on an investment in Saudi Arabia a few years back, maybe seven hundred million was a more accurate figure. No, she didn't know which country, and, no, it was none of his business why she was asking.

Chow hemmed and hawed. He ran the bank's trading desk, a big job, but he had the résumé for it. A Singaporean success story—MIT, Wharton, partner on Wall Street by thirty-two, before returning to work for his country. She'd interviewed him a half-dozen times for one story or another and turned him down for a date just as many.

"Caught me at a tough time," he said. "I'm really jammed."

And so, a carrot: "Find out," said London, "and I'll let you take me to dinner at the Gordon." The Gordon Grill, the fancy eatery at the Goodwood Park Hotel.

"Now that I think about it, it rings a bell," said Benson Chow. "Give me till tomorrow?"

"Close of trading today."

A sharp knock at the door came as she ended the call. London checked her watch as she rushed to the door. She'd forgotten what day it was. "I was just on the phone. Come in. Come in."

Astrid Sörensson Li swept into the apartment, slowing to bestow two brittle kisses on London's cheeks. She was sixty-six, an inch taller than her daughter, her thick hair more silver than blond, pulled off her forehead and gathered into a severe ponytail. She was a vigorous woman, with broad shoulders and a determined step. God forbid those who blocked her path. Dressed in a knee-length skirt and a sleeveless blouse, an essentials bag draped over one shoulder, she looked little different from the buxom, no-nonsense, Swedish schoolteacher who had swept London's father off his feet forty years before.

"I had hoped you would be practicing," said Astrid Li as she entered the kitchen, depositing the bag on the counter.

"It's almost noon, Mama. I'm working."

"I haven't seen your name in the paper for quite some time. I'd thought that maybe you'd lost your job. Then who would pay for this?"

"No, Mama, I haven't lost my job," said London. "In fact, I think I've found my next story."

Astrid Li nodded, adding nothing more to the subject as she unpacked their lunch. "Are you still working on the Fauré nocturne? It was your father's favorite."

"I've put it aside for now."

No comment. London's mother had never given up hope that she'd one day find the grit to overcome her injury and resume her career. "Grit." Her word. In the Li family's mixed household, it was her mother who had exhibited the Asian insistence on excellence. If there was a Swedish term for "tiger mom," it could be applied to her mother.

"What did you bring?" said London. "I'm hungry." She shot a glance at the trash can, hoping her mother wouldn't spy the Snickers wrapper. Too late, said the damning blue eyes.

"I made meatball soup and gravlax sandwiches…if you still have an appetite."

"Sounds good."

"And I'm not giving any salmon to that damned cat. He's fat enough already."

London noted that her mother's hand shook only a little as she set the sandwiches on their plates and poured herself a glass of Chardonnay.

"Are you feeling well?"

"Why shouldn't I be?"

"You look wonderful."

"I can still outrun you, young lady. Don't forget it."

"I won't, Mama."

"Two miles this morning."

"Wow. Good for you."

Astrid Li carried the plates into the dining area and set them on the table. "Let's eat." She shot London a sly smile. "I hear salmon goes wonderfully with candy bars."

Lunch lasted an hour. Afterward, Astrid Li packed the empty containers into her bag. There was no disguising the shaking this time.

"Mama!"

"I'm just fine. The tremors come and go. It's to be expected."

"Isn't there medicine?"

"Don't you think I'm taking it?" retorted Astrid Li. "Now, shall we talk about something else?"

"Have you fallen lately?"

"Do I look as if I've fallen? I'm fine, and I'll stay fine as long as I tell myself to. It's a question of discipline. Like the piano."

London took her mother by the arms. "Please, Mama, you have to let it go."

But Astrid Li had never asked for quarter, or given it. "If you wanted it, if you really wanted it, you could be there now. Carnegie Hall. The Salle Pleyel."

London nodded, knowing better than to argue. It had always been this way. Her mother would beat her multiple sclerosis just as London should have conquered the injuries to her hand. The Book According to Astrid Sörensson Li.

London handed her mother her bag, kissing her on the cheek. "You know I'm here if you need me. Just call."

"We see each other once a week," said Astrid Li. "I think that is sufficient. You're a busy woman. So am I."

"Yes, Mama." London didn't bother with a smile as she walked her mother to the door.

"I'll be looking for your name in the paper," said Astrid Li in parting.

After her mother left, London sat back down at her desk and got back to work. She started on the second path, turning to the pages listing members of the management teams and boards of directors. Quickly, two hits. Brunei and Indonesia, each country's minister of finance serving on the board.

She called back Benson Chow with the news.

"By the way," he said. "I was thinking, instead of dinner, how about a weekend at Amanpuri?"

Black-bottom pools. Chaise longues. The ultimate in luxury and serenity atop a bluff overlooking the Andaman Sea. And sex.

"Don't push your luck," said London, hanging up.

She dropped the phone on her desk. She'd done all she could for the moment. It was a question of waiting.

On the balcony, she gazed out over East Coast Park and, craning her neck, caught sight of the ocean.

"R," she said aloud, "where are you?"

Chapter 15

Where are you off to, then?" asked Harry Mason.

Four thirty p.m. The sounds of drills and rotors echoed off the shop's walls. A motor revved wildly, then died all at once. Sunlight streamed through the transom above Simon's office door. He tossed his travel bag onto the couch.

"Thailand. An old friend is in trouble."

"I'll look after the shop."

"I know you will. That's not why I called you in. Get the door, will you?"

Harry Mason closed the door. "You all right? You've been a royal pain these last few days."

"It's Lucy."

"Figured as much, me and the lads. Any change?"

"Still waiting for word." Simon shook his head. "This trip I'm taking…I don't want to go. Not with Lucy the way she is."

"You don't need to explain to me."

"Sure I do. I'm responsible for Lucy. She got hurt working for me."

"She loved it," said Harry, brightening. "Always talking about the little problems she helps you with. You didn't force her."

Simon patted Harry on the shoulder, a thank you. "Still…Well, like I said. I'm responsible. While I'm gone, I'd appreciate it if you could look after her. Visit her every day. Don't worry about your work here. If anything changes, call me. Doesn't matter when. Day or night." Simon drew a breath. "Her family won't…Well, we're all the family she has."

"Understood, boss."

"One more thing."

"I'm listening."

Simon chose his words with care. "This trip…I'm not exactly sure what I'm getting into. It's different from my usual line of work. Might be a little out of my depth. Anyway, there's an envelope in my desk with instructions, you know."

"Why are you telling me?"

"Believe it or not, you, Harry Mason, are the only family I've got."

Harry's face sagged, caught unawares. "Stop your blathering," he managed after a moment. "Never heard such a bunch of nonsense. You'll be fine. Always are."

"Sure I will be."

Harry considered this, unhappy to be put upon. "Christ, I didn't know you were one of them."

"One of who?"

"What's Lucy always saying? A 'drama queen.'"

Simon laughed. For some things, he didn't have a response.

"Need a lift, then?" asked Harry.

"You bet."

"Gatwick or Heathrow?"

"Heathrow."

"What time?"

"Seven thirty."

Mason looked at his watch. "Cutting it close."

Simon picked up his bag and threw a hand onto Harry's back. "We better take the LaFerrari. Let's see if we can't get us a speeding ticket on the way."

CHAPTER 16

Cannes

Monet or Degas?

Samson Sun studied the brochure from Christie's listing artworks for sale at the coming auction in London. Lily pads or ballerinas? He wasn't crazy about either. Or maybe a Van Gogh? He liked sunflowers, and the colors went well with the furniture in his bedroom. Estimated price: ninety million dollars. He wrinkled his nose. Not so much at the price. The problem with Van Gogh was that his friends back home could never pronounce his name correctly. It came out "Wan Gah," which sounded perilously close to "wanker," a name he'd been called more than once during his days at Harrow, the elite boarding school located in northwest London.

Sun dropped the brochure on the coffee table as his assistant arrived with a mug of steaming chai and a plate of figs. There was no question that he would replace the stolen work. This time, however, he would avoid the black market. Producers whose motion picture was set to screen on the last night of the Cannes Film Festival—an honor nearly equal to winning the Palme d'Or—did not keep works of questionable provenance on their walls, at sea or on land.

A sip of tea. Sun frowned. "Sugar?"

"Two packets."

He thrust his mug toward his assistant, displeased. Her name was Jen, and he'd found her bartending at the Soho House in Los Angeles, a six-foot blond gazelle who'd said she would do anything—*absolutely*

90

anything—to get into the movie business. So far, she'd made good on her word.

"Stevia," he said. "Stevia, stevia, stevia. How many times do I have to tell you?"

"I couldn't find any at the supermarket," said Jen.

"Did you ask by the French name?"

"Isn't stevia the same everywhere?"

"*Stévia,*" he said, with the *accent aigu. Stay-vee-ah.* He was proud of his ability with languages.

From Jen, a blank look.

Sun gave up. "Have it flown in," he said. "By noon."

Jen nodded and turned for the kitchen, before Sun grabbed the mug of tea. *Just this once.*

He adjusted his shirt—a loose-fitting batik his aunt had given him—and returned his thoughts to the stolen Monet. He had not yet heard from the police; then again, who was going to tell them about the theft? Still, he imagined he'd be receiving a visit in the not too distant future from an investigator interested to learn from whom exactly he'd acquired the painting. No questions asked, of course.

He was more bothered by the betrayal of a friend. He'd liked Riske. Not his usual type at all. No simpering, no sucking up, no currying favor. For once, a man who didn't give a damn about his money. Someone with whom he'd shared an authentic mutual interest. They had bonded. Or so he'd thought. In reality, Riske had been an operative sent by one of the insurance companies—Lloyd's, Swiss Re, it didn't matter which—on behalf of whatever museum the work had been lifted from who knew how long ago.

He didn't begrudge Riske doing his job. He only wished that he'd come straight out and asked him for the painting back. Unrealistic, Sun knew. But still…maybe, just maybe, he might have given it to him. A present to cement his friendship with the American with the frightening green eyes.

He enjoyed giving presents to those he liked.

On this day in May, Samson Min Chung Sun was thirty-one years old, stood five feet six inches tall, more fat than thin, horribly myopic, allergic to exercise, and congenitally ambitious. He was born on the island of Sumatra, largest of the Indonesian archipelago, to a wealthy family of planters—palm oil magnates—the youngest and sole male of six children. His father had been sent to boarding school in England at the age of seven, and so was Samson, first to Fettes in Scotland, then to Harrow, the school for British elites that before him had educated seven British prime ministers, including Winston Churchill and Lord Palmerston, as well as the poet Lord Byron, and, more recently, and of far more interest to Sun, the singer James Blunt and the actor Benedict Cumberbatch.

He was an unexceptional student, a non-athlete, not a luminary in any of Harrow's clubs or societies, not a thespian, a debater, or a chorister. And yet, Samson Sun was a presence. The rotund Asian with the Mona Lisa smile and the funny spectacles. Everyone knew him, though few could remember why. He was simply there, always with money in his pocket to make whatever occasion it might be a little better. More champagne. More pot. More anything. Over the years, he became a kind of barometer. If Sun was present, sure enough you were in the right place. If he wasn't, you'd better think twice. By some strange, unexplained process of human alchemy, he'd taken a drab hunk of Indonesian clay and fashioned himself into cosmopolitan gold.

From Harrow, he went on to Oxford, though no one understood how he could have scored well enough on his A levels or obtained the necessary recommendations from his masters. He lasted two years before his shortcomings were discovered. His dons at New College—or was it Balliol (he forgot himself sometimes)—were not amenable to offers of cashmere sweaters or cases of Cristal Champagne or weekends at Le Bristol in Paris. He was sent down.

A headache, he was fond of saying. Nothing more.

As was his skill, he turned the setback to his advantage, landing a job at a small merchant bank in the City. After that, details became nebulous. A year in Geneva. A year in Barcelona. A year in the Middle East followed by a sudden return to Jakarta. Then his path went dark altogether, until he surfaced in Hollywood with his screenplay about the *Medusa* to be produced and piles of money to make it happen.

When asked about those missing years, Sun smiled his inscrutable smile, ordered another bottle of the finest Champagne, and kept his mouth shut. Sometimes mystery was better than a thousand words.

Stewing, he opened the French doors and stepped onto the flagstone terrace. It was a gray, drizzly morning, and cold. He'd bought the villa in Mougins, tucked away in the hills above Cannes, expressly for the festival. The yacht was for pleasure. The villa was for business. The next week promised to be a flurry of luncheons, interviews, press junkets, parties, and meetings, meetings, meetings. The lifeblood of the entertainment industry. He intended to be a presence on the Croisette.

Across the Bay of Cannes, he could see the *Yasmina* at anchor. And beyond it, the Mediterranean. Somewhere out there, far over the horizon, was Libya. A distance of eight hundred miles. It didn't sound so far, but if you were on a rickety fishing boat crammed with hundreds of other desperate souls, most of whom couldn't swim, it might as well be the moon.

Sun knew all about the Mediterranean and the tide of refugees willing to risk their lives, the lives of their loved ones, their "everything" to reach a better life. He couldn't help but become an expert producing a film on the subject. The movie, *The Raft of the Medusa*, took as its subject the final voyage of the fishing vessel *Medusa*, which sank in the Mediterranean with five hundred men, women, and children aboard, only ten surviving a three-week ordeal afloat, clinging to a raft fashioned from the wreckage.

A reporter for *The Guardian* of London had chronicled the ordeal. A friend of a friend had brought the story to Sun's attention. Knowing he was angling to get into the motion picture industry, she had suggested he make it into a film. She'd even written a screenplay. The timing couldn't have been better. The refugee crisis in Syria was a cause célèbre. Another film, also about ships and featuring Africans in starring roles, had been a box-office hit a year or two earlier. Newly wealthy with unlimited funds at his disposal, Sun had taken this as his cue.

Three years later, he was here with a film.

Sun finished his tea, showered and dressed for the day. He had a lunch at the Carlton with a reporter from *Le Monde,* followed by a meeting with a Scandinavian distributor, a dapper Icelandic man with a name he couldn't pronounce.

A look in the mirror before he departed. Ivory suit. White shirt. Black necktie. And, of course, his eyeglasses: black, round, and thick, inherited from General Tojo, Philip Johnson, I. M. Pei, and now to claim as his own: Samson Min Chung Sun. *Who is this interesting chap staring back at me?*

As his fellow Harrovian Winston Churchill might have described him, Sun was a riddle wrapped in a mystery inside an enigma.

He wouldn't have it any other way.

CHAPTER 17

Bangkok

A black Mercedes-Benz sedan waited outside the international arrivals hall of Bangkok Suvarnabhumi Airport. A chauffeur in livery stood beside it, holding a sign with his name. SIRMON RISK.

"That's me," said Simon. "I think."

"Welcome to Thailand, sir. First time?"

"Yes."

"Very hot. May hottest month."

"You're not kidding." Simon had been outside less than a minute and already the heat weighed on him, the air humid and oppressive, smelling of jet fuel, woodsmoke, and a thousand foreign spices. He told the driver he'd keep his bag and allowed him to open the passenger door. A wave of air-conditioning greeted him as he slid into the back seat. A man sat next to the opposite door. Dark suit. Necktie. Neatly combed hair. A hyena's smile. Hundred to one a lawyer.

"Adamson," said the man. "George Adamson. Welcome to Thailand, Mr. Riske."

Surprise number one: Dickie Blackmon hadn't mentioned he was sending someone to meet him. Just as well. Simon was eager to hit the ground running. The men exchanged pleasantries as the car entered the freeway and headed into the city. A business card was proffered stating that Mr. George Adamson was a partner in the firm of Dewey, Cheatem, and Howe. Of course, that wasn't the name. Simon recognized the firm nonetheless. A multinational power player with offices in capitals around the world.

As a rule, Simon liked British lawyers and disliked French ones. He had less experience with American attorneys. Adamson appeared lean and eager, addicted to his stair-stepper and egg-white omelettes, more or less his own age, a man on the make. Only thing missing was a choke collar to rein him in when he got a little too ambitious. Securing Rafael de Bourbon's release might well be his ticket to the big time. Partners did not meet clients at the airport.

"Not sure if Mr. Blackmon gave you all the details when you last spoke, but here's the lay of the land. Over the last twenty-four hours, PetroSaud has turned over abundant evidence incriminating your friend Mr. De Bourbon in the crimes of which he stands accused. Emails, texts, recordings of phone calls between Mr. De Bourbon and Paul Malloy."

"Who's that?"

"Malloy was De Bourbon's superior at PetroSaud. He's the man De Bourbon was extorting."

"That was fast."

"They've been keeping an eye on De Bourbon for a while," said Adamson. "PetroSaud has gone a step further. They've engaged a cyber-security firm to dig up records of De Bourbon's having stolen confidential information. Your friend is guilty. No question."

"Is it illegal if he accessed the information while an employee?"

"No. But it is illegal to take the information from the premises. And it is illegal to threaten to make it public if he isn't paid what he believes is owed him."

"How much are we talking about?"

"Five million Swiss francs. Deferred bonus."

"I'd be upset, too."

"Mr. De Bourbon's personal grievance is beside the point. There are other means of remedy than corporate theft and extortion."

"And now PetroSaud wants the information back."

"Precisely."

"Any idea what he stole?"

"That's not our concern. Our concern is getting Mr. De Bourbon out of jail and back to his wife so he can get on with his life."

"Who are we dealing with? You said his name was Paul Malloy."

"The principal managing partner of PetroSaud is Tarek Al-Obeidi, a Saudi national, though we haven't heard from him. Right now the point man is Colonel Albert Tan."

Simon remembered the bio of Tan, which "Iron Ben" Sterling had provided. "Why is Tan involved in a garden-variety case of corporate blackmail? I see this kind of thing a dozen times a year in the UK. Disgruntled employee threatens to reveal company secrets, divulge recipe for the proprietary secret sauce. I don't recall the director of MI5 ever becoming personally involved."

Adamson shifted in his seat, avoiding Simon's gaze. He'd been in the game long enough to know how to keep secrets. Simon believed he was keeping one now.

"What else do you know about PetroSaud?" said Simon.

"Founded by Al-Obeidi and a group of international financiers a dozen years ago with the goal of selling off leases of undeveloped parts of the country."

"To?"

"Oil companies, of course. Sovereign wealth funds. Larger family offices. Minimum investment a hundred million dollars. Rafael de Bourbon was one of their top salesmen."

Simon knew how the game worked. Salesmen like Rafa worked on commission. One percent on a one-hundred-million-dollar investment was a healthy sum. "So why did he leave?"

"Excuse me?"

"Uh, nothing." Simon realized he'd been talking to himself. "How is Rafa doing?"

"Not well," said Adamson. "Conditions are taxing."

"I can imagine."

"I doubt that," said Adamson, as if he'd done time in a Thai jail himself and was the tougher for it. He pursed his lips, irritated. "Still, it's his own fault."

"Why's that?"

"I negotiated an agreement that would pay Mr. De Bourbon one million dollars and see him freed immediately and deported from the country upon turning over the information he stole from PetroSaud. All there in writing. He could have signed and walked out of the jail a free man."

"He turned down a million dollars?"

"He insisted on your counsel in the matter first."

"Who's offering him the money?"

"Who do you think?"

Simon considered this, not just why Rafa turned down the offer but why PetroSaud had made it. He gazed at the urban sprawl. There were skyscrapers everywhere, seemingly placed at random spots. Alone, in groups of four or five, and in the distance, a conglomeration—downtown Bangkok. Construction cranes sprouted like mushrooms. Ben Sterling was right. The place was booming.

He passed a large sign forbidding the tattooing of the image of Buddha. Heavy black clouds gathered on the horizon. He looked in the rearview mirror. The silver BMW that had followed them since leaving the airport remained two cars behind.

Their driver pulled into the fast lane and they came up alongside a truck with a caged-in flatbed. About twenty young women stood inside the cage, shorts and T-shirts, tank tops, flimsy blouses, each with one hand chained to a pole running along the top of the cage. Painted on the front door was a shield with ROYAL THAI POLICE, IMMIGRATION BUREAU on it.

"What did they do?" Simon asked Adamson.

But it was the driver who answered, a look to his right before glancing at Simon. "They are illegals. Rohingya. Muslims. Doesn't matter. They go."

"Where to?"

"Border. Myanmar. Laos. Cambodia."

"And then?"

The driver shrugged. "No more in Thailand. Better for everybody."

It began to rain, fat drops splatting the window. Simon looked at the women quickly becoming drenched. One girl met his gaze. She was younger than the others. Sixteen at most with long hair framing a pretty face. He read nothing in her eyes. This was the world and her place in it. Then the real rain began, a downpour. Within seconds, visibility was cut to inches. It was as if she had disappeared.

Simon returned his attention to Adamson. "What does Mr. Malloy have to say about all of this? He's the one who made the agreement with Rafa in the first place, isn't he? I imagine he's the one who supplied the incriminating information."

"Malloy is unavailable."

"Why is that?"

"He's no longer in the picture."

"Meaning?"

Adamson grimaced, avoiding Simon's gaze. "According to reports in the Swiss news, he was killed two days ago in a climbing accident in the Alps."

"Two days ago?"

Adamson nodded.

"An accident?"

No response. Simon could hear the lawyer's acid reflux shift into high gear.

"And you were planning on telling me *when?*"

"As I said, Colonel Tan is our point man."

"Change of plan," said Simon, tapping the driver on the shoulder. "Take me to the jail. I want to see Rafa immediately."

"Not possible," protested Adamson. "We haven't arranged a visit. They're expecting us tomorrow."

"Make it happen."

"Things don't work that way here, Mr. Riske."

"Tell Colonel Tan I may be able to convince Rafa to take the deal. That's what everyone wants, isn't it?"

Adamson studied Simon—*Yes,* thought Simon, *he wants this deal, too*—then placed a call. A heated conversation ensued. Simon was interested to learn Adamson spoke fluent Thai. No worries. Helen Mirren translated flawlessly. Adamson hung up, cheeks flushed. "One hour. But he's not happy about it."

"I'll be sure to thank Colonel Tan personally, if he manages to make it to the prison after his board meeting. Mekong Distillery…that's his brother-in-law's company, right?"

Adamson studied Simon. "How…*what*…you speak Thai?"

Simon looked out the window and silently thanked Vikram Singh.

The downpour ended as abruptly as it had begun. The sky cleared. The car slowed, then came to a halt. Cars ahead. Cars behind. Everywhere cars, none of them moving.

"Traffic bad in Bangkok," said the driver, as if boasting of one of the city's finest accomplishments.

Twenty minutes later, they left the highway and continued on surface streets, the traffic heavy here, too, motorbikes zipping past on either side. Their route took them through a dilapidated commercial area, almost a shanty town, palms, acacias, and jasmine growing among 7-Elevens and KFCs and open-front stores of every variety, wooden stalls, tin roofs, alleys leading to dark recesses.

They turned onto a multilane road and cleared a guardhouse. Another mile. A sign: BANGKOK REMAND PRISON.

As they passed through the gates, Simon checked behind them. The silver BMW had pulled to the side of the road a hundred yards behind them. But it wasn't the BMW that bothered him. It was the other car following them that had him worried: a beat-up white Nissan with a tall antenna and a blond-haired driver. The Nissan was no longer in sight, but Simon hadn't expected to see it. Whoever the blond-haired man was, he was good. Very good.

Iron Ben Sterling had been right.

Den of vipers indeed.

CHAPTER 18

Bangkok

Its official name was the Bangkok Remand Prison, and a handmade wooden sign posted at its entrance stated that it had been in existence since 1890. It did not look like a prison, thought Simon as he crossed the parking lot. Two long, low-slung, single-story buildings, painted a bright white with green shingle roofs separated by an asphalt path, plenty of greenery—shrubs, flowers, an abundance of vines. More like a private school or an old-time summer camp. If, that is, you didn't notice the fence topped with razor wire or the guards at every corner carrying machine guns. A reform school, then, Simon decided, for very naughty students.

Adamson charged ahead as if expecting to face an angry mob or a crush of reporters. They were met, instead, by a short, barrel-chested man in a white shirt and gray slacks offering a beatific smile along with an outstretched hand. He ignored Adamson and greeted Simon warmly, introducing himself as the warden of the Remand Prison, and after giving his Thai name, insisted Simon call him "Charlie."

The prison was divided into two camps, explained Warden Charlie as they walked to his office. One camp reflected the country's Buddhist heritage. It espoused compassion, forgiveness, and the belief that all of us are God's creatures worthy of his love. There, the prisoners were housed in clean, air-conditioned dormitories, offered classes in useful skills, like carpentry, electronics, and farming, and fed in a cafeteria run by fellow inmates, who did the shopping and prepared all meals. It was not, Warden Charlie concluded, an unpleasant environment to spend a lengthy incarceration.

The other camp was hewn from a different tree, he continued, guiding them through an armed checkpoint, double security gates, more razor wire, toward a second grouping of buildings: cinder block, wire-mesh windows, tin roofs. This camp did not espouse forgiveness or compassion, he explained, his saintly bearing replaced by a more earthly demeanor. Nor did it believe in redemption or love of any kind. This camp believed in pain, suffering, and the unremitting flagellation of the human spirit.

"No air-conditioning," said Warden Charlie as his phone rang. One look at the screen and he came to attention. Shoulders back. Chin up. A sharp glance over Simon's shoulder. A nervous smile. A hand to pat down his hair.

Simon turned to see a wave of khaki approaching, four men led by a tall, bull-shouldered officer, peaked cap, mirrored sunglasses. Colonel Albert Tan was in the house.

Tan zeroed in on Simon like a hawk coming in for the kill, stopping a breath from his chest. Off came the sunglasses. A lightning appraisal, his prey found wanting.

"I am Albert Tan," he said, a handshake to rival Ben Sterling's.

Simon introduced himself, holding the grip, giving every bit as good as he got.

"Who are you?" asked Tan, releasing him.

"An old friend of Mr. De Bourbon's."

"Are all your friends thieves and criminals?"

"Only my good ones."

Tan smiled wanly, hands on his hips. He'd let Simon get away with that kind of impertinence *for now*. His uniform sported more ribbons than a Russian field marshal: ten rows topped with a paratrooper's jump badge and a pilot's wings. Had Simon missed Thailand's involvement in any shooting wars? Tan's gold Rolex Daytona, however, was strictly civilian issue and, to Simon's eye, the real thing.

"What do you do, Mr. Riske?" demanded Tan.

"I own an automotive restoration shop in London. We specialize in Italian sports cars. Ferraris. Lamborghinis."

"You are a mechanic?"

"I employ mechanics."

"Why does Mr. De Bourbon think you have any expertise in legal matters?"

"I don't know."

"You're not an attorney?"

"Mr. Adamson is his attorney."

"And you are?"

"As I said, a friend."

Tan considered this. No one put one over on him. Then: "You've read the plea agreement. I expect you to advise your friend to sign it and to return the materials he has stolen."

"That would be my advice."

"Good. Let's get this matter concluded."

"You know, Rafa, I always imagined I'd run into you at the Dorchester."

"I swore I saw you once at Heathrow, Terminal 5. I was headed to Geneva. You were having a pint at one of the bars."

"You didn't stop to say hello?"

Weak smiles, but neither could laugh. Simon shook his head, eyes on his friend, letting him know that all was forgiven.

The room was a ten-by-ten concrete box, a fluorescent bulb hanging from the ceiling, two chairs, one battered wooden table. An armed guard stood in the corner. Simon was shocked at his friend's appearance. Cheeks sunken, eyes vacant, clothing stained with sweat, filthy. If this was what happened after four days, Rafa wouldn't last the full week.

"Dickie told me about your hotel," said Simon.

"It's nice." A glimmer behind the exhausted eyes. Rafa had always been a dreamer, eyes to the stars. "We're booked for six months."

"Tell you what. Let's get you out of here and you can comp me a suite."

"Deal." Rafa put his elbows on the table, head forward. "Have you seen Delphine? I'm worried about her. She's terribly frightened."

"Not yet. I came straight from the airport."

"Go see her. Tell her I'm all right?"

"Count on it." Simon covered Rafa's hand with his own to let him know he meant it. "Even more important, then, that we move quickly."

Rafa nodded.

Simon said that he'd read the proposed agreement and that everyone—Dickie, Adamson, and, according to the attorney, Delphine—wished for him to sign it, accept the million dollars, and turn over the information he'd taken from PetroSaud. "They want this nightmare to be over."

"What do you think?"

Simon mulled his response. "I think you were right to be careful," he said, letting the words sink in. "Tell me about your relationship with Paul Malloy."

"He hired me. Ran the Geneva office. My boss, I guess. He signed my contract."

"Was he the person you were 'negotiating' with?"

Rafa hesitated. "He gave me his word. I trusted him."

Trust. A liability in any industry. "Bad news," said Simon. "Malloy was killed in a climbing accident in the Swiss Alps the day before yesterday."

A look passed between them. Rafa shuddered, a man sentenced to a similar fate. "I did it for Delphine," he said. "She deserves better."

Simon was not there to pass judgment on his friend's actions. He'd come to secure his release, and now, it appeared, to make certain he returned to his home and family alive. He wondered if Dickie had foreseen this development. If by "proxy," he'd meant bodyguard. Of course he had. Dickie was a smart one, worldly wise if nothing else.

"Do you have what they want?"

Rafa nodded.

Simon knew better than to ask about what he'd stolen. Whatever it was, its value had been established beyond dispute. Paul Malloy's death was no accident. Colonel Tan, head of the Royal Thai Police, did not fly to a resort island to supervise the arrest of a foreigner accused of a white-collar crime. Nor did he cut short board meetings to oversee the prisoner's visits. This was about more than the theft of confidential information or a case of corporate extortion.

Simon switched to Spanish. The room was bugged. Their conversation was being recorded. Maybe Warden Charlie had a Spanish speaker on staff, maybe not. Better not to make it easy for them.

They talked for a while, barely a whisper, as much slang as they could manage. When Rafa switched to Italian, Simon followed suit, and then to German. The benefits of a European childhood. Slowly, the story came out. Rafa's precarious involvement with PetroSaud. Worse than Simon expected.

And so Simon asked: Where was the stolen information?

Rafa had a trick. He'd softly rap his knuckles on the table to emphasize a certain word or phrase. They'd practiced this years ago at bars and clubs in London, up-and-comers on the make, full of themselves, two young Turks angling for romance. Who gets which girl, who picks up the tab, and, just as often, when to duck out.

Bibliotheca. Monte Cristo. Chao Phraya. Delphine. Key.

Simon carved these words into his memory. And many more.

Even as they spoke, Simon tried not to think of Delphine, of what could have been, the decision Dickie Blackmon had forced him to make. Exposure, the loss of his job, and more. Too much, it turned out.

Thirty minutes later, Simon had an idea where Rafa had hidden the stolen information, as well as how to arrange the handoff and get Rafa out of the country safely.

Almost a plan.

Adamson handed Simon a folder with three copies of the plea agreement the moment he reentered the warden's office.

"Not yet," said Simon. "We have terms of our own."

Colonel Tan sat at the warden's desk. He had removed his hat and was smoking a cigarette. He was a handsome man—large eyes, straight nose, a military man's chin—except for his lips, a razor slash the color of raw liver. His underlings stood to either side of the desk, arms crossed, making no secret of their hostility. Behold the enemy.

Tan placed his cigarette in an ashtray. "You are in no position to make demands."

"No? Then why did you come here this evening?"

Tan rose halfway out of his chair, a finger pointed at Adamson. "I told them not to allow him to speak to the prisoner." His gaze shifted to Simon. "If it were up to me, I'd keep your friend locked up until his trial, and when he was convicted, see to it that he spent his time in a place far worse than this. Believe me, there are plenty in my country."

"You don't want a trial," said Simon. "You—and *them*—want the problem to go away. You want Mr. De Bourbon to disappear." *Like Malloy.* "I'm here to help you get your wish. It's what I do."

"Your problems have only just begun," said Tan. "You're in my country. You'll follow my rules."

"Please, Colonel Tan," said Adamson. "Mr. Riske means no disrespect. Let's at least listen to his proposal."

Tan nodded grudgingly, reprieve granted.

"First," said Simon, "Mr. De Bourbon gets moved to the other camp, given a shower, fresh clothing, and a decent meal. Mr. Adamson will stay here this evening to make sure it happens. Thank you, Mr. Adamson. Second, upon presentation of proof that he possesses the materials in question, the sum of one million dollars will be transferred to an account of our choosing. Details to follow. Third, he will be allowed to sell his hotel on Ko Phi Phi to the bidder of his choosing. Fourth, the agreement will be revised so that Mr. De Bourbon will not be charged with any crime under Thai law. It will be a civil agreement resolving a business dispute between Colonel Tan, on behalf of PetroSaud—or a person of your choosing—and Mr. De Bourbon. Finally, subject to their agreement, Mr. De Bourbon will be turned over to the custody of the Spanish embassy in Bangkok. It is there that he will hand over the materials in question and sign all paperwork. Once inside the embassy, he will be a free man with full diplomatic status and permitted to travel to the country of his choosing."

"Never," said Tan, heatedly. "You will not dictate terms, Mr. Mechanic. You are not fixing a car. Besides, you're forgetting something."

"Am I?"

"You've only addressed half the problem. Yes, we demand that Mr. De

Bourbon return the information he stole, but there's more to it than that. Mr. De Bourbon threatened to share the information." Tan consulted his phone, holding it a distance away so he could better read the text. "I quote from an email your friend wrote to his superior, Mr. Malloy. 'If this gets out, you guys are dead. I'll show the world what you really are. A bunch of fakes. I'll make sure it gets to every newspaper. And you know what reporters like to do. They like to dig. Believe me, I know just the person.'" Tan lowered the phone. "So?"

Adamson said: "There's no indication Mr. De Bourbon followed through with his threat. It was just that. Bluster."

Again Tan: "Mr. De Bourbon will remain exactly where he is until he is ready to cooperate with us fully. If he did carry through with his threat, and we find out first, the agreement is off. I give you my word he'll rot in one of my jails for the rest of his life."

Simon said nothing. He knew when he was beaten.

He rose and left the room.

Game to Colonel Albert Tan.

CHAPTER 19

Bangkok

Simon arrived at the JW Marriott hotel at nine o'clock. After his visit to the prison, the lobby was a sanctuary, an oasis of marble, lacquer, and florals. Adamson accompanied him to the front desk. He had not come to make sure that Simon's check-in went smoothly. His hungry, vulpine features had locked into a kind of fixed growl. He was not accustomed to clients questioning his advice, not at a thousand dollars an hour, or, for that matter, his integrity.

"You're walking a fine line, Riske," he'd said as they climbed into the Mercedes upon leaving the prison.

"Back at ya." Simon slammed the door, allowing Adamson to get settled. "Tell me something. Just whose side are you on?"

"You don't get it. Things work differently here. More liquid. More supple."

"So I've heard. 'Written in pencil, not ink.'"

"Exactly. They don't need to be entirely adversarial."

"Versus semi-adversarial? Tell me how that works exactly. Is it like being slapped instead of being slugged? Or is it more like consensual rape? You tell me."

"Don't be glib." Adamson shifted in his seat, intent on explaining what he meant. "Both sides can win. It's just a question of altering your perspective, of tempering expectation. We give them what they want. They give us what we want."

"Someone forgot to tell that to Paul Malloy."

"The man fell off the side of a mountain. Jesus Christ, Riske, it was an accident."

"You don't believe that."

Adamson was wise enough not to argue the point. He adopted a new tack. "Rafael de Bourbon is our concern, not Paul Malloy. Colonel Tan is a force in this country. He can be our best friend or our worst enemy."

"Tan's just doing what he's told. I'm more interested in who he's working for. Whoever 'them' is."

"He is representing PetroSaud."

"Is he?" Simon was happy not to be privy to the byzantine machinations and divided loyalties of Adamson's firm. A cover letter to the plea agreement written on the law firm's stationery listed the cities where it maintained offices. You could hop, skip, and jump from one to the next and make it all the way around the globe without getting your toes wet. Including two offices in Saudi Arabia, in Jeddah and Riyadh. That struck Simon as overkill in a country that size, its wealth notwithstanding.

All along he'd felt like there was a third party in the negotiations. Rafa, Tan, and another, for the moment, unnamed.

Adamson didn't say another word the rest of the way.

As Simon took the room key and walked to the elevator, the attorney trailed at his side.

"So, what's your plan?" he asked.

"I'm going to get my friend out of jail," said Simon.

"And you're going to follow Tan's advice."

"Do I have a choice?"

The elevator arrived. Simon stepped inside. Adamson made to join, but Simon threw out a hand. *Enough.* "Good night," he said. "We'll talk in the morning."

"And?" demanded the lawyer. "What are you going to do? Do you know where it is? What did he tell you? Riske? *Riske!*"

Simon unpacked, setting his clothes in neat piles on the bed. He'd been up over a day and he had a long way to go yet before he'd be crawling beneath the sheets. He saw a text on his phone. Dickie Blackmon. What the hell's going on over there?

No need to respond. Simon was sure Adamson had filled Dickie in. Or maybe Colonel Tan had done it himself, he mused venomously. Wheels within wheels.

Delete.

He walked to the window, gazing out over the city. Lights. Everywhere lights. A flashing neon sign circled a decorative column atop a skyscraper a mile away. The sign alternated between the Thai flag—red and white and blue stripes—and the message "Long live the King."

"Things work differently here," Adamson had said.

Correction, thought Simon, taking in the glittering skyline. Things worked exactly as they did everywhere else in the world.

He opened his laptop and looked up PetroSaud. The company's website described it as a privately owned oil exploration and production company. A list of PetroSaud executives included its managing partner, Tarek Al-Obeidi, a name Adamson had mentioned in the car. The rest of the top brass was the usual mix of Saudi nationals and their extravagantly paid minions. There was no mention of the ill-fated Malloy.

Simon showered, the hot jets relaxing his tired muscles, wishing he could stay there for an hour. He had no choice but to do as Tan advised. He had to give them back the material Rafa had stolen. He knew where it was, more or less, saved to a flash drive and hidden for safekeeping.

There was, however, a complication. PetroSaud had hired a cybersecurity firm to find what Rafa had stolen. Simon had employed similar firms. It was only a matter of time before they compiled a record of every keystroke Rafa had ever typed while an employee. Simon estimated another forty-eight hours before they had in their possession every email he'd sent, every spreadsheet he'd downloaded, and any document he'd read, commented on, or created. In the digital universe, every keystroke was immortal.

And something else.

Simon knew a little fact that Tan didn't. Rafa had made good on his threat to Paul Malloy and sent the information to a journalist. Not all of it. A smattering. Enough to entice a reporter to look further. Simon knew of the reporter and her work. Rafa had chosen well. Tan wouldn't take the news sitting down.

It was a race against time, the fuse lit, burning, as fuses do, too quickly. The flash drive for Rafa's life.

Simon dressed in dark pants and a black polo shirt, trading his loafers for a pair of crepe-soled shoes. He thought about room service—always slow—and instead scrounged in the minibar for his dinner, devouring a candy bar, some potato chips, before finding a banana and a mango in the fruit bowl. Still chewing, he accessed his map and typed in his destination. Four miles to the river, the Chao Phraya. Twenty minutes by car. More than an hour on foot.

First a call to the front desk.

"This is Mr. Riske, 1624. Could you send someone up to show me how to work the bedside control panel? I'm an idiot when it comes to these things. I just need to close the curtains."

"Right away, sir."

Two minutes. A knock at the door. Simon followed the hotelier around the room as she showed him how to adjust the temperature, turn on and off the lights, and, finally, how to close the drapes.

A one-hundred-baht tip. Three dollars. A polite bow, hands clasped in Thai fashion. *"Khop khun."* Thank you.

"Good night."

Simon counted to sixty, then left the room, walking in the opposite direction from the elevator bank and stopping at a set of double doors marked PRIVATE. Using the card key he'd lifted from the hotelier, he opened the door. Inside: an industrial washing machine, clothing hampers, trays of room service food, a housemaid eating a snack of oranges and crackers.

Simon nodded hello, putting his fingers to his lips—*it was their secret*—and summoned the service elevator. He had not failed to notice the silver BMW sliding into the hotel drive or the half-dozen men loitering in the lobby, all cut from the same cloth—dark suits, youngish, military haircuts—none wearing the silver pin sported by hotel employees. He'd have to have a word with Colonel Tan about his men's tradecraft.

He took the elevator to the first underground floor and found himself at the employee entrance, the walls bare concrete, rows of lockers, staff coming and going. Halfway across the area, he turned off Vikram Singh's software and removed the earpiece. He'd had enough of hearing how dark, hairy, and ugly he was. He passed through a set of steel doors into the parking garage. Up a ramp and he was outside. Into the night.

On the corner there was a gas station with a 7-Eleven. Beyond that, a busy intersection, traffic as congested at ten o'clock as at rush hour. To his right a cramped two-lane road, fair game for cars and pedestrians, bars and restaurants on both sides, neon galore. One of those streets in a city famous for them.

He set out, took one step, and turned his ankle in a hole in the sidewalk. He hopped up and down, wincing, but there was no damage. He told himself to be more careful. He looked up to see the silver BMW parked at the gas pump, the driver out of the car, turning to look at him. No more than ten feet separated the two.

Simon walked past him—no chance the driver knew what he looked like, not now, not when Simon was dressed differently—and crossed the street, swallowed by the foot traffic. He continued down Sukhumvit Road, one of the city's main commercial thoroughfares. A sidelong glance. A reflection in a tailor shop's window. The driver was following on foot, a stone's throw back, phone to his ear. Calling reinforcements. Simon hated being wrong.

He picked up the pace, longer strides but not rushing. Bangkok wasn't so different from London. People of every nationality passed him by. Arabs, Africans, Chinese, Indians, and far too many drunken Europeans. He resisted the invitations of several ladies, and several more who might not be. Land of Smiles.

The night was warm, 85 degrees, the heat a velvet shawl, sweat already rolling down his spine. He came to the stairs leading to the Skytrain. A blind woman sat nearby singing along to a recorded Thai folk song. An old man missing his feet lay next to her, cup raised. Simon gave each a banknote, catching sight of his pursuers, the driver now joined by another. If this went on much longer, Simon was likely to get an inflated opinion of himself.

Enough, he decided. He had places to go, people to see.

Simon looked to his left and dashed into the street, dodging cars, running down the center of the road. A check over his shoulder. He made it to the far sidewalk. No horns sounded. No drivers raised an angry hand in his direction.

He doubled back toward the hotel, catching his foot on another upturned slab of concrete. He fell forward, a hand arresting his fall. What was it with the sidewalks? He came to an intersection, a flood of pedestrians waiting to cross, blocking his way. He went around them, turning up the street, aware he was going in the opposite direction he needed to be. At least he could move faster.

The signs changed from English to Arabic. Pharmacies, nail salons, tailors, all open for business. Men in kaftans and dishdashas, women in black burkas, covered head to toe. An alley opened to his right. He ducked into it. Smoke. Coal-fired braziers. The acrid scent of roasting lamb. Tinny music blared from a storefront. The Cairo hit parade. He ventured a look behind him. A man on his tiptoes, searching. Their eyes met. Too late, Simon jumped back.

Who were these guys?

He was standing at the entrance to some kind of club: dark interior, crimson lights. Men sat around low tables smoking hookahs, the scent piquant and alluring, not just tobacco.

"Is there a rear exit?" he asked the doorman in his prison-yard Arabic.

The doorman shook his head, unimpressed. *Not for you.*

Simon thrust a thousand-baht note into his palm. Thirty dollars.

The doorman motioned him to follow.

They passed through a heavy curtain, then up a flight of stairs, the smell of incense and patchouli sweet and thick. Up again to the second floor, then along a dimly lit hallway, doors open to either side, dark-eyed women lounging on cushions. *Come in. Let me entertain you.*

"You want?" asked the doorman.

Simon shook his head. "Exit."

The doorman stood aside, duty fulfilled, and pointed to a flight of stairs, a barred door barely visible at the top. Simon ran up the stairs, giving the door a shove with his shoulder. He stepped onto a fire escape, rusted and unsteady, swaying under his weight. He turned and reached for the door as it slammed shut. He tried the handle. Locked.

He ran down a flight, both hands on the railings, metal groaning. Dead end. No ladder. No more stairs. A fifteen-foot drop to the alley. He retraced his steps, continuing up several flights to the roof.

It was a world unto itself. A tended garden, chickens in a coop, an Exercycle. He heard a door slam somewhere below him, the rickety fire escape groan. He ran to the edge of the building. A seven-foot drop to the next rooftop, the buildings cheek by jowl. He jumped and landed heavily, wiping his hands as he stood. Up again, running to the next building and the next, aware of a figure giving pursuit, thinking Colonel Tan had better give his men a raise.

He arrived at the last building on the block. One foot on the parapet, he gazed over the edge. Four stories to the ground. Across the street, a forty-story apartment building. He turned, searching the rooftop. There, hiding in the rear corner, a makeshift hovel, planks, tin roof, lights burning behind flimsy drapes. He pulled aside the curtain and entered. A man and woman sat cross-legged on a Persian rug, bowls of noodles in their laps, watching television. They gazed at him, neither evincing much surprise.

"Downstairs?" said Simon, winded, hands on his hips.

The man pointed at a door across the room.

"Thank you."

As he reached the bottom of the stairwell, he heard a door slam several floors up, another set of footsteps.

He was done running.

He opened the door to the street and let it close. He did not go outside. Crouching, he hid beneath the stairs. Footsteps echoed in the stairwell, closer and closer still. He could hear the man fighting for breath, as fatigued as Simon. The footfall grew louder. He caught sight of the man's back, an arm reaching toward the door.

Simon slid from his hiding place. Taking hold of the man with both hands, he threw him against the wall. He was young, maybe thirty. Stunned, he fell to a knee, turning to confront his aggressor. Simon hit him twice, solar plexus, chin.

The man's eyes rolled and he collapsed in a heap. Finished for now.

Back outside, Simon walked from intersection to intersection, searching in vain for a street sign. A block farther on, he saw a bridge and, to one side, a string of people descending a stairwell, disappearing from view. Reaching the bridge, he joined those taking the stairs. A rush of cool air greeted him, the pleasing scent of fresh water and plumeria. He skidded on the dirt footpath running along a broad creek. A *klong,* one of many cutting in every direction through Bangkok. Foliage everywhere—casuarinas, bamboo, palms, a jungle in the city.

He walked beside the water, the growl of an approaching motor drawing his attention. A longboat ferrying a dozen men and women, plenty of open seats, pulled to the riverbank.

"Okay?" Simon asked a young man, dressed in a school uniform, meaning could he climb aboard.

"Sure," said the high school student. "Where would you care to go, sir?"

"Chao Phraya. Bang Rak."

"Five stops."

Simon joined the queue.

CHAPTER 20

Bangkok

H ello."

"Hello, Delphine. Do you know who this is?"

"Yes."

And she knew well enough not to say his name...*just in case*. As for Simon, he knew well enough to call on the Oriental hotel's landline. Who used that anymore? Certainly not friends. He had no doubt that her cellphone was compromised in one way or another.

"Go to the lobby," he said. "Walk out the main entrance. To your right at the far side of the drive, you'll see a set of stairs leading to the river. It's a nice night for a stroll. Five minutes."

He'd met her on a frigid December day in London eleven years earlier.

He saw her in his mind, walking toward him through the high-ceilinged foyer of Chatham House. She was tall and blond and angular with skeptical blue eyes and a puckish grin. Her entire manner screamed that she was smarter, cleverer, and a damned sight better looking than the rest. If she'd been a man, Simon would have wanted to punch her in the nose. As it was, he wanted to do quite the other thing. What was he to do but say hello?

"You're not with the bank."

"God no," she said with an air of real offense. "I should hope not."

"Are we that bad?"

"I'm sorry," she said. "You were at the lecture. Forgive me. I'm hopeless."

Anything but, thought Simon.

For the past three hours he and the two dozen other members of his intake class at the bank had sat together in an auditorium at Chatham House, 10 St. James Square, and listened to a series of speakers lecture them on ethics and global responsibility.

"A dash of idealism before being sent out into the real world," he said. "I just finished my first year. They move us through the different departments, give us a taste of all the bank's activities."

"Oh, I know. It's an annual affair. Bank sends a new batch every December. I wrote it, by the way. The lecture, I mean."

"You work here…at Chatham House?"

"No one actually works in the building except for admin and staff. But, yes, I do work for Chatham House. Fellows do their research elsewhere and come to share it with other members, or, in this case, the lambs being led to slaughter."

Chatham House, officially known as the Royal Institute of International Affairs, took its offices in a bland, four-story brick building, hardly differing from those on either side, that had been home to three prime ministers: William Pitt the Elder, Edward Stanley, and William Gladstone. Its charter gave its aims as the advancement of international politics, the investigation of international questions by means of lectures and discussion, and the exchange of information, knowledge, and thought on international affairs. It was widely regarded as the finest think tank in the world.

"If you wrote it, why didn't you deliver the lecture?"

A raised brow. A look that said, *Seriously? You don't think I'd fall for that.* "You were supposed to have been impressed by the former chancellor of the exchequer and the head of the World Bank. Paragons of your world. I don't think a twenty-four-year-old doctoral candidate can compete."

"I'm not so sure," said Simon. "I'd listen to you."

"I'd make certain you did."

"I liked the talk. I did, really."

"I believed you the first time. Not sure about the second." The smile faded, her gaze much too frank. "But will you take it to heart? Me, I live in an ivory tower. You, you're out there in the real world. Where are you being posted, anyway?"

"Private banking."

"The front lines. Face-to-face with the enemy."

"The enemy?"

"The wealthiest of the wealthy. What's the minimum deposit these days? Fifty million? A hundred? To get that kind of money, you have to have set aside your morals long ago."

"That's a cynical way of looking at the world."

"Machiavellian is more like it, though I'd prefer plain realistic. You look like you understand what that means. Not one of those pink-cheeked cherubs from Eton or Winchester, are you?"

"No."

"Don't look it."

"I suppose we're getting somewhere, then."

"I can't quite see you cooped up in an office twelve hours a day."

"It's not so bad."

"Maybe you'll be the one who does something about it."

"About what?"

"Everything. Greed. Corruption. Cronyism. The yawning chasm of income inequality that threatens to bring the world to the brink of revolution."

"Right now I'm just looking forward to doing my job."

"A company man. A factotum."

"You show no mercy, do you?"

"I don't know about that." She stepped closer to him, so close he could smell her perfume, count the lashes above her eyes. "I'm always on the lookout for someone to bring over to my side."

Simon laughed. "A true believer."

She flinched, and he noted the flash in her eyes, the flush of her cheeks. "Someone had better be."

"Do true believers go out for drinks?"

"Not with the enemy."

"Not yet, I'm not. There's still a chance."

"You know…I just think there might be."

"I'm Simon. Simon Riske."

"Delphine. Delphine Blackmon."

She extended her hand, and he couldn't help but notice the chic watch hanging from her wrist. A Rolex Oyster. De rigueur for every crusading do-gooder.

Eleven years.

A heartbeat.

Simon watched Delphine descend the stairs and walk along the path toward the river, her face visible only intermittently, on and off like an old-time flicker as light from one lamp and then another fell upon it. She looked thinner, sharper, her hair cut shorter, blonder, dyed now. Her posture was more erect, her step too confident, trying to be something. A woman where before there'd been a girl.

He stepped from the shadows. "Hello, Dee."

Delphine Blackmon halted, hand to her chest. "You startled me."

Simon kept an eye over her shoulder. He caught no sign of anyone following but knew better than to trust himself. He was still wondering about the white Nissan and its blond driver. "I'm sorry. Precautions."

"So this is what you do now?"

"Not exactly."

Delphine stepped closer as if drawn against her will, a hand rising to his cheek. Abruptly, it fell to her side. Past was past. "How is he?"

"We need to get him out," said Simon.

"What can I do?"

"I'm not sure if you can do anything. Has Adamson kept you up to date?"

"Oh yes. Mr. Adamson is thorough if nothing else. He wasn't happy with how your meeting at the jail went this evening. He told me you were confrontational bordering on disrespectful. He said you offended Colonel Tan."

"He told me the same thing."

"You don't like him."

"Let's just say that he and I approach the table from different sides."

"What does that mean?"

Simon let it hang there. She knew him well enough, how he did things. "Tell me about PetroSaud."

Delphine shrugged. What do wives know about their husbands' jobs? "So long ago. Rafa turned Malloy down at first, despite the fact that he desperately needed a job. Said he didn't like Geneva. Malloy wouldn't take no for an answer. He hounded Rafa, offered him an apartment in Cologny, a car—a Porsche—expense account. Rafa ate at Le Relais de l'Entrecôte three times a week."

"Did he mention any problems? Anything that bothered him while he was there?"

"We didn't talk about work. I was traveling myself, research, writing. Mostly the Middle East, Africa. I had my own thing. Besides, you know how I feel about what you do."

"What I do?"

"You and Rafa. Banks. Financiers. Insurance companies. Private equity. The Four Horsemen of the Apocalypse."

"I don't think we're as bad as all that."

Delphine canted her head. "Wasn't my father one of your clients?"

Simon nodded. They both knew he was.

"Case closed."

"Your opinion of him runs contrary to the queen's."

"Sir Dickie? 'Sultan of Stratford.'" He heard a laugh, even if it wasn't out loud. "Yours doesn't?"

"Bankers don't comment on their clients."

"Such a convenient way to avoid examining your conscience."

Simon smiled, not about to be drawn into an argument, happy, though, that some things never changed, or at least some people. A last glance behind them. No one hiding in the shadows.

Twenty yards ahead, a walkway followed the banks of the Chao Phraya—the River of Kings—the broad waterway that twisted and turned through the city, emptying into the Gulf of Thailand fifteen miles south. Hotels, apartment buildings, offices, new and old, lined either bank. At eleven o'clock, river traffic was lively, vessels moving in both directions, mostly barges ferrying supplies up-country. Even at night, he could see that the water was filthy.

They walked shoulder to shoulder.

"Still trying to save the world," said Simon.

"I gave up a long time ago. I'd settle for educating one person at a time. Ever read any of my articles?"

Last he'd heard, Delphine was still at Chatham House, traveling the world, raising money from foundations here and there to pay for her articles about the humanitarian aid crisis.

"No. I'm sorry."

"Figures. No fast cars or pretty girls in them. Probably still reading your Dumas novels. *Count of Monte Cristo. The Three Musketeers.* Simon, my hopeless romantic." She looked away. "I'm trying to be mad at you."

"I know you are."

Delphine stopped, turned her powerful gaze on him. "You never told me why. You just went away. It wasn't fair. A girl deserves to know. Oh God, listen to me. *A girl. A woman* deserves to know. A human being with a beating heart."

"Delphine," he said firmly. They were adults. It was a long time ago. Then: *My God, she still doesn't know the truth.* Well, he wasn't going to tell her now.

"It's all right," she said. "I mean, thank goodness you walked away. I'd never have been with Rafa."

The knife twisted in his gut just as she'd wanted.

She started walking again. "Thank you for coming. I know you and Rafa aren't speaking."

"He's like a brother. Of course I came."

Delphine laughed. "You have a strange way of showing your affection. Both of you."

She threaded her arm through his. They continued on a short way without speaking. He felt the warmth of her body pressing against his. What had it been about her that had so captivated him? Her intelligence, her strength, her particular beauty? Or maybe her vulnerability despite the rest of it? She'd opened herself to him unconditionally, the first woman he'd truly known. And him…had he done the same? It had taken this long to answer truthfully. No, he had not.

"Did Adamson talk to you about Paul Malloy?" he asked.

"Just that Rafa was blackmailing him, threatening to reveal something about the company unless he paid him the bonus he was due. I take it Malloy didn't pay."

Simon stopped, turning to face her, thinking maybe Adamson wasn't so thorough after all. He told her about Malloy and the climbing accident and his opinion about it.

Delphine clutched her arms to her chest. "This changes things."

Simon nodded. The look that passed between them indicated she was of a mind with him.

"Damn him," said Delphine, meaning, of course, Rafa. "What do *you* know about PetroSaud?"

"Not enough. Look, Rafa wants to cooperate. In return for his freedom, he needs to give Colonel Tan the information he stole and was using to blackmail Paul Malloy into paying him his bonus. I think I know where he hid it. Do you know a place called Little Havana?"

"It's a cigar club. I hate it. Cohiba this, Montecristo that. He goes with some of his pals when he's in town. Comes back smelling as if he'd bathed in tobacco."

"Something about a locker?"

"Members keep bottles of their favorite liquor in them. Rum, cognac, whatever."

"Do you have the key?"

Delphine looked at him askance. "Do you honestly think he could hold on to it?"

"Rafa hasn't changed."

"No," said Delphine, without humor. "He hasn't."

"He did it for you."

"That's what he always says."

"Malloy owed him five million Swiss francs. Real money."

"Daddy has ten times that much. A hundred times."

"And so…" Simon opened his hands. "You married a Spaniard."

"The last proud man."

"He'd like to think so."

"What happens now?"

"I go to Little Havana. Find what Rafa left there. Adamson sets up an exchange. Rafa suggested bringing in the Spanish ambassador. He's a friend, I take it. We give Colonel Tan what he wants, then put Rafa on the next plane out of here."

"And our hotel on Ko Phi Phi? What about that?"

"I'm working on it. I wouldn't count on anything."

"I'm sure Daddy can do a deal. Commerce is his bailiwick."

"If anyone can, it's Dickie."

Delphine returned to her room, waited an hour as per his instructions, and came back with the key to the locker. "Little Havana is in Chinatown. You won't find a sign. It has a secret entrance." She told him the name of the street and what to look for. "There will be a doorman across the street. He's Cuban. Raúl is his name. You can't miss him."

Simon thanked her and told her he would be in touch in the morning.

"Get him out," she said. "Don't break my heart twice."

Chapter 21

Bangkok

Simon left the Oriental hotel and walked north along Charoen Krung Road. He was in old Bangkok, the quarter built nearly two hundred years earlier in the hook of the Chao Phraya River, home to Dutch and British trading houses, Chinese hongs, the province of thieves, grifters, smugglers, the flotsam and jetsam of every nationality that washed up at the end of the world. He passed along narrow roads and narrower alleys, rickety, tin-roofed shanties crowding in, neon lights reflecting off puddles in the road, everywhere stalls selling fried fish, chicken livers, and eels. The streets coursed with purpose, pulsing as the clock struck midnight, a constant human traffic. He charged ahead, a foreigner never more at home than when lost on foreign streets and surrounded by foreign people. He walked like a man pursued, but by what?

A woman, of course.

Another memory of Delphine. The opposing bookend, not the beginning but the end.

A long weekend in Paris. Late March. The first leaves had sprouted on the London plane trees lining the Champs-Élysées. Painterly clouds scudded fast and low across the sky, brushing the top of Les Invalides, cloaking the Eiffel Tower. The Seine ran full with spring melt, its waters a milky green and rough, riding high on its banks. In the Tuileries, the first tables had been set out. A hopeful ice cream vendor awaited the first customers of the year.

So Paris, as always.

It had been a weekend to celebrate. Simon had finished his training at the bank. Delphine, four years younger, had taken a new post at Chatham House, working as a research assistant helping craft papers that would shape European policy. More important, it was their first anniversary as a couple, if they were keeping track, which neither was, or so they claimed.

Simon had spent time at the Sciences Po studying mathematics and knew the city well. Where to get a cheap *ballon de rouge* that wouldn't kill a man and where he could eat like a prince for ten euros and like a king for fifteen, where he could dance all night for next to nothing and where he could find a wonderful crêpe suzette at dawn.

Delphine also knew Paris well, if from a different economic vantage point. She'd come often to shop and dine and visit museums and dance at the trendiest clubs. It was she who insisted they try the tasting menu at L'Arpège and the pressed duck at La Tour d'Argent. *Mais, il faut!* She bought him a cashmere sweater at Balibaris and tickets to La Comédie-Française (Simon's first play in any language). Of course, they went to Castel's afterward.

They made love in the morning, after lunch, before going out in the evening, as a prelude to sleep. He had only himself to give. He held back nothing.

On Sundays, they visited the Louvre. He thought of it as "his museum." As a student, he'd whiled away long, rainy winter afternoons there, a baguette smuggled inside his raincoat. What cheaper entertainment? His destination never altered. The Pavilion Denon. The paintings of the Renaissance weren't for him. Neither the Baroque. He preferred the large-scale historical works of Delacroix and David and Ingres. Works like *Oath of the Horatii,* and *Liberty Leading the People.* And his favorite, the larger than life *Coronation of Napoleon.* Delphine laughed at his taste. "Pedestrian." "Juvenile." "Cartoonish." The words bounced off Simon like water off a duck's back. Emperor Napoleon gave him a wink and let him know that he was the one with good taste.

And then, later that afternoon, crossing the Jardin du Luxembourg, an incident, in and of itself, as Parisian as buying an éclair at Stohrer. A Roma woman, a gypsy, approached the lovers, a baby in tow, her hand extended. A beggar. Delphine smiled, immediately amenable. Simon knew better. "No," he said. "Not today."

The Roma was insistent. Refusing to be put off, she came closer, crowding them, the baby crying now, as if on cue.

"Please," said Delphine. "It's all right."

Simon relented, handing the Roma a two-euro piece. Delphine nodded her approval. Thus preoccupied, neither saw the second Roma approach from behind. A man, and sly. Simon saw him only as he withdrew Delphine's pocketbook from her Hermès bag. He caught the man by the arm. There was a struggle. The tussle ended badly for the Roma, who retreated without the pocketbook, his wrist fractured. The entire incident was over in a minute.

But the day was spoiled. Delphine was unable to let it go, upset that their *rêverie* had been broken. She looked at Simon differently. Why wasn't he as bothered as she? And where had he learned to break a man's wrist as if it were a matchstick?

The call from Dickie Blackmon had come the next day. *"I know all about you. I won't hesitate to tell others. Stop seeing my daughter or else."*

Simon swept the memories aside. The past brought nothing but pain, too often in the form of truth. He'd convinced himself that his feelings for Delphine had died long ago, or at least withered absent nurture. Ten minutes in her presence and his defenses—so painstakingly constructed, so artfully reinforced, so skillfully maintained—had crumbled. One look was enough. In that look, the knowledge of all that once was and could never be. Heartbreak. Why was he surprised that he was not immune? Fool.

A laugh. Rich, well deserved. *Ah, life!* Move on.

And now, to be a friend. The chance to repay a debt. No fees, no clients, no middlemen. Simply to be of service, to give of himself. For once, an honest reason to travel halfway around the world.

Or was it?

Was Delphine the real reason he'd come? A last chance to prove himself the better man?

He dismissed the thought. Only actions mattered. He was here.

Simon veered left onto Yaowarat Road, into Chinatown. Smoked ducks hung upside down on curing hooks, tables pushed onto the streets crowded with customers slurping soups and banging tea cups, and always the motorbikes zipping past too close for comfort. He was looking for an old, immense banyan tree that dominated an intersection. He had turned off his phone, that much more difficult to follow him. He spotted the tree—one couldn't miss it—the roots as pronounced as canyons, the intertwined branches spreading across the street, blocking out the night sky, an impenetrable canopy.

He searched for a Cuban-looking doorman, saw none. He continued to the end of the block and retraced his steps, uncomfortable now, conspicuous. He slowed, the smell of cigar smoke sharp in his nostrils. He was in the right place. Or was he?

He ducked into a convenience store—two counters, fluorescent lights, selling water, chips, candy, and a variety of pharmaceuticals. He asked for Little Havana. The clerk pointed out the door, motioning emphatically, barking out instructions. Simon stepped outside, took a few steps, angry at himself, still unable to find the club.

The next instant an enormous black man was standing beside him. A head taller, dressed in a dark suit, shoulders to rival Atlas. How long had he been studying Simon?

"Raúl?"

The man nodded, stepped across the street, and pointed to a phone booth. It was from another time and another country, an anachronism— collapsible doors, rotary dial, waiting for Clark Kent, or, in this case, Simon Riske. He'd looked at it several times, failed to remark that it belonged in New York City or Chicago, not Bangkok.

Hiding in plain sight.

"1-9-5-8," said Raúl.

Simon understood at once. The final year of the revolution. December 31st. Batista out. Castro in. He entered the booth, Raúl holding the door, picked up the phone, and dialed the four digits. The opposite wall slid to one side.

One step and he was transported to Cuba back in the day. It was a high-ceilinged space, with an endless wooden bar, a mirror behind it, "El Floridita" painted in festive script—Hemingway's spot—rows of spirits, glasses on shelves. Wicker fans turned slowly overhead. A guitar quartet played from a balcony. "Desafinado." Couples danced.

The host was Brazilian, wearing a guayabera shirt. Simon explained that he was a friend of Mr. De Bourbon and that he'd come to collect something from his locker. He showed the key and asked him to call Delphine if he had any questions.

The host—a hard man beneath his Latin charm—appraised Simon. "The lockers are upstairs. To the right. I'm pleased to offer you a drink on the house."

"Another time," said Simon, then climbed a winding flight of stairs to the second floor. Darker here, leather armchairs grouped around low tables. Men, women too, smoking cigars, spirits glimmering in crystal highball glasses.

The members' lockers were tucked away in a dimly lit alcove, names engraved on gold plates. He found Rafa's in short order. The key fit. Three bottles inside. Rum, cognac, and marc—peasants' brandy. Simon ran a hand over the surfaces, then along the walls. Nothing. He examined each bottle against the amber light, saw nothing floating inside. One by one, he unscrewed the caps, checked. A flash drive, smaller than any Simon had seen, was hidden inside the bottle of marc. He used his thumbnail to free it. The size of a stamp and wrapped in plastic.

What, he wondered, had Rafa stolen that had placed his life in jeopardy and already cost another man his?

Simon slipped the drive into his pocket. It wasn't just a question of delivering it to Tan. He needed to find out its contents. He was no longer an innocent bystander but an involved party. Did Malloy deserve justice any less because Simon hadn't known him? He remembered Tan's withering glare, the promise to balance the scales of a punishment yet to come. Simon was in this, too, now.

But he wasn't the only one Rafa had drawn in.

Standing there in the alcove, smoke curling beneath the ceiling,

Simon thought about the journalist Rafa had contacted. London Li. He knew her name, every banker did. An investigative reporter whose stories appeared in the *Financial Times*. Not someone you would want writing about you.

He would have to contact her. *And say what?* A warning, that was all. *"Be careful." "Watch your back."* And what about Malloy? Should he mention him? He decided against it. Up to her to find out. She'd been given PetroSaud's name. It was all there.

Still, he was worried that to a reporter of her caliber the warning might have the opposite effect: A tap to the flanks. A goad instead of a caveat. Maybe. Maybe not. That part was beyond him.

He closed the locker and returned downstairs.

"Is there another way out?" he asked, palming the host a thousand baht.

Grease, Iron Ben had said, *makes the wheels go round.*

The host led him through the kitchen. A door to the back alley stood ajar. Simon dodged the staff and stepped outside. A rat scurried past, followed by several more. A few feet away, a raccoon stood on its hind legs, rooting in a garbage can. A dishwasher crouched on his haunches beside it, smoking. He gazed at Simon, blew out a cloud of smoke, then looked away.

Simon made his way back to Charoen Krung Road. His hotel lay a few miles east, toward the center of town. He had his phone, his wallet, his passport, everything he needed. He felt the small drive in his pocket. Almost everything.

He paused at a street corner, weighing his options. His absence would have been reported hours ago. He was officially MIA. He imagined Tan's outburst upon learning that his men had lost him and smiled. *Good,* he thought. He wanted Tan on edge, playing off his back foot. Simon's ability to move freely was an advantage, maybe his only one. Returning to the hotel was out of the question. His room there was nothing more than a gilded tiger trap.

He walked toward the river and came upon a bustling night market, row upon row of stalls selling clothing, shoes, toys, and copy watches beneath a patchwork tin roof, and at the far back corner, electronics. He showed a vendor the flash drive and his phone. The vendor wrinkled his nose, then rooted beneath his stall. A cry of victory. He stood, handing Simon an iOS–flash drive adapter. One end plugged into his phone, the other docked with the flash drive.

"Two thousand baht."

"Five hundred," said Simon.

"One thousand."

Simon peeled off a bill.

"Khop khun." The vendor clasped his hand in prayer and bowed. Smiling, he dropped a garland of flower petals around the neck of a Buddha standing watch on a table behind him. Simon had overpaid.

He continued down the aisle, finding a stand that sold mobile phones. He purchased three burners, the cheapest available, phones he could use once and discard.

He left the market, the river a block ahead, waves brushing against the shore. He turned down a shabby alley. Halfway along, a hand-painted sign hung from a bamboo pole. "The Orchid. Room 300 Baht." He didn't think this establishment was listed on TripAdvisor.

Simon ascended a flight of stairs wedged in between two shuttered stalls. There was no door, just a counter on the first-floor landing. Beneath a flickering bulb, the night clerk slept in his chair. Simon cleared his throat. The clerk opened one eye. "Five hundred baht," he said. Sixteen dollars. Nearly twice the advertised rate. Simon must be getting the presidential suite.

He placed a bill on the counter and received a key in return. "Down there," said the clerk, motioning vaguely toward an unlit corridor. Simon's room was the last on the right. The door was unlocked. A torrent of frigid air. Paradise. He turned on the light. A smile of surprise. The room was the size of a jail cell—a single bed, a chair, a sink, and a toilet—but spic-and-span, smelling of lemon floor cleaner and disinfectant. Two towels were folded neatly on the bed along with a mint on the pillow. The Four Seasons take note.

He locked the door and jammed his chair beneath the doorknob. It worked in the movies, right? He washed his face and undressed. Fatigue fell upon him like a hammer. He sat on the edge of the bed, eyes heavy. No sleep. Not yet.

Wearily, he removed the iOS adapter from its packaging. He plugged one end into his phone and attached Rafa's flash drive to the other. An icon appeared named "PetroSaud Confidential." A box opened beneath demanding a password.

Simon tried several. Rafa's birthday, Delphine's birthday, variations thereof. No joy. He turned the phone off.

He took a burner out of its box and texted Adamson. Mission successful. Set up exchange.

An answer came back immediately. Where the hell are you? Tan furious.

The phone buzzed in his hand. Simon denied the call. Another text followed. Did you get it? Call me. Urgent.

TTYL, Simon texted. He turned off the phone, dug out the SIM card, and with difficulty snapped it in two, before flushing the pieces down the toilet.

He broke out phone number two and texted Delphine. Success. All good. Get out of the country as soon as possible.

He waited a minute or two, but no reply was forthcoming. He had one last call to make. He dialed the country code 44 for England. A crusty voice answered on the fourth ring. "Hello."

"Harry, it's me."

"Evening, lad, or is it morning? Either way, you're up late."

He heard a commentator in the background. Soccer. What else? "What game are you watching?"

"A replay of the Gunners' last. FA Cup this weekend. I'm getting ready."

"You going?"

"Are you kidding? Tickets are five hundred quid to begin. I can see it better at the pub."

"How's Lucy?"

A pause. Harry Mason cleared his throat.

"Harry?"

"There was some kind of setback. A neuro-something-er-ather…

Sorry, lad, don't know what it's called. The doctor said there was some bleeding on the brain. But she said they'd caught it early and that I shouldn't worry."

"Did the doctor say anything else?"

"Only that she's resting comfortably."

Simon rubbed a hand across his forehead. "Poor kid."

"Nothing you can do, lad. It's in the Lord's hands. I'll call if anything changes."

Simon turned off the phone and disposed of the SIM card in a like manner. It was three a.m. He doused the lights and lay down. He looked up at the ceiling and whatever was beyond it. "Please," he said. "Take care of her."

Finally, he closed his eyes.

What choice did man have but to believe?

CHAPTER 22

Pleasant dreams, Mr. Riske."

The man named Kruger turned from the darkened window on the first floor of the ramshackle tenement and retraced his steps to Charoen Krung Road, heading back to a group of street vendors he'd passed earlier. Fish, eels, meatballs. He stopped in front of a large wok, oil bubbling, a vendor scooping out the deep-fried chicken feet and chicken heads with a woven ladle. He breathed in the sharp, salty scents. The smells of his childhood.

"One," he said, a finger raised.

The vendor prepared a plate of three feet and three heads. Kruger paid him and moved down the street, finding a quieter spot to eat. Not bad, he thought, chewing the feet off a wooden skewer. "Walkie-Talkie," they called the dish in his native South Africa. There, in the slums of Jo'burg, chefs prepared the dish two ways: breaded and fried or braised over hot coals. Add a little sweet chili sauce and there was nothing better.

Kruger tossed the paper plate into the trash, crouching to pick up a few cups and bottles that had missed the target. He detested litter.

His given name was Solomon Kruger Mkwezi. He was thirty-eight years old, the illicit offspring of a South African father, a supervisor at the De Beers mine in Kimberley, a member of the Xhosa tribe, as black as the coal seam he'd worked his entire life, and a German mother, the mine's director of finance, blond, blue-eyed, and built like the mighty Valkyries who adorned the prows of old-time sailing ships. "Illicit" because at the time of his birth in South Africa it was illegal for a black man and a white woman to have sexual relations. Apartheid was the law of the land. "Apartheid," the Afrikaans word meaning "apartness," a system of institutionalized segregation based on the principles of white supremacy. Being born was the first criminal act Solomon Kruger committed.

Until the age of ten, he lived with his father in a company town for miners outside the fences. Forbidden to go to the school for children of mine employees—white children—he attended local schools. Dirt floors. Thatched roofs. A blackboard. He was the only student with mixed blood. His straw-colored hair made him stick out more than his toffee-colored skin and pale blue eyes. His schoolmates made fun of his straight nose and his thin lips, teasing him mercilessly, beating him, calling him *"Wite,"* the white one. Hatred ran both ways.

He learned to fight at a young age. At first, he lost. Then, as he grew, no more. His father called him "Shaka," after the invincible Zulu chief, a symbol of pride for all black South Africans. His father taught him to box, to grapple. He gave him a set of weights and each morning supervised his training, doing calisthenics alongside him. "You are Shaka. You are a warrior."

And then, tragedy. A cave-in at the mine. His father buried alive alongside forty others at the bottom of an open pit a thousand feet deep. Shaka considered his nickname his father's lasting gift. With no family in the village, he was sent to live with his mother. It was 1992. Mandela had returned from exile. De Klerk had yielded power to the African National Congress. Apartheid was rescinded. But attitudes long ingrained were not easily dispelled. A mixed-race boy was not welcome, law or no law. Under pressure, his mother resigned her post and with her son returned to her home.

The Federal Republic of Germany was a liberal country, in politics and worldview. Still, Shaka was an outsider, struggling to learn a new language, his English scarred by a strong Afrikaans accent. He took his mother's family name but thought of himself simply as "Shaka."

By temperament, he was possessed of a short fuse and a simmering rage. An offhand glance, the wrong word, a misunderstood gesture, could set him off. People avoided him. He had few friends. He found solace in sport. His schoolmates had been playing soccer for years, real soccer—not kicking a deflated ball across a dirt field. He chose gymnastics instead. It was a good fit, the various disciplines tailor-made for an unnaturally strong and agile young man. His favorite was the rings. No one could hold the "iron cross" longer. His body grew accordingly, his arms, shoulders, and chest a tangled knot of muscle. There was talk of the national team, a trip to the Olympic Games in Sydney. An argument ended his dreams. Athletes did not shatter the jaw of their coach, no matter how badly they disagreed with him.

From high school to the army. By now he spoke German fluently, as well as English, Afrikaans, and his father's Xhosa. His language skills and innate intelligence combined with his physical prowess made him a natural for special forces, the GSG 9—the Grenzschutzgruppe 9. He thrived in the atmosphere of discipline and comradery, for once accepted as an equal. He trained with the Delta Force at Fort Bragg and the SAS at Hereford. He deployed to Kosovo and Afghanistan. In combat, he discovered his true self. He was a killer, especially adept with a knife and his bare hands. No one moved more quietly. They called him "The Wind."

An altercation with a superior ended his military career. A pattern was emerging, an inability to control his temper, a disposition to violence toward his peers, mental unrest.

He returned to his home, to the new South Africa. It was 2008. There was only one place for a man of his training. The Hawks, formally known as the Directorate for Priority Criminal Investigation, in reality the president's Praetorian Guard. A sniper, a master of hand-to-hand combat, a man in peak physical condition, Shaka quickly found himself assigned to "Night Operations," a euphemism for the death squads charged with liquidating the president's most stubborn enemies, and sometimes his friends, too.

When the minister of finance refused to pay a reasonable percentage of the funds he skimmed from the education budget, Shaka infiltrated his luxury, gated community in Cape Town and cut his throat while he slept between his two wives.

When the president's cousin, holder of a diamond concession in Kimberley, balked at a royalty fee of ten million dollars, Shaka crossed thirty kilometers of open veldt, breached a twenty-foot security fence, killed two bodyguards, and gained entry to his home in order to cut off the man's left hand. A warning, nothing more. The cousin promptly paid up.

Word of Shaka's reputation spread in those circles where men of his peculiar skill set were appreciated. One day he received a call from his former commander, General Moltke. Moltke wanted Shaka's services for a new army, a secret force charged with the protection of Europe, a rampart against the barbarian hordes. Shaka was a good German. Given the current state of affairs, surely he could appreciate the urgency of the request. The irony was not lost on him. He would be protecting Europe against people like himself. He accepted at once.

And so here he was in Bangkok, studying his hands beneath the glare of a streetlamp. The skin on his fingertips had started to go black with frostbite from his excursion in the Alps.

Shaka checked his phone. An app showed a map of the city, a pulsing red dot indicating Riske's location. He was not tracing Riske's phone. That would require cooperation from the local authorities. Strictly a last resort. Shaka disliked working with intelligence agencies, friendly or not. The same went for law enforcement. He preferred to operate below the surface. Under the radar, so to speak. Unseen and unbeknownst. The pulsing red dot came from an RFID transmitter—radio-frequency identification.

He'd tagged Riske as the American passed through baggage claim at Suvarnabhumi Airport. It had been easy enough, the sea of humanity making for the exits practically doing his job for him. A nudge from the rear. One body jostling another. A slight stinging sensation, gone before it could be questioned. It was over in a split second.

A miniature surgical instrument, what they called a "mosquito," had implanted the device beneath the skin of Riske's upper arm, a spot nearly impossible to see without the help of a mirror, the transmitter smaller than a grain of rice.

Shaka sent a text. R has the goods. Permission to intercede?

The reply: Negative. Stand down. Possible additional targets. Await instructions.

Shaka frowned. It was a mistake to leave when the target could be so easily taken. He debated disobeying the order. He could be upstairs and inside Riske's room in a minute and back on the street a minute after that. He felt a sudden throbbing at the base of his neck. *Do it,* he thought. *Get it over with. The man is exhausted. He's been on the move one way or another for more than a day. There won't be a better opportunity.*

And then, his training. Years in the military taught to obey his superiors. As much as he trusted his instinct, knew his course of action was the wiser one, he could not act.

Shaka was a servant to his past.

So be it.

Another time, then.

Soon.

CHAPTER 23

Tel Aviv

Midnight.

Lights burned in the offices of the SON Group. Danni Pine sat at her desk, frustrated, tired, at the end of her tether. She'd left the office just once since the laptop and phone had arrived from Thailand, allowing herself a shower, a nap, and a change of clothes. At some point she'd taken Luca Borgia's urgency as her own. She didn't like it when someone questioned either her efficacy or her integrity. Borgia had done both. She meant to prove him wrong.

"Major?"

"Danni?"

Danni raised her head. Dov and Isaac crowded the doorway. "If you tell me one more time you can't do it," she said, "you're fired. You can go to the Galilee. Join a kibbutz. Grow grapes. Make wine."

"We did it," said Dov, meekly. "Finally."

"Got it," said Isaac, nodding.

Danni motioned them forward.

The engineers advanced, stopping at Danni's desk. Neither man took a seat.

"Speak," she said. "You've kept me waiting long enough."

"He fragged the hard drive," said Isaac. "Used some Russian software we haven't seen in eons. Old, but good."

"We had to start from scratch, retrieve the—"

"Spare me the details," said Danni, hand raised. "What did you learn?"

A pause. Isaac looked at Dov, who cleared his throat. "He cleaned them out."

"Top to bottom. Emptied all the drawers."

"I'll need you to be more specific unless, that is, you expect me to tell Mr. Borgia that Rafael de Bourbon stole his underwear."

"Specific?" Isaac checked the tablet he used for diagnostics. "Let's see. He stole 2.7 million files, eight hundred thousand emails, and three years of text messages between PetroSaud's top executives."

"So that's who this is about? PetroSaud?"

The engineers nodded.

Danni knew the name. Over the past seventy-two hours she'd versed herself on all of Luca Borgia's businesses. She had a nose for shady dealings.

"Texts? How did he get those?"

"All digital correspondence conducted on company hardware was copied and saved to a central hard drive."

Of course it was. They did the same. "Go on, then. What did you learn?"

"You didn't ask us to read the take," said Dov.

Danni regarded him from beneath her brow. Maybe she allowed herself a hint of a smile. *Please.*

Isaac cleared his throat. "PetroSaud is a dirty shop."

"Smart, but dirty," added Dov. "And greedy."

"Essentially, they were helping sovereign wealth funds defraud their investors."

"Encouraging them, even. Instructing the fund managers how to pull off the thefts. Phony oil leases, shell companies, the whole shebang."

"How much?" asked Danni.

"Billions," said Isaac.

"Lots of billions," said Dov. "And they were taking commissions on each transaction. Big commissions."

"Mega," said Isaac.

"Is that right?" Danni tapped a piece of misshapen lead on the table.

It was the remnants of a Syrian bullet taken from her leg. "And De Bourbon...I take it he was in on it?"

Isaac shook his head. "Turns out he was the one honest guy. They tried to lure him in. He refused."

"But that's not the problem," said Dov.

"What is?"

"His bonus."

"Explain."

"De Bourbon stole the files because PetroSaud balked at paying him a bonus they'd promised him."

"So this whole thing is just so De Bourbon can get his bonus?" said Danni.

"Five million Swiss francs," said Dov. "I'd have done the same."

Danni considered this. De Bourbon's motivations weren't her concern, nor were PetroSaud's crimes. She'd been hired to retrieve information, not to deliberate on the actions of someone she didn't know. Still, she was bothered.

"There's more," said Isaac.

Of course there is, thought Danni.

"Someone else is pulling the strings. Not PetroSaud."

Danni sensed she was treading on dangerous ground. She tapped the piece of lead faster.

"The fund managers didn't keep all the money for themselves," said Isaac. "They wired a percentage of the money they stole to a bank."

"The Bank of Liechtenstein," said Dov. "Vaduz branch."

"How much?" asked Danni.

"In total, six billion dollars."

Danni swallowed. The numbers were making her dizzy. "Do we know who the account at the Bank of Liechtenstein belongs to?"

"Brick wall," said Isaac.

"Dead end," said Dov. Then, with a glint in his eye: "But we can find out."

"We can find out anything," added Isaac. "Say the word."

Danni shook her head. She had a very good idea to whom the account in Liechtenstein belonged. "And the email De Bourbon sent prior to his arrest. Did you get that, too?"

"*L* dot *L-i* at *F-T* dot com."

"A name, please, boys."

"London Li. An investigative reporter with the *Financial Times.*"

Danni spun in her chair, palming the chunk of lead. She remembered the flash of the policeman's pistol, the sharp stinging in her thigh. On that night in Damascus, she had had something in her possession the Syrians wanted. Something they were willing to kill for.

She didn't know who London Li was, but she did know the *Financial Times.* There was no more powerful a news organization. And she knew what any investigative journalist would do if she learned about sovereign wealth funds defrauding investors of billions of dollars. "What did De Bourbon tell her?"

"Not much. No names. No countries. Just a few clues."

"Is it enough to go on?"

"Yes," said Isaac, without hesitation.

"Probably," said Dov. "It would be for me."

Danni slapped her palms on the desk. Meeting concluded. It was a gesture she'd learned from her father. "Give me everything you have."

"Sent to your box before we came up," said Dov.

"You're good boys." Danni thanked the engineers and sent them on their way, telling them to get a good night's sleep and, for God's sake, to shower before coming back tomorrow.

Danni opened the drawer of the cabinet behind her and removed a bottle of Wyborowa, pouring herself a generous measure of the Polish vodka. *Ah, Signor Borgia. Ah, Luca.* Not industrial espionage at all, at least not the way she saw it. More like blackmail or extortion. Or…justice. Though not from Borgia's point of view.

She drank her vodka in one swallow, enjoying the burn, how her eyes watered. *This is why we do not do business with private individuals or enterprises.* Certainly, they had an obligation to Borgia. Without him, she would not be sitting at this desk. The SON Group would not exist. *And yet…*

The Saudis had implanted SON software in a journalist's phone and used it to read every piece of correspondence on the mobile device, track his every move, listen to his phone conversations, read his text messages, and, in the end, lure him to a meeting and execute him. Would not a journalist who threatened to expose the theft of so many billions of dollars merit a similar fate?

And what of Rafael de Bourbon?

Danni had no reason to believe Luca Borgia was a murderer. Then again, she had no reason not to. In her former profession, one erred on the side of caution or one died.

Danni knew whose name was on the account at the Bank of Liechtenstein.

And yet . . .

She poured herself another drink, then picked up the phone. The warm baritone voice answered promptly. "Luca? It's Danni Pine. I have some news. You had better sit down."

CHAPTER 24

*T*he Lion City.

London Li was playing tourist in her hometown. Phone at the ready to snap a photo, she walked down Orchard Road marveling at the glittering malls, each fancier than the last, taking in the succession of luxury boutiques. Prada, Gucci, Burberry. On and on.

London stopped at the corner, waiting for the light to turn. Mercedes, Mercedes, BMW, Porsche. The cars zipped past. Did anyone still drive Japanese cars? Oh yes, a Lexus. And every one of them slapped with a two hundred percent duty upon landing. This was the Asian miracle on steroids.

The light changed. London crossed the street, swallowed by a sea of pedestrians, most of them her age or younger, and far better dressed. She wore a pair of old shorts, a loose T-shirt, a floppy brimmed sun hat with her hair tucked up, cheap sunglasses, and a pair of flip-flops. A mainlander, people would say. A country mouse. From Chongqing, not Shanghai, bless her soul.

Orchard Road was a four-lane thoroughfare, Singapore's Fifth Avenue, Rodeo Drive, and Champs-Élysées rolled into one, with a shot of adrenaline added for good measure. The architecture, the design, the overwhelming "Wow" of it all. Everything so clean, modern, and, dare she say it… *Singaporean*. The entire area sparkled with success, optimism, the indomitability of the human spirit. Everything really was possible.

As cynical as they come, a born doubter, the devil's advocate's best friend, London couldn't help but feel a swell of pride. Fifty years ago

Singapore was another Asian backwater, located at the tip of the Malay Peninsula one degree north of the equator. For centuries it had existed on fishing, the export of natural resources—rubber, teak, a little oil—and, since 1830, the largesse of the British Empire.

In 1965, after declaring its independence, things changed. Some kind of benevolent entrepreneurial spirit swept down from the heavens and, by the grace of Buddha, Allah, Shiva, Jesus Christ—all saviors welcome—blessed Singapore with an unparalleled period of prosperity. Of course, hard work had something to do with it. Long hours. The legendary Chinese work ethic. A religious devotion to saving. In one generation, the city-state went from developing to developed, the original Asian Tiger.

Turning left onto Beach Road, she walked past the Raffles Hotel and slowed to peer through the windows of its gift shop. She wasn't interested in any souvenirs but in the reflection of the building across the street, a thirty-story steel-and-glass skyscraper that was home to the Singaporean offices of PetroSaud. Her eyes studied the entry and the three security guards flanking the revolving door. Farther along the street there were buildings just like it. Nowhere did she see another guard.

London's phone buzzed. Benson Chow's name appeared on the screen. She answered, walking into the lobby of the hotel, taking the stairs to the second floor.

"Benson."

"How did you know." A statement, not a question.

"Know what?" said London, stopping on the landing, making sure she was alone.

"The investment was seven hundred million dollars."

"You found it."

"Indonesia."

"You're certain?"

"It wasn't the only investment they made in Saudi. They dropped two more the same year. One for a billion, another for four hundred mil."

Indonesia was an oil-rich country and earned a large percentage of its GDP from the sale of oil. Therein lay the problem. Sovereign wealth funds were about diversification, mitigating risk. Loading up on one bet, putting all your chips on red—oil, in this case—did the opposite. Less diversification. More risk.

"Does that sound normal?"

"Not by a long shot," said Benson Chow. "Too many eggs in one basket. A firing offense."

"I guess a finance minister can do what he wants."

"The prerogative of autocracy."

London entered the Long Bar, taking a seat at the far end, where she could look out the window at the entry to the Beach Road tower. She'd slept poorly the night before, bothered by bad dreams. In the morning, she'd woken to find herself consumed by a terrible sense of foreboding. R was in danger.

"Do you know who brokered the sale?" she asked.

"You tell me."

"Does the name PetroSaud ring a bell?"

"Like Great Tom," said Chow, referring to the bell tower at Oxford, where they'd first met. "To the tune of two billion and change. What's going on, Lo?"

"I'm not sure yet. But if I were you, I'd consider decreasing any exposure you might have in the Indonesian SWF."

Chow swore under his breath. "What exactly are you saying?"

"I've said too much already. Anything more might put you in an unwieldy position to do your job…unless, that is, you fancy spending a year or two in Changi Prison."

"We're done," said Chow.

"Ben, one last thing."

"I'm afraid to ask."

"A shop like PetroSaud doesn't have only one client. A sharp tack like yourself might want to see if they were helping any other countries snap up oil leases in KSA."

"And if I find something…"

"Call me."

"Oh…about dinner. How about—"

London didn't hear another word. She ended the call the moment she saw a limousine pull up to the entrance of the tower across the street. A tall, statuesque woman in an orange silk dress shirt exited the back seat and turned in her direction, taking a moment to adjust her *kebaya*.

She recognized her at once.

Nadya Sun Sukarno. Indonesia's minister of finance.

CHAPTER 25

Bangkok

Twelve o'clock. Embassy of the Kingdom of Spain.

Simon looked at Adamson's text and put away his phone. He stood at the entrance to a city park a block from the embassy, surrounded by children and teachers and pedestrians on their way here and there. The day was hot, hotter than any he could remember, the midday sun beating down on his head like a branding iron. And humid, the moisture clinging to him like cellophane wrap.

He wore a cap and sunglasses. A surgical mask covered his nose and mouth to filter out the particulates that fouled the air. He did not look out of place. Every third person was wearing a mask today. A headline in the morning paper announced that Bangkok's air quality ranked as third worst in the world behind only Dhaka and Delhi. "Haze," the government called it, preferring the innocuous term to "smog." Call it what you want, thought Simon. He could hardly make out the tops of skyscrapers a mile away.

Fifteen minutes to go.

He'd woken at the break of dawn, seized by a dread and certain thought.

He'd been followed last night.

He hadn't seen anyone, not really. There were too many people and he had been moving too fast. Still, he knew.

Several times, as he'd hesitated at a street corner or slowed to check his directions, he'd sensed a ripple in the flow behind him. A shadow. A flicker. Something.

If he had any particular skill at this kind of thing, it came from his days on the streets of Marseille. Seventeen years old, a hood on the lookout for his next score, lifting a wallet, boosting a car, maybe rolling a tourist. But also on the lookout for the *flics,* who were on the lookout for him.

In the half-light of dawn, he'd closed his eyes, thinking back. There it was. A tan face. A slash of blond hair. The heavy neck and shoulders. Was it real or the figment of an anxious imagination? Even now, wide-awake, all of his senses firing, he wasn't sure.

Still . . .

Simon had learned to question his instinct at his peril. If he'd felt it, it was real.

He'd been followed. A blond man, first on the way to the prison and again after he'd left Delphine's hotel. Not a local. A professional.

If not Tan's man, then whose?

Unable to go back to sleep, he'd showered and walked to the river, where he took breakfast at an outdoor café. A strong chai tea bucked him up enough to call George Adamson and give him a rundown of his activities the night before. The lawyer reiterated Tan's displeasure at his disappearance but was not unhappy that Simon had retrieved the stolen information.

"And Delphine?" Simon had asked.

"Left on the seven a.m. Cathay Pacific flight to London."

"You should have told her to go immediately after his arrest."

"I tried. She wouldn't listen."

"You should have tried harder."

"Did you look at it?" Adamson asked. "The material he stole."

"Password protected," said Simon. "Rafa may be dumb, but he's not stupid."

"All I care is that he gives Tan what he wants, takes his check, and gets the hell out of here."

With a bow and ribbon on top, added Simon, *and a commendation to your firm for a job well done.* "Say, Adamson, you don't have a man following me?"

"We don't do that kind of thing, Riske."

"Sure you do," said Simon. "It's important. I need to know."

"No. We most certainly do not."

Simon believed him.

That was three hours ago.

From his vantage point, Simon had a clear view of the ornate black iron gates guarding the embassy entrance. Situated on several acres of open land, the embassy was an oasis amidst a concrete desert. Simon had walked past twice earlier. He'd glimpsed a rolling lawn, a tennis court, and a small lake. Set back at the end of a curving drive was a large colonial-style building with a broad veranda and two wings flanking a central residence. It was hard to see much through the fence surrounding the property.

International law declared the embassy to be Spanish territory. Setting foot on the grounds was no different from visiting Barcelona or Madrid. Once inside the gates, he was subject to the laws of Spain. That simple. But Simon knew he'd do well to keep in mind Dickie Blackmon's words: laws in Thailand were written in pencil, not ink. Five'll get you ten Colonel Albert Tan kept a Pink Pearl eraser on his belt right next to his pistol.

A check of the time. Eleven fifty-eight.

Simon clutched the flash drive in his pocket. He only hoped it wasn't too late, that unseen forces hadn't also come into possession of Rafa's purloined booty. Either way, he had no choice but to go ahead.

Eleven fifty-nine.

Time to motor.

"Here he is. The man of the hour."

Colonel Albert Tan stood in the center of the Spanish ambassador's office, resplendent in his khaki uniform, ribbons in the finest order, aviator sunglasses hanging from his breast pocket.

Simon crossed the room and shook Tan's hand, wishing him a good morning…or was it good afternoon? The Spanish ambassador, Felipe

López-Calderón, stepped forward to introduce himself and the tall, handsome man at his side, Captain Llado, his naval attaché. Colonel Tan didn't bother introducing the three uniformed men standing behind him, hands clasped behind their backs at parade rest. Simon didn't count Rafa as present.

The office was a sprawling, high-ceilinged room, dominated on one side by a heavy wooden desk flanked by the Spanish and Thai flags. A picture window behind it looked onto a manicured lawn. And on the other side of the room, a seating area fit for the king himself. In between were miles of gold carpeting.

"We are happy to be of assistance to Señor De Bourbon and our friends with the Thai government," said López-Calderón, a trim, distinguished man of sixty with a salt-and-pepper goatee.

"I told you to be here early," said George Adamson, through gritted teeth, as he shook Simon's hand.

"What, no hello or thank you?" said Simon.

"Don't press your luck," whispered Adamson. "Tan's in a foul mood. He's out for bear."

Simon returned his attention to the Thai military officer. "And Mr. De Bourbon?"

"On his way," said Tan. "First, may I ask if you have what we requested?"

"I do."

"So you weren't out all night sampling our fine city's nightlife? You had me wondering." Tan laughed, offering a few words in Thai to his associates, who smiled dutifully.

Helen Mirren translated the words no less dutifully. "A fan of ladyboys, no doubt."

Simon responded politely. "Maybe you and I can go out together. After all is said and done. Do you like Italian, or…no, I think you prefer Greek. Am I right?"

The smile left Tan's face. He extended a hand, palm up. "If you please."

Simon took the flash drive from his pocket and made to hand it to Tan, stopping at the last moment. He met Tan's eye. "Where is my friend?"

Tan muttered a command. One of his officers spoke into his phone. A door at the side of the room opened. Warden Charlie entered, Rafa beside him, dressed in his prison attire, unwashed and unkempt, hands cuffed.

"Release him," said Simon, "now."

"If you please," said Ambassador López-Calderón. "Mr. De Bourbon is a guest of the Spanish government. Restraints are not needed any longer. He is a free man, is he not?"

Tan glared at Rafa. "Not yet, he isn't." Then a word to Warden Charlie—"Unlock the dog"—who removed the handcuffs. "I'm waiting."

Rafa crossed the room and stood at Simon's side. "How are you?" asked Simon.

"Ready for a beer and a shot of tequila."

Simon patted his shoulder. "I'm sure that can be arranged. Let's get everything taken care of first."

"Delphine?"

"She left the country this morning. Better that way."

"Thank you, my friend."

Only then did Simon hand Tan the flash drive. He appeared dissatisfied at its size, somehow cheated.

Tan closed his fingers around the drive. "And now the password?"

"One moment, Colonel. There are some formalities that need attention." Adamson rushed forward, placing two leather folders on the ambassador's desk. With care, he opened each, setting down a fountain pen for the respective party's signature. "Might I ask that we receive the check?" he said, brimming with goodwill. "I have the paperwork ready. Mr. De Bourbon acknowledges turning over the information taken from PetroSaud's servers, with no admission of guilt, in return for a payment from PetroSaud of one million dollars. There's a receipt, of course. Also attached is a promise never to speak of the matter again. It's all there." He held out a pen for Colonel Tan. "Mr. De Bourbon is booked on a three o'clock flight to Doha."

"First, the password."

"First, the check," said Adamson, showing a little backbone.

Tan snapped his fingers. An adjutant handed the attorney an envelope. Adamson examined the contents. "Excuse me, but this check is not signed."

"Mr. De Bourbon owes us an additional piece of information," said Tan. "A name. A journalist, I believe. Who did you send the information to?"

Rafa looked to Simon, who nodded. Rafa had warned the journalist as best he could. There was no choice to be made.

"Okay, then," said Rafa, but still he hesitated. "I'll tell you."

Tan's phone buzzed. He looked at the screen and answered at once. *"Pronto,"* he said, his eyes locked on Simon. *"Va bene. Si. Perfettamente. Grazie, Luca. Grazie tanto. Ciao."*

Tan motioned to his adjutants. The officers stiffened as if they'd received an electric shock. A signal, to be sure.

They knew, thought Simon. Whoever "Luca" was, he'd told Tan that they'd discovered what Rafa had stolen, and with all probability, the identity of the journalist he'd told about it. Rafa was expendable.

Tan snatched the check from Adamson's hand. "A change of plan. Mr. De Bourbon won't be needing this."

"What's going on?" demanded the attorney. "Am I missing something?" Confused, Adamson looked at Rafa, then at Simon.

"You're going back to where you belong," said Tan. "Count on doing twenty years." He barked an order to Warden Charlie, who approached Rafa, opening the cuffs. "Please," said Warden Charlie. "Your hands."

"You can't arrest him," said Simon. "This is Spanish soil. He's a Spanish citizen."

"I must object," said Ambassador López-Calderón. "You have no authority here. If there is an issue, please file a protest with my government. I am at your service. In the meantime, Mr. De Bourbon is under the protection of the Spanish crown."

"You can't do this," added Adamson. "You have no jurisdiction here. We are not on Thai soil."

"Rafa, stay where you are," said Simon.

Tan ignored them, pointing at Rafa. "Do as you are told."

The ambassador slid between Tan and Rafa, arms raised, a conciliatory gesture. "Please, gentlemen. This is not the time for an incident."

"No incident. The man is a criminal, in Spain or in Thailand. I am a police officer." Tan shoved the ambassador forcefully to one side and took violent hold of Rafa's arm. The ambassador lost his balance and barreled into Simon.

Rafa fought to free his arm, only drawing Tan closer. "Get off of me. Let me go."

"You will obey!" shouted Tan, in a state of unchecked fury.

Rafa threw an elbow, catching Tan on the chin, enraging him further.

Tan's hand dropped to his holster, drawing his pistol. Rafa's hand followed it. The men wrestled for control of the handgun.

Simon untangled himself from the ambassador. "Don't! Rafa!"

Too late. Rafa was the larger man by a head and fighting as if for his life. He fell back a step, the pistol in his hand—a SIG nine millimeter—aimed at Tan's chest.

"Put it down," said Simon, approaching his friend, fighting to be heard over Tan's fevered commands, the protests of his adjutants, Adamson urging everyone to "calm down," the ambassador crying, *"Por favor, por favor."*

"Rafa, listen to me."

Rafa looked at him, then at Tan. "They can't take me. It isn't right."

A gunshot rang out. Unimaginably loud. Another. Simon ducked, dropped to a knee, ears ringing.

Tan lay on the carpet. He tried to stand, then collapsed, mouth open.

"I didn't shoot," said Rafa, a plea, eyes wide. "I didn't."

Close upon his words, Rafa's head buckled, a spray of pink—blood, brain, and bone—blinded Simon. Rafa pitched forward, a large portion of his cranium missing, dead on his feet. Simon staggered beneath his friend's weight.

Across the room, Tan's adjutants scrambled for cover. None carried a sidearm. The ambassador dropped to the carpet, hands covering his head. Adamson crouched near the desk, unprotected.

Simon wiped the gore from his eyes. There, at a side entrance to the office, stood a man in dark clothing, heavy around the neck and shoulders, blond hair. It was him. The man in the white Nissan. The man in Simon's dreams. Simon met his eyes as the man spun and pointed a heavy caliber pistol at him. Another shot. The bullet striking Rafa in the back, meant to go all the way through, forcing Simon to retreat a step.

To his left, the naval attaché, Llado, had pulled a compact pistol from his blazer. He hesitated, looking directly at the blond man, unsure what to do, then finally shot at him, missed. Then return fire. Two shots. Llado dropped like a man from the gallows.

Simon let Rafa fall to the floor, crouched, and snapped up Tan's pistol, pulled the trigger, nothing, the safety still on, thumbed it off, fired again, the bullets going wide, splintering the lintel, his ears ringing. A hornet whizzed past his ear. Close. Simon fired again. The blond man retreated from view. Simon freed the flash drive from Tan's hand, pistol raised, fired again, and ran for the double doors. A vase exploded behind him.

He was clear, running down the corridor, rounded a corner. More gunshots, but different caliber. Embassy guards? A scream. Then automatic weapons. An Uzi, crackling like fireworks. The exchange of fire went on. A cacophony.

Simon threw open the first door he came to. A Thai woman huddled beside her desk, hand covering her mouth. She stared at Simon, at the blood painting his face, and screamed. "It's not me," said Simon, out of breath, not knowing how to explain. "Someone else. Call the police."

The woman had a phone in her other hand. She nodded, indicating she'd already done so. But this was Bangkok with Bangkok traffic. Midday. It could take them ten minutes or an hour. He was on his own.

"You…you are all right?" she asked.

Simon caught a glimpse of himself in the glass of a frame. A horror show. He wiped his face with the tail of his shirt, saying that he was fine, then spat something hard from his mouth, not caring to consider what it might be. He dropped the magazine and counted three bullets remaining. His hand was shaking. He replaced the magazine, slamming it home with his palm, chambering a round. Better now. "Get under the desk. You'll be safe there."

An internal alarm sounded. A buzzer. One second on. One second off. Earsplitting. A message in Spanish. "Attention. This is an emergency. Take cover in your office."

He left the room, a fast jog down the hall, came to the entry, a two-story gallery, paintings on the walls, a wide staircase at its center rising to an exposed walkway.

"Sir, stop! Drop your weapon!" A plainclothes security man stood by the front doors, pistol gripped by both hands, pointed at Simon.

Simon raised his hands. "I'm not the shooter. He's behind me somewhere."

"Put down your weapon. Now!"

Simon bent to place his pistol on the ground.

Two shots. The guard slammed against the door and slid to the floor.

Simon threw himself against the wall as a shot struck inches from his head, shards of wood and plaster peppering his face, splinters lodging in his cheek. He dropped to the floor, peered out, saw the blond man across the gallery, fired a shot, the man ducking for cover in a hallway.

Two bullets left.

He understood now. The blond man wanted the flash drive. Simon could not allow him to get it. Battle lines had been drawn.

He surveyed the large gallery. No way could he make it to the front doors and get outside.

Simon jumped to his feet and ran for the stairs, taking them two at a time. He reached the second floor, went right, checked over his shoulder. The blond man was starting up the stairs behind him, inserting a fresh magazine into his pistol. Their eyes met.

Who sent you? Why did you shoot Tan? And, who is Luca?

No time for answers.

Simon ran down the hall, doors open to either side—sitting room, guest room, guest room. He slammed closed the doors. A distraction. At the end of the hall an exhibition room. Oils of naval battles. A mannequin clothed in a military uniform. Glass display cases. He entered the room and closed the door. No lock. He scooted a low dresser in front of the door, then moved to the windows, their handles and seams frozen with paint. On a side table, small cannonballs were arranged in a pyramid beneath a painting of a sixty-four-gun ship of the line, the *San Leandro*. He picked up a cannon ball and underhanded it through the window, glass shattering. Behind him a violent blow against the door.

Simon fired at the center of the door, rending a hole in it the size of a basketball. Nothing moved in the hall. He waited, wincing at the on-going alarm, then moved a step toward the door, pistol outstretched.

One bullet.

He listened for any movement, but his ears were a mess, still ringing and confused from the gunfire, and now the alarm. Had he hit him? The better question was how could he have missed?

A step closer. Eyes trained on the door and the hallway beyond.

Was the man dead? Where were the embassy guards? The man couldn't have shot them all.

Simon's phone buzzed. He slid it from his pocket. *Unknown Caller,* read the screen. "Yeah?"

"Give me what I want. Throw it through the door. Even you shouldn't be able to miss that."

"Who's this?"

"You know who."

"Why did you kill Tan?"

"The flash drive, please, Mr. Simon Riske, owner of European Automotive Repair and Restoration, Kimber Road, SW18, London. We know everything about you: where you live, what you do…besides chasing around the world hoping in vain to help an old friend. How's Harry Mason? Does he really think Arsenal is going to win the FA Cup? And poor Lucy Brown, still in hospital. Surrey Medical Clinic is the official name, no? Room 327 of the urgent care ward."

The words chilled Simon to the marrow. Point taken. But now was not the time to be rattled. He had questions of his own. "The naval attaché, Llado. Was he your man?"

"We have people everywhere. Thailand. England. You name it. All I want is the flash drive with the information Mr. De Bourbon stole and our business is concluded. I'm sorry your friend is dead, but it was his own fault. You know that as well as I."

"You're South African?"

"And German, if you're curious. *Sprechen Sie Deutsch, Herr Riske?* I understand you speak several languages. A man of the world. Not bad for a kid off the streets of Marseille. Quite the success story. This one, though, is beyond you, my friend. I imagine you are out of ammunition or you would have continued firing. You had me dead to rights. It's those SIGs. Bit of a hair trigger; tend to fire low. What do you say? Let's get this taken care of before the police get here. Then we can both walk out of here alive. *Komm schon, Kumpel.*"

Come on, buddy.

"You're right," said Simon. "The SIG does fire low, but then I'm not much of a gun guy. Listen, I'm feeling a little lonely in here. Why don't you come in and I'll give you the flash drive, man to man? If you have a minute, we can look at some of these paintings together. I mean, since we're friends."

From the broken window, Simon made out the wail of police sirens. Many of them. If he wasn't mistaken, he heard the thrum of a helicopter hovering overhead as well.

"Please, Simon, I hear them, too. No more time to waste. The flash drive."

"I just realized I don't know your name. You have me there."

"I'm called…Shaka."

A shadow moved in the hall. A footfall. Simon dove to the ground as gunfire ripped through the door, obliterating it, tearing into the wall behind him. Glass sprayed. Paintings crashed to the floor. The blond man peered through the door, or what was left of it, then put his weight against the base and slid the cabinet backward as if it weighed nothing at all.

Simon took careful aim. Ten steps separated them.

Dead to rights, *my friend.*

He squeezed the trigger.

Misfire.

Simon dropped the pistol as Shaka barged through the door. The man pointed his gun at Simon. He fired. Nothing. Empty. Unbothered, he slid the pistol into the waist of his pants. He wore a black polo shirt and tan slacks. For the first time, Simon took notice of his size, his muscularity. He wasn't sure which were larger, his arms or his legs. And his neck. It would take an executioner three swings of his ax to get through it.

Simon jumped to his feet. He picked up a cannon ball and threw it at him, striking the man—Shaka—squarely in the chest. The ball bounced off without effect. No underhand toss either. The man unsheathed a knife from a calf strap, the blade protruding between his middle and ring finger. A gutting knife designed for hand-to-hand combat. Simon knew at once that the man had considerable practice with it.

Fighting was not an option. At best, he would escape alive, but injured. More likely, he'd be killed, and worse, give up the flash drive. So far, five men—at least—had died for its contents. The key to why, and who was responsible, could be found in its contents, in the files Rafa had stolen from PetroSaud. Like it or not, Simon had to keep them safe. He owed his friend that much.

And so, escape.

CHAPTER 26

Bangkok

Simon ran to the broken window, diving through headfirst, landing on the gravel-topped roof covering the veranda, turning a somersault. Two steps took him to the edge. Crouching, he took hold of the gutter and dropped over the side. The gutter held. He released his grip and fell to the grass several feet below. Up and running. A straight line across the lawn. A glance over his shoulder. Shaka following, twenty paces behind.

Simon hit the fence at full stride, one foot propelling him higher, arm outstretched, hand grasping the top. No barbed wire, but curved stanchions with sharpened tips to keep intruders out. He threw a leg over and slid his torso along the rounded irons. He had nothing to grab on to, nothing to slow his fall. He plunged ten feet to the sidewalk, landing awkwardly, toppling to his side, cheek striking the pavement. Dazed, he stood, noting a drizzle of blood. His shirt was ripped. A gash from the window.

Vehicles zoomed past, right to left, a one-way street. He ran counter to the flow, arms pumping, snaking through the dense foot traffic. No looking behind him. A break in the cars. He cut across the street, dashing beneath a highway overpass. A different world here. Shade. Layers of darkness. The air cooler, a welcome breeze. Pop-up stalls selling lunch and cold drinks.

He slowed, clothing drenched, panting. He searched for the best route, not knowing where he was, where to go. Straight, he decided, wanting to remain in the shade for as long as possible.

The blow knocked him through the air. Shaka landed on top of him, his momentum causing both men to roll. Stunned, adrenaline firing, Simon made it to his feet first. He kicked his attacker viciously, a wild shot to the neck, the blow crushing his larynx. On all fours, Shaka gripped his ruined throat. Simon kicked him again, squarely in the jaw. Shaka fell onto his side, a skein of blood dangling from his mouth, a terrible noise coming from his lips.

Simon took off, following an abandoned railway track running beneath the highway. A hundred yards along, the track ended. A fence blocked his path. To his left a broad alley. Tenements on both sides, rising several stories. Air conditioners perched outside windows. Clothes hung to dry from laundry lines. And lined up, as if one to each dwelling, an endless row of motorbikes. Vespas, Hondas, Yamahas. The common transport of Bangkok's teeming millions.

He entered the alley, eyes on the locks attached to each bike, searching for a certain model. There. A U-lock. He took a pen from his pocket and unscrewed it, dropping the ink cartridge on the ground. Keeping only the uppermost half of the pen, he inserted the open end into the circular lock and turned it one way, then the other, applying pressure. The lock opened.

The bike was a Honda 125, several years old, in good condition. He crouched low and pulled a random wire from the motorbike next to it. Using his teeth, he shortened the wire to the length of a toothbrush, then exposed the copper filaments at each end, taking care to curl them neatly. Next, he found the Honda's ignition cable and unplugged the socket. Fashioning the wire into a U-shape, he inserted the exposed ends into each of the socket's connecting leads. Having bypassed the key contact, he thumbed the ignition key and the motorcycle's engine turned over.

He backed up the bike as Shaka appeared at the mouth of the alley. Another biker turned in and slowed to pass him. Shaka looked at Simon and, without hesitation, took hold of the biker's shoulders and threw him to the ground, jumping on the bike in his place.

Simon gunned the Honda, turning right at the far end of the alley and accelerating into three lanes of smoothly flowing traffic. He passed through an intersection and saw he was driving on Sathorn Road. The road grew broader still, four lanes in either direction, skyscrapers lined up like sentries on either side of the boulevard. Signs on the buildings advertised the world's largest banks and insurance companies. He drove as fast as the bike allowed, carving his own lane through the slower moving automobiles. Ahead, an intersection. Four lanes coming from each direction. He kept his wrist cocked, refusing to slow as, all around him, cars came to a halt. The light turned red a full second before he passed beneath it. Cars darted forth left and right, cutting off his path. He dodged one way, then another. Horns blared. Like that, he was through.

A look over his shoulder. No sign of his pursuer. He was clear. He slowed, moved into the right lane. Then, a squeal of brakes. A cacophony of horns. Shaka emerged from the cross traffic, off-balance, one foot dragging on the pavement.

Simon veered onto a side street. Two lanes, commercial buildings, restaurants, foliage springing up between the structures. Palms, casuarinas. Traffic in front of him came to an abrupt halt. He slid past one car and another. The road narrowed. The space between cars going in opposite directions lessened to a foot, less even, drivers playing a kind of hide-and-seek as they made their way along what essentially was a one-way street. Simon stopped repeatedly, shouting for a path to open. He could feel Shaka closing the distance between them. A glance behind him. Two cars back.

A memory from his past.

Simon, fourteen years old, on his Vespa. A broiling summer day on the narrow streets of Marseille. Cars parked cheek by jowl, one after another, every space taken. A dare. *No way you can . . .*

Mounting a Citroën parked along the Rue de Fleury, he maneuvered his bike over the top of the car—trunk, roof, hood, punch the gas—onto the next car and the next...making it ten cars before jumping back to the sidewalk.

But that was twenty-five years ago.

What choice did he have?

Simon revved the engine, pulled up the handlebars, and jumped the bike onto the trunk of the car stopped in front of him—a gold BMW, dealer plates, straight off the lot—up and over the roof, onto the hood, accelerate, and jump to the next car. Wash. Rinse. Repeat. Two cars. Three. He rode standing up, fighting for balance, wishing he had more power, not once looking behind him. A last car and he was at the front of the line. Back on the street, horns letting him know what they thought of his performance.

Simon turned onto a wide boulevard, accelerating for all the bike was worth. A look over his shoulder. Shaka remained far behind, locked in traffic, unable to follow. One trick he didn't have up his sleeve.

In minutes, Simon was on the highway, following signs to the river. He crossed the Chao Phraya, tossing his phone into the water—*Follow that, asshole!*—and headed west out of the city, toward Ratchaburi, the countryside.

Free.

For now.

CHAPTER 27

Singapore

In the trade, it was called an "ambush." Simply put, it meant approaching a subject without his or her prior knowledge and asking them pointed questions about their involvement in a crime, scandal, incident, fill in the blank—whatever story the journalist was covering. One saw it most often on television, the intrepid investigative journalist staking out a suspected criminal, waiting for him to leave the safety of his home or office, then pouncing, lights blazing, camera crew in tow, microphone at the ready.

"Sir, can you comment on . . . ?" "When did you know about . . . ?" "Did you have anything to do with . . . ?"

But London Li was a print journalist working for a respected publication. When she had questions, she called the subject, identified herself, and politely asked away. If she wanted an interview, she arranged it days or even weeks ahead of time. There were rules to follow. Professional etiquette was to be respected. London didn't do ambushes.

Until today.

Leaving the hotel, she took up position in the doorway of a leather goods store diagonally across the street from PetroSaud. The position was ideal, as she could look through the shop's window and view who was entering and exiting the building without being noticed herself. She held her phone at the ready, camera app activated and set to video. It was only a matter of waiting for her quarry to emerge.

Several times the guards turned their attention to the lobby. Convinced Minister Sukarno was on her way, she nearly dashed across the street, instinct stopping her at the last instant. One time it was a UPS man. The next, an elderly executive in the care of his nurse.

After forty minutes, a limousine pulled up in front of the building. London recognized it as the vehicle that had deposited Nadya Sukarno earlier. She left the storefront as the Indonesian minister of finance waltzed out the revolving glass door. London removed her hat and sunglasses and closed the last few steps in a rush.

"Minister Sukarno," London said, then giving her name and affiliation. "How long have you been stealing from your own sovereign wealth fund by investing in nonexistent oil leases created by PetroSaud and pocketing the proceeds?"

She held her phone high, sure she was capturing the woman's face.

"Out of my way," said Sukarno. "I'm not speaking to reporters."

London repeated the question. Then: "Why are you visiting Petro—?"

Before she could finish, a guard wrapped a hand around her wrist and forced the phone to her side. London protested, stating she was a journalist. The guard's response was to use his free hand to wrestle the phone from her grip. London resisted, having the presence of mind to keep up her line of questioning. "Why are you devoting so much of the fund to oil properties? Do you have an account with the Bank of Liechtenstein?"

Nadya Sukarno froze, a deer in the headlights.

It was then that a second security guard tackled London to the pavement. She fell awkwardly, turning her ankle, and, in the fall, relinquished her grasp on the phone. She heard, not saw, the door of the limo slam, the vehicle pull away from the curb at speed.

She pushed herself up slowly, gingerly assessing her ankle. The guard did not help her to her feet. With a victorious smile, he returned her phone. She noted that he had erased the footage of the confrontation. As far as all were concerned, the incident had not taken place.

But London didn't need the video to confirm that something spectacular had happened. Grimacing, she made her way up the street with a pronounced limp. She had gotten far more than she'd bargained for. The ambush was an unmitigated success, ankle or no.

Indonesian minister of finance Nadya Sukarno had confessed to her crimes. It was all there on her face. Plain as day.

Guilty.

CHAPTER 28

Ratchaburi Province, Thailand

Beneath a leaden sky, Simon continued across the flats of Ratchaburi Province. Buildings lined the highway. Warehouses, car dealerships, garages, supermarkets, brand-new mini-malls next to worn-out mom-and-pop stores, and every few miles a KFC and a Subway. Behind the structures stretched open fields, some planted with rice, others fallow.

He kept one eye on the road, the other behind him. Each mile from Bangkok was a mile farther from danger. He knew better than to add "and closer to safety." Two hours and a hundred miles later, he allowed himself to believe that he was alone. Shaka was gone.

He steered the bike off the highway and onto a parallel feeder road. His first stop was at a convenience store to buy an ice-cold Coca-Cola and a burner phone. He paused long enough to drink the soda, unpack the phone, and slip it into his pocket. Afterward, he continued until seeing a sign that read GAMING CENTER FORTNITE, MINECRAFT, CALL OF DUTY / INTERNET. The building was sparkling new, two stories, all tinted glass. Inside, row upon row of tables occupied a cavernous, dimly lit room, nearly every space taken by a young man, console in hand, hypnotized by the video game on his laptop. A sea of zombies. Giant screens in each corner of the room broadcast the play.

Simon asked if he could access the Internet. For a fee of one hundred baht an hour, he was handed a laptop with a card listing instructions. He paid and found an empty spot at the rear of the room. No one averted their eyes from their screen as the tall *farang* joined their ranks. Fortnite was important business.

166

After logging on, he pulled up the website for the *Bangkok Post,* Thailand's paper of record. The bloodbath at the Spanish embassy was headline news. The story read:

> At least nine persons were killed today during a diplomatic exchange when a gunman opened fire inside the embassy. Among the dead are Colonel Albert Tan, chief of the Royal Thai Police, Spanish ambassador Felipe López-Calderón, Spanish naval attaché Captain Juan Llado, Spanish national Rafael de Bourbon, and an American, George Adamson. Police are searching for a survivor and possible suspect, an American national recorded as present at the time of the attack. The man's name is being withheld currently.

Simon felt sick to his stomach. Dead. All of them. He took the four not listed to be Tan's adjutants and Warden Charlie.

He removed the flash drive from his pocket, powered up the burner, and placed a call to England. He wanted answers.

"Vikram, it's Simon Riske."

"Why are you calling from a Thai number?" asked Vikram Singh. "I only answered because I thought it might be my cousin. Did you happen to see him?"

"No time. Listen, I have an emergency. It's a long story, but I need you to hack into a password-protected flash drive."

"I can't do that."

"You can't? I thought—"

"I'm a hardware man," said Singh. "I don't play with software, at least not in a way that I'm not permitted. It is illegal, you know."

"I wasn't asking you to…well, *yes, I was.* The drive belonged to a friend of mine. He wanted me to look at the information he stored on it. He was killed before he could give me the password."

Singh answered with marked calm. Twenty years at MI5 had left him inured to talk of murder and desperate circumstance. Panic was the enemy's best friend. "And you? Are you all right? You sound, well, a little crazed."

"Not having my best day. I'm in trouble. A lot, actually. I wouldn't have bothered you otherwise. Anyhow, I'm sorry…forget I called."

"Hang on there, Simon. I said *I* couldn't help you. Let me find you someone who can."

"You know someone?"

Simon noted that Singh had placed his hand over the receiver. Then, muted, though no less clear: "Arjit! Come down to my lab. And be quick about it." The hand lifted from the receiver. "Just a minute. Arjit is on his way. He's been hacking all manner of devices since he was eight. The little bastard got into my BMW last week, reprogrammed my entire music library. He replaced my Tom Jones with Rick Astley. I was 'Rick-rolled' by my own son."

Simon smiled, appreciating Vikram's effort to make him feel better.

"Hello, Simon. It's Tiger," said Arjit Singh.

"Hey, there, Tiger. Heard you're causing your dad some problems."

"Have to keep the old man on his toes."

Simon explained that he'd come into possession of a friend's flash drive that contained important information, but he did not have the password to unlock it. In no uncertain terms, he added that the information should be considered dangerous and that several men had died because of it.

Arjit possessed his father's sangfroid. The mention that the information stored on the drive might put him in peril did not appear to faze him in the least. "Is that what you do?" he asked. "Are you some kind of secret agent?"

"Hardly," said Simon. "I was helping a friend out of a bind. Things went sideways. Listen to me, Arjit, this is serious."

"The first rule of hacking, Simon, is to keep your identity anonymous. You do know that?"

Simon reminded himself that he was speaking with a fifteen-year-old whiz kid who'd just finished his first year at Caltech, one of the world's foremost temples of science and technology. Invincible, at least in his own mind. "I guess I do."

"Here's what I need you to do. Plug the flash drive into your laptop.

I'm going to send a piece of software to your email. Download it immediately. I'll walk you through the installation. After it's activated, I'll be able to take control of your laptop and access the flash drive. Then it's a question of cracking the password."

"And you're sure no one will know it's you?"

"Only you." A pause. "We're not talking about nuclear launch codes, are we?"

"No, Arjit. No launch codes."

As soon as Simon received the email, he downloaded and installed the software. "And now?"

"Let me go to work."

"Any idea how long it might take?"

"A while," said Arjit. "An hour. Maybe more."

Simon carried the laptop to the snack bar in an adjacent room. He hadn't eaten since morning. He was starving. He ordered a bowl of curry noodles and a hot chai. The food arrived and he took it to a table nearest the window. Outside it had begun to rain. Lightning strikes illuminated a dark canvas. The water fell in sheets, hard enough to obscure the other side of the highway. He thought of the girls he'd seen in the truck—was it only yesterday afternoon? He remembered that people like them were called "stateless." Rightly or wrongly, he felt in a similarly unmoored condition. The police would be looking for him. It was only a matter of time before his name and his photograph were released.

Simon finished his food, then returned to the gaming room. There was no message from Arjit, no indication that the laptop was being controlled by someone ten thousand miles away. His thoughts went to Lucy and he considered calling the clinic. What could they tell him? As Harry Mason had said, it was in the Lord's hands.

And Delphine?

She needed to know the truth about what had happened. That Rafael had been betrayed. That he was a victim of a conspiracy perpetrated by individuals who wanted the files he'd stolen from PetroSaud kept secret at all costs. He picked up the phone and realized that he no longer had her number, that he'd saved it to his real phone, the phone that right now was lying at the bottom of the Chao Phraya.

Or did he?

He opened his wallet and found a square of white paper folded into quarters slipped in with his business cards. It was the list of contacts Dickie Blackmon had included in the packet of information he'd thrown onto Simon's desk. *"I'm old school. Prefer things printed out. Don't trust all that digital mumbo jumbo."* Delphine's cellphone was listed at the bottom.

He tapped in the number. If Delphine had left on the seven a.m. flight for London, she would still be in the air. He didn't like leaving a message, not with this type of information. Still, it was important she hear from him what had happened.

He hit SEND.

"Who is this?" a woman demanded, answering even before the first ring had ended.

"Delphine. It's Simon."

"Simon?" she asked, sounding confused.

"Simon Riske," he stated. "I wasn't expecting to reach you. I thought you were in the air."

"Simon, of course. Connection in Hong Kong. Second leg's delayed. Do you have him? Is he there with you? Put him on."

"Are you with someone?"

"What do you mean? Where are you? Simon?"

"Something happened at the embassy. Rafa is dead. So are eight others. There was a gunman. Delphine, I'm sorry."

"Dead…What are you saying? Where's Adamson? He arranged everything. He said there would be no problems."

"Adamson was killed, too. It was a setup. Colonel Tan was involved. He and others. They wanted the flash drive."

"But you…you're alive."

"I have it, Delphine. I have the flash drive. I'm going to find out who did this."

"Simon…you promised."

"Delphine…"

"I have to go. Daddy's calling. Oh God, this can't be…My Rafa."

The call ended.

Simon drew a breath, the weight of her words damning. He closed his eyes as the horror of the day swept over him. The gunfire, the blood, the shock of holding his friend's dead body.

Simon was falling, tumbling, all sense of direction lost. A collage of images blinded him; blood, everywhere blood. Worse, the knowledge that he'd failed the one woman he'd ever truly loved. He grabbed the edge of the table with both hands, tortured by the images of Rafa's wounds, unable to drive them away.

Not now. It wasn't the time for guilt, for recrimination. Too much to do.

He stared at the screen, willing Arjit to get back to him. What kind of information had Rafa taken from his former employers? All Simon knew was that PetroSaud had helped a sovereign wealth fund defraud its investors. Rafa hadn't gone into the details.

First things first. Simon had to get out of Thailand. He needed a new passport, a false one at that. But where to find one? He considered who he might call. Ben Sterling? Dickie Blackmon? He couldn't bring either of them into this. What about his old buddies in Marseille? Did La Brise de Mer do business in Thailand? Of course they did. One word: heroin. But how to contact them? Jojo Matta? No, Jojo was a street soldier. *Un petit voyou.* Not a planner. There was only one person Simon might contact. Il Padrone. The *capo di tutti capi.* Not going to happen.

Even with a false passport, he didn't dare fly out of one of the country's major airports. Customs and immigration agencies at nearly every major international airport around the world had been using facial recognition software for years. Reports varied as to its efficacy. Some claimed the recognition rate was greater than eighty percent, others, less than fifty. Either way, he'd have to disguise himself, and that didn't include wearing a surgical mask.

And go where?

The answers to all his questions lay on Rafa's flash drive.

I won't let you down, my friend. I owe you.

"Riske."

Simon turned his head. He'd been daydreaming. Had someone said his name? He checked the screen. Still nothing from Arjit.

"Riske."

Again. Clearer this time. A man's voice. A foreign accent. Dutch? No, South African.

He felt a presence behind him. A wind at his ear. He spun to look.

A blow.

Darkness.

CHAPTER 29

Singapore

The Goodwood Park Hotel was long one of Singapore's best-kept secrets. Built in the late 1800s, the hotel sat above Orchard Road tucked in its own lush enclave, a world away from the bustling commercial district outside its gates. To look at, it was a planter's country estate with broad sweeping wings extending from an elegant main entry topped with a Victorian tower. The picture of British colonialism.

Benson Chow arrived just ahead of London's Uber and was standing next to his Bentley convertible, wearing a pink open-collared shirt and a sweater draped over his shoulders in the English fashion.

London exited the compact car and crossed the driveway, her limp impossible to overlook.

"What happened?" said Benson, hurrying over.

"I took a fall," said London with a smile to make light of her injury.

"Tennis?"

"Not exactly. Let's wait until we have a drink. The story goes better with vodka."

"You should have told me," said Benson. "I would have picked you up. I don't mind crossing the bridge."

London ignored the slight, saying she had been working until the last minute. He gave her a kiss on each cheek and they walked into the lobby and then downstairs to the Gordon Grill.

The restaurant was like Benson: classy, traditional, but without much pizzazz. It was the kind of place, she thought, you took your fiancé's parents to impress them.

Benson signaled a waiter and ordered two martinis. "Grey Goose, very dry and very cold, olives."

"Three olives," said London. "Stuffed with blue cheese, if you have them. What the hell."

Benson eyed her with concern. "Are you sure you're all right?"

London put a hand on his and nodded. Benson relaxed. They exchanged pleasantries while waiting for their drinks. Work for the government was exciting enough, he said, though not especially remunerative. The economy was doing so well, throwing off such monumental surpluses, it felt as if they had too much money and not enough projects to invest it in. "After all, how many U.S. treasuries can we buy?"

Benson found the line hilarious.

London laughed with him. She'd dressed in a jade cocktail dress that made the most of her European curves, spent thirty minutes on her hair, and even dashed on a little makeup. It was a ruse, her version of a honey trap, though there wouldn't be any honey. She needed his help and, like any investigative reporter worth her salt, was going to use her every ploy to get it. She might be an award-winning journalist, but this was Asia. The #MeToo movement wouldn't get here for another few years.

The waiter set their cocktails on the table and took three excruciating minutes to discuss the evening's specials. London had already decided. The Gordon Grill was known for their steaks, and after the events of the day, she was in a carnivorous mood. The waiter departed. Benson raised his glass. "To you, my dear. May I say you look ravishing?"

London inclined her head, won over. In truth, she was thinking, *Who still talks that way in the twenty-first century?* He sounded like Lord Grantham speaking to his wife at Downton Abbey.

"To PetroSaud," she said. "May they rot in hell!" She took a swallow of her drink—far too large—and, eyes watering, set it down.

"I think you had better tell me what's going on," said Benson.

"She's here," said London.

"Who?"

"Nadya Sukarno. *Our* Nadya Sukarno, Indonesia's minister of finance, who also manages their sovereign wealth fund. I was walking past PetroSaud's offices this afternoon and happened to see her arrive."

"Here in Singapore? I hadn't read anything about her paying a visit."

"In the flesh." London went on to explain how after seeing Sukarno, she'd waited outside the offices until she left, then confronted her with questions about her involvement with PetroSaud.

"What did you ask her...*exactly*?"

"Exactly? I believe I said, 'Excuse me, Minister, how long have you been stealing from your own fund by investing in nonexistent oil leases and pocketing the proceeds?'"

"You didn't!" It was Benson's turn to take too large of a gulp. His cheeks flushed a violent hue of scarlet.

"Verbatim. And did I mention that there were three security guards posted outside the building's entrance? Why were they there? I didn't see guards in front of any other building."

"How did she take it?"

"She froze. She stopped right then and there and gave me a look I'll never forget."

"And?"

"I repeated the question. Did I tell you that I had my phone out? I was filming. I mean, obviously." London took another sip and noted that she'd finished her drink. She was feeling it, too, but at that moment, she didn't give a damn. "That was my mistake. The guards didn't like that. Not one bit. Before Mrs. Sukarno could give me an answer, they took me down."

"Took you down?" Lord Grantham was gobsmacked. Things like this didn't happen at Downton. "But you were just standing there."

"A guard tried to take my phone away from me. I wouldn't let him. We had a tussle, and a second one tackled me. I'd already shouted my name and who I worked for. He finally let me up after Nadya Sukarno had gone."

"And you have this on film?"

"Well, no," London admitted. "The guard erased it before returning my phone."

175

She might have gone on. She might have told him about the murderous look on the guard's face, her belief that he'd been expecting trouble, or the look on Sukarno's face when London had called out her crimes.

In fact, she was thinking that so far all she had done was corroborate what R had sent her. An Indonesian sovereign wealth fund managed by that country's minister of finance had, as per R's message, invested seven hundred million dollars in Saudi Arabian oil leases. She had only R's word and the copies of bank transfers, none of which would hold up to real scrutiny, to suggest that the fund manager, Minister of Finance Nadya Sukarno, had transferred the entirety of the investment to a personal account at the Bank of Liechtenstein after paying PetroSaud a generous commission.

To be honest, she had nothing.

And yet this was how every story began. Disparate threads bound by some common denominator. In this case, that denominator was PetroSaud.

"I'm sorry you were hurt for nothing," said Benson, all concern and compassion.

"It wasn't for nothing," said London. "I found out everything I needed."

"What's that?"

"A confession that she is as guilty as sin."

"But you said she didn't answer."

"She didn't need to. Her look was everything."

"And so?"

"And so I'm here with an ankle that's swollen as large as a grapefruit and the feeling that I've got my hands on the biggest story to rock the financial world since Bernie Madoff." London raised her empty glass. "Your turn."

Benson finished his drink and signaled for two more. "You were right," he said. "Indonesia isn't PetroSaud's only client. They work with a dozen sovereign wealth funds. Malaysia, India, Brunei, Kuwait—"

"Paragons of transparency."

"As well as Japan, Mexico, and a few hedge funds on Wall Street," said

Benson, naming the good guys. "There's no indication of wrongdoing. Not from where I stand."

"There wouldn't be, would there? All you're seeing is the public side of the transaction."

"All of them list their investments in the KSA on their annual reports. They're certainly not trying to hide anything."

"But how we do know if the investments are real?"

"Come on, London. How do we know they're not? The Japanese do not invest in fraudulent oil leases."

"Where there's smoke, there's fire."

"All this based on one unattributed email? You don't even know who the whistleblower is."

"Those documents are real, Benson. I know it. There's a reason PetroSaud posted security guards in front of their building. They're frightened." London wrung her hands in her napkin. "There's something else."

Benson sensed the change in tone. "Oh?"

"I received a strange email this morning, sent to my business email at the *FT*. It said very clearly that others might not be pleased if I were to look into PetroSaud and that I should watch my back."

"A specific threat?"

"God, no. More like fair warning."

"From who?"

"No attribution. I showed it to the IT guys and they just scratched their heads."

"What did it say? Verbatim."

London dug out her phone. "'Look into PetroSaud at your own risk. Others are aware of your interest. Actions will be taken.' Like I said, 'fair warning.'"

"'Actions will be taken.'" Benson leaned across the table. "Is that the first time you've gotten something like that?"

London shook her head. "Usually, it's from the aggrieved party. This came from an anonymous sender."

"So it could be PetroSaud. Ergo, the guards."

"My instincts tell me it's not."

"What will you do?"

"Do you mean will I stop looking into PetroSaud? Of course not. It's my job."

"Are you sure?"

"Do I look like a coward?"

"You most certainly do not," said Lord Grantham. Lady Grantham felt a stab of pride at his vote of confidence.

The entrées arrived. Fish for Benson and the rib eye for London. Conversation turned to other matters. The local social scene. Who was sleeping with whom. Who was making the most money. Who looked absolutely awful at so-and-so's dinner party. London was glad for the reprieve. The food was excellent.

"I have a confession to make," said Benson Chow. "There's something else I want to bring up. I was going to try to get you back to my place before I told you."

"Did you think that would work?"

"The way you look tonight it was worth a try," he said. "Anyway, forget it. This is more important than…than…"

"Go on, Ben."

"Well, I thought there might be one other thing you could look into. All those wealth funds I was talking about…at least the first ones…"

"Malaysia, India, Brunei…"

"Yes, those…they all used the same underwriter. Harrington-Weiss."

"HW's the top investment bank in the world. Why is that strange?"

"No, no," said Benson. "I mean the funds used HW *exclusively*. It's customary to spread that kind of business around. Multiple underwriters. Two at least. Usually more. I mean, we're talking about raising billions of dollars."

London put down her knife and fork. In other words, Benson Chow was suggesting the fact that all these funds had hired a single bank to handle the underwriting was highly irregular. "How many billions?"

"Four billion for Malaysia. Six for India. Two for Brunei. You'd think it would be easier to hire several banks, bigger client pool. Just saying."

"Who's the lead banker?" she asked.

"Deals this big are run by dozens of people. Besides, you know HW. All very hush-hush. Their ethos is that it's all about the firm, not the individual. I was just checking the public records, what's on the net, what the various exchanges might have. Tell you one thing, though. The teams running those deals are going to make a helluva bonus." Benson's eyes lit with greed. To an investment banker, the mere thought of a bonus was as enticing as sex with a Victoria's Secret angel.

"You can still go back to the Street," said London. "They'd snap you up in a New York minute."

"Wouldn't think of it," said Benson, affronted. "There's more to life than money."

Easy to say when you're sitting on twenty million U.S. in your private account, thought London. She raised her glass. She was quite drunk, she realized. But not so drunk as to not already be mapping out her next steps. She needed to get ahold of HW's internal phone directory. She knew one or two people at the office who might have one. Sure, teams run deals, but individuals run teams.

"Cheers to that!"

CHAPTER 30

Ratchaburi Province

Night.

Simon lay in the mud, hands and feet bound, head throbbing. A canopy of trees blocked the sky. He was aware of the sound of rushing water. The world came into focus and he saw that he was on the banks of a fast-flowing river.

Shaka kneeled beside him, slapping his cheek. When he saw Simon's eyes open, he showed him the flash drive in his open palm. "Just so you didn't think I came all this way for nothing."

Simon struggled to free his wrists and ankles.

"Not a chance," said Shaka. "Handcuff knots. It's how we tie up our enemies back home before we necklace them. Know what that is? Put a tire around their neck and shoulders, fill it with petrol, and light 'em up. You better believe they struggle." A smile at the memory. A jab to the shoulder. "You're lucky I didn't find any spare tires around here."

Simon took stock of his situation. His last recollection was of hearing his name called. He turned…and then he woke up here, in considerable discomfort, unable to move, and at the mercy of a trained assassin.

"How did you find me?"

"Trade secret."

"You chipped me," said Simon. "Where? I never felt it."

"You're too good for me, Riske." Shaka stuffed the flash drive into a pocket. "Airport baggage claim. You could perform a cavity search in there and the person wouldn't know it. A medical implantation device from Siemens. They call it a mosquito because that's how little you feel it. A friend of mine from my old outfit gave it to me. GSG 9. Mean anything to you?"

"German counterterror." Simon was more interested in why a former commando was involved with a crooked Saudi Arabian investment firm and what an Italian named Luca had to do with it all.

"Why did you kill them?" Simon asked.

"Neater that way. No questions asked."

"But they didn't know anything."

"They knew De Bourbon. That was already too much."

"What is this all about? PetroSaud?"

"*Who?* What's that, man?" Shaka stood, his knees cracking. "You're asking the wrong end of the stick. Me, I'm the sharp end."

"Should I ask Luca?"

Shaka raised a hand at Simon. "Him, you don't say his name. You're not good enough. You're like the rest, looking at the world with your eyes shut. You don't see what's happening right in front of you. He's the one with vision."

"Vision?"

"He knows what needs to be done." Shaka looked at the heavens, frustrated. "You want to know what this is about, Simon Riske? It's about purity. Preservation. Even piety, in a way."

Simon was confused. What did any of those lofty concepts have to do with ripping off a sovereign wealth fund? Once again, he was brought back to his suspicions. Who was "them"?

"Tell me, then. What needs to be done?"

"You'll find out soon enough. Everyone will. Then again, maybe you won't."

"Is that a threat?"

"No threats. Just action. I believe I'm a case in point. We do what's required."

"And that is?"

"Wait a week and you'll know. I'm sorry, there I go again."

"Colonel Tan told me that Luca was in charge," he said.

"Tan had a high opinion of himself. He didn't understand the chain of command. Only one person gives orders." Shaka kneeled on his haunches. "You want to know who's in charge? I am, Riske. See anybody else here?"

"And Malloy?"

"I told you. No loose ends. My job is to make certain done is done. No more questions asked. Now or later."

Shaka stared at Simon a little longer, then gave a last shake of his head. He'd had enough. He hauled Simon up off the ground and threw him over a shoulder, no differently than if he was picking up a Persian carpet. He walked down to the river's edge, wading into the water up to his knees. Simon could see where he was more clearly now. In the mountains, a steep hillside climbing from the opposite side of the river. Trees growing in abundance, vines falling from their branches to the ground. A rain forest or something like it.

A hundred yards downstream, two pale towers rose from the center of the river, red hazard lights blinking atop each, the water agitated, waves rising and falling, as it approached them. He guessed he was looking at some type of dam, which meant a hydroelectric power plant. Water passed through the dam, spinning giant turbines that in turn generated electricity, before being spewed out the other side, often hundreds of feet below. Not an ideal spot for an evening swim.

"Don't yell," said Shaka. "You'll just end up getting a mouthful of water, not that there's anyone around to hear you. If I were you, I'd try and get as much air as possible. You'll be under a long time."

He took another step and, with a grunt, lifted Simon with both arms and threw him toward the center of the river.

Simon landed facedown, the water colder than he'd expected. He struggled not to gasp. He felt himself moving, gathering speed, and worked to turn himself over. It was remarkably difficult. He rolled his shoulders back and forth, tried to kick his feet. Nothing. Already his air was going, his lungs constricting. A large and heavy object brushed against him, and he turned onto his back. He sucked down the warm air gratefully. A moment later, something washed across his face, cool and slimy, part of it catching in his mouth. He spat it out, shaking the rest free from his face. All the while, he fought to free himself, grinding his hands and feet back and forth, hoping the water might provide some lubricant. Quickly, he realized he was mistaken. The ropes, absorbing the water, were growing tighter as they expanded.

The current swung his feet around so he was traveling headfirst downstream. A piece of wood struck his head, something sharp poking below his eye. Reflexively, he rolled to avert it and swallowed a mouthful of water. The current grew stronger, jostling him. He felt himself rise and fall, entirely at the mercy of the river. He caught sight of the towers, closer now. Each was shaped like a gently rounded horn, a wide band of glass enclosing the control rooms. He shouted, but his voice was no match for the river. Water filled his mouth. He choked, spat it out, unable to keep from swallowing much of it.

He spun again, feet leading now, water spilling over his face, a battle to keep his mouth clear, to take a breath without gagging. For the first time he heard the turbines, a steady, low-pitched thrum. He continued working his wrists, mashing them together in a circular motion. He felt a little play, just a little, *but maybe…*

A log struck his shoulder, as hard as a body blow, turning him over, then staying with him, preventing him from rolling back. He opened his eyes, saw only black. He shifted his shoulder, thrashed. The log fell away. He turned onto his back. Air. Precious air.

And then he was angling downward, speeding faster, feeling as if he were sliding down a slope, the towers at his side, white ghosts there and gone. Steeper now. He felt himself drop and drop again, as if passing over speedbumps. A final breath. No time for a prayer. He went under.

And stopped.

Something encased his body, preventing him from moving any farther. Water continued to rush past, a torrent lifting his head clear. He looked to either side. A filter of some kind, a metallic net designed to keep larger debris from fouling the turbines. He was wedged against it, his feet tucked inside one of the perforations, somehow upright. A miracle.

The closest tower was ten yards upstream. He could see shadows moving inside the control room. He shouted. He screamed. No one could hear him. Nor could they see him. In the dead of night, he was invisible, made more so by the water rushing past him, a frothing turbulent shroud.

CHAPTER 31

Ratchaburi Province

Time passed. Minutes. Hours. He shivered until he could shiver no more. Cold left him. He grew numb. He couldn't feel his feet, his hands, nothing. He was aware of his heart slowing. His thoughts grew fuzzy. He knew he was slowly dying of hypothermia, but the thought caused him no fear. His brain had grown as numb as his body.

Consciousness came and went. At some point he began to dream. He saw a beach and a woman on it and the sun. It was very pleasant. The sun grew brighter. He wanted to look away but couldn't. It grew brighter still, until it was blinding him.

He opened his eyes and stared into the beam of a spotlight. He heard men shouting, was vaguely aware of a commotion on the walkway that circled the tower. The water passing him slowed, then grew calm. The thrum of the turbines ceased. A motor launch approached. Two men tried to lift him out of the water but were too weak to pull him aboard. One clutched his arm as the other drove the boat back to the dock, towing him alongside. As they slowed, a third man jumped into the water and cut his ropes.

Simon's feet touched bottom. Silt flushed between his toes. He tried to stand, and immediately toppled into the man's arms, the pain unbearable as blood rushed to his extremities. Tears ran from his eyes. He buried his face in the man's shoulder to keep from crying out. After a minute, he regained his strength and walked onto the riverbank. He was naked. The current had ripped off his clothing hours before.

He saw that it was almost dawn. In the growing light, the three men gathered around him. His skin was so pale as to be translucent, wrinkled like a prune. But it wasn't his skin or his pallor they were interested in. They were scrutinizing the latticework of scars crisscrossing his torso. Knife wounds, burns, bullet holes, the gash he'd suffered jumping out of the embassy window. He saw himself through their eyes. A foreigner bound hand and foot found caught in the power plant's filters, dead but for the grace of God, his body covered with evidence of extreme physical violence, a garish tattoo running the length of one forearm that all but screamed "gangster." What could they think but that he was a criminal caught out on the wrong side of a deal gone bad?

They said none of this.

"Are you able to walk inside?" one of the men asked in fluent English. Simon nodded, discovering that he was unable to speak.

With kindness, they led him inside the tower, one man assisting him on either side. Over and over, they asked if he was all right, if he needed to go to the hospital. Simon shook his head, making an okay sign with his fingers, though he was far from it.

They went to a locker room, where a shower was already running. Simon spent five minutes beneath the hot water. Gradually, he regained his strength and his senses. Then, a memory: *You chipped me.* He ran his fingers across his upper arms and shoulders. There, a hard nodule where none should be. An RFID transmitter had a limited range, no more than five miles, and a limited life span. Odds were that it was no longer functioning. But Simon was in no position to play the odds.

He finished showering and wrapped a towel around his waist. He found the men huddled in a conference room. Politely, he asked if any of them had a knife or, better yet, a razor blade. "A splinter," he said, by way of explanation.

Finally, one of the men rose and accompanied him to the snack kitchen. Simon found a paring knife in one of the drawers. Ten seconds over a gas flame sterilized the blade.

"Where is the splinter?" asked the engineer.

Simon pointed at his shoulder. "In here."

"I see nothing."

Simon sat on a chair and, with the knife in one hand and a paper napkin in the other, excised the transmitter. One, two, three, and it was out, bouncing on the linoleum floor.

The engineer picked it up, a titanium grain of rice. "What is it?"

"Top secret," said Simon. "You don't want to know."

A few seconds later, the transmitter landed in the kitchen sink and was washed down the drain. As far as Shaka was concerned, Simon was at this very moment floating his way into the Gulf of Thailand, there to stay forever.

Back in the shower room, he found a set of clothing folded neatly on a bench. Gray T-shirt, dark work pants, socks, a pair of boots, a cap. All fit him, more or less.

A bowl of noodles and a cup of hot tea waited in the conference room, complete with a napkin and utensils. Simon sat, sipped the tea, devoured the noodles. A map on one wall showed the locations of power plants across the country. One was colored with a red dot. Ratchaburi Hydroelectric Plant #2. He believed this to be his present location, some hundred kilometers southwest of Bangkok.

"The police are on their way," said one of the men, bald with thick glasses, a patient smile, and a frank manner, who'd introduced himself as "Steve." "It will take a while. We are some distance from the nearest town. I imagine you will want to tell them who did this to you."

"Yes," said Simon, though it was more of a croak. He drank some more tea and felt his throat relax. "Thank you."

He gazed out the window onto the parking lot. Four cars. A motorcycle. His mind switched into gear. He began to plot his escape. He could overpower the men, steal a car, make it to someplace where he could obtain a new passport—a false passport. Find out where London Li was, contact her, or, better yet, go there. The police could never protect her from someone like Shaka. Maybe he couldn't either.

"What happened?" asked Steve.

Simon put down his tea. He'd been working up a story, something about a waylaid tourist, a robbery…or was it a kidnapping? He was too tired to keep the facts straight. He looked at the men. All were well educated, engineers or the like. He knew his story wouldn't fly. He made a radical choice. The truth.

He told them everything, from his meeting with Dickie Blackmon in London to his visit to the Remand Prison and meeting with Colonel Tan, to the shootout at the Spanish embassy and his subsequent capture by Shaka. Along the way, he told them about himself—who he was, what he did for a living—making it clear he was not a gangster.

No one said a word. No one interrupted him. An interesting thing happened as he spoke. The moment Colonel Tan entered the story, the men shared a common look, as if each had his own history with Tan and the national police. Not a pleasant one if judged by the scowls on their faces.

When he'd finished, the men exchanged words in their native tongue. Now that he needed her, Helen Mirren had gone missing. He was unable to decipher what they were saying. By their heated tones and varied expressions, they either wanted him shot at dawn or nominated for sainthood. Simon hoped for something in between. The best word to sum up their collective mood was "confused." Simon was not a problem any of them had come across in a textbook.

A knock at the door interrupted their bickering. Steve rose and opened the door. Simon was surprised to see him place his hands together and bow. The other men shot from their chairs and followed suit. A clean-shaven head peered around the door. Intelligent eyes appraised Simon. The man said something that made the others laugh, then he entered the room. He was no more than thirty, clad in an orange-saffron robe draped over one shoulder, and sandals. A Buddhist monk.

"My nephew," said Steve. "From the local monastery. I called him as soon as I saw you there in the floodgates. To be honest, I thought you were certainly dead. I hoped he might help your spirit find its way to the next plane."

The monk bowed his head, greeting each man in turn. Their reverence was apparent. Finally, he came to Simon, who was standing like the others. He took Simon's hands as the other men spoke to him, no doubt offering a summary of the story he had just told them, some believing him, others not so sure.

"His name is Chamron," said Steve. "He is pleased to meet you and apologizes that his English is poor. However, if you speak Tibetan..."

Simon said that he did not. The monk smiled. *Touché.*

"Chamron will tend to you," said Steve.

Simon did not believe he had a choice in the matter. It was not a question of his health, but of some kind of psychic appraisal.

The monk turned his attention to him, still clutching his hands. "Is okay?"

Simon said, "Yes."

Chamron looked into his eyes and whispered for the others to be silent. He began to chant, a monotone, loud and repetitive. The atmosphere in the room grew still. Simon felt a sense of lightness and well-being come over him. He could not understand the words but acknowledged some type of bond being formed, a bridge between them, as if this man were privy to his thoughts and, more, to his soul.

The light in the room seemed to change, as if a sheer had been drawn across the windows. Simon felt himself relax and be at peace. *Yes,* he answered, *you know me now.*

The chanting ceased. The monk released Simon's hands. At once, Simon felt a current leave him, was aware of his body again, of his fatigue and discomfort.

The monk spoke softly to Steve, who translated.

"Chamron says that once you were a bad man. You were far from the healing spirit. The gods were not happy. They punish you. They put you in a dark place for long time. You came close to other side, close to the final darkness, one foot over, to leaving this plane. But you changed your ways. Inside... *in your heart...* you desired to be good, to do what is right. For you, this is still not always easy. You struggle."

Simon looked at Chamron. "When I was young, I did bad things, but no more. How do you know this?"

"Your friend."

"My friend?"

189

The monk's eyes closed as he answered. "He says that you must continue to struggle. The path is long. You are not there yet. This world needs you. Does this make sense to you?"

Simon saw that Chamron had opened his eyes and was gazing at him. "How do you know this about me?"

"He tell me," said Chamron, speaking himself.

"Who told you?"

"Your friend." Chamron raised a hand to indicate the world beyond them. "He is looking after you. Even now, he sees us. He make sure your head above water last night, no? He tell Steve to look for you."

"Did he say his name?"

"No name."

Simon nodded. Of course there was no name. There couldn't be. The monk couldn't possibly know about him. About Simon's time in prison. His time in the dark place.

"No name," said the monk once more, "but you...you call him"—here he paused, as if struggling to pronounce a difficult word; then he mouthed three syllables—"mo-see-nor."

Simon left fifteen minutes later. The car he drove belonged to Steve. The phone in his pocket belonged to Steve's secretary. An impromptu collection had netted ten thousand baht. All were to be returned or repaid at his earliest convenience. All except the blessing the monk, Chamron, had bestowed upon him. That was Simon's to keep forever.

CHAPTER 32

Rome

Luca Borgia gazed out of the window of the Mercedes saloon, bile rising in his gorge as the car turned on the Via del Colosseo and drove past the Colosseum. Traffic was worse than he remembered, and it was not yet tourist season. He knew the reason, at least one of them. It was right there in front of him, bold as day.

Near the Forum, an encampment of Africans and Arabs occupied a stretch of sidewalk and spilled onto the street. There were a hundred of them, at least, dark-skinned, shabbily dressed, loitering in and about a tent village. A souk in Rome.

A bunch had gathered around a fire burning in a garbage can, all seething glares and silent threats, roasting who knew what. A gang of miscreants if ever there was one. Even with the windows up, the foul smells penetrated the car.

Borgia knew all too well about the "Jungle" outside Calais where migrants had built a crude frontier town while hoping to cross the Channel and take up residence in England, and about the squatters in Paris who'd taken over entire neighborhoods. There had been riots in Germany. *In Germany…* where the government had practically laid out a red carpet for them, white-glove treatment and all. *"Excuse me, Farouk, would you like one lump or two?"*

Now, with detention camps filled to bursting in the south of the country, it had come to Rome. By "it" he meant the specter of un-checked immigration, though "specter" was a poor word to describe the chaotic free-for-all overwhelming his country's borders. "Catastrophe" was more like it.

He looked away. Italy had enough problems with Italians, he thought with a laugh. The last thing the country needed was more fodder for the unemployment lines and welfare rolls. More empty hands, open mouths, and idle minds. His concerns, though, went beyond the economy. He could not stand by idly and see his country's rich patrimony destroyed.

And here…in Rome, the eternal city.

Borgia curled his fists. Rome, home to Caesar and Cicero, Michelangelo and Masaccio, Cavour and Victor Emmanuel, first king of a united Italy. The cradle of Christianity…of Western art, culture, literature…if anyone cared a whit about those things any longer. Dante would have something to say about all this. He knew a thing or two about damnation and the journey to the gates of hell.

The Mercedes came to a halt at the entry to the Hassler. He climbed out and told the driver to be ready in an hour. He buttoned his jacket, gazing down at the Spanish Steps, the Fontana della Barcaccia, over the tiled rooftops. He imagined a minaret towering alongside Saint Peter's.

Never.

"Luca!"

Borgia turned to see a stocky, bearded man, in a poorly fitting suit, hand raised in greeting.

"Ah, Bruno, am I late?"

"It is I," said Bruno Melzi, Italy's minister of the interior and leader of the Italian right-wing Forza Nuova party.

The men entered the hotel salon and found a table in the far corner where they could speak freely. A waiter arrived and they ordered espresso and *cornetti*.

"It is out of control," said Borgia, dispensing with the usual pleasantries. "I tell you I almost took action myself. Bruno, what has become of our country?"

"You passed the encampment by the Forum," said Melzi, who had been a professor of engineering before entering politics.

"On our sidewalks. I saw a flag. A crescent and star."

"You are surprised? What have I been preaching about all these years?"

"They are defecating on our sidewalks. Shitting on our historic streets. It's gone too far."

"We are doing what we can," said Melzi. As interior minister, his mandate included not only policing but also sanitation. "It is a problem. We have nowhere to house them. The camps are full, and they escape anyhow. Still, they keep coming. Like cockroaches."

The waiter arrived, a Somali to judge by his elegant features. Working here in the Hassler, Rome's finest hotel.

Borgia placed a calming hand on Melzi's arm. "Please, Bruno, they are not cockroaches. They are human beings, too. I can only imagine the conditions they are fleeing. The cost, the peril, to come all this way. I salute their bravery."

"Of course, Luca. I was only saying…"

Borgia dropped a cube of sugar into his espresso. "I have every respect for their culture, as we all must, but in its rightful place. We do not share similar values."

Melzi huffed in agreement. "Most certainly not."

"They come to our open society, take advantage of our inclusive laws, our generosity and charity and goodwill toward all men, and what do they do? They establish their own rules, their own laws, which are neither open nor inclusive. Worse, they spread their restrictive, discriminatory dogmas to our own people. Do I have to mention how they treat their women?"

"Not to me."

"Like dogs. Using them only to procreate, and that they do in abundance. Like…like…"

"Rabbits."

"Indeed!" said Borgia, now that the *melanzane* was out of earshot. "Sometimes I feel as if we are surrendering to them, not just the immigrants but to all of them: the academics, the media, the communists, the entire left-leaning political mess of the eurozone. Can't they see what they are allowing to happen right under our very own noses? The destruction of the world's greatest culture, the abdication of Western democracy, the infiltration of a lesser religion, one that seeks only to dominate all others. Christ, our savior, preached that we must turn the other cheek, to be tolerant, that our first duty is to love all mankind. Their prophet preaches to blow us all to kingdom come." He mimicked pressing his thumb on a detonator switch. "*Allahu Akbar! God is great!* If this continues, there will be none of us left. Soon we will be forced to call our land 'Eurabia.' Think of it. *Eurabia.*"

"We cannot allow it," said Melzi.

"I will not allow it." Borgia finished his espresso as a familiar figure appeared in the doorway. "Ah, here is our guest."

A short, fit man dressed in the crisp uniform of the Italian paratroops crossed the salon, cap held under his arm. General Massimo Sabbatini commanded the 9th Paratroopers Assault Regiment, also called the Col Moschin, Italy's most elite special forces. He was an athlete to look at. Borgia had read something about him running a twenty-four-hour race in the Swiss Alps, covering a hundred kilometers or more. He read that commitment in his taut, tanned face as the general held out a hand.

Sabbatini sat perched on the edge of his seat, bristling with energy. "So," he said, "it is finally time. How I have been waiting."

"Soon, Massimo, soon," said Borgia. "A few days yet."

"In the nick of time," said Sabbatini. "You've driven through the city. You've seen this crime to our country. *Basta!*"

"Complaining will get us nowhere. Now, gentlemen, listen closely. The shipment is arriving tomorrow in Naples. I'll be there to pick it up."

"Luca, please, let my men. We have experience with this."

"No, no. I do not want the army anywhere near these types. You know them—there are bound to be last-minute difficulties."

Sabbatini and Melzi shrugged in agreement. They knew who controlled the docks in Napoli. Unsavory types. Gangsters.

"As soon as I have the goods, I will contact you to make the transfer. Then the rest is up to you. Massimo?"

"My men are on standby. They are only awaiting my signal."

"And Lampedusa?" asked Borgia.

The tiny island one hundred seventy-four miles south of Sicily housed the immigrant Reception Center, a processing and holding facility for refugees streaming from northern Africa. It had been built to house no more than eight hundred persons at any one time. Over one hundred thousand had poured through the facility in the last year alone.

"I have everything in place," said Sabbatini, then sotto voce: "Don't worry, Luca, our actions will be justified—welcomed, even—especially after what will have transpired the night before."

"Let us not speak of that," said Borgia. "Not yet. And you, Bruno?"

"My men control the police in Milan, Turin, and Naples. Rome is a different story, but I am hopeful that with the proper impetus, they will follow suit."

Borgia nodded grimly. "Impetus they will have. Oh yes, they will not lack motivation. Personally, I do not see how they can sit on their hands and allow the city to be so despoiled."

"Now they will have a reason to clean the streets," said Melzi.

"What more can we do, gentlemen?" Borgia stood. "I am pleased that all is in readiness. Two days, then. A spark to light the fire." He looked each man in the eye. "Prato Bornum."

"Prato Bornum," each responded.

CHAPTER 33

Pattaya, Thailand

Simon arrived at the seaside resort city of Pattaya at three p.m. Leaving the highway, he made his way toward the ocean, past shiny new hotels and soaring condos and seedy bars, past guesthouses and massage parlors and outdoor cafés and restaurants. The roads were uneven, potholed, sparkling with beach sand, kids running here and there, tangled gobs of wire looping from telephone pole to telephone pole, tin roofs, garish neon signs, and the occasional stray dog.

He knew the city by reputation only. A hotbed of sex, drugs, and vice of every imaginable variety. The world's largest bordello. In short, a hub of organized crime, or as Ben Sterling had told him without a hint of sarcasm, *"Sodom and Gomorrah with a double dash of sriracha."*

It was a sunny day, the sidewalk cafés filled with tourists drinking more than their fair share of beer, young women on their boyfriends' laps or walking the aisles looking for a lap to sit on. Music blaring, the '80s greatest hits to cater to the middle-aged clientele. He looked past the bustling tables and into the shadows, to the toughs loitering inside, street-smart runners ready to do their boss's bidding. Buy this. Deliver that. Pay off this guy. Teach that one a lesson.

Without leaving his car, he knew he'd come to the right place. In Pattaya, everything was for sale.

The drive from Ratchaburi Province had passed in a whirl of activity. His first order of business upon leaving the power plant had been to contact Arjit Singh. It had been three a.m. in London, the middle of the hacker's workday.

"What happened?" Arjit demanded. "You cut me off before I could finish. I tried to ring you back, but you didn't answer."

"Something came up," said Simon. "Just tell me if you have good news or bad news."

"Hold on a sec. First, let me know if you can get back online. I can pick up where I left off."

"Not possible. The flash drive is gone."

"More secret agent shit?"

"Something like that," said Simon. "I take it then it's bad news."

"Why do you say that?"

"Without the drive it's over."

"I cracked it," said Arjit.

"Say again?"

"Took me a while, but I got it. That's not the problem. Your friend had a boatload of files. I was halfway through downloading them when the connection broke off."

Relief poured over Simon. "But you got half?"

"A little more."

Actually, half sounded marvelous. He was in no position to complain. "What are we talking about?"

"A gazillion emails, a shit ton of files and spreadsheets, and a crap load of text messages."

"In English."

"Five hundred thousand emails, ten thousand files and spreadsheets, and a million or so text messages. Clear enough for you?"

And that is only half? "Tell me they're safe and sound."

"Tucked away in the cloud under lock and key."

"How can I access them?"

"Give me an email address," said Arjit. "And don't say Gmail."

Given events, Simon had to assume that his current email had been compromised. "I need a new one. Industrial strength. Any ideas?"

"Proton. They're Swiss. Only one thing: you have to remember your user name and password. Lose 'em and they're gone forever."

"I think I can manage."

"That's what everyone says. Give me a few minutes and I'll get it set up."

Simon promised to call back in an hour, then phoned D'Artagnan Moore, who was not as pleased to be roused in the middle of the night.

"I need you to send me some money."

"Mind telling me where you are?"

"Thailand. Heading to Pattaya."

"God help you."

"It's work."

"Something I should know about?"

"Definitely not," said Simon. "Where's my fee?"

"Pending."

"You said that last time. The painting's either authentic or it's not."

"There's an issue about the canvas. One test says it's one hundred twenty years old, another three hundred."

"So it's a fake painted before Monet was born?"

"I'm sure things will resolve themselves in your favor. Everyone has to prove their worth. Damn experts. How much do you want?"

"Twenty grand. Dollars. Oh, and one more thing. I don't have an ID with me, no passport, nothing. And I may be wanted by the national police."

"That incident in the embassy…that's not you?"

Simon didn't respond. He heard an oath. Then: "Go to a branch of the Royal Bank of Thailand. They are our correspondent. Ask for the manager. Use the name Guy Fawkes."

"You're serious?"

"You're not the first person I've had to send money to under suspicious circumstances. Tell them your birthday is November fifth."

"Of course it is," said Simon. "Guy Fawkes Day."

"Not bad for a Yank. I'll take care of the rest." D'Art paused. Then a command: "And, Simon, look after yourself."

A last call. "Hello, Ben. Sorry to wake you. I need a small favor. Maybe you can help."

"Shoot."

Simon made his request. Ben Sterling's answer surprised him.

After parking, Simon walked up the main drag, relieved to see that his fellow expats were as poorly dressed as he. He wasn't sure if he should look for the seediest establishment or the classiest. He spotted a place with a catchy name and a big footprint: Awake Till Dawn. With that much real estate, the owner was sure to be plugged in.

Simon found a seat at the bar, happy to be out of the sun. A girl joined him before he could order a beer.

"Buy me drink." She was twenty, almost pretty, with a sunny disposition, clad in short shorts and a strategically cut off T-shirt. A hand dropped onto his thigh. No beating around the bush here. "How you today?"

"I'm fine," said Simon, and when the waitress arrived, he ordered a beer for himself and a Shirley Temple for the lady. Actually, she wanted a shot of tequila.

"Me, Gate," she said.

"Gate?"

She nodded. "American name."

"Not *Kate?*"

"Gate."

Simon said he must have missed that one. The drinks arrived. He tipped the waitress and gave Gate a thousand baht to begin the process of legally changing her name. She asked where he was from, and he said, "Australia." Why not? He planned on visiting one day.

"Listen, Gate," he said. "I need a favor. I'm looking for the person who runs this place."

"You mean, in charge of bar? My boss, there." She pointed to a faded beauty seated at a far table smoking a cigarette and doing her nails.

"I mean, the big boss. The person who owns this place."

"First, I ask my boss for you."

Gate hurried to the far table. The older woman—probably his

age—eyed him, then, with great effort, rose and came to the table. "What you want?"

"A favor," he said, slipping the woman a thousand baht. "Five minutes of your boss's time. The owner."

"Who you?"

"A businessman."

Her look told him she didn't believe him. "Why you want to talk to him?"

"Personal."

"You have card?"

"Left it on my dresser." It was apparent to Simon that he was getting nowhere. He decided on the nuclear option. "Please tell him that I'm a close friend of Sergeant Rudi."

The woman's eyes didn't change, but he could sense her growing tense. "You name?"

"Simon."

"You wait here," she said. "First you buy Gate drink. Me too."

Simon ordered another round for all of them and sat back to wait. Ten minutes passed. Gate asked repeatedly if he would take her home when his business was done. Simon said, repeatedly, "Not tonight. Maybe another time."

She asked if he wanted a boy…or a ladyboy. Simon declined each.

Gate pouted. "You buy me one more drink?"

Simon obliged, thinking they should use Gate in their employee training videos. By now he was broke. Another half hour passed. He hadn't seen Gate's floor boss since their conversation. He kept his eyes on the street, checking for police. An occasional uniform walked past, keeping the peace, nothing more. Simon pulled his cap lower. One more *farang* enjoying Pattaya's hospitality. He had an hour before the bank closed. If he could find a passport, it wouldn't come cheap.

Someone tapped him on the shoulder. A middle-aged man sat on his haunches, white shirt, shorts. "Mr. Simon, please come with me." His English was good. A step up.

Simon followed the man through the bar to a suite of offices on the first floor. The floor boss waited inside a small office. "You sit," she said. "Wait."

Simon entered and took a seat. The woman left the room. He checked the door. Locked. The office was cramped and without windows. A desk, a file cabinet. A Buddha on a shelf with a wilted garland around its neck. This was not the boss's office.

Some time passed. The door opened. Two men entered. Tough and Tougher. Late twenties, as thin as rails and probably as strong, wearing jeans and T-shirts, hair cut too fashionably, razored on the sides, dressed up on top. Not the boss. Not even his deputies. They were muscle, pure and simple. He'd come to the wrong place, asked the wrong questions.

Simon hit the first man as he closed the door, a sucker punch to the ribs, knuckles extended. He followed with a jab to the chin. The man bounced off the wall, grunting, otherwise showing no ill effects.

A fist struck Simon in the kidney. He spun, vision blurring, kicked at the other man's knees, felt the kneecap give way, winced at the telltale snap of broken ligaments. A howl to alert police in the surrounding five counties as the man fell to the floor. But Simon was already turning back to the first man, blocking one punch, the other landing on his solar plexus. A hammer. Gasping, Simon threw an uppercut, connecting with bone. A tooth whistled past. The counterpunch landed wide, grazing Simon's shoulder. Simon charged ahead, a wounded bull, lifting the man bodily off his feet and slamming him against the wall. A flurry of punches to the ribs followed. The man down, writhing.

Fifteen seconds. Over and done.

He fell onto the chair, panting, head down. He was wiped.

And then, a thunderclap of boots climbing the stairs. The door flew open. A wave of olive drab stormed the room. Angry hands hauled him to his feet and flung him against the wall. His arms were pulled behind him. Steel cuffs bit into his wrists. Someone spun him around.

An officer stood before him, ribbons to rival Colonel Tan, wearing his mirrored sunglasses, too.

The national police.

"Don't move. You're under arrest."

Chapter 34

Pattaya

The policeman was sixty if a day, short and stout, a green beret tugged low over one eye, salt-and-pepper hair cut short. His name tag read SUWANNARAT.

"So I understand you are a businessman," he said, taking a chair opposite Simon. "What line of work are you in?"

"Self-preservation, for one."

The policeman eyed the two men lying on the floor with disgust and ordered his men to take them out. "Your present situation may put those skills to a greater test," he said after they had left. "Name?"

"Ledoux. Simon Ledoux."

"You're sure?" The police officer removed his beret and set it on the desk, then his sunglasses on top of it. With the same precision, he unbuttoned his pocket and removed a piece of paper, folded in quarters. With care, he spread it on his leg. "You do remember that a photograph was taken as you entered the Spanish embassy? For your ID?" He held up the photocopy so Simon could see it. Simon said nothing.

"Every police officer in the country has one of these, Mr. Simon *Riske*. On order of the king. He's quite upset, as you can imagine. Things like this reflect poorly on his country. Added to that, Colonel Albert Tan was a close friend. Practically a relative. Did you know that we only recently reinstated the death penalty? So far, the means used has been lethal injection. The king is talking of bringing back the firing squad just for you."

"I'm flattered," said Simon. "But you have the wrong man. I didn't kill Colonel Tan or anyone else."

"Says the sole survivor last seen fleeing the compound." The policeman sighed. "Really, Mr. Riske. Give us some credit. Save your story for the judge, or perhaps the king himself. By law, he can involve himself in matters like these. You'll have plenty of time to fashion something more credible than 'You have the wrong man.' A year until trial, at least. Five years until you're executed. Maybe ten. We like to appear fair-minded. The king will make sure you serve your time in an appropriate location. There's a prison up the river that we keep for our most special guests."

"This is a mistake," said Simon. "You know I'm not the killer. I was there to help my friend, Mr. De Bourbon. It was another man. Shorter than me. Mixed race. There are cameras all over the embassy."

"Disabled. All of them. Another of your business skills, perhaps…along with beating up two of my men?"

"They were police officers? I didn't know."

"Of course not. Those two aren't fit to wear a probationer's uniform. They are my employees. We are sitting in my establishment. I'm the proprietor."

"You own this place? The Awake Till Dawn?"

"And Awake Till Dawn 2 and 3."

Simon sat forward. "You're Sergeant Rudi?"

"Major Rudi these days. A bit old for the rank, but yes, I used to be Sergeant Rudi. I'm Ben Sterling's friend." The policeman told Simon to stand and unlocked his handcuffs. He held Simon's wrists for a closer look. The skin was abraded where Shaka's bonds had cut into him. "We didn't put the cuffs on that tightly."

"That's another story," said Simon.

"I'm sure we'll come to it."

"Did Ben tell you what I needed?"

"Passport and a way out of the country. He doesn't realize the trouble you're in. Do you have any kind of identification?"

Simon shook his head. "I've had a rough few days."

Rudi removed a pack of cigarettes from his breast pocket and shook one loose, tilting his head as he lit it. "Now I begin to see. Any preference for nationality?"

"Swiss, European Union, Canadian—I'm not certain where my travels may take me. I'd like to avoid any visa requirements."

"Is there anything else you'd like? Say a flying carpet?"

"Just a passport. One that meets all biometric standards and won't raise any red flags. Oh…and I need it today."

Major Rudi considered this, a long drag, a look at his boots. He exhaled and looked at Simon with a new determination. "If I were able to help you, such a document would be quite expensive. Friend or no friend. Excuse me for saying, but you do not appear to be especially prosperous at the moment. The people involved to make such a document…if I knew where to find them…the short delay. Yes, extraordinarily expensive." He dropped the cigarette on the floor and crushed it under his boot. "There is something else…"

"Yes?"

"We know that you are not the culprit. It's true that all of the cameras in the embassy were deactivated, except one."

"In the ambassador's office, I hope."

"On a separate feed. Of course, I haven't seen it. I'd prefer not to."

"Then why are you searching for me?"

"The police must be seen to be doing something. It comforts our people to know that we have some idea who we're looking for. Two of my men spotted you in the café. I had no choice but to follow procedure."

"I understand," said Simon.

"However, since you were there at the embassy, it might help if you were able to provide some information about the killer."

"I take it there's no photo of him entering the embassy."

Major Rudi grimaced. "Or the country, it turns out. A capable fellow all the way around."

"I'd be happy to," said Simon. "Though I'm fairly certain he's no longer in the country."

"Still, I'd like to be of assistance to my colleagues abroad."

"May I ask you something first? Were you close to Colonel Tan?"

"A fine officer. A credit to the Royal Thai Police and I say that without reservation. But let's say that Albert Tan and I were on the opposite sides of many issues. Do you know about his family?"

"Just stories." Simon rubbed his fingers to indicate "wealth."

"In this country, there is still very much an 'us' and a 'them.' I come from Isan, the poorest region in Thailand. I am old to be only a major. Still, for my family, it is a victory. I am 'us,' the people. Colonel Tan, he was 'them.' A member of the ruling class. Rich. A friend of the king. Two worlds, really. Why do you ask?"

"Just curious." Tan…his involvement with Rafa…whatever lay behind it all. It was too big a can of worms to open at this point. If Simon did his job, Major Rudi and the entire Thai police force would learn the reasons behind Tan's actions at the same time he did. "The man you're looking for is mixed race, thirty-five to forty years old, five feet nine inches tall. Very strong. He goes by the name Shaka. He's from South Africa and spent some time as a member of GSG 9, Germany's counterterrorism brigade. He's a trained professional."

"It sounds as if you had a run-in with him before."

"You can say that. He tracked me from the embassy and nearly killed me. Long story. If I had to guess where he's headed, I would say Singapore."

"Singapore? An arrogant bunch, the police down there. It will be a pleasure to tell them that this Shaka is on his way."

"My guess is he's already there. He probably arrived early this morning, if, that is, he took a commercial flight. He may have private transportation at his disposal."

Major Rudi wrote all this down in his police notebook. "There's more here than you're telling me. I appreciate your discretion. I have no interest in learning about what Albert Tan may have been involved in. In this country, it is often better not to know. Is there anything else you'd care to add?"

Simon shook his head, shrugged, indicating that they had better get a move on. "I'll need to get to the bank."

"Yes, the passport. I'm thinking Canadian. A trustworthy country. A man just up the road does an excellent job. You can't leave from any of the major airports, however. As I said, your picture is everywhere. We'll be keeping a close watch on flight manifests. A cash ticket will raise a red flag. I'll put in a word on your behalf, but it will be some time before your name is stricken and the watch is called off. I'm thinking a private aircraft to Malaysia—a turboprop—then the ferry across the Johor Straits. It will take longer, maybe all night, but I don't think you'll have a problem at the border." Major Rudi replaced his beret and put on his mirrored sunglasses. "I take it you are going to Singapore?"

CHAPTER 35

Cannes

Transcript from Press Conference: *The Raft of the Medusa*

Salle de Presse, Palais des Festivals et des Congrès, 21 Mai 2020

Participants:
Thor Axelsson—Director
Samson Sun—Producer
Mohammed Al-Jumani—Actor / Himself
Mohammed Tabbi—Actor / Himself
Mohammed Zafrullah—Actor / Himself
Jean Renaud—Directeur du Festival

Jean Renaud: (Introduction) *The Raft of the Medusa* is a film of
extraordinary compassion that chronicles one of the most terrible
tragedies of the last twenty years, brought to life not by professional
actors but by the very individuals who suffered through it and
survived. You are all familiar with the story. Today, I am proud to
stand beside the team behind this magnificent work of art. Dare I
say, "a masterpiece of its kind." With us are Thor Axelsson, the
director, Samson Sun, the producer, and three of the principal leads,
who play themselves. None of the actors speaks English or French,
so please direct your questions to either Mr. Axelsson or Mr. Sun.

New York Times: I was hoping you could comment on your development process. Most independent films take years to come to the screen, yet you've boasted about going from concept to completion in eighteen months. Considering this is your first film, that's quite a feat. How did you do it?

Samson Sun: As you know, everything begins with the story. When I received the screenplay, I immediately knew that it could be not only an important film that speaks to one of today's most urgent issues but also an exciting thriller and box office smash. There was no reason to delay. When Samson Sun decides to do something, he does it.

New York Times: This is the screenwriter's first film. It is safe to say she is an extraordinary talent. How did she find you, or vice versa?

Sun: You know Hollywood. It is all about connections. A mutual friend knew that I was searching for the right film to be my first. He put us in contact. As you said, she is an extraordinary talent. Of course, I had my own comments about the script. We worked together to bring it to the screen as quickly as possible.

Der Spiegel: Whose idea was it to use the real survivors of the ordeal rather than professionally trained actors?

Sun: It was the screenwriter's idea from the beginning. She had first approached the subject as a documentary. But very soon she realized that the story could be more fully told if dramatized. When she asked what I thought of the idea, I said it was brilliant.

Der Spiegel: Of the survivors who appeared in the film, only three were granted asylum in the European Union. The others were sent back to their home countries. How did you find them?

Sun: It wasn't easy. (*Laughter.*)

The Guardian: How did the actors hold up during the filming? Given the emphasis on re-creating the events as accurately as possible, did any suffer from post-traumatic stress by reliving such a terrible experience? I'm referring specifically to the graphic depiction of cannibalism.

Thor Axelsson: They are remarkable human beings. I can answer for them and say that to a man they have put the events behind them. Remember, a movie set is a busy place. While what you see on film is harrowing, the actors are surrounded by a crew of professionals. So much is going on out of sight of the camera that the men were able to maintain a division between fiction and reality.

The Guardian: A follow-up. It had been reported that there were naval vessels from France, Spain, and Italy all in the area at the time of the ship's initial fire and sinking. None responded to calls for search and rescue when the *Medusa* was reported missing two days after it had sunk. Do any of your actors harbor ill will toward those governments?

Sun: We are here to discuss the film. We know of no proven, purposeful actions taken by any of those governments not to come to the *Medusa*'s assistance. As we show in the film, no distress call was sent. This is not a political statement but a humanitarian one.

The Guardian: Does Mr. Al-Jumani wish to comment?

Sun: No. He does not.

Le Figaro: Two of the actors were among those survivors not granted asylum due to their past affiliation with terrorist organizations, namely Al-Shabab and Ras-al-Islamiya. Did you feel any responsibility—one way or the other—about hiring them?

Sun: Film is art, not politics. Whatever ties these men might have had in the past with any such organization are just that: in the past. During the course of shooting, I came to know all of them. They are remarkable human beings. As I mentioned, we had a hard time finding a few of them. Two were in Egypt and one in Sudan. Several had scattered across Europe. All had gainful employment and had started families. Enough talk of politics.

Le Figaro: And two of them were not given visas to come to France…even with the festival's backing—

Sun: A travesty.

Le Figaro: —amid ongoing concerns about their current activities.

Sun: Enough.

Variety: Much has been written about the financing of the motion picture, namely that you yourself paid the entire fifty-three-million-dollar budget.

Sun: Not me personally. My production company, Black Marble. But you are correct. We financed the picture on our own. When I believe in a project, I am not afraid to prove it.

Variety: So little is known of your background, Mr. Sun. You are a young man. Can you let us in on the secret of your vast wealth?

Sun: Hard work, plenty of play, and Samson Sun a very happy boy.

Jean Renaud: One more question, ladies and gentlemen.

Daily Mail: Will you all be attending the premiere?

Sun: Of course. We are family.

Chapter 36

Gothenburg, Sweden

Mattias dug his hands into the pockets of his reefer jacket and crossed Andersmark Park, head lowered to combat the howling wind. Mid-May and it felt like December. Already five years in Sweden, and he still wondered if he'd ever get used to the cold. He missed his home and the hot, dry winds of the Sahara more than ever. It was just past three in the afternoon and he was on his way home from work as an apprentice baker. He liked the job, despite having to rise at two a.m. each morning. The bakery was warm, smelled wonderfully—a far cry from the mud-brick ovens and open fires of his childhood—and he respected his boss, Mr. Nordstrom. The cardamom buns were the best thing he'd ever eaten. The clients, when he worked at the counter, were uniformly welcoming and seemed to care deeply for his well-being. Of course, they knew his story. Everyone in Gothenburg did. At least as much as anyone who hadn't been there could know it. It was better that way. Some things even the most forgiving people could not come to understand.

Mattias stopped by school and picked up his twin sons, Lucas and Leo. They had names from home, too, but he wanted them to be as Swedish as possible. The color of their skin, even diluted by half, made things hard enough. Not that the Swedes would admit to it. They thought their society to be colorblind. Almost, thought Mattias, warmth in his heart. It was a wonderful country and he was ever grateful.

He gave each of the boys—already four years old, *inshallah*—an almond-paste cake and held their hands as they crossed Ulfspargattan.

His home was one of a dozen row houses, two stories, large windows, painted a bright barnyard red to stave off the bleak Scandinavian winters. His rent was twelve hundred euros a month, more than a third of his monthly salary, but the government gave him some help, and Gitte, his wife, chipped in when she could.

She was working at the kitchen table when they entered, a writer, of course, waiting to be published. But talented, Mattias thought, though as a child he'd never read a novel. Novels were *haram*. Forbidden. He was permitted to read only one book, the Koran, and by fourteen, he had memorized it. Gitte rose to greet them, kisses all around, then tea and snacks, before settling the children before the television. Two hours a day. Not a minute more. That was the rule.

Dinner was at six o'clock sharp, early because of Mattias's schedule. Tonight: turkey meatballs, gravy, lingonberries, with egg noodles and black bread. The IKEA special. If Gitte didn't make it as a novelist, she could find work as a cook. Mattias was still getting used to having enough to eat. His full belly felt like an affront to those without.

That evening, Mattias insisted on clearing the table. No one looked twice at the scar running the length of his forearm as he gathered the plates. His boys called it "the caterpillar"—pink, reticulated, and uneven. He'd learned to keep it hidden at the bakery. One too many a customer had been unable to stifle a gasp. *"Grusig,"* one had said. Gruesome. He didn't want to make anyone uncomfortable. He didn't like being reminded either. The nightmares still came, all these years later.

A last sip from the jar—the water hot, murky, dizzy with grease and dead flies. Whose would it be? The rusted gutting saw wasn't enough. Mattias's hands were stronger. One man lived, the other died. Survival on the open water.

Mattias kissed the children good night at eight o'clock. Gitte would tuck them in at ten, after reading them a story. His life was a fairy tale. A Western fairy tale, but so what? To know that his children would want for nothing…that was enough. More than he could have dreamed of.

He went upstairs and got ready for bed, kneeled, said his prayers. Twice a day was enough. If his bed faced east, west, north, or south, he didn't know. He was sound asleep when Gitte slid in next to him, pressing her cool body against his back, wrapping an arm around him. Her kiss barely registered.

He woke at one fifty-five, five minutes before the alarm sounded. Rising from bed, he padded to the bathroom. The tile floor was warm beneath his feet…heated from beneath. A wonder. He showered and dressed, clothing laid out before bedtime so as not to wake Gitte. He looked in the mirror. Sharp cheekbones—though nowhere near as sharp as before—slim lips, liquid eyes, the regard of a warrior. Forever and always. *Inshallah. God is great.*

Only now did he alter his routine from the one he'd followed these last years.

Let it begin.

Mattias left the bathroom and opened the bottom dresser drawer. He found the roll of bills tucked into a pair of socks. Three thousand five hundred euros, all that he'd saved since coming to Sweden. There was more, much more, but he wanted her to know that this was from him and him alone.

He placed the roll in Gitte's drawer, in the wool socks she wore for cross-country skiing. She would find them at the right time. He put on his belt and shoes, then took a look at this woman who had captured his heart. Blond, a little heavy, a gap between her front teeth, rosy cheeks—as different from him as chalk from cheese. Or perhaps, snow from coal. And yet…love.

Then, no hesitation in his step or his heart, he left.

His phone and wallet and passport remained on the dresser.

A man waited downstairs. It was the man from the mosque. A Saudi. His name was Abdul. "Sheikh Abdul," Mattias called him. As always, he was perfectly dressed. Suit, necktie, an overcoat that would cost a month's wages.

"Tonight is the night," he said. "Peace be unto the Prophet."

"May peace be unto him," said Mattias.

"Did you check your wife's bank account?"

Mattias said he had. One million euros transferred from the Bank of

Liechtenstein, though he could neither pronounce the name nor had any idea where the place might be.

"Do not worry," said Sheikh Abdul. "I will look in on your wife from time to time. She will want for nothing. As it should be."

A car drew up. A man who could be Mattias's brother sat behind the wheel. Mattias said goodbye to Sheikh Abdul. He had memorized his instructions long ago. He knew where to go, what to say, and what was expected of him. It was really not so difficult.

"Shut the door, Ibrahim," said the driver, using Mattias's birth name. "It's freezing."

Mattias slammed the door and put on his safety belt. "How far?"

The driver gave him a look. "You better have taken a wicked piss, my brother. We're going to be driving a long time."

And despite himself, Mattias laughed.

It was time to give back.

Allahu Akbar.

God is great.

CHAPTER 37

Singapore

London Li hadn't been in the bullpen for a month. It was just past nine as she made her way across the floor of the *Financial Times* office in Singapore, offering a "Good morning" or "How are you?" to the journalists she knew (too few) and several she didn't. She went from desk to desk, speaking with reporters who had written pieces on Harrington-Weiss over the past few years and who might have contacts at the secretive bank. Doing so, she managed to put together an organigram of sorts with names and positions. Ivan S., head of investment banking. Sheila G., capital markets. Freddy N., equity research. It was a start.

Just as an army needed perfect cooperation between its branches—infantry, artillery, intelligence—to mount a successful invasion, a bank needed the same to underwrite a billion-dollar bond issue. No one person did it all.

In addition, London asked who the big players were these days, the alphas. Only a top dog could go to the Indonesian minister of finance and convince her that HW and HW alone should underwrite her sovereign wealth fund to the tune of six billion dollars.

For all the power a bank's name might bring to a deal—the clout of a long history and the allure of a burnished reputation—in the end, finance turned out to be a people business. Deals were closed on the power of personality. The highest paid bankers, the highest ranking execs, the "big swinging dicks," didn't get to where they were by sitting at a desk crunching numbers. You would never see an equity analyst seated in the royal box at Wimbledon. But if you knew who to look for, you'd see the top dealmaker at Barclays, and ten to one, he'd be joined by a face you'd seen on the cover of *Vogue* magazine.

London knew plenty of these bankers. To a person, they were brilliant, charismatic, larger-than-life characters who filled any room they entered. Personalities in their own right. Whatever "it" was, they possessed it in spades. Like she'd said, "alphas."

In the space of a few hours, she'd assembled a list of six executives at Harrington-Weiss who might have overseen the deals in question.

She found an empty desk—there were too many for her taste—and called HW's public relations department. Stating that she was doing an article on the firm's work with Asian governments to raise money for the SWFs, she asked to interview the bankers who ran the deals. The PR person was all too happy to help, though unfortunately interviews were out of the question. HW policy. She could, however, provide answers to any of London's questions on an unattributed basis, and, *whoop-de-do,* even hand her a quote from the chairwoman of HW Asia herself. How did that sound? Was two weeks soon enough?

London hung up the phone, middle finger raised to express her gratitude.

"That for me?"

London lifted her eyes to see Mandy Blume, *FT*'s managing editor, arms crossed, glaring at her.

"HW. Jerks."

"Not getting anywhere? You could have asked me." Mandy was fifty, blond, battered, and as elegant as the day is long, a longtime expat who'd gotten her start chasing celebrities for a Fleet Street tabloid before making the jump to the respectable side of the street. The side where women didn't show their boobs on page 3. Mandy's husband, Michael, ran HW Asia's foreign-exchange desk.

"Really?" said London. *"Really"* because it was verboten to mix the personal and professional sides of a journalist's life.

"You working a story? I haven't seen you around in a while. Don's about to type a letter with your name on it. Give me something positive to tell him so he'll tear it up."

Donald Manning, the publisher, was the executive responsible for all hiring and firing decisions.

"Are you serious?" asked London.

Mandy didn't bother saying yes or no. Her look said it all.

"I think I have a big one," said London.

"How big?"

"Madoff times ten."

Mandy raised a skeptical brow as she pulled over a chair from a vacant desk. *Prove it.* She was dressed in a pencil skirt the color of clotted cream and a flashy striped men's dress shirt, opened a button farther than her mum would like. Her hair was teased and frosted and fell about her face in a perfectly controlled chaos that had to cost London's weekly salary. It was good to be married to an I-banker. Her skin was pale and papery, decorated with a network of lines no amount of makeup could conceal, the result of thirty years smoking Players, a habit she'd only recently broken. Instead of a cigarette, she held a pencil between her fingers and tapped it on London's desk. "And HW's involved?"

"Looks like it."

"How sure are you?"

"A hundred percent," said London, eyes locked on her boss. "I'm sorry."

"Fuck." Mandy exhaled angrily. In that instant, she abandoned her married name and everything that went with being Mrs. Michael Blume, and returned to being simply Mandy Rosen, the girl they'd called "Rupert's meanest dog." "I'm ready," she said. "Spill."

London leaned closer and gave Mandy a detailed summary of everything she had to date: the email from R that had put her on PetroSaud's trail, Benson Chow's corroboration that the Asian fund mentioned had to be Indonesia's, followed by her own suspicion that if there was one, there had to be others—and there were. In fact, seven sovereign wealth funds had worked with PetroSaud, though their complicity in any illegal act remained to be seen. And finally, Benson's bombshell that every one of the funds involved with PetroSaud had been brought to market by Harrington-Weiss, and Harrington-Weiss alone. Somewhere in there she tossed in her encounter with Nadya Sukarno and her belief that the Indonesian minister of finance was as guilty as sin.

"You think Michael knows who ran those deals?" asked London.

"Of course he does," said Mandy. "I'm always amazed a sixty-story office building is big enough to hold all those egos. No one does a billion-dollar deal without making sure everyone in the firm knows about it. Probably hires a brass band to march up and down the hallways trumpeting the news. You'd think people that smart and successful would have a little self-confidence. Hardly. They are the most insecure, hypercompetitive assembly of geniuses you've ever seen." Mandy laughed thinly. "Of course, I can't ask Michael. I mean, I won't."

London hadn't expected any different. "I was thinking of dredging up the prospectuses from all the offerings. Research has to have copies. I'll bet we'll come across a common name, someone at HW who worked all the deals."

Mandy wagged a finger at London. "Wrong side of the animal. You're looking at the ass, not the snout."

"I don't get it."

"You never worked at a bank, did you?"

"No."

"When a client closes a deal, an IPO, a secondary offering, if they acquire a company or sell off a division…or"—and here, she looked directly at London—"if they complete a successful investment fund, *a billion-dollar one,* they throw a party."

"A party?"

"Champagne, caviar, beef Wellington, white truffles…*tous les accompagnements.*"

London smiled. "I see now."

"Ten years ago I would have added coke and hookers. Alas, times have changed." Mandy sighed. "Anyhow, my love, no self-respecting investment authority would throw a party without inviting the press."

"If your picture doesn't land in the paper, did the party even take place?"

"Not the papers. The glossies. The gossip bibles."

"The *Tatler*," said London.

"Bingo."

London crowded in beside Mandy Blume, both seated at the managing editor's battleship-sized desk, eyes glued to the twenty-seven-inch screen of her iMac Pro. The door was closed, the blinds drawn. For the past hour they had scoured back issues of the *Singapore Tatler*, Asia's preeminent chronicler of high society, searching for photographs taken at parties celebrating the closings of investment funds for (in order) Indonesia, Malaysia, Brunei, and India. London, for one, was growing tired of looking at so many magnificently bejeweled, begowned, and be-dinner-jacketed men and women, all of whom appeared to be having the times of their lives. They were a cosmopolitan, multinational, multiethnic lot. They had one thing in common. They were rich. Filthy rich.

She and Mandy found their man early on. *It had to be a man.* Tall, raven-haired, severe, never a smile, not handsome, but a command- ing presence, whose laser-like black eyes bored holes in the camera. Whenever there was royalty—a king, queen, prince, or maharajah—he was present, hobnobbing with the select few, nearly always the only "commoner" in the photograph. Whenever there was a head of state— president, prime minister, chairman—he was there, embraced as an equal. The pictures had been taken over the course of four years, but to their eyes he was everywhere at once. The thread that bound them all together.

Or, as London put it, the common denominator. And, yes, he was an alpha.

Hadrian Lester, vice chairman of Harrington-Weiss.

"It's 'Lecter,'" said Mandy. "That's what they call him at the firm. He's a serial killer. He eats the competition alive."

"I hope not with fava beans," said London.

"Oh yes," said Mandy. "And Chianti, though I've heard he prefers Château Pétrus at ten thousand euros a bottle."

"I know who he is," said London. "He's married to that Europop singer. Beatrice something."

"He must be doing it for love, then," said Mandy, rolling her eyes. "Son of a bitch."

"He's in on it, all right. Maybe the instigator. He has to be."

"You don't think it's the other one, the Saudi? The smiling Arab?"

There was another face that had been present at all the parties, though not a banker. Tarek Al-Obeidi, the managing partner of PetroSaud, slim, silver haired, dignified, with a smile that could melt an iceberg.

"No," said London. "He couldn't get in the room where it started. It had to be Hadrian Lester giving the pitch. PetroSaud came afterward, once they agreed to use HW. 'And by the way, you might want to consider using my friends in Saudi Arabia if you'd care to line your own pockets.'"

"He has balls, I'll give him that."

"Big brass ones," said London. "By the time Lester brings up PetroSaud, he's already felt them out. He knows who's clean and who isn't. The one thing HW stresses is discretion. I'm sure he tiptoes right up to the line before crossing it."

"He really is a devil."

London stepped away from the desk, stretching her arms. A hunch came to her. Really just an inkling. Something she'd seen in the pictures that caused the rest of it to make a little more sense.

"Do me a favor, boss. Type three words into the search bar. Humor me."

"Shoot."

Mandy Blume typed as London said the words. The results appeared. Mandy's face dropped. "I have to tell Michael."

"You can't."

"We're ruined."

"Not yet."

Mandy sobbed. Tears began to flow. London put her arm around her managing editor. The words she'd asked her to type were "PetroSaud Hadrian Lester."

The first result read: HARRINGTON-WEISS VICE CHAIRMAN JOINS

Board of Saudi Arabian Investment Firm PetroSaud. Dated one month before the Indonesian deal.

The smoking gun.

"Nail 'em," said Mandy, gathering herself. "Crucify the bastards."

London said she would do her best. One question continued to nag at her, as it had for the past week.

Who was R?

CHAPTER 38

Singapore

As Hadrian Lester gazed from the window of his office on the fortieth floor of the Harrington-Weiss tower looking out over the city of Singapore, past the downtown core and the cricket fields, over Sheares Bridge, and east to the airport, he was thinking about prison.

In February 1942, the Imperial Japanese Army, under the command of General Tomoyuki Yamashita, swept down the Malay Peninsula and crossed the Johor Straits to lay siege to the British colony of Singapore, known as the "Gibraltar of the East." Eight days later, the British surrendered. Fifty thousand troops were taken prisoner. Winston Churchill called it the "worst disaster" in British military history. Some of the prisoners were shipped to camps in China, Burma, or Japan. Most, however, were incarcerated nearby at the prison complex at Changi, where the current airport had since been built.

Lester's grandfather, Flight Lieutenant Robin Lester, had been one of those imprisoned there. As a child, Hadrian had listened to his grandfather's stories describing the deplorable conditions. Little food, severe overcrowding, rampant disease—malaria, beriberi, dysentery—and, of course, the rats. Rats that grew as big as cats and as mean as tigers with teeth every bit as sharp. The stories had given the boy nightmares for years. Changi was hell on earth.

And so, today, when Hadrian Lester thought of prison, he imagined the horrors of Changi.

Never, he swore to himself.

"Mr. Lester, I have Minister of Finance Sukarno for you."

Lester walked to his desk, placing a hand above the receiver as he composed his thoughts. His father had been a military man, too, and before joining the bank, so was he, also a pilot, flying Harrier Jump Jets out of RAF Lossiemouth and, later, off the carrier HMS *Illustrious*. He operated under one principle: *"L'audace. Toujours de l'audace."*

He snatched the receiver and put it to his ear. "Calm the fuck down, Nadya," he stated slowly in his warm, princely tone. "I have everything under control."

"The man killed in Bangkok worked for PetroSaud, and now I've learned another of their employees died in Switzerland just last week. Don't tell me to calm down."

"Rafael de Bourbon was a blackmailer and a lousy one at that."

"What about the reporter? She's called my office three times this morning. They know."

"They don't know anything."

"She asked me about the oil leases in Saudi Arabia, Hadrian. The leases you instructed me to buy. You promised nothing like this would happen. You gave me your word."

"Darling, nothing is going to happen. I'm making the entire problem go away."

"When?"

"As we speak."

"But how…I don't want to ask too many questions, but this reporter… she's with the *FT*. I've heard of her. She sends people to jail."

"Nadya, how much have I made for you?"

"Hadrian, please, don't change the subject."

"How much?"

"I don't know. A billion, maybe."

"Higher."

"Two."

"Higher."

"Four billion dollars."

"And change," said Lester. "And we have another fund on deck. The biggest yet, don't we? Anyone asking questions about that?"

"That's all well and good, but—"

"Calm, my dear. You didn't think there might be a few questions? Really?"

"Well…"

"And I'm here to take care of them. Why do you think you pay me so much?" A laugh to soothe the rawest nerve. "Here's what you're going to do. Ignore the reporter. Forget about what you saw on the telly about Bangkok. Dreadful things happen. None of our concern." He paused, excited now. "Why don't you buy yourself something nice? A new Gulfstream. I know just the designer who can really trick it out for you. Or maybe a yacht like the one you bought your nephew. Better yet, why not the Hope fucking diamond? God knows you can bloody well afford all of them. Now listen, I've got a bank to run. Be well. Beatrice and I send love." Pronounced *Bay-ah-treee-chay* because his wife was Italian. *"Ciao, bella."*

Lester put down the phone, sighed with feigned exhaustion.

A finger snap later, his secretary came back. "London Li, *Financial Times. Again.*"

"Where did she get my direct number?" he muttered, then once again the soul of politeness. "Tell her *again* that I am otherwise occupied but that she should feel free to contact Debbie Whatshername in investor relations who'd absolutely adore helping her."

"Yes, sir."

Lester placed his hands on his hips, his face set in a scowl. Journos: hated 'em. In fact, at the moment Lester hated pretty much everyone who wasn't family or a close friend. Nadya Sukarno wasn't the only one rattled. He'd had calls from Kuala Lumpur and Malaysia, and from his boss, Sir Ian, asking if there was anything to be worried about. And all of it because of a minuscule bonus that a hired hand in Geneva had pocketed for himself. Greedy little peckerhead. Lester wished he could have pushed Paul Malloy off that cliff in Switzerland himself.

He turned, running a hand over his hair, and caught sight of himself in the mirror. White shirt. Navy-blue tie. Charcoal suit. A fighter pilot's posture. A man in charge. He liked this uniform a helluva lot better than an orange one with a number stenciled on the back.

He slid his phone from his pocket—what time was it in Italy, anyway?—placed a call, speaking Italian. "Luca, old man, we need to act. I'm worried about Nadya."

"Is he with you?"

Lester kept his eyes to the floor. "Yes, he's here in my office."

"Do as I told you."

"You're sure…reporters, messy business."

"Nothing else to be done. And this time tell him to keep things manageable. None of this savage nonsense. Nice and neat."

"Understood."

"I know you're worried, Hadrian. In a few days, this will be behind us. The world will have more important things to think about."

"Cheers to that."

Luca Borgia lowered his voice. "Did you put the shorts on?"

"A hundred mil in our joint account. Mostly index funds. Dow, DAX, Hang Seng, Nikkei. All the big ones. I'm guessing markets will tank five to seven percent Monday morning before bouncing back."

"Is this considered insider trading? Wouldn't want to do anything illegal."

"Just admirable foresight. Something like it was bound to happen sometime."

"Exactly my thoughts, Hadrian. Anyhow, I will see you and Bea soon enough. Give her a kiss from me. And remember, tell him it must appear to be an accident. Like our friend, Malloy. He's a commando, for goodness' sake. It shouldn't be too hard."

"I will and I will."

"Prato—"

"Luca, stop. Remember, I'm just in it for the money."

Lester hung up. Forcing a smile, he poked his head out of the office. "Darling, get me that journo on the line…London Li. I'm going to make her day."

A minute later, Lester's phone rang. He swooped in to answer.

"Ms. Li, Hadrian Lester. What a pleasure. Tell you what. Why don't we meet and have a chat? I understand you have some questions about a few of the sovereign wealth funds we've brought to market…No, not here. I can't spend every hour of the day cooped up in this velvet birdcage. How about Tanjong market? My schedule opened up unexpectedly. We can talk as we stroll, maybe grab a bite. *On me*…or does that count as bribery? How does four o'clock sound? Perfect. Cheers."

Lester dropped the phone in the cradle. When he turned, the smile was gone from his face. He strode across his palatial office and looked at the man seated by the window. "Well, well, Mr. Kruger," he said. "Looks like you're back in business. The boss is none too happy with how things went in Bangkok. Asked me to tell you not to muck it up this time. 'None of this savage nonsense' were his words. She's the last of our problems. With her out of the way, it's smooth sailing. Oh, and if you can find a way to gather up her papers, computer, that sort of thing, all the better. Tanjong market. Four p.m. Not far from here. Know it?"

The killer's pale blue eyes met his. Damned unnerving, though he'd never admit it.

"Here's an idea. Don't you boys in South Africa have some type of dart gun you can use?" Lester mimicked putting a tube to his mouth and blowing. "Nice and neat. Curare, isn't it? Oh well, you know better than me."

Shaka smiled. *Not a bad idea, but…* "Actually," he said, standing and approaching Lester, menace in his eyes. "We natives have something better than a blow dart. It's called a panga. Like a machete, but longer and sharper. Very helpful in the bush where I come from." He threw a hand up and took hold of Lester's neck, measuring it, squeezing and squeezing harder. He could lift the man off his feet if he wanted to. "A tall runt like you, I could take your head off in two blows. Chop. Chop. Maybe not as neat as you'd like, but more fun."

He released Lester and walked to the door. A look over his shoulder. *One last thing:* "Don't ever tell me how to do my job."

Chapter 39

Singapore

Simon stood on the sidewalk looking up at the apartment building. A tall metal gate guarded access to the driveway. An attached mesh door to admit pedestrians was locked. He walked a short way down the block, considering his options. It was past one in the afternoon. The sky was growing hazy, clouds moving in from the south, the salt tang from the Straits of Singapore sharp in his nostrils.

It had been a difficult night. On Major Rudi's advice, he'd chartered a twin-engine turboprop to fly down the Malay Peninsula. An hour out of Pattaya, they hit rough weather. A cell of thunderstorms forced them to seek out the nearest airstrip. Winds buffeted the plane up, down, and sideways. The stall alarm sounded, as loud as a foghorn. With an unsteady grin, the pilot assured him this was only moderate turbulence. That was when the water bottles and the maps and everything that was not secured bounced off the ceiling. Simon thanked him and made use of his air-sickness bag. He decided that he and the pilot had different definitions of "moderate." Twelve hours later, his forearms still ached from clutching his armrests. Until then, he'd thought himself a good flyer.

The pilot put down on a jungle airstrip, having to buzz the runway twice in order for his radio to remotely activate the landing lights. There was no tower. On the ground, they'd sought refuge inside a large palapa hut, no windows, the rain slashing horizontally through the place, drenching them. The pilot tasted the wind, let Simon know that they were not going anywhere soon, lay down beneath a wooden picnic-style table, and, after flicking away a centipede as long as a bobby's nightstick, declared that there was room for Simon, too.

With nowhere else to escape the downpour, Simon lay down beside him, where he spent hours reading through Rafa's stolen files. He flitted between emails, texts, memos, notifications from financial institutions, and much more. It didn't take much time for him to gain a clearer picture of PetroSaud's activities. The company had been created as a front to camouflage theft on a massive scale. It wasn't entirely dishonest. It actually conducted a fair amount of reputable business. In other words, it really did sell leases to extant wells. But Rafa hadn't died to protect the honest side of the business. He'd been killed to stop outside parties from learning about the other side.

Like any good piece of thievery, at its core it was simple. You want money, rob a bank. You need wheels, steal a car. In other words, go to the source. The plan had been hatched by an executive at HW named Hadrian Lester, who with the help of a friend in Switzerland, a Saudi national named Tarek Al-Obeidi, had set up PetroSaud with the express purpose of stealing money from sovereign wealth funds. What made it so ingenious was how few people were required to steal so large an amount of money. Three: Lester, Al-Obeidi, and the individual who ran the wealth fund. Each took their cut. Later more were brought in, namely Rafa's colleagues, like Paul Malloy. Simon had worked in a bank. He knew that Lester had to have a few helpers at HW on his payroll as well. Lots of intelligent people would be reading the documentation. If no one else, the legal eagles at the investment bank would spot something amiss. But not right away.

One element, however, defied Simon's every effort to understand it. Lester had insisted that fund managers transfer a significant portion of their ill-gotten gains to a numbered account at the Bank of Liechtenstein—flagged in the "special instructions" box of wire transfers as either "PB" or, on two occasions, "Prato Bornum." Intrigued, he'd looked up the term but was no more satisfied than before. It was only when he remembered Shaka's words at the riverbank that he began to have some understanding of what he might be looking at, however vague.

Finally, he'd fallen asleep.

At dawn, under clear skies, they took off for Johor Bahru, landing at an abandoned airstrip on the eastern edge of the Malay Peninsula two hours later. There was no customs control and Simon took a taxi to the ferry, then crossed the channel and touched foot on Singaporean soil. A tense moment as Simon's passport was scanned by immigration control and the machine failed to read its biometric chip. Officials were summoned to diagnose the problem. At one point five men in the navy-blue uniform of Singapore Immigration and Checkpoints Authority huddled around the errant machine. Standing there like a sheep led to slaughter, Simon remembered Major Rudi patiently unfolding the sheet with his likeness on it. Strangely, he felt only calm. It was too late. He couldn't run. If Thailand had shared Simon's likeness with its neighbors, he would be identified and arrested.

It was not to be. After a few knocks, the reader came back to life. Simon's passport sailed through with flying colors. Down came the stamp.

"Welcome to Singapore, Mr. Ledoux."

Khop khun, Major Rudi.

Khop khun, D'Art, for sending the twenty thousand in U.S. "grease."

A thirty-minute taxi ride took Simon across the island, north to south, to London Li's apartment: "14 Fort Road, unit 6F, purchased by London Li 12 July 2019—for S$2,100,000," stated the publicly listed property records.

Yesterday he'd sent an email to her *FT* address. It had read:

Rafael de Bourbon, Spanish national killed in the Bangkok embassy shooting, was the individual who supplied you with confidential information regarding crimes he discovered while an employee of PetroSaud in Geneva, Switzerland. His murder, that of Paul Malloy, another PetroSaud employee, in Switzerland several days earlier, and the other victims killed at the Spanish embassy yesterday were ordered to prevent knowledge of PetroSaud's role in helping multiple sovereign wealth funds defraud investors of billions of dollars from becoming public. Others know of your involvement. Your life is in imminent danger. Seek protection.

Upon landing this morning in Malaysia, he'd phoned the *FT* at the first available moment and left a message on London Li's voice mail.

He had not attached his name to either message. He had to assume her email had been compromised, as he'd assumed his own was. For now, Shaka and those he worked for thought Simon dead. He did not want to disabuse them of the notion.

As of yet, he'd had no response to either communication.

A gate squeaked and Simon turned to see a man passing through the side entrance. Simon moved quickly, catching the handle before the gate closed and entering the compound. The front door to the building stood open. He walked in uncontested and took a waiting elevator to the sixth floor.

He knocked, checking his phone, seeing that she had still not responded. "Ms. Li. Are you home?"

He waited an appropriate time, then tried the door. The handle turned easily. Unlocked. Simon opened the door warily, cocked his head to listen. The place was silent except for the thrum of the air conditioner. He stepped inside and closed the door behind him.

It was a small flat, modern, aggressively clean. He had a view across a sitting area—L-shaped sofa, stone coffee table, Kentia palms in the corners—and into her bedroom. An upright piano stood against the opposite wall. The sheet music was for a Chopin nocturne. It was also upside down.

He noted that the pillows on the sofa and chair were askew. A man's touch, to be sure.

Someone had been here before him.

Adjacent to the sitting area was an open-style kitchen, as large as a sailing boat's galley. He found a recently used Keurig in the trash and a fresh banana peel. London Li was in town. To be safe, he slid a carving knife from the block. He'd been premature to believe the apartment to be unoccupied.

He crept toward the bedroom. The queen-sized bed was neatly made. The night tables bare. Something tickled his nose. His eyes began to water. He buried his face in the lee of his arm and muffled the sneeze, and the one after it. On the terrace were two bowls, one with water, the other dry food. London Li was a cat lover. But where was the cat?

He continued down an abbreviated hallway. In an alcove, he found a home office. The desk was immaculate, not a single paper, pen, or rubber band in sight. Several drawers were not entirely closed. A cursory check showed them to be empty…and the file drawer cleaned out. Not her doing. Already he knew that.

Simon kneeled to look under the desk and noted a piece of paper that had fallen over the back. He stretched his arm and freed it. He switched on a reading lamp. The front page of a prospectus for a Malaysian investment fund called Future Malaysia being led by Harrington-Weiss. He was not surprised. A reporter of London Li's reputation would jump to investigate fraud of this magnitude. Rafa had chosen well.

Then he saw it. On the desk's matte-black surface was a hair. Blond, slightly kinked, short. He didn't require confirmation, but there it was.

He sneezed again, blinking back tears.

A door at the end of the hall led to a bathroom. He turned on the lights. A look. A gasp. He shut the door. He had found London Li's cat. It lay in the toilet dead, its head turned all the way round.

Chapter 40

Ingolstadt, Germany

Razor wire.

The first thing Mattias noticed was the tall, forbidding mesh fence surrounding the complex of stucco buildings and the dense coils of razor wire running from end to end atop it. It took him a moment to spy the second fence inside the first, this one not as tall, and with doors cut into it. Security guards stood nearby—no weapons but sturdy white batons hanging from their belts. He didn't know how many people wandered the enclosure—hundreds, maybe a thousand. Some men had gotten up a game of soccer, playing on a patch of grass run to dirt. They were mostly black, though he saw a few white faces.

Omar, his midnight chauffeur, found the parking lot. A sign on the main building read, IMMIGRANT PROCESSING AND ANCHOR CENTER, INGOLSTADT.

Mattias walked into the building alone.

"We are full." A young bearded man sat at a metal desk littered with notebooks and papers. "You must go to the police station and register. They will take you to another camp at the far side of town. Not as nice, I'm afraid. We do what we can."

Mattias showed his Swedish passport. "I'm not here to register. I came to visit a friend."

"Three hours," said the young man.

"Excuse me?"

"Visits are not to last more than three hours. If your friend leaves now, he may miss lunch. The cafeteria closes at one p.m. No exceptions. Dinner is not until five o'clock. We are not responsible."

"We plan on having lunch together," said Mattias.

"Name."

Mattias gave the name of his friend and his refugee number.

"Sit," said the man. "I will notify his barracks. It will be a few minutes." Mattias took a seat. *Thank God,* he thought. The sheikh had found him.

He'd approached Mattias five months earlier at the local mosque, one of just two in Gothenburg. It was after Friday prayer; the Iman had preached a sermon on sacrifice and forgiveness. Mattias was collecting his shoes, dreading the bitter cold of the December afternoon that awaited him outside.

"A fine sermon. There is another verse I might add. A verse particular to you. 'Nothing you've ever given has gone unnoticed. Every sacrifice you've made, Allah has seen it.'"

The man was sixty, of medium height, with a trim beard and deep-set mournful eyes, and by his dress, wealthy. From his accent, Mattias placed him as a Kuwaiti or, perhaps, a Saudi.

"Me?" said Mattias. "But I've made no sacrifices. Allah has blessed me with abundance."

"But it was not always so, was it.... *Ibrahim?*"

Mattias regarded the man with interest. How had he known his true name? Why was he, Ibrahim, of interest to this rich stranger?

"You have suffered greatly," the man continued. "It is only right that Allah bless you with what you kindly speak of as 'abundance.'"

"I'm sorry, but we have not met."

"My name is Abdul Al-Obeidi. You are Ibrahim Moussa, survivor of the *Medusa* tragedy. It is an honor. Would you believe that I have traveled all the way from Jeddah to speak with you?"

"Truly, I would not," said Mattias. It had been a long time since he had heard his given name and he was uncomfortable at being the subject of undeserved flattery. "But you are here, so I must. I hope I do not disappoint you, Sheikh Abdul."

"You? You do not have it in your heart to disappoint another."

"I try my best," he said earnestly. "For my family, at least. I'm afraid I fail Islam."

"You are here for Friday sermon. That is what is most important. I am a man of the world. I know that our earthly commitments make piety—at least as the Prophet defines it—difficult." A smile. A complicitous pat on the shoulder. *I am not perfect either.* "Will you join me for tea?"

"I cannot, Sheikh. I must return to work."

"Please. I will not keep you long."

Mattias checked his watch. He was due back at the counter in a quarter hour. "But quickly."

The two men crossed the street and entered a nearby café. The sheikh ordered tea for the both of them. He returned from the pastry counter with two *mille-feuilles.* "I cannot resist them," he said. "Please join me."

Mattias thanked him but declined. He no longer had a sweet tooth. The sheikh ate one of the cream-filled pastries in three ravenous bites, leaving a rime of custard on his beard. "I can't help myself," he said. "A treat."

Mattias relaxed at the show of informality.

"I will be brief," the sheikh went on. "I need your help, Ibrahim. It is for something I know you have never considered but for which only you and a few others are qualified."

"What others?"

"The others who were on the raft. Allah has chosen you to honor him."

"How can we do that?" said Mattias, unable to disguise his bitterness. He was hiding an important fact from the sheikh. He was no longer a believer. Yes, he had survived a terrible ordeal, but he had come to view his survival as a matter of luck, not divine providence. Certainly not a reward for his piety. What he had done on the raft flew in the face of all that was pious. He had abandoned the bounds of accepted human behavior. He had fought, he had killed, and worse.

He had become inhuman, a savage, a primitive far beyond the Prophet's purview.

Mattias rose, upset. The sheikh placed a hand on his. "Please. I understand. I do."

Mattias heard something in the man's voice he had not heard before. He sat. "All right."

For an hour he listened to the Saudi. The sheikh's voice had a hypnotic quality, his eyes beacons of faith. Mattias quickly forgot about his job. The sheikh told him a story about a hero called to perform a task far beyond his abilities. The hero was a common man, a man born to faith but who over time, beaten down by life's broken promises and failed dreams, had grown estranged from God. He was not a brave man, but when presented with adversity, he had responded bravely. God could not judge him for doing what any of his creatures would do to survive. Was God not in some way responsible?

"Are you speaking about me?"

"You are a hero."

"I am not."

"Not yet, perhaps. I wish to give you a chance to become one. A chance to turn your suffering to the advantage of others."

"But how?"

And so the sheikh told him.

Mattias was too stunned to give an immediate answer. He promised to consider it. To his surprise, he needed only a short time. He agreed. Days, not weeks. The fact was, he had been looking for an avenue of escape for years.

A chance to be a hero.

Thanks be unto him, the Prophet.

An hour later, Mattias had collected his friend. For a while they drove in silence. Ingolstadt was behind them. They'd passed the cities of Augsburg and Ulm. Paris was a further six-hour drive.

For the first time Mattias acknowledged the butterflies in his stomach, the cord of unease tugging at him. The trip could end only one way. Strangely, he was not at all frightened. He'd seen too much for that. If anything, he felt exhilarated, eager, optimistic even.

He turned in his seat. "So," he said, "how was it?"

"Not so bad, I guess," said Hassan, the new arrival. "If you like sausage."

A moment. A look all around. The men broke into laughter.

CHAPTER 41

Naples

If Rome was bad, Naples was a catastrophe. Not because refugees crowded the streets, but because trash did. Trash everywhere. Piled on sidewalks in heaps ten feet high, overflowing *cassonetti,* clogging gutters.

Luca Borgia placed a handkerchief over his nose and mouth as they passed through the Spanish quarter, the city's worst, and turned down the Via Santa Chiara toward the harbor. Sometimes he thought the entire country was falling apart. It would be easier if he stayed at the Castello dell'Aquila and tended to his roses, rode his horses through the magnificent countryside, and made love to his mistress.

And then?

Sooner or later the country's ills would land on his doorstep. Perhaps not a trash strike. The Camorra didn't control Umbria, not yet anyway. But the tide of unrest and unemployment, the degradation of decent family values, the forfeit of native culture, and the adoption of foreign ways. Yes, one day it would arrive. Italy was being invaded, as surely as if the Goths had returned to her shores, bringing with them their barbarian ways. Borgia saw himself as his country's staunch defender, standing at her borders with sword and shield to drive them back.

They turned onto Calata della Marinella and drove along the docks. At the sight of the water and ships and the boats crisscrossing the harbor, he felt a shell form around him, a second skin to keep the dirt off him.

Sicily had the Mafia. Calabria, the 'Ndrangheta. And Naples, the Camorra.

The Port of Naples was one of the oldest and largest in all the Mediterranean, built around a crescent-shaped harbor many considered one of Europe's finest natural anchorages. Seventy thousand vessels came and went each year. Five hundred thousand shipping containers loaded and unloaded. Thirty million tons of cargo. And not a single thing moved without tribute being paid.

Borgia continued past the passenger terminal—shiny and new, buffed to a gleaming white perfection, four cruise ships at dock. Past the automobile terminal, crowded with the five-story-tall oceangoing ferries that connected Naples to Palermo, Corsica, and Sardinia. And into the gritty heart of the port, the commercial cargo and container terminals. An iron and steel jungle of cranes and winches and tractors. Nothing shiny and new here.

"Number 37," said Borgia to his driver as they passed one warehouse after another, old brick buildings, no two alike.

He rolled down the window of the van and let a blast of sea air into the compartment. The morning was exceptionally clear. In the distance, Vesuvius, the volcano whose eruption had destroyed the city of Pompeii, appeared close enough to touch, its blue-gray slopes iridescent beneath an admiring sun.

Ahead, a squadron of vehicles was parked at odd angles at the water's edge. A half-dozen men milled beside them. Slobs to look at: blue jeans, shirts untucked, beards that hadn't seen a razor in days.

The van drew to a halt. David, his driver and bodyguard, turned to face him, blazer hanging open, holster and weapon visible. "You need me?"

"Thank you, David, but I'll be fine. After all, I haven't paid them yet."

Borgia climbed out of the van. *May the ghost of Zeffirelli look down upon me,* he thought as he threw out his arms and muscled a smile into place.

"Toto, Peppe! *B'giorno!*"

Hugs all around. Kisses, even, as Borgia greeted each in turn. The names typed on their files at police headquarters were Salvatore Rinaldi and Giuseppe Nassa. Both were captains, or *capi,* in the Camorra.

Unlike the Mafia, which was organized vertically, with one capo—the *capo di tutti capi*—overseeing all elements of the criminal trade in Sicily, the Camorra was organized horizontally, numerous clans operating independently, and often in competition with one another. This made doing business unpredictable and dangerous.

It seemed like an hour passed with the men talking about soccer and the trash strike, now in its sixth week, but not their concern. Toto and Peppe worked the ports. Trash collection was someone else's business.

Talk turned to shipping. Business was not good. European economies were faltering across the board. Even Germany. And then, to make matters worse, the Chinese, undercutting them all with cheap transport costs, the price per container at a historical low.

Finally, they got down to business. Shipments from the Middle East. But not before a tirade against the Americans and the ongoing sanctions imposed on the Islamic Republic of Iran. It turned out Iran was a big buyer of Italian olive oil.

"And Libya," said Toto. "What a mess!"

Toto Rinaldi was a lumbering bear of a man, a few inches taller than Luca, a gray stubble covering all three of his chins, hair dyed a black that would make Berlusconi blush, with great hams for arms proudly on display this fine morning.

Toto was Luca's connection to the Camorra. Somehow it turned out they were distantly related, cousins of cousins and so on. Toto had done ten years for strangling a man with his own hands.

"Total chaos," he went on. "Everyone fighting everyone else. One's a warlord, another's a chieftain. They were better off with Qaddafi."

"About Libya," said Peppe Nassa, a short, lithe man dressed entirely in black, with a clean-shaven head, all brooding glances and pained expressions. "There was a problem with the plastique."

"Ah." It was the first Borgia had heard of any problem.

"The factory you mentioned was bombed out last month."

"Destroyed," said Toto.

"Burned to the ground," added Peppe.

"I hadn't heard," said Luca.

239

Peppe nodded. "We didn't learn about it till we showed up and the place was a pile of ashes."

The factory in question, Società Libica Prodotti Esplosivi, the Libyan Explosives Company, manufactured the plastic explosive called Semtex under license from the Czech manufacturer. There was plenty of Semtex to be had in Europe, but it was essential that Borgia purchase plastic explosive made in Libya. Chemical tags placed in each batch identified the place of manufacture.

"That complicates things," he said.

"Of course, we didn't stop there," said Peppe. "You place an order, it's our job to fulfill it. It's what we do, after all."

"We always keep our word," said Toto. *"Famiglia."*

"But…" Peppe made a face.

"The price," said Toto.

"How much?" asked Luca.

"Double."

Toto placed a hand on his heart. "Best we could do."

Luca had contracted to purchase one hundred kilograms of Libyan-manufactured Semtex at a price of one thousand euros per kilo. The unexpected difficulties in the supply chain would cost him an additional one hundred thousand euros.

"Out of the question," he said. "We agreed upon a price. I expect delivery at that price. If you come to me to buy a stallion and that stallion runs away or, God forbid, dies in a stable fire, I must find you another equal animal at the same price. You said it is your job to fulfill, then fulfill…but at the price agreed upon."

"Libya is a war zone, Signor Borgia," said Peppe. "These are not ordinary circumstances."

"A war zone," said Luca, dismissively. "A few skirmishes, perhaps."

"A true war zone," said Peppe, offended. "Artillery, machine gun fire, fighter jets."

"Fine, if you say so. If circumstances were ordinary, I could have flown down myself, knocked on the front door, and placed my order. It is exactly because these are unordinary circumstances that I contacted you."

Peppe's face darkened. He was not a man accustomed to being insulted.

"Signor Borgia, I'm sorry, but that is not true," said Toto, as diplomatically as he knew. "I saw the factory with my own eyes. A bomb from a plane landed directly on it. Many people died."

"You were there?"

Toto nodded. "With Peppe."

Luca looked between the men. Both nodded gravely, testifying to the tragedy. "I'm sorry," he said. "I had no idea. My thanks."

The men bowed their heads. Apology accepted.

"So where did you find my merchandise?" asked Luca.

"We have friends there, of course. They looked around. A little here, a little there. It was difficult, but we get what you want."

"And the rest?" Semtex was not the only item he'd asked for.

"The rest…no problem," said Toto. "Very easy."

"At the price we quoted," said Peppe.

Luca bit his lip, stepped toward the water, a man forced into making a decision against his better judgment. He had no choice but to pay. He made a note to tell Bruno Melzi. The police could deal with Peppe Nassa later.

"Any other problems I should know about?" asked Luca.

The Neapolitan gangsters shook their head.

"Well, then, gentlemen. I appreciate the risk you took on my behalf." Borgia returned to the van.

"How much more?" asked David.

"One hundred thousand."

"Half what you expected."

"Family," said Borgia, and the men shared a look. He opened a briefcase and counted out an additional one hundred thousand euros, placing the bills in a satchel containing the amount originally agreed upon.

Besides Semtex, he had purchased one hundred Beretta semiautomatic handguns, ten thousand rounds of ammunition, fifty hand grenades, and fifty KA-BAR knives.

It took thirty minutes to load everything into Borgia's van. As he closed the doors, Peppe came close. One final question. "May I ask what all this is for?"

"Friends in the north," said Borgia. The north: cradle of right-wing politics, bastion of anti-labor, anti-communist, anti-immigrant supporters. Heirs to Benito Mussolini. *Il Duce.*

Toto and Peppe nodded approvingly. After all, they were not bad men. They would not want to see the weapons used for the wrong purposes.

"*Arrivederci,*" said Borgia. "*Grazie tanto.*"

"*Arrivederci.*"

CHAPTER 42

Singapore

Shaka arrived at Tanjong Pagar market at three o'clock. He strolled past the stalls and vendors and hawkers, just another tourist. He'd traded his dark suit for khaki shorts and a T-shirt, a baseball cap covering his hair. He ignored the glances thrown his way, both admiring and apprehensive. Sun's out, guns out. Deal with it.

The market was one city block in length, a pedestrian-only thorough-fare crowded with stands selling food, electronics, clothing, you name it. It was a lively spot, colorful banners fluttering in a soft breeze, lights strung overhead, and chock-full of visitors, their sights and senses drawn in all directions. In every way, the market was perfect for his work.

He made a circuit of the block twice, familiarizing himself with its layout. Should London Li come directly from her office, she would approach from the southeast. He found an ideal vantage point tucked behind a stall preparing fried squid—plenty of activity here, steam spiraling into the air, excited voices, woks shaken and drained with flair. Far too much going on for the eye to pick out a lone man keeping watch for his prey.

It went without saying that come four p.m. Hadrian Lester wouldn't be anywhere near the Tanjong market. It wouldn't do for the vice chair-man of one of the world's most important banks to be in the vicinity when a prominent journalist dropped dead on the pavement.

Shaka felt the mosquito pressing against his leg. The device resembled a staple gun, but finer boned and fashioned from high-tensile titanium. Originally, Siemens, the German industrial conglomerate, had designed

243

it to inoculate livestock. Years later, the device was appropriated by his country's intelligence services and modified for other, less bucolic, uses, namely to track adversaries and, when necessary, to kill them. His other pocket carried a pellet filled with a lethal dose of potassium cyanide, contained safely in a stainless-steel caplet. The job called for a "wet insert," meaning he would have to load the pellet into the mosquito immediately before use.

Cyanide acted as an oxygen suppressor, blocking the cells' ability to absorb the molecules from the bloodstream. Within seconds of ingestion, the victim would feel light-headed, disoriented, then lose control over her muscles and collapse. Unconsciousness and death followed quickly. Sixty seconds at the most.

Shaka sat down on a bench behind the stall to wait. One last task to attend to, then back to Europe. He had booked himself a seat on the midnight Swiss Air Lines flight to Rome via Zurich. All in all, a productive trip, the redundancies in Bangkok notwithstanding.

He checked his watch. Thirty minutes yet. He looked at the picture of London Li on his phone. A half-breed like him. Sexy as hell. All he had to do was keep an eye out for a woman with hair the color of warm caramel.

It shouldn't be too hard.

Chapter 43

No, sir, once again, I cannot tell you if Ms. Li is in the building. She is not answering her phone. You're welcome to call the main number and leave another message. I understand that it is a matter of some urgency. If you'd like, I'd be happy to call again on your behalf in a quarter hour. Until then, you may take a seat in our lounge."

Beside himself, Simon walked to the seating area in the lobby of the Mapletree Anson tower, home to the offices of the *Financial Times*. *"A matter of some urgency."* Yes, thought Simon, you could call it that. *A trained assassin twice as strong as Superman is looking for one of your journalists and he isn't hoping to fill her in about life on the planet Krypton.*

He sat down, eyes taking in every corner of the lobby. No amount of cajoling or persuasion was going to get him past the reception. He watched a procession of employees enter, each in turn running an ID badge over the turnstile. The guards, he noted, were keeping an eye on him. Even if he could steal a badge, he'd have to find another way in.

A clock high on the wall read 3:45.

He checked his phone. Still no response from London Li to his email or his voice messages. Most likely, the email had never made it to her inbox, had been filtered out for one reason or another and sent to a file reserved for spam or junk. As for his voice messages, either she hadn't checked them or she thought he was unhinged. If he received a message from an anonymous woman telling him to stop looking into an important matter and immediately seek protection, he would delete it without thinking twice. *If you're going to tell me my life's in danger, you'd better have the courtesy to leave your name.*

Simon gave a last look around the building and stood. This wasn't going anywhere. There was only one thing to do. If Mohammed couldn't go to the mountain, he would bring the mountain to him.

Once outside, he walked around the corner and called the *FT*'s main number.

"*Financial Times* Asia. How may I direct your call?"

"Yeah, listen," said Simon. "There is an explosive device in your office. You have five minutes until it goes off. Consider this fair warning. Bang!"

He ended the call. Eventually it would be tracked back to him, but the phone was a burner and he hadn't left his name on any of the messages for London Li. Anyway, he didn't care about "eventually." He crossed the street and took up position where he could see into the ground floor of the tower. Almost immediately he noted a flurry of activity. Guards opened all sets of doors, locking them in place. Emergency lights in each corner flashed blue and white. Workers began streaming out of the building and congregating in the entry plaza, first in a trickle, then quickly, a torrent.

Simon had studied photographs of London Li he'd pulled off the net. She was a striking woman, Eurasian, maybe thirty years old, her most recognizable feature her toffee-colored hair. By now, nearly two hundred people were milling about the plaza. She was not among them.

He brought up a list of the *FT* management. If London were actively working the story—and all evidence pointed to the fact that she was—she would certainly have discussed it with a managing editor. There were two: Anson Ho and Mandy Blume. He looked at their pictures.

He saw Blume at once, standing at a far corner of the plaza, nearest the walkway leading into the building. She was a blond, elegantly bedraggled woman who reminded him of an aging rocker…if, that is, the rocker had traded her denims and lace for a cream-colored skirt and snazzy blouse. He made eye contact with the woman as he approached, taking her by the arm and leading her away from the others.

"Excuse me," said the woman. "Just what in the—"

"Where is London Li?"

"Wait." An effort to free her arm, to no avail. "Who are you?"

"A friend. Someone who wants to make sure that she's safe. My name is Simon Riske. Has she told you about PetroSaud? Has she mentioned the name Hadrian Lester?"

"Riske…Are you R?"

"R is dead. His name was Rafael de Bourbon. He was killed in the embassy shooting in Bangkok two days ago. I was there. Rafa— Mr. De Bourbon—had agreed to turn over information he'd taken from PetroSaud in exchange for his freedom and—"

"Why would he do that? I'm not following you—Mr. *Riske,* is it?"

Simon fought down his desire to hurry, to blast through the story. It was imperative she understand what London had gotten herself into. "PetroSaud owed Rafa a five-million-Swiss-franc bonus. When they didn't pay, he threatened to make public what he knew about them— information he'd gathered while an employee of theirs four years back. The stuff you guys are figuring out about Indonesia and Malaysia and Brunei."

Mandy Blume's face darkened. "How do you know we're looking into those countries?"

"Let me go on." Simon was not about to admit he'd entered London Li's apartment. "PetroSaud didn't bite. They had Rafa arrested and jailed in Thailand. Just before, he sent London Li a note giving her clues as to what went down. Rafa was killed because of what he knew. So was a man named Malloy, who was his boss. I have proof that the killer is here in Singapore…*right now.*" He leveled his gaze at the woman. "He's here to take care of London Li."

"'Take care of'?"

"Kill her."

Blume was having none of it. "It was you who called in the bomb threat?"

"I couldn't get upstairs. She isn't answering her phone or responding to my emails. Do you know where she is?"

"Yes, but I won't tell you."

Simon took her by the arms. "Look at me. I have the files Rafa took from PetroSaud. Thousands of them. Emails, texts. This story is bigger than any of us think. It goes beyond defrauding the funds of billions. Ms. Blume…*Mandy*…you have to trust me. I'm an investigator, too. A different kind, but we're after the same things, you and me. I have every reason to believe an attempt will be made on London Li's life today…at any minute. This is happening now. Call her. Tell her to find a policeman and stay close to him. If she can't, she needs to come here."

Mandy Blume stared at him, disbelief and fear softening to acceptance. "I don't know if she'll answer. She's meeting someone. It's about this."

"Who? Where?"

"I can't tell you."

"What is it that you don't understand?" demanded Simon. "London Li's life is at stake."

"You better not be lying to me, you son of a bitch." Mandy Blume shot him a withering glance. "She's meeting with Hadrian Lester. Tanjong market. Four o'clock."

"It's a setup. Lester is part of it. At the top, I think. No way he'd talk to a reporter. He knows everything that's going on. Call her."

Blume put her phone to her ear, shaking her head a moment later to indicate that there was no answer. "London, this is Mandy. Call me as soon as you get this. I know this may sound crazy, but you need to get somewhere safe. Find a policeman and stay with him. Just do it. You're in a great deal of danger. Hadrian Lester is not coming. Call me."

"Where is Tanjong market?" asked Simon, feeling the seconds running out, desperate to act…to do something, anything.

"Three blocks that way. Shall I call the police?"

"Yes…no…do what you want. I have to run."

CHAPTER 44

Singapore

London Li arrived at the southeast entrance to the Tanjong market precisely at four p.m. She rarely came to this spot during the week and was surprised to find it every bit as busy as on the weekend. Mostly tourists, she noted, meandering here and there, slowing at every stall, enjoying the colorful sights and enticing smells. This wasn't an ambush. It was an interview, strictly on the record, and she'd prepared accordingly. She'd committed to memory details of every fund HW had managed over the past five years. Amounts, dates, principals. And the flip side as well. Where and how the fund managers had invested the billions raised, especially when the investments involved PetroSaud.

She had been reminded that sovereign wealth funds derived the largest part of their funding from the country's own surpluses: gains from foreign currency transactions, unspent taxes (as rare as the concept may seem), and bond issues. It was the fund manager's duty to invest the proceeds to benefit the shareholders—in this case, the country's own citizens. Norway, to take an example, ran a fund valued at over one trillion U.S. dollars, or two hundred thousand dollars per citizen. The idea, then, that Hadrian Lester had used his position and influence to funnel billions of dollars into PetroSaud's phony oil leases enraged her. He wasn't stealing from the rich and giving to the poor. He was stuffing his grubby hands into the pockets of every taxpaying citizen and snatching their hard-earned money for his own personal gain. It was abhorrent.

For the moment, however, London had only supposition. Photos taken at celebratory dinners did not constitute hard evidence. R's

249

stolen information, while admissible in court, simply wasn't enough. She had a big fat handful of speculation, as substantial as fairy dust. It was a conspiracy theory that any defense lawyer worth his salt could deconstruct with his hands tied behind his back. It was her job, then, to convince Hadrian Lester that she had more than fairy dust, more than a theory, that she already possessed evidence that would undeniably implicate Lester and HW, and thus convince him to tell her the truth.

No small task.

She wandered through the market, eyes peeled for the tall, dark-haired banker. The time was five minutes past four. Though the market was not exceptionally large, maybe a hundred paces end to end, it was a hectic, bustling sieve. In her excitement at landing the interview, she'd failed to specify an exact location. How silly it would be if she somehow missed him. It was always the reporter's fault.

London felt someone bump into her and stumbled. She turned rapidly, ready to savage the offender. "Excuse me," she said with malice.

A wizened amah smiled apologetically, taking her grandson in hand, scolding him. London smiled belatedly, waving at the little boy. *You need to calm down,* she told herself.

Her phone buzzed and she saw that she'd received a voice mail from Mandy. *What now?* She looked everywhere for Hadrian Lester. How difficult could it be to locate a six-foot-three-inch *gwai lo* banker in a dark suit? She decided that it was best to wait in one place and let him come to her.

Her phone buzzed.

Mandy. *Again.*

London brought up the voice mail and read a transcription of the first message. *"... this may sound crazy ... you need to get somewhere safe. Find a policeman ... You're in a great deal of danger. Hadrian Lester is not coming."*

Lester wasn't coming? How did Mandy know? Had he called her?

Only then did London digest the rest of the message. The important part. *"You're in a great deal of danger ... find a policeman."* The words didn't go with the Mandy she knew. Not one bit. Mandy was the last person to be afraid of anything, the rebel who proudly spit in the eye of authority.

But this wasn't about Mandy. It was about her.

"...in a great deal of danger..."

A bolt of fear, as cold as ice, ran the length of her spine. She had no idea what the message could be referring to, but whatever it was, it had shaken Mandy. London appraised her surroundings with a new wariness. Nothing had changed. She sensed no evil vibe. Everything appeared normal. The little boy who'd bumped into her stood a few feet away, gazing at her. She tried but couldn't muster a smile.

She recalled the anonymous email warning her to be careful. *"Others are aware of your interest..."*

She started up the pavement, heading north, hoping to see a policeman, finding it hard to remember the last time she'd seen a uniformed cop on the streets. She threaded her way through the stalls, her steps assuming a hasty rhythm, something inside her...something she had no control over...urging her to hurry, to get clear of the market.

Ahead, a woman cried out. A commotion. A ruffle in the crowd.

London froze, not knowing if she should go forward or back.

She was dressed in black jeans and a tan stretch T-shirt, her hair pulled back into a ponytail. The glasses had almost thrown him off: large black frames that gave her a professorial look. Then again, Lester had said she'd be coming from her offices at the *Financial Times*.

Shaka left his position behind the busy food stall and moved slowly up the row of stands behind London Li. Next to him, a family of Americans had gathered around a chef making noodles from scratch. Shaka paused beside them, pretending to look on as the chef spun the mass of dough between his fingers, stretching it and dividing it, twirling it in the air until he'd created a latticework of slim noodles that stretched from arm to arm.

From the corner of his eye, he saw the reporter check her phone. Her bearing changed in an instant. Her motions grew jerky, head turning this way and that, eyes flitting here, there, everywhere. Whatever she'd read or seen on her phone, it had rattled her. She left the spot where she'd been standing for the past few minutes and started toward him. With one stride, he could reach her. He could snap her neck and be five steps away before she dropped to the ground.

Do it, he told himself, fingers tingling. *Now. Be done with it.*

The woman looked directly at him, then spun and walked in the opposite direction.

Shaka gave pursuit. His right hand dropped into his pocket, fingers closing around the mosquito. He slipped the device from his pocket, thumb cocking the hammer. Deftly, he nicked the cap of the cyanide cartridge and pressed it into the barrel.

He lengthened his stride, closing the distance between them. His eyes searched for the best spot to hit her. The base of the neck? Maybe higher up, near the jawline? Or the forearm? He couldn't risk penetrating her clothing, for even a small amount of the toxin might be lost on the fabric.

He drew closer, close enough to see how the strands of her hair were different colors, to note the fine texture of her skin. She was a beautiful woman. A shame.

He noted a commotion at the entry to the market. A ripple in the current of shoppers. He saw a uniform, now two, and cupped the mosquito in his palm. Then relief. Not police officers. Bus drivers, coffee cups in hand.

Shaka smiled to himself. A last step, close enough to smell her perfume, to see the downy hairs running along the nape of her finely shaped neck. He reached out a hand. There, he decided, just below her perfectly shaped mole...

"Shaka!"

Simon grabbed the man from behind and spun him around. He held a can of Mace in his hand, a silent gift from one of the police officers in Mapletree Anson plaza, and he sprayed it in Shaka's eyes, a prolonged blast from a distance of inches. Shaka grunted, his head jerking to one side, cap falling to the ground. His right arm lashed out, and Simon saw something shiny and silver in his palm. Not a knife, but a weapon all the same. He was sure of it. He caught Shaka by the wrist, but even incapacitated he was too strong to control. Bending at the waist, Simon twisted the man's wrist, forcing Shaka's arm to his side. At the same time, he swept the assassin's feet out from under him, causing him to topple onto his back. As he went down, Shaka struck out with his left hand, balled into a fist, the blow landing on Simon's cheek, stunning him. For a moment, he relaxed his grip. Shaka shook his right hand free, rolled, was on his feet.

Steps away, London Li looked on in horror.

"Go!" shouted Simon. "Get out of here."

But instead of running, she came closer, as if drawn to the spectacle, oblivious to the fact that her life was in peril.

"Go!"

The crowd parted. There were no cries; there was just an orderly retreat from the altercation, whatever its cause. Singaporeans were restrained in all things. All except an elderly hawker who, having decided that Shaka was the troublemaker, advanced on him, loosing a torrent of Chinese invective. Simon lunged at the old man, driving him away. Too late. Shaka staggered forward blindly, his right hand swinging in a wide arc, landing on the old man's neck. The hawker fell back, a welt on his skin. He cried out in pain, but the protest died in his throat. His mouth opened wider. He collapsed to his knees.

An arm's length away, Simon sprayed the Mace once more into Shaka's face, a five-second blast, the South African recoiling, hands flailing, calling out, "Riske. You're dead."

Simon hit him in the jaw, an uppercut with everything he had, momentum carrying him off the balls of his feet. Shaka fell to the ground. Simon landed on his chest, knee to the sternum, driving the wind from him. He had liberated a further item from the Singaporean cop—handcuffs—and he threw one on Shaka's wrist, clamping it as tightly as he could—payback for the brutal knots that had bound his hands and feet two nights earlier. The other cuff he attached to the leg of a dining table planted in the pavement.

The hawker fell against Simon, then slid to the ground. Foam issued from his mouth. His body spasmed. He lay still, eyes wide. There was no mistaking the scent of bitter almonds.

Simon took a handful of Shaka's hair. "Guess I can hold my breath longer than you thought," he said. He slammed his skull against the pavement, once, twice. Shaka fell unconscious.

Simon got to his feet, face flushed, dizzy with rage. He took London Li by the arm and started toward the south entrance to the market. "Don't you check your messages?"

She fought to free herself. "What just happened? The old man…he's dead." A confused look, turning to consternation, then anger. "Who are you, anyway?"

"I'm the one who told your boss that you were in danger."

Finally, she yanked her arm free. "Mandy?"

Simon nodded. "That man back there…it was you he was after."

"My God. It's true. What you said."

"Yes," said Simon. "It is." They reached the main road. "Which way?"

"Where are we going?"

"Somewhere far from here. We need to talk."

London Li started to the left, then stopped abruptly. "You didn't tell me your name."

"Simon Riske. With an *e*."

CHAPTER 45

Herzliya, Israel

Are you seeing this?"

Danni Pine stared, transfixed, at the screen high on the wall of the Café Bohème in Herzliya where a cable news channel broadcast images of the Spanish embassy in Bangkok. A procession of gurneys leaving a side entrance. A line of ambulances. Horrified onlookers. A cordon of police officers. Then photographs of the victims. The sound was off, but it made no difference.

Her father, retired General Zev Franck, founder of the SON Group, looked over his shoulder and stared at the screen for a few seconds, long enough to digest what was going on and decide he didn't need to see any more. He was a trim man, seventy years old, with a crust of white hair, his lined face tanned a nut brown, sparkling brown eyes ready for a fight. "Terrible," he said. "Didn't know that kind of thing went on in Bangkok."

"One of the people killed was Rafael de Bourbon."

Eyes fixed on his daughter, Franck evinced no emotion. He required no explanation as to who Rafael de Bourbon was or why he might be of interest to the both of them. Though he no longer took an active role in the company, he spoke with his daughter at the close of every business day to review all open dossiers. He'd followed her work on behalf of Luca Borgia every step of the way.

"It was Borgia," said Danni.

"We don't know that."

Danni set her napkin on the table. "Did you know?"

255

"Know what?"

"That he was a gangster."

"Please, Danni. This business…this has nothing to do with him."

Danni pointed at the screen. "He did that."

"Do you think I would have taken his money if I thought he was a gangster?"

Danni regarded her father, sitting there in his linen blazer, his fancy sunglasses and Gucci loafers. In that instant, she saw that he'd changed. Maybe he'd seen too much, done too much, hurt too much. Before joining Unit 8200, he'd been a founder of Israel's targeted assassination program. When she'd first joined the Mossad, he'd spoken to her of his victories and his mistakes, happy to be freed from the bonds that forbade discussion of such matters. These days, he talked about his new Mercedes or his newer Swiss watch or his culinary excursions to London and Paris.

"I think you've lost your bearing, Papa," she said, taking his hand.

"What's that supposed to mean?"

"You forgot where True North lies."

"My daughter, the poet." Franck freed his hand.

"Look at you. Your jacket costs as much as a major's monthly salary. Brioni, right? You have your gold Rolex and your Italian loafers. You look like you belong with Fredo Corleone in Havana."

"It's a Breguet, by the way. And I'd prefer it if you said I belong with Michael in Lake Tahoe."

"God knows, it happened to me. It's like rot. You get used to doing whatever you think is necessary, breaking every rule, breaking the law, ignoring your conscience. It's easy to believe that the means—no matter how twisted, how depraved, how ugly—are acceptable when the end is Israel. After a while you forget everything you know about right and wrong. There's just the mission."

"Danni, please, this isn't the place."

"You used to talk about them. The families of the targets. Wives, sisters, mothers, children. The 'collateral damage.' God, I always hated that term."

"It had to be done," said Franck. "I won't apologize."

"I don't want you to. There was no alternative, at least not at the time. But after a while it stopped bothering you."

"It never stopped," said Zev Franck solemnly. "Never. I just chose to forget."

"And now? We're not protecting Israel anymore. We're business-people. We make a product and we sell it. Daddy, the information we provided to a client led to a man's death. Luca Borgia ordered Rafael de Bourbon's killing."

"You don't know that."

"I read some of the take."

"Danni, the first rule is—"

"Never get involved in a client's business. I know. But Borgia is a thief. De Bourbon threatened to expose him. Now he's dead."

"It is not our concern."

"We are accomplices."

"Why are you telling me this?"

"Because I need your permission."

"For?"

Danni leveled her gaze at her father. After a moment, he looked away. She saw something in his features she'd never before seen. Shame. It came to her then that it was him, that it was her father who'd given the Saudis the software that had led to the journalist's death.

Zev Franck stood and buttoned his jacket. "You'll do it no matter what I say." He turned to leave. "But it's a mistake."

"And Daddy...not a word."

CHAPTER 46

Singapore

Simon waved down a taxi at the corner of Gopeng Street. He held the door as London climbed in. She slid across the seat, pale, shaken. "What just happened?"

"Take a breath. It's going to be okay."

London threw her shoulders back, lifted her head. "Okay," she said. "I'm okay."

The driver asked her where she would like to go.

"Mapletree Anson tower," she said, then to Simon: "We can talk in my office. I have to tell Mandy."

"No," said Simon. "Not there."

"What do you mean?"

"Not safe. People saw you back there. At the outdoor market. We have to think some were taking pictures, video even. You're a prominent journalist. Someone may have recognized you."

"So?"

"They'll tell the police. The police will come to your office."

"And I'll tell them what happened."

Simon turned in his seat, facing her. "Okay, then. Tell me what happened."

"I went to Tanjong market to meet Hadrian Lester—at his instruction. You showed up and stopped a man from trying to kill me."

"Is that what happened?"

"You told me it did."

"And it's true. Every word. But I'm not sure the police will be so quick to believe you or me."

"But the old man…the hawker…he's dead."

"And the poison that killed him was meant for you."

"That can't be…*How?*"

"Hadrian Lester set you up."

"He's the vice chairman of Harrington-Weiss."

"And who are you investigating?"

The taxi arrived at the office tower. Police vehicles lined the curb, officers everywhere. The evacuated employees still milled about the plaza, not yet allowed to return to their offices.

"What's going on?" asked London. "Why is everyone from the office outside? Look, there's Mandy." She opened the door, only for Simon to lean across her body and slam it closed.

"Bad idea," he said. "We don't know that the guy back there is the only one who wants to hurt you."

London sank back in her seat. "This is a little much for me to take in. Who did you say you were?"

"My friend, Rafael de Bourbon is R," said Simon. "He was killed in Bangkok two days ago by the same people who want you dead. Among them, Hadrian Lester. I was there. I witnessed his death. Go back to your offices and inside of ten minutes you'll be speaking with the police, half an hour at the outside. Tell me something. Do you think a man like Hadrian Lester—rich, powerful, connected—has friends in the Singapore police department?" He waited until she said yes, however reluctantly. "Bet on it," he went on. "I came here as quickly as I could to tell you face-to-face that you are in danger. I think I've been proven right on that count. It's up to you. Trust me or trust Hadrian Lester."

London considered this, then nodded. "All right, then. I think I understand."

"Right now we need somewhere safe to stay for a while. Just a few hours while we figure things out."

"My apartment."

"Out of the question. We have to assume they have it under surveillance."

"They?"

"Lester. The people he's working with. The ones who sent a man to kill you."

"We can go to my mother's. She has a small home ten minutes from here."

Simon shook his head. "We can't bring her into this. Don't you have a friend? Someone who's not a relation."

London considered this, then barked orders to the taxi driver. The car made a U-turn and headed south, toward the water. "I know just the place."

"Where are we headed?" asked Simon.

"Sentosa Island. A friend's apartment. It's a security building. We'll be safe there."

Simon looked at the reporter. She stared back, arms crossed, eyes beseeching the world. *Why is this happening to me?*

And he hadn't even told her about the cat yet.

The apartment of Mr. and Mrs. Michael Blume took up one half of the forty-second floor of the Drake Court Luxury Condominiums on Sentosa Island. Three bedrooms, four baths, in three thousand square feet. A mogul's palace by Asian living standards. And decorated like one. Ming vases, lacquered screens, marble floors, jade carvings.

Simon and London sat with Mandy Blume in the living room. A picture window offered a view of the Singapore Straits. Vessels of every size plied the water from shore to horizon. Tugs, freighters, motor yachts, cutting white swaths through the dark blue seas. But mostly there were the big boys. The Panamax-class container ships—nine hundred fifty feet long, piled to tipping with thousands of rectangular containers— and the supertankers, low and sleek, longer still, some reaching fifteen hundred feet, moored to offshore gas lines or heading to all points bearing cargos of Indonesian and Malaysian oil. It was a view into the bloodstream of international commerce.

The time was just past six in the evening. Mandy had arrived ten minutes after them, heeding London's plea for a safe place to rest up. She gave them a second cup of tea and a third dram of Irish whiskey as Simon explained in a level of detail appreciated by the two journalists (both taking notes as he spoke) the events that had brought him from England to Thailand, and now to Singapore. He concentrated on what he considered the salient moments: the meeting at the Bangkok Remand Prison and Colonel's Tan's evident allegiance to a higher master, his retrieval of the flash drive secreted in a bottle at the Little Havana, the feeling even then that he was being followed, and then the shooting at the Spanish embassy. He saw no need to describe the horror of it, instead drawing attention to the moment Tan received the call from an Italian named Luca, how everything spun out of control after that. He touched only lightly on the rest: his flight from Bangkok, the call to Arjit Singh (no names given, of course), his subsequent capture by Shaka and loss of the flash drive, and finally his escape out of Thailand.

London, in turn, briefed Simon on the fruits of her investigation thus far, though most of it he already knew from his conversations with Rafa and his more recent perusal of the files stolen from PetroSaud's servers. She was as smart as she was pretty but cold and machine-like in her summation. Impressive and a little intimidating. A force.

"This story promises to be the biggest instance of financial fraud in the past fifty years," she said in closing. "We're looking at over thirty billion dollars of stolen money."

London gauged him and Mandy for their response. Mandy expelled a breath, though she hardly looked pleased. If HW went down, and there was a good chance it would given the scope of Hadrian Lester's malfeasance, her husband would be out of a job, and all this—the vases and teak and jade—might vanish in the blink of an eye. Or rather, the bang of a judge's gavel.

"He can't be doing it alone," said London. "He's got to have help, in compliance for one." Compliance, the much-hated division of any financial institution charged with making sure its employees follow the letter of the law. "No way all of those funds' investments with PetroSaud pass muster without someone looking the other way. This has been going on for too long to keep hidden. Lester has to have men at every level of the operation."

"Agreed," said Simon. "But there's more to the picture. This isn't just about money. There's something else tying all these countries, these fund managers, together. PetroSaud is only one side of it."

"It's Lester," said Mandy Blume. "He's behind it all. Scoundrel."

"He's part of it," said. Simon. "Maybe a big part, but not all."

"How do you know it's about more than money?" asked London.

"A couple of things," said Simon. "Hear me out."

London and Mandy nodded, pens at the ready.

"The involvement of Colonel Albert Tan, for one. His behavior made clear he wasn't acting only as a representative of the Thai police. He wasn't there to oversee Rafa's arrest. He had skin in the game. Why else would he fly to Ko Phi Phi to personally take Rafa into custody? Why would he leave a board meeting to make sure he was present when I met with Rafa in jail? Why all the goons following me? I don't know if I can explain. He had orders to make sure Rafa didn't get out of the country. My guess is that they came from Luca. Oh, and I checked…Thailand isn't one of Hadrian Lester's, HW's, or PetroSaud's clients. It's something else entirely. Then there's Juan Llado, the Spanish naval attaché killed at the embassy. Llado knew what was going down. In fact, I'd bet he was the one who disabled the cameras. He had a clean shot at Shaka…or whatever his real name is…He didn't take it. He hesitated."

"But Shaka killed him," said London, checking her notes.

"He also killed Tan and Rafa and George Adamson. Like he tried to kill you and me. 'No more questions.' His words."

"What will happen to him?" asked London.

"Jail, I hope," said Mandy. "For a bloody long time."

"I called a contact in Thailand," said Simon. "The man who helped me get out."

"Major Rudi," London volunteered.

"Yes, I told him the Singapore police had the embassy shooter in custody. I'm sure he alerted his colleagues."

"You don't appear especially relieved," said Mandy.

"Properly skeptical," said Simon. "Whatever is going on is bigger than us...the law-abiding public. Bigger than a scheme to rip off lots of money. If Tan, chief of the Royal Thai Police, was involved, why not the commissioner of the Singapore police? Or the head of the army? The prime minister?"

"We're talking thirty billion dollars," said London. "How much bigger do things have to get?"

"I can't say. But when an assassin lectures me on ideas like purity and piety and preservation, my ears prick up. Those are dog whistles for extremism."

"You're reaching, Mr. Riske," said Mandy Blume. "We're journalists. We prefer to let facts speak for themselves."

"You're probably right," said Simon, not liking her high-and-mighty act. He knew plenty of bent journalists, too. "I'm just a guy who fixes cars for a living."

"There you are, then," said Mandy. "You said it, not me. Let's stick to what we know and can prove."

But London held him with her eyes. Two hours ago she'd escaped being killed by the narrowest of margins. She no longer possessed the luxury of relying solely on the facts. Facts offered scant protection against a global conspiracy that had put her squarely in its sights.

"Go on," said London. "You have more to say."

"May I use your computer?" he asked.

"Desktop is in the study," said Mandy.

The three moved into the Blumes' study. Dark, wood-paneled, leather-bound volumes lining the shelves—they hadn't changed rooms but continents. The air-conditioning blasted so hard, Simon shivered. He slid the keyboard closer and accessed his new email account, bringing up the last message from Arjit Singh, which included an attachment titled "PRF," for "PetroSaud recovered files."

"So far you've seen only the files Rafa sent London. As I said, there are a few more."

"How many?" asked London.

"Total? A million. Give or take." Simon saw a look pass between the two women, equal parts disbelief, astonishment, and joy. The Holy Grail. "Emails, texts, spreadsheets, banking instructions, the works," he continued. "Rafa downloaded them from the company server his last day of work four years ago."

"A million?" said Mandy. "This is all happening a bit too quickly for this old broad. I need a ciggie."

"And you're certain they are authentic?" asked London.

"As certain as I can be. Have a look."

"Oh, we will," said Mandy, taking a filtered cigarette from a box on the desk and hoisting a heavy silver lighter.

"My first concern is whether you can use them in court," said Simon.

"If the documents are real, they are admissible," said London. "It doesn't matter how we came upon them, whether we found them lying on the street or were handed them on a silver platter. We're not dealing with privileged information…you know, communications between a lawyer and client, that kind of thing. Otherwise we're in the clear. When all is said and done, Mr. De Bourbon will be regarded as a whistleblower. I hope that is some consolation to his family."

Simon nodded, thinking of Delphine. Cold comfort. "What I've seen of the files validates what you know about the Indonesian and Malaysian funds. It looks like those were the first ones that involved PetroSaud. We can come back to those later. Now we need to concentrate on the other thing."

"The dog whistle," said Mandy, caustically.

"I think they call it 'Prato Bornum.'"

"Prato what?" said Mandy.

"Sounds Latin," said London.

"In fact, it's the medieval name for Zermatt, Switzerland," said Simon. "You know, where the Matterhorn is. 'Prato' means source, or a wellspring. 'Bornum' means 'the place where it begins.' Put them together and you have 'Here, where the spring originates.' The 'spring' refers to the river that flows through the town of Zermatt down to the Rhône Valley."

"The place where the spring originates." London considered this. "A place of purity, preservation, and piety. I think I'm getting the drift."

"So am I," said Mandy. "And I don't like it one bit." She drew from her cigarette. "Apologies, Simon, if I was a bit snide. Comes with the territory. Trust is a four-letter word."

"Apparently, there is some kind of spiritual affiliation with the spot," Simon continued. "A sacred link to the past."

"And how did you figure this out?" asked London.

"To an extent, luck. As I was looking through the files, I saw the initials 'PB' and the words 'Prato Bornum' in a few places. In one, Hadrian Lester tells Tarek Al-Obeidi, PetroSaud's managing partner, that a portion of the money used to buy the false oil leases had to be sent to an account at the Bank of Liechtenstein and flagged 'Prato Bornum.' I thought it sounded odd, so I did a word search. After that, it was a question of putting two and two together. Like I said, the files are four years old. That's about the time PetroSaud got involved with the Indonesian sovereign wealth fund."

"Future Indonesia," said London.

Simon read from the screen. "Here's another from Lester. 'Tarek, it is essential our team is on board with larger objectives, PB, and do not balk at payment.' And another: 'T, spoke with NS. She's a firm believer in the cause. Provided all her account information at BOL. She will wire funds from her cut.'"

"'NS' must be Nadya Sukarno," said London.

"Seems you were right about her being guilty as sin," said Mandy. "But what's the cause?"

Simon went on: "There are numerous mentions of Prato Bornum, but the one I found the most interesting is a note sent to Al-Obeidi from an email handle, 'Aquila'—that's Italian for 'eagle.'" Simon brought up the flagged message. "'See you at meeting of principals at the Crillon in Paris. Prato Bornum, Luca.'"

"'Meeting of principals,'" said London. "Fund managers?"

"Or believers in the cause," said Simon. "Like Nadya Sukarno."

"The cause of purity, piety, and preservation."

"So then," said Mandy, waving her cigarette, "who the hell is Luca the eagle?"

"That's the sixty-four-thousand-dollar question," said Simon. "That's the second time I'd heard the name. Like I said, Colonel Tan took a call from a man named Luca immediately before he reneged on the deal to free Rafa. Tan spoke Italian with him. My guess is that Luca had managed to get his hands on the information Rafa had stolen and no longer required his cooperation to get it back. He was expendable. When I asked Shaka about Luca, he became upset, telling me I wasn't fit to utter his name. It's clear that 'Luca the eagle' is the man in charge." Simon stood from the desk, crossing his arms. "Something else Shaka said bothers me. When I asked him what he and Luca, and those behind this, were going to do about purity, piety, and preservation, he told me that I and the rest of the world would find out next week."

"Next week?" said London, writing feverishly on her notepad.

"Was he boasting? You know…puffing out his chest?" said Mandy.

"In my view, he was referencing a threat."

"Did he say anything specific?"

"Not about that. He just told me to take a deep breath and threw me in the river."

Mandy touched his arm. "Lucky dear."

Simon thought of the monk, his words about a guardian angel looking after him. "Very lucky."

"I don't suppose you can let us make a copy of the files," said London.

"They're yours." He regarded Mandy. "There is something you can help me with."

"I knew this was coming," said Mandy, then with abundant gratitude: "Of course I'll help. I'm all ears, Mr. Riske."

"I want to talk to Hadrian Lester. Now. While he's off-balance and before he can lawyer up. Do you know where he is?"

"No, but I know someone who does." Mandy stamped out her cigarette and picked up her phone. "Michael," she said when her husband had answered. "Need a favor. Don't ask any questions. You have two minutes to tell me where I can find Hadrian Lester."

Mandy hung up. She gave London a nudge, head inclined toward Simon. "He certainly sounds like he knows what he's talking about. Bit of a ruffian, though. Not bad looking if you go in for that type." Her eyes painted Simon up and down, saying that she, Mandy Blume, very much went in for that type.

"Sorry," said Simon. "I didn't have time to stop at my tailor."

"I'll give you some of Michael's things. He's a bit bigger around the waist, smaller other places, otherwise they should do nicely."

The phone buzzed and Mandy snatched it to her ear. "Thank you, darling," she said. "Won't ask again." She ended the call. "As of ten minutes ago, Hadrian Lester, vice chairman of HW, can be found at the SKAI Bar on the seventy-fifth floor of the Stamford Swissôtel presiding over a cocktail party to announce HW's newest piece of business. It's another sovereign wealth fund. Guess what? Future Indonesia 3."

Chapter 47

Singapore

Situated at the southernmost tip of the Malay Peninsula, straddling the equator, the South China Sea to one side, Indonesia and Indian Ocean to the other, Singapore has for centuries been a crossroads of trade and commerce. Arabs came from Jeddah, Indians from Delhi, Chinese from Canton, and Malays from the jungles to the north. Two hundred years ago, the British arrived to add a few drops of Western blood to the mix. More than any other country, Singapore was founded on the precepts of peaceful coexistence. All peoples and all religions were to be treated with equanimity and respect. If its residents shared a common deity, its name was prosperity.

So it was that in a ten-square-block perimeter one could find an authentic Chinatown, an Indian market that might be mistaken for its cousin in Mumbai, and an Arabian souk seemingly transplanted from old Mecca.

Near the souk, the Islamiya Fashion Boutique on Arabiya Street has offered the finest in Arabian menswear to a discerning clientele for over one hundred years. Its current proprietor, Faisal Faisali, a native Saudi, took ownership of the store in 1965, the year Singapore declared its independence from Malaysia. His timing was fortuitous. As the years passed, not only did Singapore grow wealthier, so did the countries of the Arabian Peninsula. Oil made the Arabs rich. Trade, the Singaporeans. There was a demand for new and fancier clothing. After all, what good was being rich if you were not able to show those around you?

Faisali's offerings grew in style, color, and fabric. Traditional cottons were supplanted by fine Egyptian weaves and even finer Chinese silks. The standard men's garment—the dishdasha, or thobe—became more decorative, with gold piping and filigree, ivory buttons, and cuffed hems. The keffiyeh, or ghutra, as it was called in Saudi Arabia, the square piece of cotton worn on the head and secured by the agal, also saw a flowering in design. Red, white, black, red checked, green checked, on and on.

If Faisali had to keep a larger stock, so be it. Sales from his three-hundred-square-foot store multiplied tenfold over the years and, along with prudent investments in real estate, had made him a wealthy man. No match for the sheikhs from the oil-rich kingdoms, but a millionaire many times over. Not bad for a street merchant's son who had grown up selling dried almonds in Jeddah.

So it was with a feeling of abundant goodwill that he greeted the couple who stormed into his establishment at twenty minutes past six in the evening. The man was American, of average height and evident vigor with broad shoulders and eyes the color of bottle glass. The woman was Eurasian, quite beautiful, if excessively businesslike, but weren't they all?

"How may I help you?" Faisali asked in his most refined English.

The man responded not in English, or French (another language Faisali spoke with fluency), but in his own Arabic. And not any Arabic, but the Arabic of the street. One might even say of the lower classes. In no uncertain terms, he described the articles of clothing required for him and for her, and that he wanted them as quickly as possible. To underscore his demands, he placed a fat stack of currency on the counter.

Faisali eyed the wad of bills and clapped his hands for his assistants to join them and get busy. He liked a man who knew what he wanted.

"But of course, Sheikh," said Faisali, after he had slipped the currency into the deepest pocket of his dishdasha. "It is my pleasure."

CHAPTER 48

Singapore

Not *another cocktail party.*

Hadrian Lester pasted on his most patient smile as he circled the SKAI Bar near the top of the Stamford Swissôtel. He said hello to all the usual suspects, making note of the VPs who had arrived early to get a head start on the weekend's festivities. Demerits for all. The gathering was being held to celebrate the kickoff for HW's third Indonesian sovereign wealth fund, appropriately titled "Future Indonesia 3." He spotted Wing Lo, the deputy chief of compliance, holding court by the bar outside, or rather he spotted Wing Lo's newest wristwatch, one of those million-dollar monstrosities tennis players and race-car drivers were wearing these days. He'd have to have a talk with Lo about toning things down. He was a salaried employee, not even a partner.

It was a beautiful spring evening. A few clouds here and there. A gentle breeze smelling of plumeria even seventy-five floors up. The view was unsurpassed, the city core to one side, the ocean to the other, limitless really. He walked to the railing. Directly below, some nine hundred feet, was St. Andrew's Road and the Padang, the grass fields where old man Raffles himself had played his polo. He took a step back, stomach reeling. It was a long way down.

Hadrian greeted Sir Ian, the firm's Scottish chairman, recently arrived from New York. Had he come to congratulate him or did he smell fire? A few feet away, a smashing brunette wearing a gold sheath of a cocktail dress gave him a wink. Helluva rack, too, if he might say.

"Hello, there," he said, sauntering up next to her. "What's a nice girl like you doing in a shithole like this?"

She put her lips to his ear. "Hoping to take home a tall, dark, handsome stranger and do very nasty things to him. Know anyone?"

"Just the bloke," he said. "Standing right in front of you. Mind if I give the goods a check?"

Without permission, he gave the woman's buttocks a firm squeeze. "Stop it," said his wife, Beatrice, feigning alarm. "People will talk."

"Let them. I hope about something other than finance for once." He kissed her. "*Buona sera, Contessa.* You look absolutely *incantevole.*"

Hadrian got them each a flute of champagne. Moët & Chandon Brut. Save the DP for when the fund closed. He'd prefer something stronger, an entire bottle of Johnnie Walker came to mind, but it didn't do to drink at these events. He gave his phone a quick look. Still no word from Kruger. He'd been tempted to hustle over to Tanjong market himself to learn what happened, but he was far too busy to leave the office. The process of minting money was a twenty-four-hours-a-day job. Besides, no news was good news, wasn't it?

"Listen, dearest, be a sweetheart and give Sir Ian's balls a little tickle. He's absolutely in love with you. Buff up the company stock, as it were. Maybe he can help me put a 'sir' in front of my name one of these days. 'Sir Hadrian.' I like the ring of it."

Beatrice Lester moved off and engaged Sir Ian in conversation.

Hadrian surveyed the setup. They'd put a table in one corner stacked high with prospectuses and manned by a new hire from Kenya by way of the London School of Economics—with a serious set of tribal tom-toms. Some idiot had insisted on making a banner that read FUTURE INDONESIA 3 in a font more appropriate to an action movie than a six-billion-dollar investment vehicle. Still, he really shouldn't be too upset. The firm would bonus him twenty mil up-front, with the real action coming on the side. A hundred-mil commish from Nadya and something similar from the firm he and Tarek had set up in Zurich to peddle investments in rare earth minerals. They were done with oil leases.

It was then he saw the sheikh. Royalty, at first glance. The elegant

271

white thobe, virginal ghutra, black-twine agal. Three-day beard. Sunglasses. And sandals to prove he was keeping one foot in the desert with his ancestors. That sealed it. A Qatari.

Hadrian could spot a prince at five hundred paces, tell you the branch of his family at a hundred, and give you his net worth at fifty. This was one of the new breed, which meant any man under sixty. Educated, cosmopolitan, probably an expert at one thing or another: drove fast cars, climbed tall mountains, collected signed first editions, though by the look of him, this one was a sportsman. None of that indolent Arab posture for him. The "Saudi slouch," Lester called it.

The sheikh had his wife with him, or one of them, clad head to toe in a black abaya and niqab, not even her eyes visible, and standing a respectful step behind him. Might as well be the Middle Ages. Barbarians, thought Hadrian, but who was he to judge?

He approached the sheikh, introducing himself in the little Arabic he knew. "Peace be unto you, and welcome."

The sheikh responded likewise, his Arabic rough and guttural, a peddler's tongue, which marked him as one of the obscenely rich.

"Tamani Al-Thani," he said, before switching to English, thank heavens. "What does a man have to do to get a drink around here?"

An Al-Thani. Good God. The Qatari royal family. He'd nailed it. The Al-Thanis made the Al-Sauds look like paupers by comparison. Controlled nine percent of the entire English equities market. Owned half of London, including Harrods, the former U.S. Embassy in Sloane Square, and the Park Lane Hilton. Oil reserves of twenty-five billion barrels. And loads of natural gas. It was his lucky day.

Lester escorted him to the bar. "What may I offer you, Sheikh?"

"Jack Daniel's. On the rocks." Tamani Al-Thani lifted his drink. "Where the hell's Tarek? He told me I had to come to this thing."

Perfect English, but of course. Probably went to Andover or Deerfield, one of the elite academies where the richest one percent sent their offspring to inoculate them against the lower classes.

"Did he? I believe Mr. Al-Obeidi is in Zurich at the moment. I hope you aren't inconvenienced."

"I'll catch up to him sooner or later. He told me about the new fund. Said something about you having an interest in investing with us. I run my family's natural gas concessions."

Not his country's. *His family's.*

Hadrian pulled a face, not impressed. "I'm afraid Indonesia is a bit overweighted in the energy sector. We're looking to diversify."

"Pity. Between you and me, we're about to announce a new find. Biggest yet. We're looking for partners to develop it. Tarek was certain you'd have an interest, Lester. You know, get in on the ground floor, so to speak."

"Hadrian, please."

Al-Thani ignored him. "Mentioned that Minister Sukarno would most likely come aboard as well. Oh well…up to you. Perhaps another time."

The Qatari finished his drink and grunted a command to his wife.

"Don't be hasty," said Hadrian. "HW is always interested in a profitable venture."

"Don't make me twist your arm."

"Not at all. If Tarek suggested I should take a look…"

"In fact, I may have some documentation in my suite."

"You're staying here?"

"Royal Suite. Cramped, but it will do. Why don't we have a look? I think you'll find it quite remunerative. Make my visit worthwhile. Keep Tarek out of the doghouse. You'll be back in ten minutes."

Hadrian checked the room. He was due to give a speech at seven, just something off the cuff. He looked at his phone, wondering once more why the hell Kruger hadn't checked in, finding it impossible to imagine something had gone wrong—*who could stop a man like him?*—then thinking there was just time to hear the sheikh out. If he was a close friend of Tarek, he had to be crooked as the day was long. New gas fields. Ha! Maybe he was even telling the truth.

"Shall we, then?" said Tamani Al-Thani.

"After you."

*　　*　　*

The three got off at the seventy-third floor. The sheikh led the way into the suite, his obedient wife bringing up the rear. They walked through one room to the next, arriving at a sprawling sitting area big enough to hold the Glastonbury music festival. Cramped indeed.

"Sit down. Get yourself a drink," said Al-Thani. "Be right back." The sheikh disappeared into the bedroom.

Hadrian dropped into a quilted armchair. The sheikh's wife sat nearby, facing him. Frankly, he was surprised she was present. Then again, Qataris prided themselves on being quite modern in certain respects, the abaya notwithstanding.

"Enjoying your stay?" he asked the woman. "First time in Singapore? Amazing city, isn't it?"

The woman didn't respond. He caught a flash of her eyes behind the gauzy veil. It was nice to know that there was a human in there. It was hard to tell much about her figure. At least she wasn't one of those beasts of burden you so often saw trailing behind her husband. As big as camels some of them.

He heard the door to the bathroom open, adjusted his posture. This was business. Back to being vice chairman of the most profitable investment bank in the world. If Al-Thani wanted him as a partner, Hadrian damn well planned on driving a hard bargain.

A fit, well-dressed man entered the room. Dark suit, broad shoulders. Then he noted the three-day stubble, the green eyes he'd glimpsed behind the sunglasses. *Could it be?*

"Sheikh Al-Thani?"

The woman lowered the hood of her abaya. She wasn't an Arab at all but a striking Eurasian woman. In fact, he recognized her. Lester felt his stomach drop.

"I'm sorry," the woman said, "but he's not really a sheikh."

"Actually, the name is Riske. This is Ms. Li. We're going to have a little talk."

CHAPTER 49

Singapore

Simon sat perfectly still. Blood coursed through his veins as it never had, making his heart pump wildly, flushing his cheeks, bringing a terrible pressure behind his eyes. If he moved, if he lifted a finger, he would lose control.

You, he thought. *You did it.*

He had not been prepared for the flood of emotion unleashed by the sight of Hadrian Lester, the knowledge that he was one of the men responsible for Rafael de Bourbon's death and the carnage in Bangkok. He'd met more than his share of white-collar criminals—they were his stock-in-trade, so to speak. A thief was a thief, whether he stole a thousand, a million, or a billion. The only thing that changed was the cut of his suit and whether he wore it on the left or the right.

But Lester was a murderer. He'd sent Shaka to kill London Li. Simon had every reason to believe that he knew about the embassy in Bangkok. Oh yes, he knew, thought Simon, having read the slew of emails between Lester and Al-Obeidi and Sukarno and all the other fund managers he was in cahoots with. Lester was the mastermind, or at least one of them. Nothing happened without his knowledge. It went without saying that he would go to any lengths to prevent the discovery of his crimes.

There he sat, close enough to grab by the throat and strangle. Simon stared at the man—smug, confident, arrogance oozing from his every pore—not knowing that his world had changed. Simon saw through Lester and imagined Rafa, looking at him in the ambassador's office, bewildered, frightened, wondering who had shot Colonel Tan if it wasn't him, realizing, of course, in that short, agonizing moment, that he was next, and then the gunshot, the weight of Rafa's body falling against him, the viscera splattering Simon's face.

The shock had been too immediate to register. Seconds later, Simon had been running for his life. But now, fifty-some hours later, it came to him. The horror. The anger. The rage.

Simon considered killing him. Not as an abstract thought. *What if . . . ?* But as the next action he might take, as if hefting a stone in his palm, assaying its weight, readying to throw it. He could use the paring knife he'd found in the mini bar. He would stab him in the chest, making sure to point the blade upward to nick the heart. It would not be the first time he'd killed a man.

Twenty years ago he'd cut a man's throat in a steaming prison shower, slit it with a razor blade clenched between his teeth. He knew what it felt like to have blood run over his hands. Then, he hadn't had a choice; it was kill or be killed. Not for a second had he felt remorse. In fact, he hadn't felt anything except relief—an obligation fulfilled.

It was this thought that prevented him from acting. The knowledge that he would feel no better afterward.

He felt the stone drop from his hand. Another day, perhaps.

"What do you want?" Lester was saying. "I've got one hundred people upstairs waiting for me. Let's make this quick."

"They can wait," said Simon.

"Who did you say you were?" Lester pointed a rude finger at him, one more underling to be ordered about. "Her, I know. Oh hell. I don't have time for this nonsense. Goodbye, then."

Lester rose from his chair. Simon hit him in the stomach before he'd taken a step. A steam piston to the gut. Lester doubled over, the wind knocked out of him. Simon grabbed him by the collar and manhandled him back into his chair, yanking him upright.

"I said they can wait. Now sit still and pay attention like the gentleman you never were."

"You can't..." Lester blustered as his breath came back to him. "I'll call the police."

Simon slapped him across the face. "You'll do what I tell you."

Simon looked at London. "You need to leave now. Mr. Lester and I are going to have a private talk. Man to man."

They'd discussed it earlier. Lester was never going to talk voluntarily. They could accuse him of all the crimes in the world. They could brandish evidence, drag up Rafa's ghost to testify, and still Lester wouldn't say a word. London could write her story. She could expose Lester, PetroSaud, Harrington-Weiss, and all the others. Eventually, charges would be brought. Lester would be arrested. No question. But between now and then, time would pass. Months. Maybe a year. Simon needed answers now. This minute.

On the banks of a river in southwestern Thailand, Shaka had all but admitted it. It was happening now. It was up to Simon to find out what and put a stop to it.

"I've changed my mind," said London. "I just realized that he tried to have me killed. I'm staying." She looked at Lester. "As you can see I'm alive. The man you sent after me—I believe his name is Shaka— is in police custody. I don't need to interview you any longer. Mr. De Bourbon made sure we'd have everything we needed."

"De Bourbon…who's that?" said Lester, looking between his two captors. "Never heard of him. What do you want, anyway? Think I scare easy? I was in the military for ten years. Pilot. Had my share of scrapes."

"Now you'll have another to compare them against," said Simon. "I'm guessing they're going to come up shy."

He pulled up a chair so the two men faced one another, in fact were uncomfortably close to each other.

"De Bourbon…name doesn't sound vaguely familiar?"

Lester shook his head furiously as Simon took Lester's right hand in both of his, separating the fingers, massaging each one. "What are you doing…now, hey there, stop this…"

"You asked who I was. The only thing you need to know is that Rafael de Bourbon was my friend. When he died, I still owed him a favor."

Meeting Lester's gaze, he grasped the middle finger and wrenched it violently clockwise. The bone fractured, the sound as loud as a nut-cracker crushing a walnut. Lester's cry was louder still.

London Li looked on passively, as if she'd witnessed this kind of thing a thousand times before.

"Go ahead," said Simon, as the banker groaned and whimpered. "The suite takes up half the entire floor. Your party is above us. They won't hear a thing. Anybody else does, I'll take my chances. We'll be finished by the time security arrives."

"What do you want? Is it money? Tell me how much. Done deal. Ten million. Twenty." He tried to smile, friend to friend, his pain making the smile a grotesque facsimile. "What will it cost me to make this go away?"

"Right now, I could ask you for it all and you'd give it to me."

Simon grasped the ring finger, gave it a little shake to let Lester know what was coming, then twisted it viciously. Another crack. Another horrible protest. Lester began to cry. Perspiration ran down his forehead mingling with his tears.

"Come on, then," he pleaded. "Tell me what it is you want…anything. Be reasonable."

"Reasonable?" Simon took the index finger. Lester cried out before he'd done anything to it. "Is two enough? Or should we move on to the fingernails and really get this party started?"

"Two's enough!"

Simon let go of the man's hand and Lester held it to his chest, trembling, breathing labored, pain creasing his features.

"You, sir, are done. Out of the game. Finished. For your information, Rafa copied over a million files from PetroSaud's servers. Your name is everywhere. You know what you did. Ms. Li thinks it's going to be the biggest case of financial larceny in the last fifty years. Once murder is thrown in, you'll be looking at twenty-five years, no parole. They'll all be fighting for you. My guess is that you'll end up in the States. New York. Are you getting this?"

As he spoke, London Li passed along a variety of documents, first the ones that Rafael de Bourbon had sent in his initial email high-lighting the monies stolen from the first Future Indonesia fund, then other documents highlighting other crimes. Lester studied them with increasing interest, his eyes shifting occasionally to Simon, then back to the damning evidence.

"We know all about the money," said London. "How you stole it from the different funds by creating false investments with your associates, wiring money in and out, and back to managers like Nadya Sukarno, all the while taking your cut. It's all there. Wire instructions. Bank transfers. Commission statements. Notes confirming the wheres and whats and hows. I commend your bookkeeping. It's going to be very helpful."

"All that," said Simon, "that's Ms. Li's side of things. Me, I want to know the bigger picture. I have just two questions. What is Prato Bornum? And, who is Luca?"

Lester fidgeted, face red, sniffling, struggling to regain a measure of dignity. "Riske…that's your name, right? Listen to me. I wasn't kidding about the money. Go someplace quiet, out of the way. Maybe they won't find you, but I doubt it. These people you're asking about, they're everywhere. Government. Military. Finance. Europe. Asia. The States. Ask me, they're all a little crazy. Think the world's coming to an end because of a few immigrants, refugees, whatever. Me, I'm in it for the money. But them…they think otherwise. It's all about stemming the tide. More than that, I don't know. I don't want to know. Now, please, I'll wire you twenty million. Got the cash in my account. You two can split it. Go away." He leaned closer to Simon, speaking to him as if London weren't in the room. "If she thinks they're going to allow her to write her story, she's got another think coming. She may try, but they'll get to her. Christ, they'll buy the bloody *FT* if they have to."

"And Luca?"

"Don't ask."

"We're past that point."

"Please. Just go. They've been planning this for years. They won't let two nobodies get in the way."

"I want to know it all. Hear me? Everything. What's Prato Bornum?"

"Load of bullshit. Like I said."

"That's not going to cut it."

"I always told him. I'm only in it for the money."

"Tan wasn't in it for the money. Llado wasn't in it for the money. Too many people are already dead because of Prato Bornum. Don't tell me it's a load of bullshit."

"They want to clean things up. Send people back to where they belong. Tighten up borders. It's out of control. That's what they say. Me, I live here. Everything couldn't be more *in control*. But in Europe, the States, other parts of Asia, it's a free-for-all. People think they can go wherever they like and expect others to care for them. It's bankrupting the system, the poor countries dragging the rich ones down to their level, not bothering to solve their own problems. You've seen the pictures. Internationalism is finished. Isolationism is the order of the day. Everyone to his own. White to white. Brown to brown. Yellow to yellow."

"Sounds pretty dull," said Simon. "I wouldn't want to live in a place where everyone looks like you."

London said: "And so you make them send hundreds of millions of dollars to the Bank of Liechtenstein. What's the purpose of those transfers?"

Lester's eyes darted to London's, then ducked away.

Yes, Simon thought, *we know about that, too.* "What is happening in a few days' time?"

"Nothing. No idea. What do you mean?"

Simon backhanded him. Very hard. Lester raised his hands to protect himself, too late. They remained up, trembling.

"Let's try that again."

"I don't know. It's his deal. No one knows except him."

"Luca?"

"Why do you ask me if you already know?"

"Luca who? Or don't you want to tell me because you think it might put your life in danger? Sorry, my friend. Your life is in mortal danger right this second." He grabbed a handful of Lester's hair. "Talk to me."

"All I know is that it's going to be in Europe. Italy, France, Germany. I don't know where exactly. He's got them all lined up and ready to go. The money is for them. Payoffs."

"To who?"

"Prato Bornum. *Them*. Military. Government. Police. Businesses. He said it's 'a spark to light the fire.'"

"What's that supposed to mean?"

"I don't know."

"Guess."

"A lot of people are going to die."

"When?"

"Soon."

"When?"

"Goddammit. I don't know. This weekend maybe."

"Is it or isn't it?"

Lester nodded. "Tomorrow. Maybe Sunday."

"You have to do better than that."

"That's all I know. He only told me so I could short the market."

Simon drew a breath. Had he really said, "short the market"? It wasn't enough to be complicit in the death of innocents; Lester planned on profiting from it. It was all he could do not to pummel the man.

London appeared shaken. "You…you…" She looked to Simon. "Break another finger. Break his neck. Go ahead. Do it."

Lester met their gazes unrepentantly.

"Who's Luca?"

"Family."

"I want a name."

"I told you. Family. That's why he can't hurt me. He's my brother-in-law."

"Your wife's side?"

"Beatrice…she's his sister. Luca Borgia."

London's face creased in surprise. It was a name she recognized.

"What the hell else do you want?" said Lester.

"Nothing. We can take it from here. It's over."

Lester gave them a look, all hate and disgust. "It's not over until he says it's over."

281

Chapter 50

*N*o *time like the present.*

Danni Pine popped her head into accounting. "Anyone home?"

Goldie Levin answered without lifting her eyes from her work. "Busy."

Danni entered the office and took up position in front of her desk. "Ahem."

Goldie raised her eyes, met Danni's gaze. "Sit. I'll be with you when I can."

Goldie was sixty if a day, a wrinkled, gray-haired refusenik from the former Soviet Union and, if Danni wasn't mistaken, this company's second employee, not counting her father. Danni could intimidate software engineers. Clients she could tell what to do. But Goldie? Not a chance. The woman might as well have founded the company instead of her father.

Danni studied the calendar on the wall showing a photograph of the Galilee. She looked at pictures of Goldie's family. She picked up an old action figure of Moshe Dayan. Where in the world had the woman found that?

"So," said Goldie, at length. "To what do I owe the honor?"

Danni smiled as politely as she knew. "I need to check the billing for a client."

"Name?"

"Borgia, Luca. It might be under a corporate name. Central Umbrian Enterprises, I think."

Goldie typed the name into her desktop. "Borgia, Luca M. Ten days left on the billing cycle."

"I need to close it out today."

"Bills go out at the end of the month."

"Humor me."

"I'll have to add the remaining May days onto June. Messy."

"Goldie!"

The accountant's eyes opened wide.

"Send a copy of Borgia's bill through today's date to my personal email. I'll forward it to the client myself. I need to add a personal note. If it isn't there by the time I get upstairs, I'm going to confiscate Moshe Dayan here."

Goldie froze. "You wouldn't!"

Danni left the question unanswered.

She stopped in the lab on the way upstairs. Dov and Isaac stood at the whiteboard working out a problem. With a whistle, she motioned them to follow. The men dropped their markers then and there. Danni was already feeling better about her authority.

Luca Borgia's bill for the month of May was at the top of her inbox when she sat at her desk. She opened the attachment, noting that Borgia was paying her company a monthly retainer of twenty thousand euros, with add-ons for special projects. At least he was paying full freight. She closed the message, then sent Goldie a note thanking her.

"We have a problem," she began, after the engineers had shut the office door and taken up their spots opposite her desk. "Normally, we don't look into our clients' affairs; what they do with our software is their business. However, a situation has come to my attention where we can no longer turn a blind eye."

"Bangkok?" said Dov.

"You saw?"

"Who didn't?" said Isaac.

"Yes," said Danni. "Bangkok. We were right to worry."

"Has he done something like this before?"

"Borgia? Who knows?" said Danni. "Does it matter?"

"And the other one," said Isaac. "The journalist."

"London Li," said Danni. "That's my concern."

"And so?" asked Dov.

"We are going to take a deep dive into Borgia's affairs."

"For who?" asked Isaac, not yet grasping her intent. "I mean, who's the client? MI6? CIA? Spanish intel? Thai police?"

"We are the client," said Danni. "SON. Me. You. Dov. All of us."

The engineers squirmed in their chairs. For once, they were faced with a concept of which they had little experience, one that no computational skills could solve.

"Suggestions, gentlemen?"

"Pegasus?" said Isaac.

"Pegasus," agreed Dov.

"Pegasus," stated Danni with the finality of an auctioneer's hammer.

Pegasus was the SON Group's most powerful hacking tool, initially developed in conjunction with Unit 8200 and the United States National Security Agency. The first iteration had been stolen by the Shadowbrokers, an anonymous international hacking collective, and made available to one and all on the web. SON had built the second and third iterations themselves. It had quickly become their bestselling product.

In short, Pegasus was a piece of spyware that, when installed on a phone, laptop, or desktop using the iOS operating system, gave them—the SON Group—total and complete control of the device. Pegasus tracked calls, collected passwords, reported the device's location, read text messages, and allowed its user to gather information from every program installed on the device. WhatsApp, Viber, Facebook, Instagram, Skype—anything and everything, including taking control of the phone's camera and microphone.

All that was required was for the target to open a file with the spyware secretly attached to it. Pegasus did the rest. In this case, that "Trojan" file would be Luca Borgia's May billing statement.

There was one problem. All Borgia's devices were equipped with software designed to search incoming mail for exactly such hidden attachments. Danni knew this because SON had sold him the software, and subsequently installed it.

Danni laid out the dilemma they faced. "Can you get around it?"

Isaac and Dov exchanged looks. "An hour?"

"Forty-five minutes."

"Get me a hack in thirty and you boys can take the rest of the day off."

Dov made a face. "And do what?"

CHAPTER 51

Singapore

Hadrian Lester left the elevator and walked unsteadily into the SKAI Bar. His hand throbbed beyond imagination. One eye was swollen shut. He suspected his nose was bleeding…*who else's blood could it be on his shirt?*…and his ribs ached horribly.

It was over.

The words caromed around the inside of his battered skull like spiked pinballs.

Over…over…over.

The reporter had the files…a million of them, good God…Shaka was in custody. And Riske…whoever he was…the man was relentless.

It was over. At least for Hadrian. He imagined the press, the harassment, the trials, the sheer pain of all that was to come. All of it would come out. Every sordid detail. There were too many people involved. One person would talk, then the next, then it would be a mad race to see who could save their skin first, who could cut the best deal, who could get the least prison time. But there would be no deal for him. Not for the man at the top. For the man at the top there was only the guillotine.

Luca, of course, was insulated from the whole thing. Neither Riske nor the reporter, Li, would find his name anywhere. Not on an account, an email, a text, nowhere. He gave the orders. Hadrian followed them.

Luca could take care of Riske. Of that, Hadrian was certain.

"Christ, man, what's happened to you?" It was Sir Ian, eyeing him not with sympathy but alarm. Can't have the vice chairman wandering

286

in here looking like this. It doesn't do. What would they think in Edinburgh…or Glasgow…or wherever the fuck Sir Ian was from?

Hadrian kept walking, the sky a shade of indigo, clouds lounging beneath the stars. On the equator, darkness came in a hurry. By now, his presence had been noted and commented upon, word spreading through the crowd like wildfire. Heads turned. Conversations stopped dead.

"Hadrian, what is it? What has happened?" Beatrice hugged his side, trying to lead him away. He rebuffed her.

"Not now, darling. Just one thing I have to do." He smiled.

"But…your face. Who hit you? Hadrian! Please. Talk to me. Darling."

"Please." Italians. So emotional. Actually, it was one of the things he loved most about her.

He pressed on, steadying himself against the bar, aware of all eyes on him. Drawing a breath, he continued past the seating area. If he looked carefully, far out on the horizon, past where the planes were taking off and landing, he could see Changi.

He squinted and it came into view. All of it. The prison walls. The barbed wire. The rats with their long, sharp teeth.

Never.

With a nimbleness he didn't know he possessed, he placed one hand on the rail, a foot on the bench next to it, and vaulted over the wall seventy stories and nine hundred feet above the earth.

Never.

CHAPTER 52

Singapore

Borgia," said Simon. "Luca Borgia. That's who we're after."

"I can tell you all about Borgia. I interviewed him five years ago."

"Wait, you know him?"

"As well as I know any of my subjects. He's one of Italy's wealthiest men. The Borgia family has holdings in industrial concerns all over the country—the world, really. They're worth billions."

"I've never heard of him."

"They're quiet, Simon. The epitome of old money. They like to control things from the shadows. He's the principal landowner in the region of Umbria. We're talking tens of thousands of acres. He lives in a castle there. It's called the Castello dell'Aquila."

"Did you say '*aquila*'? As in 'eagle'?"

London nodded.

"'Luca the Eagle.' I saw that handle on a few emails."

Waiting for the elevator, Simon handed her Hadrian Lester's phone. "Look what I found."

"You took his phone?" said London. "That's theft."

"He left it on the table."

"No, he didn't."

"I may have lifted it."

"You do that? You pickpocket people?"

"Handy skill, if you want to know. I'm going to give it back to him the next time we see each other. It's what friends do."

"Do friends give friends their passcode?"

"One-one-one-one."

"It isn't!" She punched in the code, then looked at him, wide-eyed. "How?"

"Parlor trick," said Simon. "Actually, I caught him checking his phone when we were upstairs. Guys like him, who have to check it a thousand times a day, tend to keep it simple."

She ran through the apps. "It's a gold mine."

"Admissible?"

"For this, you need a warrant."

"I won't tell the police if you won't."

The elevator arrived. They entered and Simon punched the button for the ground floor. "Did you hear him? Something bad's going down."

"What do you think? Another 9/11?"

"With all the money that's being shifted between accounts, I wouldn't doubt it. And soon, this weekend."

They looked at each other, not sure how to handle the responsibility with which they'd been burdened.

"Do you think Lester called the police?"

The elevator slowed. The doors opened. "I don't want to wait around to find out. Let's move."

Simon scanned the open floor as they moved across the lobby. There was no sign of anything amiss, just the lazy ebb and flow of guests and business people and staff. They walked outside. A line of taxis was drawn up to their left.

"And now?" asked London.

"You write your story. Put those guys behind bars. The quicker the better."

"What about you? What next?"

Simon took back Lester's phone, bringing up the executive's daily agenda. "Lester and his wife are booked on the Singapore Airlines 23:55 flight to Switzerland," he said, showing London the screen. "Connecting flight to Nice. Room at the Hôtel du Cap-Eden-Roc. Nothing but the best."

"Think he's going to meet Borgia?"

"That's what I aim to find out."

"You're going, too?"

"Maybe I'll get a seat next to Lester. We'll have plenty of time to get to know each other better. You know how it is when you're flying. People say almost anything to another passenger."

"Don't you think Lester is going to tell Borgia what happened?"

"You mean about me breaking his fingers? I hope so. It might stop Borgia from doing whatever it is he has planned."

"Do you believe that?"

Simon laughed bitterly. "Not for a second."

The porter blew his whistle. A taxi pulled forward, a silver Mercedes.

"Go ahead," said Simon. "Take this one."

London looked at him askew. "I'm going with you."

"As much as I'd like the company, I don't think that's a good idea."

"And I'm supposed to care?"

"Pardon me? A few hours ago you came this close to lying on the pavement dead of cyanide poisoning. You're staying here, where you'll be safe."

"Pardon me? It was me Rafael de Bourbon contacted to look into PetroSaud in the first place. My involvement in all this predates yours. And by the way, who do you think you are to tell me anything about how I should live my life?"

"Look Ms. Li…London…I don't care what you do, one way or the other. I do care that you stay alive, if only to break this story. Rafa deserves that."

"Do you have any idea how patronizing you sound? As if I need a man to keep me safe."

"Man, woman, as long as it's someone who can see a threat coming."

"The man who tried to kill me—"

"Shaka. He's a professional assassin. And yes, that's for real."

"Shaka. He is in jail. We don't have to worry about him any longer."

"We don't know that for certain."

"He was handcuffed to the ground. There were witnesses. This is

Singapore. Not Thailand or Malaysia or any of those places where laws can be bent to suit the richest party."

"And your point?"

"Our officials are not corrupt. I thought about what you said earlier, about Lester having friends in high places. It doesn't wash. Not here. The police will keep Shaka in custody until he stands trial."

The porter stepped forward and opened the rear door. "Please, madam, sir."

By now, there was a queue behind them.

"Thank you," said London.

"After you."

Without warning, a thunderclap.

Closer and louder than any Simon had ever heard. A shock wave passed through him. A blizzard of glass peppered his face. Metal shrieked. Tires exploded. Screams.

Inexplicably, Simon was on his behind, half sitting, half lying on the pavement, London next to him, both of them dazed but unhurt. Slowly, he gathered himself, the tremendous boom fading, the very air itself vibrating.

Hardly more than a foot away, a body lay on the crushed roof of the Mercedes taxicab. A man in a dark suit. He'd landed on his back. His head lolled to one side, eyes open, staring at Simon. But for a trail of blood running from his mouth, Hadrian Lester looked remarkably peaceful.

Simon helped London to her feet. A moment to come to their senses, to fully realize what was before their eyes. London circled the ruined car, hurrying to help the driver pinned inside. With Simon's help, and that of several bellmen and porters, they pulled the man free. By some miracle, he was unhurt except for some cuts on his forehead. He saw his car, the dead man on it, and collapsed.

Simon approached London. "Come here."

"What is it?"

"Just come here."

She approached warily. With a handkerchief, he wiped away several flecks of blood on her cheek. She lifted her chin, eyes on his. "You sure you want to go?" he asked.

London nodded, but a moment later, backed away, as if she'd gotten a shock. She walked to the next taxi. "My apartment is on the way to the airport. Am I allowed to get my passport?"

CHAPTER 53

Latina Air Base, Italy

Caesar led his legions to victory at the Battle of Vosges.

Mark Antony at the head of his cavalry routed the Gauls and their king, Vercingetorix, at Alesia.

And Luca Borgia, no less a champion of his people, would expel the barbarian hordes from the shores of Europe.

Borgia sat in the passenger seat of the van as it cleared security at Latina Air Base, an hour south of Rome, and drove onto the tarmac. A Piaggio turboprop sat on the runway, engines spooling, loading ramp lowered. Near it was parked a jeep. General Massimo Sabbatini, clad in his navy-blue utilities, beret cocked on his head, jumped down and started toward them. A squad of his men waited close by.

Borgia left the van. The two men shook hands. It was not a day for pleasantries. They were preparing for war.

Sabbatini ordered his soldiers to unload the van. In minutes, a stack of crates man-high stood next to the loading ramp. The paratrooper read from a clipboard. "Four crates Semtex at ten kilos per crate. Two crates hand grenades at twenty grenades per. Two crates Beretta nine-millimeter pistols at ten pistols per. Two crates ammunition. All here." He caught Borgia's air of concern. "What is it?"

"I don't want them getting their hands on the materiel."

"No question of it. The plastique cannot be detonated without the proper equipment. We will defuse the grenades and remove the firing pins from the pistols."

"No mistakes," said Borgia.

Sabbatini placed a hand on his upper arm. One soldier's word to another.

It was a clear, pleasant afternoon. The air base, on the Lazio plain, looked east toward Cassino and south toward Pompeii. Borgia fancied himself a student of history. At such a place Pompey had fought Caesar and lost, signaling the end of the First Triumvirate. Borgia had no illusion. He was not the next Caesar. But like Caesar, he viewed himself as an expression of the people's will, the vox populi. Through him, their voices would be heard. He was not the only one who had had enough.

Turin. Milan. Lampedusa. Ingolstadt. Dijon. Copenhagen. Madrid.

Equal shares of explosives and armaments purchased from Libya had been sent to each city. In each city, members of Prato Bornum would see that they were properly used. Police. Military. Intelligence agencies of one stripe or another. Bloodshed was necessary, but Borgia had instructed his colleagues to keep it to a minimum. Enough blood would be spilled come tomorrow night to spark his plan into action. The other cities were meant to be symbolic, to let the public know that no one was safe. Not in Italy. Not in Germany. Not in Denmark. Not in Spain. And not in France.

Poor France, thought Borgia. Yet again she would suffer the most, but if it was any consolation, many of the victims would not be French.

There had been one last shipment, and this was the most important. It had left his possession an hour after he had acquired the materiel from the gangsters Toto and Peppe, on the Naples docks, and had been placed aboard a private jet and flown to, of all places, Switzerland. Fifty kilos of plastic explosives packed in a lead-lined stainless-steel case, ensuring the plastique's chemical signature remained invisible to even the most sophisticated scanner.

From the airport outside the Swiss capital of Bern, a courier had ferried the case south along Lake Thun before turning due west and heading into the Simmental Valley. His destination was the resort town of Gstaad, elevation 3,445 feet, in the canton Bern. It was a ninety-minute drive. Once there, he navigated toward the famed Palace hotel, and past the hotel to a chalet not much smaller.

The chalet belonged to Arabs, the Al-Obeidi family, originally from Dhahran. Tarek Al-Obeidi had served as managing partner of PetroSaud and, more recently, headed up the newly formed International Rare Earth Consortium. His older brother, Abdul Al-Obeidi, age sixty-one, had chosen a different profession. For the past twenty years he had served as the deputy chief of the Mabahith, the Saudi secret police.

It was Abdul Al-Obeidi who the day before had made sure the doors to the chalet's subterranean garage stood open so the courier could enter and off-load his sensitive cargo undetected. Abdul Al-Obeidi had phoned Borgia soon afterward to give him a firsthand description of the work being done.

Swiss law demanded that every home have a secure, airtight room on the ground floor or, preferably, the cellar to serve as protection against a nuclear attack. The *luftschutzbunker* was large and high ceilinged, its concrete floor and walls painted a glossy battleship gray, a reinforced steel door one meter thick guarding entry and exit, anti-gas filters built into the ceiling. A worktable had been erected in the center of the room, no more than a thick plywood sheet set atop sawhorses. It was a temporary construct, to be disposed of after use. Four military-style vests rested on the table's surface. The vests were made from molecular-weight polyethylene, black, with pockets on the left and right and a larger one across the back, all designed to house Kevlar plating to protect the wearer against bullets and shrapnel. These vests, however, would be used for quite the opposite purpose.

On the floor beside the worktable was a tall plastic garbage bin filled with an assortment of nails, nuts, bolts, washers, screws, hinges, steel balls of various diameters, and razor wire, the last designed to slice off appendages and cause death by exsanguination to those not in the blast's immediate vicinity.

A gray, elfin man dressed in baggy trousers and a shabby cardigan stood by the table, hands in his pockets, as the explosives were brought in. He moved quietly and carefully, and with his trim mustache and scholarly glasses could have been mistaken for a shy-mannered country physician. In fact, in his earlier days he had practiced medicine as the chief of cardiology at Baghdad General Hospital. His career ended the day the Americans invaded Iraq. For the past sixteen years, he had specialized in the building of suicide vests and explosive belts for the Sunni insurgency. He was known by all as "the Doctor."

The Doctor opened the case and removed the bricks of plastic explosives, each individually wrapped in navy-blue plastic and weighing two and a half pounds, or approximately one kilo. When he had finished stacking the bricks, he chose one and peeled off the thick wrap. The plastique was colored a bold, unmistakable orange. Semtex.

He knew what it was capable of, the destruction it could inflict. In an enclosed space, even a large auditorium, the effects would be impressive.

Four vests used in unison in such a space.

The Doctor could only imagine the result.

All this Abdul Al-Obeidi had told him. Borgia had been grateful for his enthusiastic narrative.

He turned to General Sabbatini. "Shall we go through it one last time?"

"The plastique will be cached in an empty fuel reservoir next to the principal dormitory. At last count, the place is filled to bursting."

"How many?"

"Eight hundred in a building meant to house one hundred fifty."

"Have you identified any agitators?"

"Easy enough. All they do is complain, the lot of them. Not enough food. Not enough soft drinks. Their rights aren't being respected. We have no right to hold them so long. Some are more vocal than others."

Borgia handed Sabbatini a piece of paper folded in half. "A list of phone numbers. Make sure they are on the agitators' phones...even if they don't have one yet."

Sabbatini slipped the paper into his breast pocket. "That shouldn't be a problem. Their quarters are inspected several times a day. Guards have duplicate keys for all the lockers."

"Will your men be on the island?"

"Security on Lampedusa is handled by a private contractor. My troops will helicopter in upon receiving word of the incident. I have it on good authority that we will receive a tip that another attack is about to occur."

"There will have to be casualties," said Borgia. "Italian blood must be spilled."

"At least it will be quick. A warrior's death."

"Patriots," said Borgia.

"It will appear as if the agitators detonated the Semtex themselves. Later the pistols and grenades will be found, what's left of them. It will be all the proof we need."

"More than enough, one hopes."

"And Melzi, our distinguished minister of the interior?"

"Everything is set for Torino. His men have identified several terrorist cells. The cells have been provided similar stores of explosives and weaponry. The chemical signature of the plastic explosives will be the same across the board. It may take a few days, a week even, but there will be no denying a high level of coordination between the groups. Only one conclusion can be reached."

"A revolution," said Sabbatini.

"A failed revolution." Borgia's phone rang. His sister. He sent the call to voice mail. The phone rang again. "Will you excuse me, Massimo? Family."

"Of course."

Borgia walked out of earshot. "What is it, Beatrice? Really."

She was hysterical. "Hadrian is dead. He killed himself. He jumped, Luca. He jumped."

"'Trice, calm yourself." Borgia turned and saw that Sabbatini was watching him intently. It was critical he not betray the slightest worry. "What do you mean, he's dead? I spoke with him earlier."

"He had been beaten. His face…his eye. There was blood on his shirt. He walked right past me and jumped."

"Jumped? I don't understand."

"From the top of the hotel."

"*Gesù e Maria.*"

Borgia managed to calm her and listened as she relayed the events more clearly. There had been a party of sorts, a business gathering to launch one of HW's new funds. Hadrian Lester had gone off to speak with an Arabian sheikh. She didn't know who the man was or what they had discussed. Lester had returned twenty minutes later looking as if he had been severely beaten. Worse was his mood. He had been distant, inconsolable, utterly bereft, as if something terrible had befallen him.

"A sheikh? You're sure?"

"Yes."

"Was it Tarek?" he asked, even though he was certain Tarek Al-Obeidi was elsewhere.

"I don't know," she answered unsteadily. "I don't think so."

Borgia told his sister to find a friend and stay with her. He would call back shortly. He ended the call and gestured to the paratrooper. Two more minutes. He dialed the number for Kruger. The call went to voice mail immediately, indicating that the phone was powered off. Kruger never turned his phone off when working.

Hadrian dead. Kruger MIA. Something was wrong.

Next a call was made to the Singaporean minister of defense, General Teck Koo. *One of us.* General Teck answered promptly. Borgia related that a man who did some work for him had gone missing in Singapore. No reason for concern, but he was hoping Teck could check if he was in the custody of the authorities. A small problem: he doubted that the man had valid identity papers on his person. He offered a brief physical description. A word about his nationality. And, finally, if Teck did locate him, could he see that the man was released in the shortest of delays. After a labored silence, Teck agreed.

Borgia ended the call. He refused to panic. Setbacks. Nothing more. Had not Caesar lost a quarter of his legions before conquering the Germanic tribes? He drew a breath, though not entirely successful in camouflaging his anxieties.

"Everything okay?" asked Sabbatini.

"My sister. She fears her husband may be having an affair. She is distraught."

"Women." Sabbatini shrugged. A subject about which he knew too much.

Borgia managed a laugh, even as the enormity of the problem hit home and his bowels turned to water. Sabbatini clapped him on the back. The men watched the last crates being loaded onto the aircraft.

"We will be in Lampedusa by eight. A routine supply run. By midnight, all will be in place."

The men clasped hands. Years of discontent. Months of plotting. The day had finally come.

"Just a few more hours," said Borgia.

"And you?"

"Leaving in the morning."

"Be careful."

"You're not going to wish me luck?"

"Buona fortuna," said General Massimo Sabbatini. "Or should I say, 'Break a leg'?"

Chapter 54

Umbria

The call came three hours later as Luca Borgia was driving through the Umbrian foothills, approaching the Castello dell'Aquila.

The number appeared on his automobile's information screen.

Relief.

"Kruger?"

CHAPTER 55

Tel Aviv

*K*ruger? *Where are you?"*

Inside the software lab on the second floor of the SON Group's offices in Tel Aviv, Israel, fourteen hundred miles from Italy, Luca Borgia's voice rang out from the high-performance Piega loud-speakers.

"Utram Road. Standing in front of the Singapore Metropolitan Detention Center."

"Sounds like they're next door," said Isaac.

"Quiet." Danni patted Isaac on the back and pulled up a stool to sit beside him and Dov.

She'd counted on Luca Borgia to be a responsible businessman, and Borgia did not disappoint her. Minutes after receiving his May billing statement (nine days early), he had opened it, presumably scanned the contents, and saved it to his personal files. The Pegasus spyware was set free. For the past hours Danni and the combined team of the SON Group had been making a deep dive into Luca Borgia's world.

For all intents and purposes, she might have been holding Luca Borgia's phone in her hand. At her whim, she could access any app on it without the need for a pesky user name or password. In the parlance of spies, she "owned" him.

Borgia's image was displayed on a color monitor mounted on the wall. He had placed his phone in a dashboard holder, and she could see him in his camel-hair jacket and pink shirt, his forehead fairly glistening with

301

perspiration. She also knew his location to the nearest fifty centimeters as relayed to SON by the Global Positioning System that formed the heart of his Maps app.

A second monitor showed a map indicating his current location—traveling along Autostrada E35 in Central Italy. Thanks to the Maps app, they also knew that his home was the Castello dell'Aquila, the location where he parked his car most nights.

"*What the hell happened?*" Borgia demanded.

"*Riske.*"

"*You said he was finished. I believe your words were 'fish food in the Gulf of Thailand.'*"

"*He must have big lungs.*"

"*I don't see anything amusing about this situation.*"

"*You had to be there.*"

Isaac put the call on a five-second delay. "The other one, Kruger… Dutch?"

"South African," said Danni, who had an ear for accents. "Not Afrikaans. A native, I'd say. A tribesman."

Isaac turned off the delay. Once again, they were live inside Borgia's phone.

"*Listen to me,*" said Borgia. "*Hadrian Lester is dead. He took a dive off the top of a hotel right in front of my sister.*"

"*On his own?*"

"*Apparently. Suicide.*"

Danni recognized Lester's name from the emails De Bourbon had stolen from PetroSaud.

"*It's him,*" said Kruger. "*Riske. He saved the reporter.*"

"*General Teck Koo said you killed a seventy-year-old hawker. I told you to keep things nice and neat.*"

"*It couldn't be helped.*"

"*You said the same about Bangkok. That turned into a bloodbath.*"

"*It couldn't be helped.*" Kruger's irritation was evident, as was Borgia's.

"*So you say. Well, at least you have the flash drive.*"

"*When I tracked down Riske, he was in an Internet lounge. The flash drive*" *was inserted in his laptop. It would be wise to assume he downloaded some, if not all, of its contents."*

"Colonel Tan told me the drive was encrypted."

"If it's encrypted, it can be decrypted."

"For now, that's not a concern. The files are four years old. We're tied off on this end. All the better Hadrian's dead."

"I wouldn't share that sentiment with your sister."

Danni could see the mean smile on Kruger's face, whoever he might be. She didn't think it would be a good idea for him and Borgia to be in the same room, at least for now.

"So you believe it was Riske who beat him up?" said Borgia.

"Who else?"

"Which means Hadrian talked."

"People always do."

"Jesus Christ," murmured Borgia.

"How much did he know?" asked Kruger.

"Too much. He wanted to short the market. He promised me we'd make a killing. A hundred million at least."

"So he knew it's going down this weekend?"

"Yes."

"You didn't tell him anything more?"

"God no."

"You're sure?"

"Yes, dammit," said Borgia. *"This man Riske, does he know about our plans?"*

"Before, no. Now, I wouldn't be so sure. And remember, he knows your name."

Borgia could be seen banging the heel of his hand against the steering wheel. *"We're twenty-four hours away from changing the world,"* he said. *"We cannot allow this man, whoever he is, to interfere with our plans. Do you understand me?"*

"I do."

"Find Riske and the woman. This story ends now."

The call ended. Luca Borgia shook his head repeatedly, grimacing, frowning, baring his teeth. Danni had never seen a man so worried.

And she, in turn, felt worry's cold, dry fingers tighten their grip around her own neck.

Danni rose from the stool and paced the room. "He's planning an attack and it's going to take place within the next twenty-four hours."

"You should see some of the stuff we pulled off his phone," said Dov. "He's out there to the right of Attila the Hun and Genghis Khan."

"Some of our own countrymen share those beliefs, if I'm not mistaken," said Danni.

"So, what do we do?" asked Isaac.

"Get me a list of everyone Borgia has phoned in the past thirty days. Cross-check it against emails with those names. Tell me what you find." She turned to Dov. "Can we get into the Maps app...I mean into the measurement and reporting functions?"

"Sure."

"I want to know everywhere Borgia's been during the last month."

"You got it."

Danni moved closer to the two engineers. "It's imperative we find out what Luca Borgia has planned. And when we do, we tell Simon Riske. Everything else comes to a halt. Do I make myself clear?"

The men nodded.

"Okay, then." Danni drew a breath, charting out the next steps. "First thing, we contact that journalist and let her know that her life is still in danger."

CHAPTER 56

Singapore

Lights burned inside the sixth-floor apartment at 14 Fort Road. From his position outside the building's gates, Shaka made out shadows moving behind drawn curtains. Someone was home. Someone who believed he was still locked up and, therefore, that she was safe to pursue her investigation. He hoped that London Li had a guest. It would make things easier.

Shaka moved toward the entry. The night was hot and sticky, his shirt clinging to his back. The flags in the apartment building's forecourt hung limply. A car emerged from the garage. The gates to the compound opened slowly. Shaka slid inside as it passed him and turned onto the street.

In the lobby, a concierge sat at the reception, hypnotized by his phone. Shaka circled the building, descending the ramp to the underground garage, walking to the elevator alcove. A key was required to summon the lift. There was no indicator to show what floor either of the two elevator cars might be on. He waited a minute, then another, growing impatient. It was late. Most residents were probably home and tucked in for the night. This was Singapore, not Jo'burg.

"This story ends now." Borgia couldn't have been any clearer.

Shaka tapped his foot, willing an elevator to come. Even now, London Li might be leaving her apartment, taking Riske with her.

"Screw it."

Shaka turned and ran back up the ramp and crossed the forecourt to the lobby. The door was unlocked. He went inside. There was a waiting area to one side with a couch and a glass coffee table. The concierge glanced at him, then went back to his phone. He was young. Twenty, skinny as a rail, his collar a few sizes too large for his thin neck.

Shaka walked to the counter, smiling in greeting. He threw out an arm and wrapped his fingers around the little man's throat, crushing his larynx as he might crush an aluminum can of soda pop, lifting the man off his feet. Angry at himself, at the concierge for doing his job, he tossed the man onto the ground, then rounded the counter and broke his neck. He couldn't stand the writhing and wheezing. A set of keys dangled from the man's belt. Shaka removed it.

The sixth-floor corridor was dim and deserted. As he advanced toward London Li's apartment, motion sensors activated the lights. He put his ear to the door. Silence, then voices. Footsteps.

Shaka pulled his knife from his ankle sheath, slipping the blade between his ring and middle finger. He tried the door. Locked. There were too many keys to try one at a time without alerting the reporter. He couldn't knock, as they would see him through the peephole.

He took a step back, recalling the apartment's layout, rehearsing his moves. Living area, kitchen to the right, past that a bedroom, an office area, and a bathroom. He studied the doorway and lintel. Both were wood, unreinforced. He lifted his leg, drew a breath, and with all his strength, aided greatly by the knowledge that should Simon Riske or London Li get one step closer to Luca Borgia, to jeopardizing the work of Prato Bornum, he, Solomon Kruger, would be a dead man, kicked the door at a spot immediately below the handle. The frame splintered. The door flew inward.

Shaka entered the apartment. Living area: empty. Kitchen: empty. Bedroom: empty. They were in her office. Of course they were. He charged down the hall, fist cocked, angled horizontally, the fat blade facing outward.

A man came out of the bathroom. Tall, dark haired. He held a plastic bag, a cat's paw dangling over its lip. Seeing Shaka, he froze. A handyman or janitor wearing dark coveralls. He was not Simon Riske.

Shaka peered into the office alcove to his left. Empty. The journalist was not here either. An unimaginable rage surged through him. He advanced on the man, who was shaking now, eyes blinking behind his glasses. One of his earbuds fell out. He must have been singing as he cleaned the apartment. It was his voice Shaka had heard.

"Keep things nice and neat."

Shaka let the knife drop to his side. With his other hand, he hit the man in the jaw. He fell to the floor unconscious, the dead cat sliding out of the bag.

Sixty seconds later, Shaka was back on the street walking down Fort Road.

Where were they?

CHAPTER 57

Singapore

Simon walked alongside London through Terminal 2 of Singapore Changi Airport. It was nearly eleven. At the sales counter, he'd purchased two business class seats on the midnight flight to Zurich and onward to Nice. The clerk informed him with a gracious smile that he must be a lucky man. Until a minute before, the flight had been entirely sold out. They'd just that second had two cancellations.

"Imagine that," Simon said.

He had traded Michael Blume's ill-fitting suit for an outfit from a men's boutique in the airport's vast shopping emporium. Heather trousers, a navy polo shirt, and navy zip-up jacket. He carried a leather valise with toiletries, a change of socks and underwear, sunglasses, and a second outfit. He'd even found a pair of driving shoes like he wore at home.

"What happened at the embassy?" London asked him.

"I told you," said Simon.

"How were you the only one to make it out?"

"How did I make it out?" Simon shrugged. "Dumb luck."

"I don't think so."

"He just shot the other people first. It could have just as well been me."

"Do you feel guilty?"

"Shouldn't I?"

"Of course not."

"At least now I'll have something to discuss with my therapist."

"You don't strike me as the type."

"Really? You probably know him. Dr. Jack Daniel's of Lynchburg, Tennessee."

"Who…oh, very funny. That's no way to solve anything."

"Well, then I have you to talk to."

They walked past an indoor waterfall, four stories high, some kind of engineering wonder, a little rainforest surrounding it, a fine mist cooling the air.

"You know," London said as they approached the security barrier, "I haven't thanked you properly."

"Really you don't have to. I was only—"

"Without the flash drive, we'd have a much more difficult time proving the case against Lester, HW, and all his co-conspirators. Rafael de Bourbon only gave me enough to get started. What I'd dug up was more supposition than anything else."

"It wasn't me. It was my friend in London, the kid who was able to break the code. He's the person to thank."

"I'm not used to people who don't like talking about themselves."

"There are a few of us left."

"When this is over, I want it all. Every last detail."

"Or else?"

"I'll do to you what you did to Hadrian Lester."

Simon stopped walking. "Promise?"

London, looking at him a second too long, was standing a little too close. He could feel her body touching his. She nodded, her eyes saying, *Oh, I promise. I'll do worse, even.*

London's phone buzzed. She broke away, yanking it from her pocket. "Text," she said. She read it, her face clouding.

"What?" asked Simon.

London read it aloud: "'Solomon "Shaka" Kruger has been released from the Singapore detention center. On orders from Luca Borgia, he is to find and kill you and Simon Riske. Take appropriate precautions. Signed, Gabriel.'"

"Do you know a Gabriel?"

London shook her head, eyes glued to the phone, fingers banging at the screen. Who is this?

A response came back immediately. Keep your phone on for further messages. Others are now involved.

Please. Who is this? she typed once more.

No further text came back.

"Shaka is out," she said.

"I heard."

"Do you believe it?"

Simon didn't answer, his expression saying enough.

"He can't be, I mean…" London trailed off, shamed by her boasts about her countrymen's incorruptibility. "Of course, you're right. We have to believe it."

"These people," said Simon. "Borgia, Prato Bornum, they mean business."

"What does he mean, 'others are now involved'?" London asked.

"Not sure," said Simon. "We have to assume that Gabriel is a friend. My guess is that he is an intelligence professional."

"From where? Singapore?"

"Right now it doesn't matter. What's important is that he or they know about Borgia."

"But how?"

"There's always a way, London. You know that." Simon motioned toward the security line. "Let's make our way to the gate. I'll feel better once we're there."

London began to check around her. "This is the airport. There are police everywhere."

"Lester said that Prato Bornum came from all levels of government, business, the military. If Gabriel is correct about Shaka having been released from jail, it's not a big leap to imagine someone helping him get into the airport. It's not like there's only one way in and out."

"You're scaring me."

"That makes two of us."

"What are you going to do if you see him?"

"Let's go," said Simon. The fact was, he had no idea.

They reached their gate fifteen minutes later. Most of the passengers had already arrived. Seating in the waiting area was limited. Simon led them to a far corner against the windows. Their aircraft, an Airbus 380, the largest commercial airliner in service, seemed almost to press itself against the glass. Simon surveyed the area, then excused himself to place a call, moving several strides away. He checked his watch. Four thirty in London. Harry Mason answered on the first ring.

"There you are."

"Thought I'd better check in."

"Glad you did. Just got off the phone with Lucy's clinic."

"Is she all right?"

"Doing a bit better, actually, last I heard. But I wasn't talking to the doctors. Billing."

"Christ." More jolly news.

"They wanted to let you know that they'll be needing another fifty thousand pounds at the end of the month. Sooner if possible. Do you have it?"

Simon said he did. Barely. "Tell them not to worry. I'll wire it in the morning."

"Got it."

"What about her condition? They promised to know more by now."

"No change, but apparently that's something."

"Have you seen her?"

"Was by the clinic yesterday. She has some color in her cheeks."

"Was her mother there?"

"No. No one mentioned seeing her either."

"All right, then."

"Am I allowed to ask where you are or when you'll be back?"

"Far away and as soon as possible."

Simon ended the call, noting that London was also on her phone. Probably her editor.

The first boarding announcement was made. Simon suggested they be among the first in line. He picked up his bag and walked to the gate, where an agent had begun scanning boarding passes. A group of well-dressed passengers swept past in the first class line, entering the aircraft through a designated door. Among them, a proud, iron-jawed woman with jet-black hair in traditional Indonesian dress.

"Did you see who that was?" said London. "Nadya Sukarno."

"Two guesses where she's going."

"Zurich with a connection onward to Nice and a room at the Hôtel du Cap-Eden-Roc."

"It's going to be quite a gathering."

"The Cannes Film Festival is going on right now, isn't it?"

"It is."

London watched as Sukarno disappeared down the gangway. "I remembered something. I took a look at all the earnings reports issued by HW for its first Future Indonesia fund. One of the investments they made was in a film company, Black Marble. I thought the beta on that one was a few standard deviations above the norm."

"The 'beta'?"

"The risk. You have to be crazy to invest in the movie business, right?"

"How much did they put in?"

"It didn't say, only that they held a majority stake in the company."

"I know a little about Black Marble," said Simon.

"You do?"

"It's run by a man named Samson Sun. Strange guy. That answers my questions about where he got his money."

"Sun is Sukarno's nephew. He's been popping up in the local papers' entertainment pages."

"That right? I did a small job with him just last week."

"You're joking!"

"File it under 'small world.' He invited me to the premiere of his first movie the final night of the Cannes Film Festival."

"Do you remember what it was called?"

"*The Raft of the Medusa.*"

"Like the painting?"

"You know that one?"

London gave him a look. Who didn't know that one?

Simon was thinking back to the afternoon in the Louvre, admiring the painting, an enormous canvas, the figures depicted larger than life, and Delphine saying it was too gruesome, which of course made him want to study it longer. "Apparently, the movie is about a boat that went down in the Mediterranean five years back."

"The *Medusa*. It was a big story. Five hundred refugees drowned. Only ten survived after a harrowing ordeal. I'm not surprised they turned it into a movie."

They boarded the aircraft and took their seats on the upper deck. No sign of Sukarno. Business class not quite up to her standards. Why should it be when you can afford ten thousand dollars a seat?

After stowing their bags, London consulted her phone again, looking up all mentions of the film. There was a transcript of an interview with Samson Sun and the cast, most of whom played themselves. Simon recalled seeing them on the boat, seated at Sun's table.

Chapter 58

The luxury towers at 22 Drake Court, Sentosa Island, stood on a rise at the end of a long drive, surrounded by dense forest on every side. Shaka crouched among the trees, draped in shadow, waiting for a car to approach the gated entry. Besides the gates, there were walls to keep intruders out. He could scale them easily enough. But a place like this had cameras, trained security. He needed a better way to get inside. Headlights approached. The sound of a well-tuned motor. Shaka felt his heart beat faster. "Come on."

Someone had told Simon Riske about London Li's rendezvous with Hadrian Lester. It couldn't have been the journalist herself or Riske would have warned her not to go. Therefore, it was someone else. Someone close to her. Someone at work. Most likely her boss. It took Shaka all of ten minutes to find the *FT*'s webpage and learn the name of its two managing editors: Anson Ho and Mandy Blume. He checked publicly listed property records and found addresses for both of them. He looked for pictures of them. Ho was Asian, light-skinned, probably fifty. Blume was European, blond, rough around the edges. Then— *Bang!*—he saw it. A photograph of Mr. and Mrs. Michael Blume taken at a black-tie dinner given by Harrington-Weiss. He had no doubt who Simon Riske had spoken with.

The car slowed, dimming its high beams. A BMW. Four doors. The gate began to open. The car came to a halt.

Shaka dashed from the shadows, assaulting the car as if it were an enemy vehicle, throwing his elbow through the driver's window, needing a second blow before the safety glass crumbled and fell away. He thrust his knife into the man's chest, once, twice, three times. With his free hand, he opened the door and folded the driver, dead or close to it, headfirst into the footwell of the passenger seat, the car still in gear, beginning to pull forward. He slid into the driver's seat and closed the door.

The gate stood open. He continued up a long curving road, then to the left into the covered garage. No keys at Drake Court. Magnetic keycards.

He parked the car, then took the elevator to the forty-second floor. The doors were stronger here. He partially covered the peephole with a corner of his thumb and knocked.

"Coming." Then: "Who is it?"

"Simon Riske."

The door opened. The blond woman held a phone to her ear, saying, "Simon? But I thought you were—" the words catching in her throat.

"Hello, Mandy. We need to talk."

CHAPTER 59

Paris

Mattias rolled into Paris early Friday evening. A pewter sky hovered low, the streets slick after a spring downpour. They'd come from the east, across the German plain, over the Rhine, through Saarbrücken, then into France. Omar, the driver, had found asylum in Sweden like him. Hassan, whom they'd picked up at the refugee center in Ingolstadt, had been denied entry to Europe after the tragedy. His path had led him to Syria, Greece, then northward up the Balkan Peninsula—Macedonia, Albania, Croatia—and finally, after seven months, Germany.

To look at, the three were brothers. All came from North Africa. Mattias and Omar from Tunisia, Hassan from Mauritania. Their features were markedly European—straight noses, prominent cheekbones, slim, well-defined lips. Their eyes, though brown, were light. It was the color of their skin that marked them as foreigners.

Mattias called out instructions as they drove. Straight on the Boulevard Macdonald. Left on Rue d'Aubervilliers. He had never been to Paris, and though he knew it as a great world capital, he was unimpressed. To him, it was an endless parade of soot-stained concrete, abominable traffic, and hostile faces.

"Porte de la Chapelle," said Omar, banging his hand on the wheel. "How hard can it be to find?" Traffic slowed and he laid on the horn, to no effect. In his former life, he'd been a taxi driver, an excellent one in his own estimation.

"Right at this street," said Mattias, motioning for Omar to turn. "And here, right again." It was at Porte de la Chappelle on the northern rim of Paris that the immigrants had taken up lodging.

Omar spun the wheel. The car disappeared into the shadow of the Périphérique, the elevated eight-lane highway that circled the city perimeter. They rounded a corner. In an instant, they'd reached their destination.

In the dank, shadowy enclaves beneath the highway, a patchwork encampment of domed tents had been set up, hundreds of them, multi-colored mushrooms springing from every crevice for blocks. Their occupants milled about in droves, spilling onto the streets, unmindful of the traffic passing within inches. The smell of burning wood and unwashed hordes penetrated the car.

"Keep going," said Mattias. "Turn left here. Find a place to park, then we can call him."

"A place to park," said Omar, surveying the uninterrupted line of automobiles filling every space. "You might as well ask me to fly to the moon."

They made six circuits of the surrounding area before finding a space. Omar killed the engine and the three men climbed out of the Volks-wagen Polo. It was a small car for the tall men and the long drive had been taxing. They stretched and clapped their arms and joked around. Mattias spotted a boulangérie and went inside to buy them sandwiches and drinks.

"You must pay," shouted the clerk, his arms gesturing for him to get out.

"I have money," said Mattias in his soft voice.

"Pardon me," said the clerk. "I was rude. It's just that…" He shrugged, motioning to the camp city outside his window.

Mattias purchased three cheese sandwiches, soft drinks (Fanta orange—his favorite), and an éclair for them to split. His companions devoured the food as if starving.

Omar tried the number for Mohammed, then frowned. "No longer in service."

"He said he was selling cigarettes," said Mattias.

"In a kiosk? He doesn't have a work permit."

"I think he meant on the streets. Loosies."

"Spread out," said Omar. As the driver, he had assumed the role of de facto leader.

Mattias crossed the road and started along a band of asphalt skirting some of the tents. The men were from everywhere. Tunisia. Algeria. Egypt. Libya. Sudan. Somalia. Ethiopia. "Do you know Mohammed from Tunis?" he asked over and over again, stopping at each knot of immigrants. It was like asking a European *Do you know Pierre from Paris?"* The answer was either a laugh, a dark look, or a simple "No."

He continued another two hundred meters, arriving at the end of the encampment. He found no sign of Mohammed and, to be honest, was no longer sure he remembered him. It had been a long time and not something he cared to remember. Still, a small, wiry man with an eye patch shouldn't be too difficult to find.

"My friend, my friend, come here." Three men looked him over. Not immigrants; locals, Parisians, though one might have had Middle Eastern blood. He knew their types, regardless. Bad news. They spoke to him in English. "Who are you looking for?"

Mattias's English was good. "A friend. I couldn't find him."

They didn't bother asking the man's name. "You have a job? Doing something here? Anything?"

"I'm from Sweden," said Mattias. "I'm not staying."

"Sweden. Pretty girls."

Mattias said, "Yes," and turned to leave. One of the men blocked his path. He was shorter than Mattias, but thick. "Maybe you work for us," he said. "Give your friends something to smile about. A little fun. You can make a lot of money. Understand?"

Yes, Mattias understood. Drugs. "Excuse me, but I must go."

A hand in his chest stopped him. "Have a look. If you want, take a smoke. Good stuff."

The hoodlum opened his palm to reveal a small plastic canister with ugly pale rocks inside. Crack cocaine or methamphetamine. "We front you. You sell it. Pay us later."

"Before you go back to Stockholm," said a second man, to his friends' amusement.

"No, thank you. Really. I must go."

The men closed in, the thick man pressing his chest against him. He smelled of garlic and cigarettes, and mostly of perspiration. Mattias held his eyes. Something inside him tensed. He was not afraid of fighting. He was not afraid of anything anymore.

The hoodlum backed off, offering his colleagues a disappointed shrug. "Out," he said. "On your way, Swede."

They found Mohammed two hours later, returning from Clichy, where he had spent the day selling cigarettes for one euro apiece. He had gotten fat over the years but still wore his eye patch. Mattias remembered him without it, on the raft, after the Ghanaian had torn his eye out. They'd killed the Ghanaian the next day.

"Should I get my things?" Mohammed asked.

Mattias had forgotten how young he had been back then, just a boy. Ten, eleven. The youngest on the raft. He hardly looked older now. Mattias threw an arm around his shoulder. "I don't think you'll need them, do you?"

The four men burst into laughter and climbed into the small automobile for the long drive south.

CHAPTER 60

Above the Bay of Bengal

Two hours aloft.

The miniature plane icon on their seat-back monitor showed them to be cruising at a speed of 540 knots at 39,800 feet over the Bay of Bengal. They both had enjoyed a drink before dinner. In fact, they'd enjoyed two. Gin martinis per London's suggestion. Who was Simon to say no? It was the first real meal he'd had in days. A filet for him, béarnaise sauce, pommes soufflés. Fish for the lady. Pan-roasted sea bass with black bean sauce, a vegetable medley. The lights had been dimmed. Beneath a lavender canopy, they'd toasted their future with a snifter of cognac. Hennessy, this time Simon's choice. For the remaining ten hours of the flight, they declared themselves safe, out of harm's way.

"What's this?"

"What?"

"On your arm."

Simon adjusted his sleeve, pulling it lower. London slid it right back up, keeping her hand on his arm, her long, slim, beautifully manicured nails tracing the waves, the anchor, the grinning skeleton draped around it. "'*La Brise de Mer,*'" she said, almost too quietly to be heard. "Is that right?"

"It's French," said Simon, leaning closer. She'd tucked her oversized glasses in her hair. Her breath smelled sweetly of the liqueur and mint. "It means 'ocean breeze.'"

"*Mais, je parle français, Monsieur Riske.*"

"Of course you do."

"Were you a bad boy?"

"Depends on how you define 'bad.'"

"I think you know." London reclined her seat halfway. Simon matched her. He had been trying not to look at her, not that way. He knew she valued her intellect over her beauty. She'd already called him "patronizing." He didn't want to add "lech" or just plain "rude" to the list. Yet here they were, face-to-face, the world and all its pain and sadness far below.

So he looked. At her eyes, her lips, her hair, her skin, the notch at the base of her neck, at the cleft of her breasts. She was exquisite, every feature demanding attention, inspiring a gasp.

"Let's just say I wasn't always the gentleman I am now."

"You mean the gentleman who sprays Mace in a man's face, hand-cuffs him to a table, and slams his head onto the pavement until he's unconscious? The gentleman who knows how to break a man's fingers to force him to talk? What did you used to be? A hardened criminal?"

"Well," said Simon, "yes."

"You're kidding, right? *You're not?*"

"This," he said, pointing to the tattoo, then running his fingers over the back of her hand. "This was my outfit. The police referred to us as 'organized criminals.' Not the Mafia, exactly, but what passes for it in Corsica and parts of the South of France—Marseille, in particular."

"You're from Marseille?"

"Long story. Born in the U.S., parents divorced early. Grew up in London, then shipped to France when my father died. I guess we can blame it all on the French."

"They usually are the cause of most problems," said London.

"To the French," said Simon, lifting his snifter.

"*Chin-chin,*" said London, touching her glass to his. "Before, when I said I wanted to thank you...I really wanted to thank you for saving my life. So thank you."

"It's what gentlemen do."

She gazed at him, closed her eyes and opened them, her lips parted. It was a look every gentleman recognized, and only a scoundrel ignored.

Simon kissed her.

"And you?" he said, after.

"Me?"

"No tattoos? History of organized crime? Lengthy prison sentences?"

"Not unless Beethoven, Bach, or Brahms were gangsters."

"Music."

"Piano."

"No wonder your hands are so beautiful."

"Look closely. Broken knuckles. A car door. End of career."

"I'm sorry."

"So was I. Not anymore."

"Me neither, then. We wouldn't have met."

"Move to Singapore?"

"Probably not in the cards." Simon raised his eyebrows. "*London…* London?"

"Ditto." She continued to look at him, mischief and maybe something else in her eyes. "I have a secret."

"Oh?"

"I'm a bad girl." She kissed him, longer this time. She raised her seat back, unclasped her safety belt, and stood, brushing her body over his as she made her way to the aisle. "Coming?" she whispered in his ear, a nip on the lobe.

Simon watched her walk to the lavatory. It was the big one, the one for handicapped passengers. He waited a moment—no wheelchairs, walkers, or flight attendants in sight—then rose.

He knocked once, softly.

Like a gentleman.

Chapter 61

Jerusalem

Transcript of conversation / Names of participants redacted

Time: 16:15 GMT

"So?"

"The Doctor is hard at work caring for his patients."

"Are they giving him any problems?"

"None. He's looked after these kind of things—patients, that is—before."

"Will they be well enough to leave the hospital tomorrow afternoon?"

"The Doctor asks if all five must leave at the same time. One is giving him a bit of trouble. Nothing serious, mind you, but given the type of medicine involved, he would like additional time."

"Out of the question. We have only one ambulance free."

"I will tell him. He wanted you to know that the patients are remarkably robust. Some of the strongest he's operated on in years. He thanks you for the medicine. He says he is certain that upon their release, the patients will be more than able to accomplish any task you have in mind."

"Convey my thanks to him."

"What is the latest time he can stop treatment?"

"The ambulance will arrive at nine a.m."

"Can you delay it?"

"It is a six-hour drive to their home. Rain is forecast for the first part of the journey. Under no circumstance can the ambulance travel at speeds greater than the limit. Part of the route is under construction. There may be a slowdown."

"Why not fly?"

"We can't risk anyone seeing the patients. As you can imagine, security in and around their home is stratospheric."

"To be expected."

"Will you be coming, my friend?"

"Sadly, no. I must return home. My master had been asking for me. It doesn't do to keep the young prince waiting."

"I had so hoped to see you."

"Next time."

"In a better world."

"Thanks be unto God."

"Ciao, my friend."

"There it is."

Danni ended the playback and set down the transcript. She was not in the offices of the SON Group but inside a SCIF—a sensitive compartmented information facility—at a Mossad outstation in the hills above Jerusalem. It was midnight. Seated across the table from her was Avi Hirsch, deputy director of Operations, Covert.

"Am I allowed to ask where you got this?" Hirsch was a sallow, hatchet-faced fifty-year-old, a lifelong veteran of the "office," as its members referred to Israel's foreign intelligence service.

"A client."

"Really?" Hirsch looked at her askance. He'd known Danni for twenty years, give or take, had been one of her first trainers upon her intake and her case officer on several ops that ran beautifully and several that did not. "Tell me something, Major Pine, since when do you install your software on a client's phone?"

"Long story," said Danni. "I saw something I shouldn't have. Maybe I even looked for it. I decided to do something about it. I'm not the devil, you know."

"You had some of us fooled," said Hirsch. "Keeping to yourself, pretending you don't know us."

Danni offered a weak smile. Guilty as charged. She'd declined Avi Hirsch's requests for help on more than one occasion. Her company didn't give away its software for free and the Mossad was notoriously tightfisted. "So, what do you think?"

"What do I think?" Hirsch said, giving a nasty laugh. "I think those two men, whoever they may be, are talking about building bombs. Explosives. Whatever you want to call it. It's obvious, isn't it? 'Patients' are explosive devices."

"Agree," said Danni. "I'm thinking vests. A concealed explosive device of some kind. An IED. Whatever they're discussing, it's sophisticated and requires some degree of expertise."

"And it's being transported tomorrow morning at nine a.m. local time—wherever that may be—for what sounds like immediate use." Avi ran a hand across the back of his creased neck. "Jesus, Danni, you're laying a real-time situation in our lap."

"'The Doctor,'" she said, an eyebrow raised playfully. "Suppose that isn't just a clumsy codename. Suppose that's what he's really called. Ring a bell?"

"Syria," said Hirsch. "We were running an operation against a terrorist named Al-Adnani, the self-proclaimed leader of the Islamic State in Iraq and the Levant. I think it was 2015."

"Aleppo," said Danni. "They had a guy who made their bombs—IEDs, vests, little pressure cookers that could take down a small house. An Iraqi. We had him on tape. He was good. They called him 'the Doctor.'"

"I remember," said Hirsch. "Do you really think it's the same man?"

"Why not?"

Hirsch lit a cigarette and leaned his chair back, balancing on two legs. "Anyway, you've gotten our attention. It's not something we can ignore. Are you ready to tell us the name of your client?"

Danni set her clasped hands on the table. "Luca Borgia. Italian industrialist. Billionaire. Right-wing fanatic. Bankrolled the Northern League for years. Old-school fascist. A latter-day Mussolini with a great head of hair and a beautiful blond mistress."

"I thought your shop sold only to governments."

"Borgia is family." Danni explained the Italian's ties to the company, giving Hirsch an edited version of the events that had brought her to the smoke-filled room in the middle of the night.

"So the first voice is Borgia," said Hirsch. "I wouldn't have said he's Italian. Maybe a Swiss who'd gone to school in the States."

"The second's a Saudi," said Danni. "I'll tell you that for nothing."

Avi Hirsch nodded ruminatively. "I'm tempted to say I know him. Maybe it's just a hunch, but I'm guessing he's one of us. A professional."

"If we're right about the identity of the Doctor, that would figure. Can you run the recording through the VP database?"

"VP" for "voiceprint." The Mossad maintained a library of several thousand voiceprints belonging to individuals deemed worthy of interest to the Jewish state—politicians, military officials, public figures with some tie to Israel, and, of course, terrorists.

"Easier if we run the Saudi's cell number," said Hirsch. "We have a few people at Saudicom. But since you've been such a sweetheart to bring this information to our attention, we'll do both. Like I said, he sounded familiar. And not in a good way. He gave me a bad case of heartburn. I make it a point to follow my gut."

Danni forwarded him a copy of the recording. "All yours."

"Anything else you want to tell me?" asked Hirsch.

"Someone else is on to Borgia. Actually, there are two of them. A reporter for the *Financial Times* Asia named London Li. Solid record. Won some awards. And an American named Simon Riske, some kind of fixer out of London, used to be a banker, runs an automotive restoration operation these days. He was at the embassy in Bangkok when the shit hit the fan."

"And he got out?"

"The sole survivor. Apparently, he was a friend of De Bourbon."

"And they're giving chase?"

"Looks like it."

"To what effect?"

"Like I said, the whole thing is tied to a fraud. One of those involved was the vice chairman of Harrington-Weiss, a man named Hadrian Lester. Lester is dead. Killed himself a few hours ago. Jumped from the seventieth floor of a hotel in Singapore apparently after meeting with Riske, who'd beaten him up or tortured him in some way."

"Riske told him something he didn't want to hear."

"Probably that he knew about Lester's involvement in the fraud."

"Sounds about right. Something made Lester jump." Hirsch pulled a face. "Seventy floors. I'm impressed."

Danni laughed.

"This guy, Riske, he a pro?" Hirsch asked. "Retired Agency? FBI? Blackwater?"

"Not that I know," said Danni.

"Maybe we should hire him."

"Another day, Avi." Danni tucked a strand of hair behind her ear. "Borgia with Lester's help sicced an assassin on the woman, London Li. A man named Kruger. Riske broke up the play. Borgia's ticked off. He's sending Kruger after both of them now."

Hirsch wrote down the names, then summoned an assistant. "Run them down," he said, tearing the sheet from a notepad. "I want everything you can find. Trade favors if you need to. This is important."

Then to Danni: "Any idea where these two crusaders are as of now?" asked Hirsch.

"Last known location in Singapore. That was several hours ago. Kruger's a South African dual national. I did some checking. Possibly former German military. GSG 9. Dishonorable discharge."

"How many South Africans named Kruger can there be in the German military?" Avi Hirsch pushed back his chair. "This is some can of worms you're dumping in my lap. I'm tempted to have you recalled to active duty so you can help clean it up."

"I'm tempted to accept."

Hirsch stood, tucking the transcript under one arm. "If it gets out that we knew about this—and believe me, it will—and this attack succeeds, which given the time constraints, it will, there will be hell to pay that we didn't stop it."

CHAPTER 62

Back in Europe.

Simon walked down the concourse, keeping close to London. He had insisted they wait until half the passengers had deplaned before joining them. He made sure they didn't walk too quickly or too slowly, two faces in the crowd among a hundred others. He traveled often to Switzerland for his work. The feeling that he was back on familiar territory relaxed him, even with the specter of a free Shaka looming over them.

It was early Saturday morning, just past six local time. The long, immaculately clean walkway felt like a sanctuary, the dampened footsteps and the quiet hum of conversation lending the airport the hushed, respectful atmosphere of a modern church.

"But he's still in Singapore," said London. "Right?"

"He got into Thailand with the help of his friends. He could get into Switzerland." Simon nudged her shoulder. "And don't say, 'But the Swiss…'"

London smiled weakly. "Never again."

Simon had passed the flight reading Hadrian Lester's emails, learning everything about the man: his work, his family, his mistress, his tennis game, and, of course, the fraud. The emails went back months, years. There was nothing about the attack, nothing about Prato Bornum, and much too little about Luca Borgia, other than the usual family exchanges.

But there was plenty about Lester's criminal activity. It was all there,

329

writ in excruciating detail, even if it wasn't admissible as evidence. There was nothing they didn't know already. Almost nothing. Still, those first emails between Lester and PetroSaud back when it all started came as a shock. Small world indeed.

They descended the escalator and joined a throng waiting for the tram to the main terminal. Simon kept his eyes on the passengers lining up behind them, on the faces coming down the elevator. It was easy enough. The rough-and-tumble crowding of the Far East was a thing of the past. Nowhere did he see the thick blond hair, the coffee-toned skin, the blue eyes and massive neck. But this wasn't the place, thought Simon. Shaka would wait until he had them somewhere to his advantage, somewhere he could kill them and get away scot-free. And if Shaka knew they were stopping in Zurich, he knew they were continuing to Nice.

If he knew . . .

Of course he knew.

They boarded the tram for the ninety-second ride to the main terminal, greeted along the way by a hologram of a woman standing beneath the Matterhorn flanked by two flag-twirling countrymen. Prato Bornum was everywhere.

They took the stairs up a floor to the transit lounge. Shops, boutiques, kiosks, and cafés lined both sides of the hall. More passengers here, foot traffic headed in every direction. They consulted the monitors for their connecting gate. Simon stopped to change the rest of his Singapore dollars into Swiss francs. He checked his mail, seeing a note from Harry Mason about the new hospital bill. He opened the attachment and frowned. Fifty-two thousand nine hundred pounds. The second this thing was over he was going to drive to D'Artagnan Moore's office, turn him upside down, and shake him until every last pound, dollar, and euro fell from his tweed pockets. He was done with the art world.

"Two hours till our flight," said Simon. "Let's grab a tea and go to the gate."

London put a hand on his arm. "If he's here, he'll know where to look for us."

"At least we'll see him coming."

Simon couldn't see Shaka trying to take them inside the airport. It was too public, the space too confined, in effect a sealed environment. At the outdoor market in Singapore, he could hit them and run, the open spaces his ally.

Or might he wait until Nice? The airport was smaller, less guarded. Watch for them to leave the terminal, follow them to a hotel…

It was pointless to guess. There was no way to map out every scenario. Simon would have to keep his wits about him.

They stopped at a café and ordered tea and coffee and fresh croissants. He slathered his with butter and honey. London followed suit. No country had better bread. Simple pleasures.

They arrived at their gate at ten minutes before seven. One couple had arrived before them, looking every bit as tired as Simon felt. He studied them all the same. The man fifty, a paunch, wearing a houndstooth trilby; the woman a few years younger, a frosted blonde, trim, hard-bitten.

Simon set down his bag at the row nearest the window and sat looking toward the wide concourse. London sat next to him, laying her head on his shoulder, the touch of her stirring memories of their passionate tryst. He didn't know if sex was better at forty thousand feet, but it was certainly fiery. Quick, uninhibited, and fiery. No time to worry about pleasing or impressing. Every man for himself. She had matched him every step of the way, maybe even led. Taboo obviously worked for her.

"I've been thinking," he said. "Maybe you can help me out. Prato Bornum—the one pure source—it's about closing borders, restricting immigration. Keeping undesirables out."

"Purity, piety, and preservation."

"But the movie, *The Raft of the Medusa,* is about the plight of refugees. I mean, ten out of five hundred survive. Pretty tough deal. Without having seen it, I'm going to say it's a sympathetic depiction of their plight."

"Yes."

"Well, if Nadya Sukarno is a majority shareholder in Black Marble and she bankrolled her nephew, presumably she knew what the film was about."

"Presumably."

"Why would she allow him to make a movie that espouses everything that Prato Bornum is against?" Simon waited for an answer. None came. "I don't get it."

But in his mind an idea had taken root. It was all interconnected. Borgia, Lester, Sukarno, Prato Bornum, and Samson Sun. All of it of a piece.

"This weekend," Lester had said.

But what? Where? When? How?

An announcement played over the public address system. "Lufthansa flight 564 to Nice is now departing out of Terminal A, gate 67. Passengers are requested to take the escalator to the lower level and await the bus for transport to the aircraft."

London picked up her bag.

"Wait," said Simon, placing a hand on her arm. "Terminal A is for commuter flights. Regional jets. Turboprops."

"So?"

"We're on an A320."

"It's a gate change. Everyone's going."

The couple he'd noticed earlier had stood and were gathering their belongings. A few others trickled out, following the signs to the escalators.

"Do you see anything?" asked London. "Is it him?"

Simon pulled up the Flight Tracker app on his phone and tapped in the flight number. A list appeared showing data for the past ten days: departure times, aircrafts, gates. "Lufthansa flight 564, an A320 out of Terminal B. Every day." He lowered the phone. "We're blown."

"What do you mean?"

"They know we're here. Someone's waiting for us at the new gate."

"Shaka?"

"Him. Someone like him. *Them.*"

"But how?"

"Your passport, maybe. Flight manifests. Did you tell anyone we were coming?"

"Just Mandy."

"Mandy? When?"

"Last night. When you called your office, I phoned to tell her where we were going. She's my editor. It's what we do."

"Call her," said Simon. "Now. But calmly. No stress."

London called Mandy Blume's cell. It rolled to voice mail immediately. She shook her head.

"Call the office," said Simon. "It's one in the afternoon in Singapore. She should be there."

London dialed the *FT*'s main number, identified herself, and requested to speak to Mandy. A moment passed and she signaled that Blume was coming on the line. Simon stepped closer. London held the phone so he could hear. "Mandy…Oh, Anson, hello. I'm calling for Mandy."

"Mandy's dead," said Anson Ho, co-managing editor. "She and her husband were murdered last night. I'm sorry."

"What? That can't be. I spoke with her at eleven. Anson, what happened?"

"Someone got into their apartment. Look, I don't have any more details. The police are here. I can't talk now. We're all in shock."

London dropped the phone to her side, the color drained from her face. "We did this."

"No, we didn't. It's just how things played out. I'm sorry."

"I'm going to be ill."

Simon placed his hands on her arms. "Not now, you're not. You can be sad later. Tonight, tomorrow. Right now, I need all of you."

Of course emotion overruled logic. "Why did they do this?" said London. "Oh, poor Mandy."

Simon gripped her tightly. "It's going to be all right," he said. "You need to believe that."

London nodded, not believing it. Not for a second.

Then he saw them. Two men standing a ways down the concourse, one older, silver-haired, the other younger, fit. Both trying hard not to pay attention to them, sneaking a look now and then. And then there was the couple a row of seats over who also hadn't heeded the announcement yet. They stood fussing over a carry-on. Maybe fussing too much. And what was that bulge in the man's blazer? There, beneath the arm.

Simon pulled up a map of the airport on his phone, running his finger over the layout. Outside. They had to get outside. And from there? He studied the map more closely. It took him a moment, but he spotted a path. Yes, just maybe. He looked at London, at her shoes. "Can you run in those?"

"Run? I guess."

He put his mouth to her ear. "Listen to me. We got lucky last time. Not going to happen again. This time it's all or nothing."

"I get the point," London said sharply.

Simon forced a smile. "Sorry. Didn't mean to…well, you know."

"I'm ready."

"Leave your bag here. Just you and me flat-out."

"But I don't see anyone."

"They're here. Believe me."

"Not my laptop. It has everything."

"London."

She nodded, gathering herself. "Where are we going?"

"Just follow me."

Simon rose wearily, stretching, looking at his watch. "Excuse me," he said, approaching the couple in the next row of seats. "Are you on the flight to Nice?"

Hesitation. A look passed between the man and woman. "Yes, we are," said the man in the trilby hat, a German speaker, heavy accent. "Holiday. We are about to head down to the new gate."

"I doubt that."

Simon shoved the man against the window, one hand at his throat, the other delving inside his blazer, finding nothing, no gun. Only a fat wallet. The man offered no fight, his eyes blinking wildly. *Who is this madman?*

Simon released him, framing an apology. "I'm sorry...really I—"

The woman hit him, a fist to the cheek, staggering him. He fell back as she dug her hand into her handbag, eyes narrowed, a ball of will. He grabbed her wrist as she brought a pistol out of her bag, the gun a stainless-steel semiautomatic. He slammed her hand against the window, using his free hand to forcibly pry it from her fingers. She kneed him, missing by an inch, bruising his thigh. The man—*her husband*—hit Simon with a chop to the back of the neck. Simon spun, pistol-whipping him across the face, opening a gash to the bone, the man tumbling onto a bank of chairs. Simon looked back at the woman, kicking her in the sternum, her body colliding with the window, her head striking the glass with force. She collapsed.

The two men surveilling them approached hastily, caught unawares by Simon's attack. Simon brought the pistol to bear. "Don't even think of it," he said, in German, walking toward them. "Down on the floor. Now. On your belly, arms extended."

The men raised their hands and complied. Simon kicked the younger man in the ribs, crouched, took their pistols, slid them across the floor. "Put them in the trash," he called to London.

London gathered up the guns, holding them by the muzzle as if they might scald her, rushing to the trash, dropping them in.

By now, several passengers had gathered, concerned. Simon fired a shot into the ceiling. The people took off running. Europeans knew how to react to an active shooter. He found a pair of handcuffs and cuffed the men together, then struck the younger man at the base of his skull, rendering him senseless.

Simon scrambled to his feet.

"Now what?" said London.

"Outside. Follow me."

Simon headed down the concourse, London at his shoulder, passengers peeling out of their way. He pushed through a set of double doors leading to a gate on the lower level and descended a flight of steps to a waiting area. The room was deserted. Windows on all sides. The tarmac and runways beyond. He tried the doors. Locked. He kicked the handle and hopped back. "That hurt."

A folded wheelchair was propped near the agent's desk. He hurled it at the window, shattering it, then finished the job with a cylindrical metal trash receptacle, wielding it to clear off the remaining shards of glass.

Footsteps behind them.

"They're coming," said London, glancing over her shoulder.

Simon jumped over the transom, helping London. They were outside. He headed left toward the bonded warehouses, delivery docks. He hugged the terminal building, all manner of vehicle passing them. Fuel trucks, vans, baggage carts. At the sound of a siren, he turned his head. A police cruiser, blue-and-whites flashing, barreled across the airfield, effectively blocking their path.

To their right, fifteen meters across the tarmac, was a freestanding concrete shed, candy-striped barriers surrounding it—DANGEL, a prominent construction company, stenciled across them—the shed door open.

Simon ran to the shed, vaulting the barriers. London found her way through. A sign on the door showed a lightning bolt. *"Vorsicht. Heizung. Strom."* Danger. Heating. Electricity.

"In here."

Simon entered the shed, closing the door after London, using the pistol to break off the door handle. Stairs led belowground to a high-ceilinged corridor that appeared to run endlessly in either direction, a strip of fluorescent bulbs high on the wall providing a dim, stuttering light.

"What is this place?" asked London.

Simon pointed to a large-bore steel pipe running along the center of the ceiling. "Runway heating. Hot water passing through the pipes melts the snow and ice during the winter."

"Which way?"

Simon pointed to the right.

"But that's away from the terminal."

"Hope so. There has to be an access point at the other end."

"And from there?"

"We'll see. We have a better chance the farther away we are."

"But they'll know we came in here."

"Eventually," said Simon. "But not which way we're going. There are three runways. That's a lot of exits to cover. Feeling lucky?"

"You said our luck had run out."

"Did I?"

They began to run, London setting the pace, the corridor indeed endless, passing one junction then another, similarly endless corridors stemming from each. Already fatigued, Simon began to wonder how long runways were. Two thousand yards? Three thousand?

He pulled up, placed a finger to his mouth. Voices. The patter of running feet. Closer. Closer. Fading. Fading. Gone.

"You good?" he whispered.

"Just go," said London.

"You first," he said.

London set off. It was apparent she could run faster and farther than he could. He redoubled his efforts but still found himself fighting to keep up. Minutes passed. Then far, far away, a shaft of natural light. Finally, they arrived at the end of the corridor. Stairs led to a door, ajar, as was the other, a sliver of sky visible.

Simon slowed, then stopped, hands on his thighs. He dropped the cartridge and counted the bullets. Seven. He couldn't shoot a policeman. Shaka was another story.

London regarded him, hands on her hips. *Ready when you are.*

"Okay," he said, straightening up, then charging up the stairs, out the door. "Come on."

They stood at the very end of the runway, fields of spring grass on either side, farther out a fence. A kilometer beyond that, a village. He looked to all points of the compass. No sign of their pursuers. He'd been wrong about their luck.

They crossed the tarmac, a jet barreling at them, landing gear lifting off the asphalt, nose climbing into the sky, the silver belly sliding overhead, jet blast flattening the grass, buffeting them, the noise ungodly.

At the fence, Simon gave London a foot up. She clambered over the wires nimbly. He followed suit, not quite so. A path led through a forest. Ten minutes later, they stood in the center of the village of Glattbrugg. It was eight o'clock. They had been running for an hour.

They walked to the train station and climbed into a taxi. "Forty-five Grossmuttstrasse," said Simon. *"Schnell, bitte."*

"You know your way around Zurich?" said London.

"Did I ever tell you what I do for a living…I mean, when I'm not doing this?"

The Garage Foitek in Zurich-Urdorf served as the official Ferrari dealership for the city of Zurich. Similar to the high-performance Italian sports cars they sold, the building was new, shiny, and sleek. Sacha Menz, the manager, spotted Simon passing through the doors and rushed to greet him. "Simon Riske, what are you doing in my town without telling me in advance?"

"Hello, Sacha. Flying visit. Can we talk?"

"Of course. Come into my office."

"Actually, the lot is better."

"Whatever you say. You look rather serious. How can I help?"

At 9:03, Simon and London left the dealership, turning left onto Birmensdorferstrasse, Simon at the wheel of a red 2015 F12 Berlinetta. The car belonged to the Grand Tourer class and was the fourth fastest road car Ferrari had produced, with a 6.3 liter, naturally aspirated V-12 engine capable of generating 730 horsepower with a top speed of 280 miles per hour. In short, an ass-kicker of the first order.

In minutes, Simon had them on the A4 driving south through the Sihltal in the direction of Zug. He kept his foot to the pedal, passing where it was safe, and often where it wasn't. There were radar traps everywhere—cameras carefully hidden to record your speed—and he knew that his friends at the dealership would be receiving letters from the traffic authority very soon containing photographs of an F12

Berlinetta with Simon and London visible inside the cockpit and their speed emblazoned across the bottom.

He wasn't thinking about the fines, however. Of course he'd pay them, though he'd never be legally allowed to drive in Switzerland again. He was thinking about something else altogether.

It had been too easy.

CHAPTER 63

Cannes

A light rain fell on the Côte d'Azur. Samson Sun left his villa in the hills above Cannes at nine for the short trip into the city. He was a cautious driver and negotiated the winding road well below the speed limit. By the time he reached the bottom of the hill, a line of cars ten long stretched behind his Bentley, including a tractor. He paid them no heed. With less than twelve hours to go before the premiere, he did not intend on risking injury.

He turned right onto the Rue Jean de Riouffe, pleased to be back on a straight, flat road. Traffic moved slowly toward the coast. It was the festival. He saw the first sign of it soon enough. Policemen in fluorescent vests stood in the median, directing traffic. Accompanying them were soldiers dressed in blue utilities, armored vests, machine guns cradled to their chests. He had made sure his credentials were visible, hanging from a lanyard around his neck.

Traffic came to a halt, and he checked his appearance in the mirror. His head was newly shaven, and was as smooth and white as marble. His glasses were polished and in the sleekest order. No suit today, but white linen trousers and a billowy black shirt with a scarf tied at the neck. He was a pirate ready to storm the Barbary Coast. A Chinese Captain Blood. Errol Flynn, beware!

It promised to be a busy day. Lunch at the Martinez with an American film executive. Tea at the Carlton with a French distributor. Then home to get ready for his big night. A facial. A manicure. A massage, if there was time. At five p.m., a car would arrive to take him to the Palais des

Festivals. There would be a press call, then the walk on the red carpet, a speech to the audience before the film began. And then, voilà: the world would get to see the wondrous project into which he'd put his very heart and soul.

But before any of that, a visit to the office of festival security.

A roadblock at the Boulevard de la Croisette stopped traffic dead. Traffic barriers lined the sidewalk. More soldiers patrolling. Policemen advanced on his car from every direction. All necessary, thought Sun, feeling safer because of them.

Several years earlier, on a warm summer night in Nice, a terrorist had commandeered a large truck and mounted the Promenade des Anglais, the broad pedestrian thoroughfare bordering the sea that ran the length of the town. Driving at high speed, he had mowed down hundreds of tourists, carving a mile-long path of death and destruction. Over eighty innocents were killed; dozens more injured, many severely. The French would not permit a second occurrence.

Sun extended his credentials through an open window along with a letter from festival organizers. The letter instructed him to appear that morning no later than eleven o'clock with two forms of government-issued identification at the office of festival security, where he would be issued a second set of credentials and tickets that would allow him to attend the premiere of his own movie.

The policemen moved the barrier aside and gave him directions where to park. Sun squeezed the Bentley through the gap and drove the short distance to the Palais des Festivals. The road ran parallel to the sea. Even with the rain, the Croisette bustled with activity. Banners hung from every streetlamp. Great billboards looked down on the street advertising one film or another. Reporters from television channels and entertainment journals around the world could be seen doing stand-ups in front of cameras. Executives strode imperiously to their next meeting. And there it was: the billboard for his movie. As he'd insisted, the largest billboard on the Croisette. It mirrored the film's namesake in the Louvre, a still showing the refugees clinging to a raft, really just an assemblage of debris from the sunken ship, hardly seaworthy, one man clearly dead, another half conscious, most strewn in poses of despair, but among them, one raising an arm high in the sky, head held high, and there at the far edge of the picture, the very, very top, the faintest outline of a ship. Salvation.

Toto, thought Sun, tremendously excited by it all, *we're not in Jakarta anymore.*

Sun parked in the subterranean garage behind the Palais and took the escalator to the main building. He found the security office tucked away in the rear of the ground floor. Thor Axelsson, the film's Icelandic director, had arrived before him, along with members of the production team and film crew. Sun was quick to note that some personages were missing.

"Where are the boys?" he asked the director, referring to the principal actors, "the four Mohammeds" who portrayed themselves in the film.

"On their way. A bit of a drive."

Sun had arranged for the four African actors to stay at the Ibis Motor Lodge just outside of town. It wasn't the Carlton, the Martinez, or the Du Cap, but as first-time actors they could hardly demand the finest lodging and amenities. The cost to transport them from their homes in North Africa and the Middle East was already astronomical. Further, he wasn't sure they possessed the requisite social skills to stay for days on end at one of the five-star hostelries that lined the Croisette.

There was a last reason. He didn't want any of his actors to get into trouble. Sun had the Indonesian's instinctive misgivings about those with darker skin. He'd seen them on the film set, and their crude behavior had done little to change his opinions. Either way, it was easier to keep them outside of town and bring them in for the premiere and any other press functions. He didn't want anything to spoil his big night. Samson Sun had every intention of returning to Cannes in the future. Next time, it would be with a film boasting big-name stars. A-listers only.

There was a commotion in the anteroom. The sound of furniture banging. Raised voices. Sun clutched his shirt to his throat as a pair of soldiers barreled into the room, followed closely by the four Mohammeds. Several uniformed policemen crowded in behind them.

"Please," said Sun, presenting himself to one of the soldiers. "Is there a problem?"

"These men, they work with you?" The soldier was broad and red-faced and brutal, with a tattoo running up the side of his neck and arms as large as cudgels. His name tag read, GALLONDE.

Sun nodded furiously.

"None has brought with them proper identification."

"That's impossible," said Sun. "We submitted copies of their identifications before traveling. All of them have been issued credentials."

The four Africans showed the badges hanging from their necks.

Gallonde paid them little attention. "Every person visiting the festival is required to carry two forms of government-issued identification with them while inside the festival perimeter. The badges are not enough."

Sun frowned. No one had ever asked him to show anything other than his festival credentials.

Gallonde picked out Mohammed from Tunis and Mohammed from Algiers, grabbing them by the collars. "These gentlemen have only their passports. Both will expire in less than six months. This, too, is a violation. They should not have been allowed into the country." The soldier then pointed to Mohammed from Marrakech and Mohammed from Alexandria. "And these two only have their refugee cards. No passport. The photographs are insufficient." He exhaled angrily. "They could be anybody!"

"Officer Gallonde," Sun began, in crisis mode, "I thank you for your diligence, your courtesy, and your professionalism. Let me assure you that these men are who they appear to be. You have my word."

"They are actors? Really?" Gallonde appeared unconvinced.

"The stars of my film."

Gallonde didn't like it, not one bit.

Thor Axelsson, the director, stepped forward to attest to the fact. "We worked together many months. They are who they say."

Just then the door to the office flew open. In rushed Jean Renaud, the festival director, in a state. He made his way to Gallonde and rattled off a barrage of questions, his indignation apparent, accosting the soldiers and policemen before they could respond.

Turning to Samson, he offered a heartfelt apology, on behalf of himself, the festival, and the French Republic. Samson realized he still had a lot to learn about groveling. Renaud then returned his attention to the offending officers, shooing them out of the room.

On his way out, Gallonde gave Sun and the rest of them a scathing glance. He would remember them. *Just try and get out of line. See what happens.*

With the help of Jean Renaud, Sun, the actors, the director, and all other interested parties were issued their credentials and tickets for the world premiere of *The Raft of the Medusa,* to take place at the grand Palais des Festivals that evening at six o'clock. TENUE DE SOIRÉE was printed on the bottom of the tickets. Black tie obligatory.

A last member of the creative team had not come for her credentials: the film's screenwriter, M. L. De Winter. But Sun knew her to be a capricious and temperamental sort. She had phoned the day before with a promise to attend. Sun didn't really care one way or the other. He was planning on wearing an ivory tuxedo from Tom Ford and looking sensational. He, Samson Sun, would stroll down the red carpet alone. The photographers could take as many pictures of him as they liked. It was going to be the most memorable night of his life.

CHAPTER 64

Gstaad, Switzerland

It was called the Chalet Edelweiss, and what the name lacked in originality, it made up for in splendor. Sitting atop a grassy hillock and framed by a wooded mountainside, the Chalet Edelweiss was three stories high, as wide as a European city block, and built in the traditional Swiss style with extended eaves, painted shutters, and window boxes filled to overflowing with geraniums. A flagstone terrace circled the home. The red field and white cross of the Helvetic Confederation flew on a pole in the garden, snapping in the fresh breeze. The only thing missing, thought Danni Pine as she gazed up at the house, was Heidi, Peter the Goatherd, and Grandpapa blowing his alphorn.

It was 9:15.

She was late.

But then, when had an Arab ever been on time?

Danni continued on her walk up the road. She was dressed to *"go wandere,"* as the Swiss called hiking—in knee-length shorts; a flannel shirt, sleeves rolled up to her elbows; sturdy boots with conspicuous red woolen socks; wraparound sunglasses to shield her eyes from the sun; and a knit watch cap to conceal her black hair. She walked with her hands dug into her pockets, a rucksack dangling casually from one shoulder. As she walked, she whistled tunelessly if only to distract herself from her fatigue.

It had taken Avi Hirsch and his unsleeping team less than thirty minutes to identify the name, occupation, and approximate location of Luca Borgia's correspondent. The phone belonged to the vile personage of Abdul Al-Obeidi, deputy chief of the Mabahith, the Saudi Arabian secret police, and the call had been placed in or near the town of Gstaad, high in the Bernese Oberland. Hirsch had required an additional thirty minutes to scour Al-Obeidi's file and discover that his family owned property in Switzerland in or around the same location. Namely, the Chalet Edelweiss, purchased for five million Swiss francs in 1989, currently valued at twenty-one million.

A private jet was commandeered from the air force and lifted off with Danni, its sole passenger, at 4:25 a.m. local time, landing at the Gstaad regional airport, the Flugplatz Gstaad-Saanen, at 8:20. She had with her a change of clothing and a bag of tricks Hirsch had provided for the occasion.

Danni continued another two hundred paces until well out of sight, then cut through a cherry orchard separating two homes and circled to the rear of the chalet. She sidestepped down the hillside, taking care to move from one tree to the next. She saw no indication of activity. The windows were closed, some shuttered. Every few steps, she stopped and listened. Only the chirping of the birds and distant roar of cars zooming along the Schönriedstrasse marred the calm.

Slipping off her rucksack, she opened the top pouch and removed a matte black Glock 18, making sure the extended thirty-three-round magazine was in place, slipping a second mag into her pocket. The pistol was capable of firing in fully automatic mode at twenty-rounds per second. She wasn't the most accurate shot. She flicked the fire selector to FULL AUTO. Better safe than sorry.

Next she removed a handheld TPD—a trace particulate detector—to check the air for explosive isotopes or chemical taggants emitted by all plastic explosives. She turned it on, checked that it was functioning properly, and stuffed it into her pocket.

She wore an earpiece and a mike on her collar, and via secure phone spoke to Hirsch, who was in the ops center in Jerusalem. "Going in."

"Careful."

She folded down the brim of her cap, revealing a miniature GoPro camera. "Getting it?"

"Clear as a bell."

Ten steps took her to the back door. A lightning glance through its paned windows. No one. She tried the handle. Locked. She kneeled. Out came the electric lockpick. She tucked the pistol into the waist of her pants, inserted the pick into the jagged opening, hit the charger. The lock yielded.

She freed her pistol and entered the house.

Stop. Listen.

Silence.

A long hallway. Wood floors. Doors on each side. Open one. The next. Pleading for the planks not to creak. The rooms empty.

Into a great hall. A stairway hugging one wall. One step, then stop. Across the hall, a door standing ajar. A light burning behind it.

Danni dashed to the door. Another stairway, this one leading to the basement. Concrete stairs. Thank goodness. The smell of damp earth, closed quarters. And then something else. Men's cologne. Danni held the pistol tighter, her finger resting on the trigger.

Down the stairs. Another corridor, a string of bare bulbs burning overhead. A great steel door at its end, one meter thick at least, and standing ajar. She drew out the TPD. The readout flickered, red numerals climbing steadily: *600...700...800*. The isotope count was off the charts. Plastique for sure. Semtex or C-4.

She entered the bunker. A worktable set on wooden sawhorses. Fragments of wire, batteries, and little slabs of putty. No, not putty. Plastic explosives. Orange, meaning Semtex. Her boot sent something skittering across the floor. Nuts, bolts, nails, ball bearings. A plastic garbage bin lay on its side.

"He was here," she said, so quietly as not to be heard at all.

"Careful," said Hirsch, his voice scratchy, distant, reception weakening. *"Langsam."*

Danni came closer, scouring the bits and pieces of bomb-making materiel, and picked up a small circuit board, hardly the size of a playing card. She recognized it as a component from a cellphone. It was used to detonate an IED or a vest by placing a phone call to initiate the charge, usually in cases the bomber might lose his or her nerve. She slipped her own phone from her pocket and snapped a picture of it, sending it to Avi Hirsch and the boys at the office. A navy-blue plasticine wrapper lay by her foot. She bent to pick it up. A label read, SEMTEX. PRODUIT DE LIBYE. Product of Libya.

She took a picture of this, too.

Across the floor, a toolbox sat, still open, and in disarray, not yet straightened up by its owner. Danni froze, her every nerve on edge. *You left trash behind. You left tidbits of wire and electronics behind, even explosives.* But no one ever left his toolbox behind.

She turned and there he was. An older man with a bit of gray hair, half-moon spectacles, and wearing a cardigan vest. Ten steps separated them. The pistol in his hand was pointed squarely at her chest.

"You aren't Abdul's daughter," he said.

"No," said Danni. "Quite the other thing."

She raised her gun.

Chapter 65

Cannes

Mattias and the others had arrived at the safe house sometime after five a.m. The rustic stone cottage sat high on a forested hillside ten kilometers above the town of Grasse. A man had been waiting in the drive. It was Sheikh Abdul from the mosque in Gothenburg. He had greeted them as if they were family, directing them to park the car inside a hay shed, before leading them inside and feeding them an early breakfast of warm milk, coffee, baguettes, and fruit.

After a fitful sleep, Mattias rose to meet the morning of his final day. As he stepped outside onto a gravel terrace, a warm drizzle falling, he smelled the fragrant air. It was the smell of lavender and saffron and thyme. Grasse was the world's most important manufacturer of perfume, and most of the ingredients used were grown in the area. He looked to the south, to the body of water that began some twenty kilometers distant and stretched to the horizon. The Mediterranean lay calm and placid beneath a low, gray sky. His thoughts drifted to the water, to a sunny day five years ago.

Once the sea had tried to kill him…

The *Medusa* sailed from the port of Sirte on September the sixth. It was a blustery, blue sky day, strong offshore winds, whitecaps as far as the eye could see, the boat swaying at dock, making passage of the gangplank hazardous.

When Mattias had arrived at the dock, he believed that he had come to the wrong place. The boat he was to travel on—the *Medusa*—already appeared to be full. Every square inch of the deck was packed with men and women standing cheek by jowl. And yet, two hundred more waited to board. It made no difference. The handlers continued to hurry the passengers aboard, forcing them into a cavernous hold belowdecks. It was into this dark hell that Mattias descended for the three-day voyage.

He had barely set foot inside when the stench overcame him. Everywhere men and women were vomiting, already nauseated by the boat's violent pitching and rolling. Though it was blustery on deck, no wind penetrated the fiberglass hull. The temperature inside was 90 degrees and rising. There was no water to drink other than the liter bottle he had brought with him. And no food, except for the packet of nuts and dates he had stuffed into his small travel bag. The single toilet was broken, overflowing with waste. Still more passengers came aboard.

Mattias, born Ibrahim Moussa, had arrived in Sirte a day earlier, after a month's journey from the city of Nemharat in the Atlas Mountains, 1,200 miles to the south. He was twenty-one years old, a son of a sheepherder, tall and lean, hungry for life's rewards but without the education, the barest minimum of wealth to be anything more than what his father had been, and his father's father. Disease had ravaged the flock. Summers were hotter; winters colder. Two years before, he had traveled to Nemharat for work. At first, he'd found a job in a leather-tanning factory. The work was grueling, twelve hours a day, six days a week, a thirty-minute break for lunch, usually tea and bread, his monthly salary two hundred dollars, eight dollars a day. Of this, half he sent to his family. He lived in a boarding house. Men slept in six-hour shifts, then made way for the next, fifty in a room, one toilet, an outdoor shower that often did not work.

One day he was fired. No reason given. He remained in Nemharat for a year, doing odd jobs to survive. Selling tea on the street, digging graves, cleaning the abattoir. Even for these jobs, competition was fierce. He lived on a dollar a day, often going without food.

And then he met a man from his hometown who promised he knew a way to change his life for the better. He would send Mattias to Europe, where he could get a job that paid him enough to send two hundred dollars to his parents each month and still have more than enough to live in his own apartment, buy new clothes, eat three meals a day, and perhaps even go to a restaurant or see a movie. One did not have to be a citizen or have a passport. It sufficed to land on their shores.

Mattias would be an asylum seeker. On arrival, he would be placed in an immigration facility—this the man described like a fairy-tale castle: clean beds, hot showers, a cafeteria, even women—and after two weeks, he would be released and allowed to find a job or, as was often the case, given one if Mattias was intelligent enough. The man could see that he was. Mattias was tall and handsome. He had straight white teeth, and did he not speak English, at least a little? A fortune awaited. All he had to do was work up the courage to leave. With luck, there were a last few spots available on a fine vessel leaving in a month's time.

But first, money.

It was not cheap to travel. The cost was three thousand dollars. Impossible, thought Mattias, his heart aching to miss such an opportunity. Three thousand dollars was a year's wage, two years' even. He could never come up with such a sum. The man from his village was undaunted. Surely Mattias's family had saved. And if they had not, the man had another proposition. He would lend Mattias a portion of the cost. Mattias would pay him back after he found employment in Europe. If not, his father could help repay him. Did his father not own five hundred sheep?

There.

Soon after, the deal was agreed upon. One thousand dollars up front, paid in cash—the family's entire savings, every last cent. The balance to be repaid over the next two years at a fair rate of interest, to be determined, naturally, by the prevailing market.

Taking in the chaotic scene around him, Mattias knew that the man had lied. What was he to do? There was no choice but to continue.

The *Medusa* finally left the dock at two p.m. The first day passed in a haze of misery. With no room to lie down, he stood the entire time, hemmed in on every side. Mercifully, the sea calmed. The epidemic of seasickness abated. A boat passed their way, offering water and food, though at astronomical prices. The mood aboard the ship soared. In a day's time, their feet would touch European soil.

Mattias was the first to notice the problem. It was late on the second day, nearing dusk. The sound of the ship's engine had changed. Its steady rhythmic chug had slowed. More troubling, it had developed a persistent cough, like an old man suffering from tuberculosis. He sensed the decrease in the ship's progress. The sound of the waves slapping the bow waned, the boat felt lower in the water.

He began to worry.

With difficulty, he made his way toward the stairwell, sliding and cajoling and worming his way closer and closer. His fingers could nearly touch the railing when suddenly the boat listed to one side. People toppled onto one another. A hue and cry came from topside. The acrid scent of smoke and fire stung his nose. Through the hatch, he saw a plume of smoke as black as night lifting into the air. Then, shooting up, tall, angry flames.

Panic.

Fear spread as if everyone was stung by the same hornet. In a rush to stand clear of the flames, the passengers above crowded to one side of the boat. Already unstable, the boat listed madly to port, her gunwales sinking below the surface, water pouring onto the decks and down the hatches, all kept open to allow precious air into the hold. The engine died altogether. The boat ceased moving. Unbalanced, making no forward progress, the boat became unseaworthy. In seconds, the *Medusa* lay on her side, taking on water, the ocean pouring over the gangway, flooding belowdecks.

Mattias hauled himself topside, fell, was trampled, got to his feet, fell again, and was struck in the head by a loose piece of equipment—he never knew what. The boat was sinking. From the hold, screams. Then an explosion as seawater engulfed the overheated engine.

Mattias found himself in the water. Unlike nearly all the others, he could swim; in fact, he was a strong swimmer, having grown up in the mountains and spent summers fishing and swimming in their crystalline lakes. The top of a storage locker floated past. He took hold of it, kicking to distance himself from the vessel as it slid below the surface, only the captain's bridge visible now. Then it, too, was gone.

Where was everyone? He had reckoned that at least four hundred persons had boarded the *Medusa*. Heads bobbed here and there. An arm reached for the sky, then went under. A few shouts for help, then no more.

Mattias spotted a small raft, hardly larger than a bathtub, a half-dozen men clinging to its sides. Other men held on to pieces of the boat that had broken off or floated away on their own. Fifty yards away, looking like a jaundiced iceberg, a large jagged slab of fiberglass rose out of the water.

Slowly the survivors congregated. Men. Only men. Pieces of the boat were lashed together, the iceberg—actually a section of the stern blown off when the engine exploded—the raft, the locker, a barrel, several life jackets, an oar, anything buoyant. A makeshift life raft was built, eight feet in length, ten across. Bottles of water that had come to the surface were gathered. From the beginning, there was no food apart from what the men had on their bodies, and that was now ruined by seawater.

Thirty-three men survived the initial sinking. All those belowdecks drowned immediately. Most above deck could not swim and perished soon after.

Of the ordeal, Mattias remembered little. The memory was too painful to recall, like placing his fingers around a white-hot teapot. It was easier that way. Others had told the stories.

It was a slow descent into madness. The lack of food, the absence of drinking water, the gradual loss of hope as day after day passed. Men succumbed to their thirst, gulping down saltwater, sinking into delirium. One swam off in search of a boat he was certain was nearby. *He could see it!* Another claimed he would ride a dolphin to shore.

Each morning they woke to find one less face.

There was more. The violence, the depredations, the primitive evils as the men set upon one another. And then, cannibalism. Men devouring the flesh of another. There was no fire. No time to dry the strips as jerky. Just a few knives to flay a dead man—the upper arm and thigh yielded the most—the pieces eaten raw. The liver, too. It was such a knife, one with a serrated edge, that left the scar on Mattias's arm.

And then one day—their twentieth at sea—a boat appeared. A vessel of the Italian Coast Guard. They were saved.

Ten of five hundred three.

The incident became known as *The Raft of the Medusa,* named after a painting Mattias had never heard of and, certainly, never wanted to see. The *Medusa* he had known was enough.

Five years had passed since.

In that time, he had fallen in love, started a family, found gainful employment and an occupation he enjoyed. A baker—who would have dreamed it?

So why a suicide vest? It was not jihad. Martyrdom was a word that held no meaning for him.

At his core, there was a black, festering hole. Since he'd set foot back on land all those years ago, he'd been more dead than alive. The passage of time had changed nothing. Thoughts of revenge were never far away. Over time, they had grown ungovernable, ever demanding his attention. He came from a cruel, unforgiving land, a land where words mattered little. Only actions.

So why the vest?

Because, as the sheikh had said, it was his chance to turn his suffering to the advantage of others. The world must know that there were others like him. Others with little or nothing. But people all the same. Human beings with the same hopes and ambitions and dreams as any other. They must not be forgotten.

Did a man need a better reason to wish to make a difference? By his actions, he would give those left behind hope.

And, of course, there was the money. The second part of the sheikh's promise to him. But his soul did not wish to contemplate his sins when it had so little time left.

CHAPTER 66

Cannes

Simon's route took him past Zug, along Lake Lucerne, and through the town of Altdorf—no sign of William Tell or Gessler—then into Gotthard tunnel, spitting him out in the Tessin, then skirting Lugano before entering the lake district of Northern Italy. The change upon crossing the border was marked: the roads rougher, litter strewn in the weeds, buildings run down, covered with graffiti. Past Milan, then a straight shot to Genoa and the Mediterranean, 200 kilometers per hour all the way, the Ferrari's V-12 purring like a tiger on the prowl.

At the four-hour mark, they reached the coast. Snarled weekend traffic cost him an hour. It was nearly two when they crossed the border into France just before Menton, jumping onto the autoroute that wound through the mountains above Monaco, the Tête de Chien offering a mute greeting, before returning to the sea at Nice for the last few kilometers to Cannes.

Home again.

The villa stood at the end of a short drive off the main road. To look at, it was a modest dwelling, typical of those on the Côte d'Azur. White-washed walls, clay-tile roof, wrought-iron fixtures over recessed windows. Old, billowing pepper trees shaded the walk to the front door. Simon took the heavy ring knocker and banged twice.

The door opened. A slim, blond woman hardly old enough to drive gazed at him dully. "You called about delivering some contracts?"

"Something like that."

"I'm Jen. Samson's assistant. I'll get him."

"Do that."

They had stopped first at the port, looking for the *Yasmina,* only to be told that Samson Sun was not aboard. Simon had said something about being an executive for a film studio and that he must have mixed up where they were supposed to meet. The skipper had taken one look at the Ferrari, at London in the passenger seat, and given Simon the address of where Mr. Sun was residing for the length of the festival.

Simon walked into a spacious living area: high ceilings, exposed rafters, art on the walls, sliding doors leading out to a manicured grass terrace. Beyond soft, rolling hills, the Mediterranean beckoned under a royal-blue canopy.

"Not bad," said London.

"Not bad at all," Simon agreed.

As they admired the view, Samson Sun entered the room with an audible clearing of his throat. He was dressed for the premiere in an ivory tuxedo, a black silk scarf draped around his neck. "Excuse me," he said. "You can't barge into someone's home without their permission."

Simon turned. "Hello, Samson."

Samson Sun didn't miss a beat. "Riske. Where's my painting?"

"It's not yours. It belongs to the Rijksmuseum of Amsterdam."

Sun bristled at the suggestion, then seemed to think the better of it. "At least I know it was authentic," he said, his good-natured self once again.

"Don't be too sure," said Simon.

"Back for another? Look around…No Monets. I bought the place with all furnishings. If you see something else that's been stolen, help yourself." He took note of London. "Who's your friend?"

Simon introduced them, leaving out that she was a reporter for the *Financial Times.* Sun took to her, as he did to all beautiful women, gripping her hand too long, asking her why in the world she was with Simon when she could be staying at his, Samson Sun's, villa. The Sun charm offensive.

"I'm not here to talk about art," said Simon. "I'm here to take you up on your invitation to the premiere."

"Too late. All the tickets are spoken for."

"Two just came free."

"What's that supposed to mean?"

"Hadrian Lester and his wife won't be attending," said London.

"Who?"

"Come off it, Samson." Simon stared at the man. "Didn't your aunt tell you? Lester's dead."

"Aunt Nadya?" said Sun tentatively. How did Riske know her? "She might have mentioned something." He took a few steps and fell into an oversized armchair. "What are you here to talk about, then, if it isn't art?"

"Like I said, your movie."

"What about it?" asked Sun, already softening, gesturing for them to take a seat on the sofa across the room.

"We looked at your press conference online," said London. "It's your first film. Where did you get the idea?"

"The screenwriter. M. L. De Winter. She approached me—a friend of a friend—hoping to make it as a documentary. I suggested it might work better as a drama."

"Tell the story on a more personal level," said Simon.

"Yes," said Sun, smiling a bit. "Indeed. That's the beauty of the film, of film itself. It allows the viewer a glimpse into a character's heart, as well as their mind."

"So the film is sympathetic to the refugees' situation."

"Asylum seekers," said Sun. "Fleeing from oppressive regimes. How could it not be?"

"And your aunt was okay with this?"

"My aunt? What does she have to do with my film?"

"I think we both know her political views."

"She can be a bit conservative," said Sun. "So what?"

"I'm just wondering," Simon went on, "since Future Indonesia is a majority shareholder in your company, Black Marble Productions, and since your aunt is not only Indonesia's minister of finance but also manager of its sovereign wealth funds, why she would agree to finance a motion picture that lionizes the plight of individuals with whom she has a fundamental disagreement. The money to finance your motion picture, *The Raft of the Medusa,* it came from your aunt."

"How would you know that?"

"Public knowledge," said London. "It's in the fund's annual disclosures. You see, Mr. Sun, we've been taking a close look at Future Indonesia and at Harrington-Weiss lately."

"Who is 'we'?"

"I'm sorry," said London. "Mr. Riske failed to tell you that I'm an investigative journalist for the *Financial Times.*"

Sun shifted in his seat, uncertain how to view Riske or London: friend or foe. "I'm a motion picture producer. I have nothing to do with my aunt's affairs either in government or in business. If she decided to finance my film, it's because she realized it represented a good return on her investment."

Simon laughed, the banker in him rebelling at the suggestion. "How many films ever make money?"

"This one will, I promise you."

"So your Aunt Nadya gave you free rein to make any movie you wanted?"

"Of course," said Sun. "She recognizes my skill as a creative professional. One might even say genius."

"That's not the way I see it," said Simon.

"You're a glorified mechanic, some kind of thief. What would you know about the movie business?"

"Very little, but I know lot about you."

Sun swallowed, offering a nervous smile to London, adjusting his scarf, his glasses.

Simon stood up from the sofa and approached Sun. "I know, for example, that you worked for a finance and investment company named PetroSaud. I know that it was you who came to Tarek Al-Obeidi and

Hadrian Lester with the scheme to defraud your country's sovereign wealth fund."

"P-preposterous," stammered Sun. "Really…"

"You see, I don't think your aunt had any say in it at all. How could she? The money she stole from Future Indonesia…you thought it was yours."

Simon set Lester's phone on the table near Sun. "That belonged to Hadrian Lester. Last night on the flight from Singapore, I spent eight hours reading his old emails. They go back years. It's all there. I don't need to remind you. After all, you're something of a 'genius.'" Simon kneeled in front of Sun, hands on the chair, effectively imprisoning him. "You worked with my friend Rafael de Bourbon at PetroSaud's Geneva offices. It was you who told Paul Malloy not to pay him the bonus he was due. Do you remember what you did?"

Sun didn't answer. He had somehow become smaller, weaker, the real person minus the clothes and the house and the trappings of his stolen wealth. Suddenly, he looked like an overgrown child playing dress-up.

"You suggested that Malloy invest the bonus in your company," said Simon. "In Black Marble."

Sun's expression hardened. Though the room was cool and pleasant, he had begun to sweat.

"Did he?" asked Simon.

Sun hesitated, then shook his head.

"Smart man."

Simon stood quickly, eliciting a gasp from Sun. He strolled around the room, needing a minute. "It all started in that office. All of this. You, Rafa, Malloy, Lester, your boss Tarek Al-Obeidi. I'm missing someone. Oh yes, Luca Borgia. The big boss. You met him there, too, didn't you?"

Sun nodded. He might not really be a genius, but he was smart and canny. He could see where this was leading.

Simon continued: "I wonder what Luca Borgia will say about all this. That it was you who gave Malloy that lousy advice. That it was you who started this whole chain of dominos. Borgia is Al-Obeidi's partner, has been for years. You know what happened to Paul Malloy, don't you? And Rafa?"

The first real look of concern. "Why would I? I'm busy working."

"You don't read the papers? Look at CNN?"

Sun shook his head, eyes moving between Simon and London, preparing for bad news.

"Your aunt didn't tell you?"

"No."

"They're dead. Borgia had them killed."

"That's ridiculous."

"Malloy took a fall off a cliff in Switzerland last week. Rafa was killed in the shooting in Bangkok, or didn't that piece of news penetrate your Hollywood bubble?"

"This is true?" said Sun, looking to London in hopes she might say otherwise.

"This is true," she said.

"Borgia is cleaning up your mess," said Simon. "We're here because of you and your petty actions."

"And me? You think he'll kill me?"

"You tell me. You know Borgia better than I do."

Sun bit his lip, a hand caressing his smooth scalp, eyes darting here and there. The plotting and scheming and conniving had begun.

Simon went on: "I'm afraid that after word gets out of your involvement not only in defrauding your own country's funds but also in setting up investments to defraud many others, you won't be producing many more movies. Unless you can produce them from jail."

"If, that is, you live that long," said London.

"Did you come here to threaten me?"

Simon sat down in a rattan chair near Sun. "I came to ask you if you are part of Prato Bornum."

"What's that?"

"You tell me."

Sun pulled a face. "Prato what?"

Simon considered this, not taking his eyes from Sun. He was as dishonest as the day was long, functionally amoral, incapable of discerning right from wrong, concerned only with furthering his own best interests. *But*…he wasn't a killer.

"Has anyone come to you and asked you to do anything out of the ordinary regarding the premiere of your movie this evening?"

"I don't understand the question. I have nothing to do with the premiere, other than to attend it and speak to the audience."

"Samson, listen to me. This is your chance. Your one opportunity to mitigate all the crimes you committed at PetroSaud. If you can tell me anything about the attack that Luca Borgia has planned this weekend…anything at all that might help us to stop it…I'll make sure your efforts won't go unrecognized. The court looks favorably on contrition and cooperation."

"Attack? What in God's name are you talking about?"

"You don't know?"

"Who do you think I am? I'm a creative professional. A motion picture producer. I'm stunned. First you tell me Luca Borgia wants to kill me. Now you speak of an attack. What kind of attack? What am I to say?"

"We don't know yet," said Simon. "My guess is that it's tonight. At your premiere."

Sun hauled himself out of his chair and walked to the bar, taking a bottle of Pellegrino from the fridge. "I tell you this right now, Mr. Riske. No one is going to interfere with the premiere of my motion picture."

Simon went to the bar and took a bottle of mineral water for himself and for London, opening them, and handing one to her. He returned his attention to Sun and said: "Has Luca Borgia ever had any involvement with your movie? Think about it for a second."

Sun shook his head violently. "Never. Why would he? I barely know him. It's been years since—" He stopped.

"Since what?" asked London.

"It was years ago…"

"Go on," said Simon.

"He might have been the one who told my aunt about the documentary."

"The documentary?"

"They were at lunch. His foundation had been approached by a British researcher who wished to make a film about the refugee crisis, in particular the story of the *Medusa*."

"M. L. De Winter?"

"Yes. Aunt Nadya said Luca was laughing about it, saying the woman was certainly barking up the wrong tree. Of course I immediately recognized it for what it was: a tremendous idea."

"Of course you did," said Simon.

"Did Borgia know your aunt well?" asked London.

"A little too well from what I gather," said Sun, dripping sarcasm.

"They were intimate?"

"If that's what you call rutting with a brute like that, then yes. He seduced Milady, too. I've never forgiven her."

"Milady?" said Simon.

"Our screenwriter. That's her first name. Milady De Winter. It's her nom de plume. You know, from the novel. *The Three Musketeers*."

Simon gripped the bottle harder, sure it would shatter, wondering if his shock was visible. He'd suspected it for days now, had dredged up one excuse after another not to believe it. Here it was. Proof. Alexandre Dumas couldn't have come up with anything better himself. *Small world*.

Sun's eyes left his, newly engaged by something else. Something behind Simon. A look of surprise, then terror. There was a wet whisper, a fléchette blown from a dart gun. The left lens of Sun's eyeglasses shattered. He staggered. Blood, dark as wine, flowed from the ruined socket. The diminutive producer toppled over backward, lay motionless on the floor.

"Hello, friend," said a smooth, South African–inflected voice. "Good to see you again."

CHAPTER 67

The vests looked smaller than Mattias had imagined. Black nylon. Sleek. Professional. A succession of pockets circling the waist. A zipper and straps to secure it. He saw no wires; then again, he would not be responsible for detonating the explosives contained inside it.

Four vests for four men.

"Once you put it on," explained Sheikh Abdul in a kind, patient voice, "you can never again take it off. After I have secured it, you must consider yourselves as having died and entered paradise. Do not be frightened. It will be easier this way. You will feel freer. What is there to worry about? Your soul has already passed to a higher plane and joined your ancestors. Your destiny is assured. You will feel only peace. The pains of this world are behind you. We should all be so blessed."

Mattias stood inside the bedroom alongside the men with whom, in the space of a few hours, he would end his life. The four looked on with rapt expressions. None appeared frightened. They had made their decision long ago. They would be happy to be finished of it.

"When you are inside the great palace," the sheikh continued, "you will take your seats and wait for the film to begin. It is essential that every last member of the audience be allowed to enter. Even one more infidel's death will please Allah. Ten minutes after the film has begun, you will rise from your seats, walk to the aisles, and take up your assigned positions, each of you occupying one corner of the auditorium. You will feel nothing. Perhaps a last pleasant sensation of warmth. It will be Allah embracing you to his bosom."

The sheikh looked from one man to the next, blessing them with his regard. "Questions?"

No one said a word.

"Who shall be first?"

Mattias stepped forward. He wore only his underwear, socks, and T-shirt. The vest might chafe his skin. It was essential that each man appear relaxed and comfortable. They had been ordered to smile as they strode the red carpet. To wave. To be the picture of happiness. Later, all would comment on their fearlessness. The world would know the Magnificent Four.

Sheikh Abdul lifted one of the vests in his hands solemnly, as one might lift the Koran during prayers. Mattias turned and placed his arms through the openings one at a time.

"Remain absolutely still," said Sheikh Abdul.

The sheikh came around to face him, carefully zipping up the vest, stopping just shy of the bottom of his neck. The vest was heavier than Mattias had expected, twenty pounds at least. He could feel the shrapnel inside the pockets, and he thought there must be a lot of it for it to poke through the fabric of the vest. This made him happy. He hoped his vest was the most powerful ever constructed.

The sheikh stepped closer, the tips of his fingers white as he closed the final snap. With care, he opened the breast pocket. Inside was a small flat red button affixed to some type of circuit board. The sheikh pressed the button very hard. A tiny bulb flashed red three times, then burned green steadily.

Mattias felt no differently now that he was dead. He had made his peace when he left his wife in their bed in Gothenburg. To his mind, he had died long ago, somewhere in the middle of the Mediterranean Sea.

The sheikh kissed him on both cheeks, then once additionally. "Peace be unto you, my son. *Inshallah*. God is great."

*   *   *

Thirty minutes later, Mattias walked to the front door followed by his friends. All were dressed in fine evening wear. Dark jackets and matching trousers. Shiny black patent-leather shoes. A white collared shirt and bow tie. All had showered and shaved earlier. No beards were allowed. None had ever looked more handsome.

There came a knock at the door. A man Mattias had never seen entered and handed Sheikh Abdul a package. A moment later, he was gone. The sheikh opened it and removed four laminated badges, each attached to a beaded-metal lanyard. He examined the pictures on each and handed them out in turn.

Mattias studied the picture on his badge, knowing that the man was dead. The sheikh had told him it was necessary. The actors could not be trusted. Surely they had been corrupted. Mattias did not know how they had been killed. It did not matter. The sheikh knew about such matters. Once he had let slip that he was a professional. Mattias only worried that someone might find them before the premiere. Then what?

He did not recognize the face on the badge, nor did he remember it from the raft. The man, Mohammed Tabbi, resembled him only in passing. They shared the same high cheekbones, the same shape of the eye, a similar nose and cut of the jaw. Nothing more. Were anyone to place it beside Mattias's face, the game would be up in a matter of seconds. But Mattias knew that he looked at men from his part of the world differently than a European might.

Minutes later, a van arrived. The sheikh escorted them from the cottage and helped them climb aboard. The vest was unnoticeable. Mattias might look a bit stockier than usual, but he was a thin man to begin with. Now he looked average. He breathed in the evening air, exulting in the sharp fragrances. Dusk was beginning to settle. The sky was yet a rich and welcoming blue. Through the back window, he saw Sheikh Abdul waving goodbye.

Mattias raised his hand and smiled.

CHAPTER 68

Cannes

Last I saw, you were lying on the ground handcuffed to a table leg," said Simon.

"It seems we both have a unique talent for looking after ourselves."

"I haven't learned how to let myself out of jail yet. You have me there."

"You need a better class of friends."

"I like mine just fine," said Simon. "Mind if I turn around?"

"You think I would shoot a man in the back?"

Simon turned, hands raised, held away from his body. He didn't want any mistakes. He was acutely aware of the pistol stuck into the waistband of his pants, hidden only by his untucked shirt. Had he chambered a round?

"It's over, Kruger," he said, trying to sound reasonable, unthreatening. "It's all coming out. Everything Borgia has been up to these past years. It's done."

"Says who?"

"The evidence is overwhelming," said London. "Hadrian Lester knew it. He decided to take the coward's way out."

"Lester," said Kruger with contempt.

"You can help us stop it," said Simon. "Where is the attack taking place? Shaka, please."

"You've got it all wrong. I'm here to make sure the attack takes place. Once you and the lady are gone, it will be easy to clean up the mess."

"Others have seen the files," said London. "It's all saved to the cloud. My newspaper has it all. No one can suppress the information."

"And we will find those people and make sure we put an end to their activities. It's what we do." Shaka smiled inquisitively. "Riske, tell me, how did you discover my name?"

"It's not just us. Others are involved. Governments. Intelligence agencies. They know all about Borgia and what he's planning. There's still time."

"Chain of command. First thing you learn in the military. Colonel Tan forgot it. He tried to tell Borgia what to do. Me, I don't bother with the bigger issues."

"A loyal soldier."

"Meine Ehre heisst Treue," said Kruger, echoing a Nazi slogan. My honor is loyalty.

"I thought the Germans ditched that one after World War Two."

"We are who we are," said Kruger.

"Why did you kill Mandy?" asked London.

"She was the only person I could think of who might have had an idea where you were. I couldn't allow her to inform you. Besides, she'd have written the story in your absence."

"So will someone else."

"We'll see about that."

"And at the airport?" said Simon.

"Borgia insisted on giving the Swiss a shot at you. He didn't want you to get a step closer. To your credit, I was confident you would slip through their fingers."

"Especially since you weren't there to help them."

"I owe you, brother." Shaka shook his head, eyes narrowing, sizing Simon up. "Too bad you can't come over to our side. Mr. Borgia would like you."

"The feeling isn't mutual."

"Not to worry. I wouldn't allow it to happen. You might steal my job."

"Doubtful. I prefer something with a little more security. I've got a feeling you're about to become unemployed."

"I see things differently." Shaka tossed Simon a small metallic box with a digital readout on its face. "Radioactive isotope detector. One of our boys painted you at the Zurich airport. Uranium-239. A little spray on your clothing. Done quickly. No smell. Virtually unnoticeable. Extremely rare. We can get a read on its signature at three kilometers. Don't worry, sweetheart, it won't kill you. We only use a little bit. And, no, we didn't follow you from Zurich. Why bother? We knew there were only a few places you might go. We picked you up on the autoroute coming into Nice, then at the port. From there, we didn't need a damned thing; we could see you from a mile away in that red machine."

Simon lowered his hands, a sign of capitulation. He needed to distract the man, just for a second. "And now?"

Shaka checked his watch. "Show's beginning soon. Did you figure it out?"

"I think so."

"Clever bastards. I'll give them that. The last people you'd suspect. The actors. Mr. Borgia is convinced all will go smoothly. It's my job to be on-site in case it doesn't." He crossed the room, the pistol hanging at his side. An invitation. "Here's what happened: You came to confront Samson Sun about his activities working for Hadrian Lester and PetroSaud. Sun broke down. Frightened for his freedom, he pulled a gun to shoot you. You were also armed. It appears that no one survived." A smile. "Darling, will you move closer to Mr. Riske. I don't think Samson Sun was *that* good of a shot."

"Stay where you are, London," said Simon.

Shaka raised his pistol, the fat barrel of the noise suppressor pointed at him. "Time to say our farewells."

A gunshot. An ear-shattering crack.

Shaka fell forward, off-balance, a gaping hole below his shoulder, gore everywhere. In a moment, the blood had drained from his face. A second shot. Plaster exploded from the wall inches from Simon's head. Simon threw himself to the ground. Kruger fell to a knee, fired a shot into the floor. Slowly, he raised the gun, eyes locked on Simon.

A third shot. Shaka's head dissolved in an opera of blood, bone, and brain. He fell face down on the carpet.

A tall, fit woman clad in black pants, black T-shirt, hair pulled back, advanced into the room, large-caliber pistol held in both hands. She moved the pistol to all points of the room. "Was he alone?"

"Yes," said Simon. He hadn't even cleared the pistol from his waistband.

"Everyone okay? You, there?"

London said she was, then was sick on the floor.

"And you?"

"Still in one piece." Simon pointed to the hole in the wall inches from his head. "You almost got me."

"I've always been a terrible shot." She stood above Shaka, appraising his corpse without emotion. She had done this before.

"Do we know each other?"

The woman lowered her pistol. "My name is Danni."

"Simon Riske."

"Yes, we know."

Simon recognized the accent as Israeli. "We?"

"Gabriel sent me."

CHAPTER 69

Antibes

Luca Borgia hurried through the park-like grounds surrounding the Hôtel du Cap. He saw the man seated alone on a bench set among a copse of olive trees. Young, Middle Eastern, dressed in a suit and tie—if not a client of the hotel, an associate or friend of one.

"I came at once when I saw the text," said Borgia. "What is it?"

"I have a message from Abdul Al-Obeidi."

"Why didn't he call?" asked Borgia, sensing at once that all was not well.

"Please sit. The Doctor is dead. Killed this morning at the chalet in Gstaad. An assassination."

"Who?"

"As always, we suspect the Jews."

"But how?"

"We must assume our lines of communication are compromised. My superior asks that you no longer contact him until such later date as specified."

"And tonight? Are we to go ahead?"

"There is no indication that the French security forces are taking additional actions."

"Do you know this for certain?"

"We have men at the highest level of their security apparatus. I have spoken to Sheikh Abdul. The chosen ones are on the way."

The man took a flip phone from his pocket. It was the kind of phone one purchased for thirty euros at a kiosk or convenience store.

"The number has been programmed into the phone," he said, handing it to Borgia. "The battery is fully charged. When you are ready, simply hit the 'send' key."

"And it will send a signal to all four?"

"Simultaneously." The man made the sign of an explosion with his hands. Then he rose and walked away.

Borgia watched him go, weighing the course of action he must take. The vests had arrived. The bombers were on their way to the festival. He looked at the phone. He could place the call now. End it once and for all. It would be worse if they were captured alive. They would be made to talk, to reveal all they knew. There was the location of the safe house, the identity of the man they knew as Sheikh Abdul. They would disclose the payments. The money would be tracked down to a numbered account at an offshore bank in the Caymans or Liechtenstein or Vanuatu, one of thousands maintained by the Saudi Mabahith. More proof.

He thought of calling Kruger. Had he killed Riske? Was there anything he, Borgia, needed to know? That was impossible. If his phones were compromised, then so might be Kruger's.

Theoretically, Borgia was safe. He'd done nothing wrong. He could pack his bags, climb on his jet, and be home for a late dinner. For the moment, however, he didn't care about being safe. He cared about Prato Bornum. He was so close.

And Caesar? Would he walk away on the cusp of his greatest victory? Never.

Neither would Luca Borgia.

He looked at the flip phone.

One call.

A spark to light the fire.

371

CHAPTER 70

Cannes

Simon pushed the Ferrari through the hills above Mougins. He knew these roads, had learned to drive on them from Marseille to Monte Carlo, and in the backcountry, too. Single-lane macadam tracks, no safety railings. Nothing between him and a five-hundred-foot fall over a sheer cliff. Cannes, Antibes, Juan-les-Pins were prime territory for a young car thief. Nothing taught you how to drive better than being pursued by a dogged cop, or a dozen of them. The prospect of jail, or worse, was ample motivation to keep the pedal to the metal.

Simon felt the same urgency as they neared Cannes, driving as fast as he thought safe, maybe a little faster. His mind was racing as rapidly as the car, but not ahead. He was speeding through the far more treacherous alleys of his past, advancing on the black heart of Delphine Blackmon, or as she now called herself, Milady De Winter.

He should have known.

She lay facing him on her immense bed, their legs intertwined, her head propped on an elbow, eyes staring down at him as if he'd committed a crime. Her naked torso glistened with sweat, her nipples erect. "Jesus, where did you learn to do that?"

"Do what?"

"That. I'm still shaking."

"Seminar at the bank. Management wants to ensure we keep our clients satisfied."

"Satisfied? That's one way of putting it." She ran her hands across his chest, tracing the latticework of scars, pressing against the ridges of muscle. They'd been dating for three months. He'd told her his story that night, about his past, about prison, his return to the law-abiding world. Not all of it, but enough. She kissed him, her breath sweet, her mouth no longer a cauldron of desire. Her hand went lower. She liked holding him, squeezing him until he responded, then instructing him what he was to do. She liked being in control.

"Now I'm going to teach you something," she whispered.

"Oh?"

"Don't…move…a muscle."

She pushed him onto his back and mounted him, waiting for him to stiffen entirely, then using him as an instrument, pressing herself against him, riding him, her motions near violent, without the least inhibition, until she gasped and shuddered and rolled off of him. She didn't care about his pleasure. That one had been for her and her alone.

Delphine.

He'd never met a woman like her, a woman of such wide and varied appetites, all of them pursued with a passion bordering on the fanatical. Sex stood at the top of the list.

She hadn't gathered her breath before she found the remote and turned on the television. Politics came in a close second.

"All those people with nothing. No one lifting a hand to help them."

Simon didn't need to open his eyes to know that she was talking about the unrest brewing in Venezuela. She'd traveled to Caracas the month before and had returned determined to expose the dictator's crimes.

"Isn't that their government's responsibility?" said Simon. "I mean, they have oil. Tons of it."

"'They' have nothing. The government supremos keep all the money for themselves. I'm sure you have plenty of clients from there."

"A few," said Simon. "Maybe I should frog-march them down to the basement and summarily execute them."

"It would be a start."

Simon laughed, though part of him thought she wouldn't mind one bit.

"And if the government can't help…or won't?" said Delphine. "Then what? Is it really every woman for herself? Every child? Have we come to that?"

"But we do help, Delphine. The Brits, the Americans, the EU. They provide billions in aid."

Delphine reared her head. "We should give billions more."

"All I'm saying is that sooner or later people have to solve their problems themselves."

"And if they can't? What if they need someone to solve them for them?"

Simon sat up, seeing that she was crying.

"Sometimes I just feel so damned helpless," she said. "I can't do anything about it."

"But you can," said Simon. "*You are.* All your work helps. Everything you write. It makes a difference."

"You believe that?"

"I do."

A disgusted laugh. A scowl. She pushed herself away from him. "As if words matter. One day, I'll show you. I'll prove to you I can."

Simon had had the answer all along.

The slow winter afternoons at the Louvre. The visit to the museum his last day with Delphine. He'd looked at the painting a hundred times, she for the first time. *The Raft of the Medusa* by Théodore Géricault. It was a giant canvas, sixteen feet by twenty-three. Survivors of a shipwreck clinging to a sinking raft, hardly more than a few planks lashed together, adrift on a rising sea beneath a turbulent sky. And yet...*hope.* There, at the top of the picture, far, far away, a sail illuminated by a shaft of sunlight. *A ship! Salvation!* One of the survivors, marshalling all the strength that remains in him, has pulled himself upright and raised a hand, waving a tattered shirt. A final desperate gesture. *Save us!*

And the ship had done just that. The men on the raft had been rescued. The painting, like Samson Sun's eponymous film, was based on a true incident.

And Delphine? All she'd said was that the painting was too gruesome. Surely it must have affected her, yet she'd said nothing more.

It had been right there in front of him all this time.

*   *   *

"Simon!"

Danni's voice brought him back to the present as the front wheel wandered off the asphalt. He jerked the wheel, correcting the path of the automobile. In the back seat, such as it was, London braced herself. But Danni was as relaxed as if they were taking a Sunday drive. She spoke in even tones, briefing him on how Israeli intelligence had come to be involved, beginning with her company hacking into Rafael de Bourbon's phone and laptop, then turning their attention to Luca Borgia, going on to describe what she had discovered at the Chalet Edelweiss.

She showed Simon the circuit board she'd found, explaining that it was commonly used in explosive devices detonated remotely by cellphones. She'd counted over twenty Semtex wrappers. She guessed there were at least three vests, maybe four. There could be more. She was not an optimist.

"Have you alerted the French authorities?" asked Simon.

"We talk to Paris. Paris evaluates the intel. They phone Cannes. In the meantime they tell us, 'the police are already on highest alert.'"

"You didn't tell me how you knew where we were."

"The same way we know about Borgia and the chalet in Gstaad."

"My phone?"

"Did you receive any strange emails recently? Something out of the ordinary or anything with an attachment."

"A hospital bill. But it was from Harry Mason. He works for me."

Danni shrugged unapologetically. He'd taken the bait. "I've been told you have some expertise in these matters."

Simon nodded. It was pointless to ask any more questions. The Israeli intelligence apparatus had turned its spotlight on him. They possessed as formidable a surveillance capability as the United States National Security Agency or British General Communications Headquarters, GCHQ. What they wanted, they got.

"For what it's worth, thank you," he said. "Mr. Kruger was not in a merciful frame of mind."

"Yes," said London. "Thank you, thank you."

Danni smiled, an amusing memory. "You were right back there."

"About what?" said Simon.

"That he was about to lose his job."

Traffic on Rue Jean de Riouffe moved slowly. It was after five. The premiere was slated to begin at six. Fifty-four minutes by the car's digital clock.

"Do you have any more information about the attack?" asked Simon.

"We were hoping you might be able to help," said Danni.

"It's going to take place at the premiere. Kruger said as much."

"I had a live feed from your phone. I heard." Cannes to Jerusalem back to Cannes. The new way of the world.

"Last night on the plane, I had an idea," said Simon. "I thought I had to be sick to imagine it, but it makes sense now that you told me about the vests. It's the movie, *The Raft of the Medusa*...well, the actors in it. Four of them are survivors of the tragedy. North Africans. Muslims, I'm guessing. They all have to have badges to get into the premiere, meaning they've already passed security checks. No one is going to stop them from entering the theater."

"Like the Bataclan," said Danni, referencing the ISIL attack on the crowded Parisian theater in November 2015 that had left ninety dead and dozens wounded.

"Worse," said Simon. "The Grand Auditorium in the Palais seats more than two thousand people."

"Four vests in an enclosed space. Fifty kilos of Semtex. It would be the Bataclan twenty times over."

"Just get Borgia," said London. "You said you know where he is."

"We do."

"At the Du Cap," said Simon. "They're all meeting there."

Danni's averted glance told him he was correct. "I have no authority," she said. "I can kill a bomber. The French won't like it, but they won't throw me in jail for the rest of my life. Luca Borgia is a different story. He's a billionaire, one with powerful friends. Our efforts have to be on stopping the bombers. Borgia, we get later." She looked sidelong at Simon. "Don't worry. We don't forget. Ever."

"What about killing the cellphone service," said London. "Cut that and a call can't go through."

"If we had two days and a judge's court order, that's a fine suggestion. Or do you want to sabotage every cell tower nearby? Good luck with that."

"And a mobile jammer?" said Simon, referencing a handheld device capable of disrupting all cellular communications in a limited area.

"I don't happen to have one on me," said Danni. "Do either of you?"

They arrived at the first roadblock. A policeman waved them toward an auxiliary road heading away from the Palais. Simon counted five shock troops milling behind him and an armored personnel carrier parked down the block.

"Without credentials, we can't get close," said Danni.

"*We* can't," said Simon. "*They* can." He pointed to the group of soldiers, clad in navy-blue utilities, vests, berets, submachine guns worn against their chest.

Danni narrowed her eyes, considering this. "I don't see any female commandos."

Simon gunned the motor, speeding down the street. He turned to her. "I'm looking at one."

A few blocks farther along, Simon pulled the car into an illegal space. It was quieter here. A typical Saturday afternoon at closing time. Only a few people about, most already at home, making dinner, preparing for a night out on the town. All three climbed out of the car, Simon offering London a hand.

Danni brought up the Pegasus app on her phone. "Borgia's still at the hotel. Room 302."

"I want to go," said London. "I can't help here. I'll do whatever I can to find him and let you know."

"That's a good idea," said Danni. "You sure?"

London said she was.

Danni went on: "If he's going to detonate the vest, he won't be using his own phone. He'll know that we can trace the call."

"And if I find him and he has the phone?"

"Don't shut it off. Don't do anything except put it in your pocket and keep it away from Borgia."

"London, you don't have to do this," said Simon.

"It's really no different from what I do for a living. Track down people. Pressure them into speaking with me."

"You want the gun?" asked Simon.

"And do what with it? Shoot myself in the foot?"

"Take it," said Danni. "You never know."

London held out her hand. Simon gave her the pistol. She tucked it into her belt and covered it with her blouse. Fast learner.

"Have you ever shot one?" he asked.

"Aim and pull the trigger. If it comes to it, I doubt I'll be far away from the target." London turned her attention to the car. "I'm more worried about this monster. I haven't driven in years."

"Don't worry," said Simon, patting the hood. "A Ferrari practically drives itself."

"Why don't I believe you?" London slipped into the car and adjusted the seat. She started the ignition and touched the accelerator, jumping at the engine's aggressive response.

"Go fast," said Danni. "Go very fast."

It was five twenty-seven Saturday evening.

The van moved slowly down the Croisette, the Palais in sight ahead, situated next to a large promenade, the ocean beyond that. They had been stopped once already, a policeman putting his head inside the driver's window, asking where they were going and to see their badges. "Palais," the driver answered. "Red carpet." All four held up their credentials and smiled as they'd been instructed. The policeman radioed a superior. A moment's pause, then he waved them forward. Barriers were moved aside. The van continued on.

Mattias wiped the sweat from his forehead. It seemed to him that they were in a country at war, so great was the number of soldiers lining the sidewalk. Behind them, a crowd of onlookers gazed at the van, at the dark faces inside it, many standing on their tiptoes, a hundred phones taking their photograph.

"Smile and wave," Sheikh Abdul had instructed them.

Mattias smiled and waved. Inside, though, he was a mess. His earlier pious certainty had begun to fade as soon as they left the villa and started the drive to Cannes. A new thought had come to him, growing with every minute, threatening to paralyze him. Worse than dying was the prospect of arrest, of spending the rest of his days in a prison cell. The worry ate at him as surely as acid eats through steel, attacking his confidence, his will to see the act through.

They passed beneath an imposing billboard advertising the movie. *Their movie.* They pointed at it and commented, awestruck. Mattias regarded himself, dressed in a tuxedo, driving along the Croisette in Cannes. For a moment, he forgot his concerns, forgot the vest strapped to his chest, and half wondered if he really was an actor. If that dark face on the billboard was him. Even at this distance, fame was intoxicating.

"Are you frightened?" asked young Mohammed.

"Of what?" said Mattias, astounded that his voice did not falter. "Either way, we will be at peace by the end of the day."

Mohammed nodded. He did not appear as convinced.

The van slowed and came to a halt. A second set of barriers blocked the road. Policemen swarmed the vehicle. The driver rolled down his window. Another policeman banged on the passenger-side door. The driver lowered that window as well.

"Credentials. Everyone."

Mattias and the others held them up.

"Give them to me."

Mattias took the badge from his neck. He looked at his friends before handing it to the driver, who in turn gave them all to the policeman. Mattias remained still, silently praying as the policeman examined the badges, taking pains to compare each to the four men seated in the van. The policeman's face darkened. Something was not right.

"Out," he said, speaking English. "Everyone out of the van."

The driver remonstrated in French. They were already late. Can't the man see, these are the film's stars! What could possibly be the matter?

The policeman opened the sliding door. A half-dozen soldiers stood behind him. They held their submachine guns away from their chests, barrels pointed to the ground, fingers resting on the trigger guards. Mattias could sense their apprehension, excitement even. Finally, a little action.

The policeman continued to study their badges, waiting. Mattias felt as if he were chained to his seat. To exit the van meant capture. Jail, if they could remove the vest. Either way, failure.

"Come now!"

Another policeman fought his way into the group and stuck his head inside the van, eyeing them with malice. He was blond and red-faced and brutal, a tattoo running up the side of his neck. He retreated, took the man with their badges aside. It was not a friendly exchange. The blond policeman snatched the badges from his colleague and thrust them at the driver. "Okay," he said. "See? I learned how to be a nice guy."

He gave Mattias and the others a withering look and slid the door closed.

Mattias saw his name tag as they passed through the barrier and toward the red carpet.

GALLONDE.

The soldiers were young, barely out of training, perhaps nineteen or twenty. They stood at the corner of Rue Pasteur and the Boulevard de la Croisette, marking the far perimeter of the security zone. Barely one kilometer from the Palais, Simon felt as if he were in a different city altogether. The sidewalks were nearly deserted. The occasional car passed by. A few shops had lowered their shutters, eager for the workday to be done. Even the grand hotels looked quiet, the Martinez, the Carlton.

Danni approached the soldiers at a jog, halting, a hand to her chest. She had let her hair down and untucked her shirt. Even with her muscular arms, veins popping, she appeared every inch the worried mother. "My daughters are locked in my car," she said breathlessly. "I don't know how I did it. Please, can you help?"

Only one of the soldiers spoke enough English to understand. "Your children are in the car?"

Danni nodded, leading the way, explaining that she was a tourist from Israel. Did they know Tel Aviv?

The soldiers exchanged a few words as they followed her across the street and into a parking structure. She pointed at a Peugeot station wagon. "Please. Can you open the door? I'm so scared."

The soldiers neared the car, heads bent, trying to peer inside.

Simon moved from his position behind a concrete pillar, striking the larger man with the butt of Danni's pistol. He dropped. Before his smaller colleague could react, Danni crushed the man's knee with a kick, spun him round, and placed him in a headlock, holding him until he fell limp, and then a while longer to make sure he remained unconscious.

It was over in fifteen seconds.

The harder part was undressing them. Even unconscious, the soldiers fought like lions, it being nearly impossible to pull the uniforms off their limp limbs. Simon's uniform fit him well. Danni's posed the bigger problem, but after rolling up the sleeves and stuffing the trousers into the tops of her boots, she looked the part. The vests, berets, and Heckler & Koch MP5 submachine guns completed the trick.

Simon used the soldiers' flex-cuffs to bind their hands behind their backs. He stuffed a sock into their mouths to keep them quiet. He ran up the aisle until he found an unlocked car and, with Danni's help, stuffed the soldiers into the back seat. He hoped it was enough to keep them out of commission.

"Now?" he asked.

"We do what every soldier here has been taught. We protect the Palace."

They set off at a jog toward the festival, slowing when they reached the first barrier, passing through without contest. The number of soldiers grew as they neared the second barrier. Few addressed them. Simon nodded and grunted, *"Salut,"* pouring on the Marseille accent. With his two-day stubble and brooding looks, no one thought to question him.

They arrived at the second barrier a minute later. The system was simple enough. Residents, business owners, and credentialed visitors were allowed inside the outer perimeter. Only credentialed festival-goers were allowed inside the second barrier. There was a third barrier on the far side of the promenade. Only those persons holding tickets to the film were granted entry to the Palais des Festivals.

Simon and Danni walked past the steel traffic barriers, maintaining the attitude of soldiers on patrol. Turning left, they crossed the esplanade adjacent to the Palais. A large number of people came toward them, many of them photographers busying themselves packing away cameras.

Simon began to jog, but Danni put an arm on his.

"Calm," she said.

Simon slowed his pace to a brisk walk.

They were late.

London gripped the wheel of the Ferrari as if holding on to a bucking bronco. The car was too fast, too powerful, too savage for her to control. A tap of the accelerator sent it hurtling down the road far too rapidly, the throaty, violent engine delivering frightening vibrations through her body. She could feel the tires gripping the asphalt—feel them—and this unholy communion between road and car and driver left her far too exhilarated, fearing for her life.

She followed the coast road out of Cannes, past the smaller marinas, and into Juan-les-Pins. The route veered south as it navigated the Antibes peninsula, gentle hills rising on her left, the scent of heated pine flooding the car. *Faster,* a voice urged her. *We haven't enough time. We're relying on you.* But was it Simon or the madly capable Israeli woman? Or both of them? Defying her every instinct, she kept her foot on the pedal and her mouth closed in case any second she might scream.

A sign popped up for the hotel.

No! She was going too fast to make the left-hand turn. Traffic approached in the opposing direction. *Faster!* Clenching her jaw, she yanked the wheel to the left and pressed the accelerator, the Ferrari leaping forward like a prisoner escaping her bonds as it cut across the oncoming lane, the roar of the motor more than loud enough to drown out the protesting horns.

Up an incline. Right onto the Boulevard J. F. Kennedy. She spotted tall pillars guarding the hotel drive. Still driving much too quickly, she turned too late, then overcorrected, the nose of the car narrowly missing one pillar.

She was there.

London braked much too hard as the Ferrari skidded to a halt in front of the Hôtel du Cap-Eden-Roc. Originally built as a private mansion in the style of Napoleon III, the hotel resembled a grand nineteenth-century country house. Leaving the car running, the muffled roar of the motor an affront to the pristine calm, she ran up the stairs and inside.

"Room 302," she shouted. "Mr. Borgia is in trouble."

A bellman hurried over. "Excuse me, madame?"

London hurried past him, searching for the elevator. "It's an emergency. He phoned me. Please. We must hurry."

The staff of the front desk, located in an alcove immediately to her left, reacted immediately.

"One moment, madame." A concerned hotelier went straight to a back office. A minute later, a well-dressed man emerged, rushing to her side.

"Mr. Borgia, you say? Something is the matter?"

London nodded, still gathering her breath. "I believe he's had a heart attack. Quickly, we must check on him. Room 302."

The manager looked at London, tears streaking her cheeks, a woman in distress, then at the Ferrari, idling by the front stairs. He had been trained that a client was never wrong. He had also been trained that a guest's privacy was inviolable. A final look at London's imploring gaze, her state of distress. "Follow me, please."

They rode the elevator in silence, except for London's imprecations that they must hurry. *"Il faut se dépêcher."*

They alighted at the third floor. The manager led the way, key in hand. By now, two members of the security team trailed behind them. The manager rang the doorbell, waited, then waited no longer. He inserted his key and opened the door. London barged past him, through an entry hall, through a grand living room, calling his name— "Luca!"—no sign of him here, and into the bedroom, light streaming through the tall glass doors, a view across a canopy of pines to the ocean beyond.

The bed was unmade, the sheets tangled. A peach-colored satin camisole lay on the floor; beside it, a pair of panties and stockings. Men's clothing was folded neatly on the chair. No sign of Borgia.

London halted, unsure how to proceed. Wrongly, she'd assumed that she would find Borgia in his room. Somehow she felt betrayed. She realized she was still on a high from the ride in the car, some kind of adrenaline rush. It came to her that she had no business here, but there was no time for doubt. No room for hesitation. Lives were at stake. *We're relying on you!*

"Luca, are you all right?"

Then she heard it. The sound of a shower coming from the bathroom. She opened the door, slipping the pistol from her waistband. Clouds of steam filled the room. She advanced a step, then another. A woman stood inside the glass stall, face to the jets, washing her hair. She sensed the intrusion and turned her head. Eyes open, she saw London and the gun. She recoiled, hand covering her mouth.

"Is he here?" asked London, opening the shower door.

The woman looked at her unashamed, her gaze forthright, defiant. "Who are you?"

"Is he here, dammit?"

"At the premiere," said the woman. English. Educated. But why wasn't she more frightened?

From the bedroom, the manager called out: "Madame, is everything all right?"

"Yes," said London, still staring at the woman, feeling as if she should know her. "I'm fine."

London called Simon from the hotel lobby. "He fooled us. He's at the premiere."

CHAPTER 71

Cannes

The van stopped.

The door slid open violently. A woman motioned for everyone to get out. "Come," she said, her English heavily accented. "They are waiting. Please. Quickly." Then: "But where are the others? There are more, no?"

Mattias left the van and, with his friends, was escorted along a narrow walkway and onto a broad red carpet at the base of even broader stairs leading to the Palais des Festivals. A legion of photographers faced them, shouting incomprehensible instructions. Omar put an arm around his shoulder, so Mattias put an arm on his, and on Hassan to the other side. Mohammed followed suit. The four stood like this for what seemed an eternity, smiling as flashbulbs popped and photographers yelled for them to turn this way and that. One of the escorts kept looking back toward the van, as if expecting someone else to join them.

Mattias felt exposed, vulnerable, certain that at any moment someone would remark on the bulk beneath their jackets. But no. There was only applause and the intermittent flash of the cameras.

And then it was over, as quickly as it had begun. Another woman accompanied them up the stairs and into the auditorium, showing them to their seats situated in the center of the cavernous space.

Mattias sat on the aisle—he would lead the attack—keeping his gaze lowered as the auditorium filled up. He was no longer able to smile, no matter how he tried. He apologized silently to Sheikh Abdul. He felt as if all eyes were on him, as if he were the subject of a thousand policemen's scrutiny. *They know,* a voice whispered repeatedly inside his head. He shifted in his small, tight seat, his discomfort growing. More and more people filed into the auditorium, seemingly in little hurry to take their places. He could only sit and wait, each second a minute, each minute an hour.

All the while he felt as if the vest was closing around him, tighter and tighter, squeezing the air out of him. He wanted it to be over. If only they'd given him the detonator. His thumb twitched, seeking out something to press, a button to push. He looked to his left. Omar's eyes were half closed. A low keening noise came from his lips. He did not look well. Mattias nudged him with an elbow, but it had no effect. Young Mohammed was rocking gently back and forth. Surely someone must notice. How could they not?

Mattias tapped his feet, his hands drumming the armrests. A furtive look to all quarters. No one was paying them notice, most too busy chatting among themselves. It wasn't possible.

He could get up now. He could run out of the theater. They would have to detonate the vests then, whoever "they" were. His breath came faster. Anything was better than the waiting.

Suddenly, applause.

A man mounted the proscenium. His name was Renaud or something like that. He began to speak in French, then switched to English. Five minutes passed as he introduced the movie, apologizing that the director and producer had been taken ill. Mattias only half heard what he was saying. His heart was beating furiously, blood pounding between his ears, deafening him. He felt hot, unbearably hot.

A hand landed on his shoulder. Mattias jumped. A red-faced man seated behind him said, "Congratulations. I am happy for you. A triumph!"

Mattias tried to respond. He wanted to say "Thank you" or "*Merci,*" or "*Tak*" like he did in Sweden. His mouth would not work. He was mute. After a moment, he turned to stare at the screen.

And then, miraculously, the lights dimmed. Music.

The film began.

Ten minutes, thought Mattias.

Ten minutes and he would be free.

Simon and Danni crossed the esplanade adjacent to the Palais and headed to the red carpet.

The Palais des Festivals was a modern travertine-and-concrete building with sweeping panes of glass soaring from ground to roof—all right angles and dramatic planes. A broad set of stairs, red carpet running up its center, led to the entrance of the Grand Auditorium. A banner decorating the Palais's façade read FESTIVAL DE CANNES, with the year's specially designed logo—a dove in Picasso's hand standing atop an old-fashioned film projector.

The staging area where celebrities stood for their photographs was deserted, somehow forlorn, a ballroom after the ball. Press, photographers, technicians were packing their wares, dismantling lights, stowing gear. It was ten minutes past six. The film ought to have begun.

Simon and Danni climbed the stairs. Plainclothes security guards stood by the doors to the Grand Auditorium. Simon walked to the center door. "We need to go inside."

The guard looked him over, then at Danni. "Is there something the matter?"

"Open the door."

The guard registered the tone of Simon's voice. This was real. It was happening now. A man he should believe. "How can I help?"

"No commotion," said Danni. "Everything very easy. No warning."

The guard nodded. He was fifty, trim, with steel-colored hair cut close to the scalp. Ex-military, Simon guessed.

"Where are the actors sitting?" asked Simon.

"Row twenty. The first four seats on the aisle. Easier for them to reach the stage afterward."

"Get another man," said Danni. Then: "Can you shoot?"

"Yes. I can."

"They're wearing vests," she said. "Remote detonation."

The color drained from the guard's face. He spoke into a hand mike. A few moments later, another man arrived, similarly dressed in a blue blazer, gray slacks, necktie. "This is Michel. I am Jean-Marc."

Danni addressed the men. "We find them. We kill them. We get everyone out."

The men nodded, recognizing Danni's authority without question. Her Israeli accent told them everything they needed to know.

Danni took the safety off the submachine gun and turned the fire command to semiautomatic. Simon followed suit, placing one hand under the stock, the other on the grip, a finger inside the pistol guard.

"Can you shoot?" Danni asked.

Simon nodded. "I can."

On a screen bigger than any he'd ever seen, Mattias stared up at the *Medusa* docked in the harbor at Sirte. Hundreds of men and women crowded the deck. One by one they boarded. He remembered the crush of humanity, the heat, the sweat, the hand in his back shoving him forward against his will.

The camera zoomed in on a familiar face, Mohammed Tabbi. He was from Algiers, Mattias remembered. He had been the joker of the group, the only one who had retained any semblance of good nature and humanity until the end. It was he who had killed the Ghanaian who had taken the boy's eye. He had strangled him.

Mattias felt for his badge. It was Mohammed Tabbi's credentials he was wearing. Somewhere, at this instant, the man lay dead. Mattias felt sick. To his left, Omar, the driver, was weeping silently. Young Mohammed watched the film through hands covering his eyes. Sheikh Abdul had not considered their reactions when he recruited them. He and his masters had not asked themselves how the survivors might feel upon reliving such a vivid, nigh perfect, depiction of the ordeal.

The *Medusa* was leaving port. Her deck was filled far beyond capacity. All those black faces on the white boat. Anyone could see it was not seaworthy. How could they have let it set sail? It was a miracle the boat had made it as far as it did.

Mattias could sense the audience's discomfort. Just watching made them complicit. Several persons nearby turned their heads to glance at him, at the others who had been on that boat. A murmur of disbelief swept the dark auditorium.

Where were you then? Where was your outrage? Your simmering sanctity?

"No!"

He was not aware of shouting, that it was his own voice lifting above the voices of the actors, of the boat's motor, of the haunting music hinting at the disaster to come.

A hand grasped his arm.

He shook it loose.

If the boat had turned back then, it would have been all right. No one would have died. He wanted to yell at the skipper, at the mates, to stop. The emotions churning inside him were unexpected and overwhelming and beyond his control. He shifted in his seat. He was acutely aware of the vest. It was too tight, stealing his breath, crushing him to death.

Was it time yet?

He checked his watch. Seven minutes. He couldn't last another three. He stood, his friends clawing at him. Angry voices told him to sit down; then other voices speaking Arabic: "It is not time."

"Let me go."

On the screen, a man vomited belowdecks. A woman held her baby to her breast. Doomed, both of them. It was all coming back to him. The heat. The smell. The certainty of impending disaster. Mattias could not bear to watch a moment longer.

He stepped into the aisle. Which way to go? Heads turned toward him. Concerned voices. Always just voices. Words. Never actions.

There was no going back. He knew that now. Let God take him here.

"Allahu Akbar!"

*   *   *

From his seat in the front row of the balcony, Luca Borgia was among the first to take note of the disturbance. He sensed the man's distress before hearing him cry out, before seeing him rise from his seat and lurch into the aisle. Borgia's initial response was one of frustration, anger. The man was moving too early, disobeying his instructions. It was enough to make Borgia perch on the edge of his seat, eyes entirely focused now on the four bombers directly below him.

Still, for a moment, Borgia did not stand, did not try to get out of the building. He'd had no choice but to come. His presence was proof of his innocence as much as his guilt. Who could ever point a finger and accuse him of being involved? He was there. He was a victim, if not of bodily wounds, then of trauma. There was more, of course. He wanted to be there. He needed to hear the explosion, to feel the concussion, to witness the carnage. It was essential the public's outrage be his own. How else could he gain the visceral justification for his actions? The refugees— the invaders, as he thought of them, the cockroaches—really were that bad! If not tonight here in Cannes, then another time, another place…perhaps even worse.

Then the words. "Allahu Akbar!"

Borgia watched as the four men left their seats, two dashing to the front of the theater, hardly more than shadows in the darkened auditorium. One jumped onto the proscenium, his silhouette visible as it cut across the screen, his intent clear.

By now, Borgia was moving, too, up the balcony aisle and through the doors to the upper mezzanine. The shooting began as he reached the stairs. First one shot, then a dozen all at once. He did not slow, his hand delving into his pocket as he descended the stairs. Fingers found the phone, taking it into his palm. Reaching the lobby, he made himself stop and slipped the phone from his pants.

Outside again. Safety.

He flipped the phone open. The sun's glare prevented him from reading the number on the screen. He turned to block its rays, brought the phone to his eyes. Yes, it was ready. He lifted his thumb.

*   *   *

As he entered the auditorium, Simon heard the man cry out.

He saw him at once, standing in the aisle fifty feet away, shouting. Two more men ran past the man toward the front of the theater. Another had reached the stage. The bombers.

The images on the screen froze, then went dark. The overhead lights came up. Distressed voices ruffled the crowd. People turned in their seats. *Something was wrong.*

"*Restez assis,*" shouted Simon. Stay seated.

The first gunshot came from behind Simon, then it seemed everyone was shooting at once. A furious firefight, even if all the bullets were aimed at the four North Africans. Screams. Pandemonium. Danni was running past him down the aisle, kneeling, shooting one of the bombers in the head, then rising, turning, shooting the man still in his seat a second time, a third. Jean-Marc and Michel, the security guards, had reached the front of the auditorium. Simon lost sight of them as the audience rose and frantically sought to escape. More shots. Before Simon could bring his weapon to bear, the attackers were down. All of them.

He looked toward the lobby, seeing a man running out the front doors. The first to leave. Fifty years old. Tall. Black hair. Roman nose. It was him.

Luca Borgia.

"*Borgia!*"

The man slowed, but only for a second, before continuing. He held something in his hand.

But Simon was already outside, running down the stairs in close pursuit. "Borgia," he shouted again.

This time the man turned. Simon recognized him from the dozens of photographs he'd looked at online. Borgia reached the bottom and began to run across the red carpet, haltingly at first, then faster. Simon caught him in ten strides and tackled him to the ground. Borgia landed on his back, wriggled free. He held a phone in his open palm.

His thumb came down on the SEND key as Danni's boot crushed his wrist.

Borgia screamed.

The phone dropped from his hand.

Behind them, men and women streamed out of the theater. A column of soldiers charged up the stairs. Sirens came from every direction. Mayhem.

Simon picked up the phone. A ten-digit number blinked on the display. He looked toward the auditorium—waiting for the terrible cataclysm—then back at the phone.

The call had failed.

Simon closed the flip phone and placed it in his pocket.

"Is it you? Riske?" Borgia climbed to his feet, clutching his shattered wrist. "I'm going to the police. I'll tell them what you've done."

Simon pressed the machine gun to Borgia's stomach. "You," he said, thinking of Rafa, then of the others.

"We're done," said Danni.

Simon shot her a glance, not understanding. "We can't leave him here."

"We're done," she said again. "Let's go."

"Yes, go," said Borgia, threateningly. "Leave. But I will find you, Riske. Count on it. We know all about you."

Simon lowered the weapon. Danni was right. They were done. The bombers were dead. They had stopped the attack. No innocents would die tonight. What else were they to do? The cellphone by itself constituted no proof. On what grounds could they have Borgia arrested? If the Italian could have Kruger freed from a jail in Singapore, he would have himself released within the hour by a French magistrate.

"We're done," said Simon.

"Believe me," said Danni, taking his arm. "He isn't going anywhere. Are you, Signor Borgia?"

"Who are you?" demanded Borgia.

Danni put her face close to his. "I am the angel of death."

There was a flash of blue, a glint of silver. Borgia grunted as the knife entered his chest. Danni wrapped an arm around him, ramming the blade home, twisting it. Borgia's eyes widened, and she noticed that one was blue, the other brown. His mouth fell open. A skein of blood poured forth.

Danni left the blade inside him.

They were ten steps away when he fell to his knees, dead.

Epilogue

Simon set the neatly wrapped package on the table. "Hello, Delphine," he said. "Brought you a present."

It was one o'clock. The restaurant Bibendum on Fulham Road in Chelsea was nearly full. It was one of Simon's favorite spots. He liked the food and the décor, which changed according to the season. Today, the fifth of July, the colors were yellows and oranges—something to do with growth and abundance. Mostly, though, he liked the memories the restaurant evoked. He had a history with the place.

Delphine Blackmon offered her cheek. Simon bent to kiss her, then took his place across the table.

"We missed you at the service," she said. "I didn't know he'd come from such a small town. So remote."

"I'm sorry," said Simon. "I couldn't get there." It was all he wanted to say.

He'd had his own service for Rafa. One Friday evening not long after he returned, he made his way to the Blackfriar. He bought two pints and set them on the bar where they used to sit. Guinness for himself. Stella for Rafa. He hadn't known what to say, so he'd thanked him silently for the good times they'd had. It was enough. Upon leaving, he gave the untouched beer to a young man in an almost decent suit. A banker, probably a trainee. Rafa would have liked that.

"What's this, then?" With care, Delphine unwrapped the plain brown paper. Inside was an old hardcover copy of Alexandre Dumas's *The Three Musketeers*.

"Or should I call you 'Milady'?"

Delphine put down the book. "She was always my favorite character."

"She was a spy for Cardinal Richelieu. She tried to betray the king. I believe that made her the villain."

"That's one way of looking at things. She also knew how to look after herself. She didn't rely on husbands, lovers, or *friends*. For a woman in the seventeenth century, that was something." Delphine set down the book. She looked at Simon forthrightly and without apology. "How long have you known?"

"Long enough."

"The first time I saw the painting I was with you."

"I remember the day."

Delphine's eyes shifted to the distance. "I didn't like it. It scared me. Still does." She looked back at him. "I guess it stayed with me."

"Guess so."

Simon ordered a DeLap—grape juice, soda water, a large chunk of lime—a thing he'd picked up from a former flame.

"You're looking prosperous," she said. "Business good?"

"Very. Smart money is figuring out that the right sports car is a better investment than the stock market or real estate."

"Doesn't that spoil the fun?"

"Fun is for purists. I'm more of a mercenary these days. My bank account comes first. People want to pay me a half-million pounds to restore a car, I don't care what they do with it afterward. Drive it in the Gumball Rally or keep it under lock and key in a bonded warehouse. Their choice."

"My, that doesn't sound like you at all."

"It's been a tough couple of months."

"You're not the only one."

"Spare me the crocodile tears."

"And I thought you'd invited me here to cheer me up after all I'd been through." She sipped her mineral water, eyes locked on his. "Now that I'm a single woman."

Simon laughed dryly. "Isn't six weeks a little short as far as periods of mourning go?"

Delphine put down her glass and sat tall, appraising him. "You know, I think I rather prefer you this way."

"What way is that?"

"Stripped of all illusion. You were such a wide-eyed dreamer."

"Maybe I just prefer to see the better side of people."

"In Bangkok you asked if I still wanted to save the world. I hate the world. I only want to save myself. It's you who can't resist helping the damsel in distress."

"Is that why you made sure your father asked me to help Rafa?"

"That was Rafa's doing. He always looked up to you so. Simon this, Simon that. Simon for sainthood. Still, even you couldn't save him."

Simon adjusted his napkin as the server brought his drink. He squeezed the lime and took a sip. Had Bangkok been only six weeks ago? So much had happened since.

Luca Borgia's death remained unsolved, his involvement with the attempted attack shrouded in mystery. Hints, rumors, nothing more. Sometimes silence told one more than a thousand words. The right people knew. That was all that mattered.

Despite an abundance of CCTV cameras in and around the Palais des Festivals, none had captured an image of the culprit who had stabbed him to death. Secretly, Simon thought that such images existed but certain powers had made sure they remained hidden from public scrutiny. Then again, what did he know? What had Samson Sun called him? *"A glorified mechanic"*? Simon liked the title. He was thinking it would look nice on his business card.

London Li had published her exposé about Harrington-Weiss, PetroSaud, and the sovereign wealth funds that had defrauded investors of billions. The story had made her a worldwide celebrity. A day didn't go by when she couldn't be found on at least one cable channel somewhere around the world. Simon hadn't been to Singapore in the interim. And London hadn't come to London. Ah well…they'd always have forty thousand feet.

He looked across the table at Delphine. She'd never looked better: sharply turned out, sophisticated, radiantly intelligent. It was easy to see why he'd fallen in love with her, his first true love. It was only now, years later, that he was able to see the other side of her. The cynicism, the distrust of human nature, the congenital pessimism. Maybe he'd loved her because she possessed so many qualities alien to him. She was his dark side, albeit with a nice ass and a great pair of legs.

"Did you know?" he asked.

"What?"

"That your lover was a terrorist."

A gasp. A look of horror. "You can't think that I knew Luca was going to use my screenplay as a means to mount some kind of large-scale attack. That I'd say nothing if I had."

Simon looked away. The restaurant was bustling, and he enjoyed the efficient orchestration of food and service and ambience united in pursuit of a common goal. Not unlike a perfectly tuned motor.

"When did you meet him?" he asked.

"Years ago. I was on one of my fundraising jaunts for Chatham House. Working at a think tank is more about raising money than anything else. He had a humanitarian foundation in Rome. I pitched him the story of the *Medusa* as a documentary film Chatham House could make. We'd put his name on it as executive producer. Buff up his image. He turned me down on the spot."

"You thought he'd turned you down. In fact, he'd passed you along to Samson Sun via Sun's aunt, Nadya Sukarno. He owed Sun a favor. It was Samson Sun who'd come up with the idea of how to use PetroSaud to steal billions."

"How could he know that I'd write the screenplay?"

"You probably talked him into it after you had sex."

"I ought to slap you."

Simon wanted to ask her if she knew about Prato Bornum, but he knew she'd say no and he wasn't in the mood to listen to any more lies.

Delphine went on: "The film will do more good than all the articles I've ever written put together."

"If you still believe those things, how could you be with a man like him?"

"You think I'm some kind of Eva Braun."

"Not 'some kind.'"

"You really are being a prick today."

Simon smiled. Maybe he was. If so, he was enjoying it. "Did Rafa know?"

Delphine's eyes flared. Her cheeks colored, and for a moment Simon thought she really was going to slap him. As quickly, she calmed. After all, it was just Simon, and she'd known him forever.

"He suspected. He's not dumb."

"So you rubbed his face in it. What was he supposed to do, especially after your father put some of his money into the hotel?"

"That's why I could never have been with you. It always has to be about the truth. The whole goddamned truth."

Simon leaned closer. She was right. All he wanted was the truth. "Tell me one thing. Why didn't you go to the premiere? You were there at the hotel. It was you London Li saw in the shower. So why? It was your movie, after all."

Delphine didn't answer. For once, she was at a loss for words. He could see it made her angry.

She eyed him smugly, sliding to the edge of her chair. "You want the truth. It wasn't Daddy's idea to make you leave me. It was mine. I knew I could never be with someone like you. Someone who saw the world in black and white, when I saw it in a continuum of grays. Someone so…so *uncomplicated*. I told Daddy that you'd treated me badly, then let slip that you'd been in prison in France. A bank robber, no less. I pleaded with him not to say anything. I told him that I still loved you. But I knew him. Just like I know you. I knew that he'd do everything in his power to protect his only daughter."

Delphine folded her napkin, set it neatly on the table, then rose. Her step as she left the restaurant was not the least bit hurried. As always, she refused to live life on anyone's terms but her own.

The black Rover idling at the curb across the street from Bibendum pulled a sharp U-turn as Delphine left the restaurant. The car's driver was a woman, fortyish, fit, with raven hair and glacial-blue eyes, though both were concealed by a wide-brimmed hat and sunglasses. The car was not hers. It had been stolen the day before from a car park in Immingham, several hours' drive from London. As a precaution, she'd been sure to change the plates. She was nothing if not professional.

The woman followed Delphine for a city block before opening the glove compartment and removing a small pistol with a large noise suppressor attached to its snout. A nine-millimeter hollow-point bullet lay snugly in the chamber. She had been working on her shooting these past weeks and felt confident that one would be enough, especially at close range. The light turned red. The pedestrians stopped at the curb. The woman pulled up alongside Delphine.

"Excuse me," she called out. "Can you help me with directions?"

Delphine barely glanced in her direction. "I'm sorry, I'm busy."

"Please. I'd be grateful."

Maybe it was the foreign accent. Maybe it was her sad, pleading tone. Delphine Blackmon sighed as she approached the car. "Just this once," she said, lowering her head toward the open window. "What is it, then?"

As the Rover sped away, the driver smiled to herself. She was right. One shot was enough.

"Knock, knock."

Simon opened the door and poked his head inside the hospital room. "Lucy?"

The bed was empty, sheets thrown back. He had called ahead, as was his custom. The nurse at reception had said she was expecting him.

"Lucy?"

Four weeks had passed since the doctors had removed her from a medically induced coma, judging that her cerebral swelling had decreased sufficiently. Another week passed before she began speaking. Since then, she'd made remarkable progress.

Her motor functions had returned more slowly. Five days earlier she had begun feeding herself. Walking, however, still posed a challenge. Her casted leg didn't help matters.

A toilet flushed. The door to her private bathroom opened. Out walked Lucy, balancing on a pair of crutches.

"Look at this!" Simon rushed forward.

"I'm fine, thank you very much," said Lucy, in a proud and nearly polished voice. The accident had somehow robbed her of her Cockney slur. But her eyes remained fixed on the floor, her face a mask of concentration. He stood to one side of the room, ready to help if needed.

"Take them," she said.

Simon accepted the crutches, setting them in the corner.

"Let me help you get into bed."

"No, let me!"

Simon turned to see Lucy's mother, Dora, hurry from the bathroom. She was dressed in a knee-length skirt and short-sleeved blouse, her hair done nicely. Simon was quick to notice the absence of a pall of smoke.

"Hello, Mrs. Brown."

"Dora, please. And hello to you, Simon."

Dora Brown lifted her daughter onto the bed. "Would you look at her?" she said, beaming. "Almost as good as new."

"I'm going to be better than new," said Lucy, lifting her eyes to Simon.

"Yes, you are. I don't know what to say. This is a good day."

Dora Brown pulled a chair close to the bed for Simon and took a seat on the sofa beneath the window. "Lucy and I have been talking. We've decided we're going to take a trip to Paris when she's recovered. Just the two of us."

"Is that right?"

Lucy nodded. Her hair had begun to grow out. If anything, it was blonder than before. "Mum's never been. It will be the first time for both of us."

Dora Brown sat, hands clasped in her lap, smiling beatifically.

"This may help." He took an envelope from his jacket and gave it to Lucy. She needed a moment or two but managed to open it and take out the check that was inside.

"Ten thousand quid. Cor!" The Cockney hadn't totally vanished.

"Your fee from the job. D'Art called yesterday afternoon. The experts finally confirmed that the Monet was authentic."

"But you're already paying so much. I can't. It wouldn't be right." Lucy handed back the check.

"Yes, it would," said Dora Brown, plucking the check from her daughter's fingers.

Simon laughed and gave Dora a hug. He hadn't been this happy in a long time.

They talked for an hour, mostly about the shop and Harry Mason and the new paint room that was being installed the next week.

"Will we still have to scrape the old paint off?" Lucy asked.

"'Fraid so. Some things you have to do by hand."

Finally, he decided it was time to leave. He kissed Dora Brown on the cheek. She said she was returning to look after Lucy on the weekend. He turned to Lucy. "See you tomorrow, kiddo."

"Don't call me that."

"You'd prefer?"

"'Darling.'"

Simon kissed her forehead. "Goodbye, Miss Brown."

Outside, the last clouds had moved off to the east. The sun shone down on the green fields of Surrey. On a day like this anything was possible. He walked to his car, taking a moment to check that his wiper blades were on properly.

His phone rang. He looked at the screen.

"What is it, D'Art?"

"Simon, you must come to my offices immediately. You'll never guess who is here."

"That important?"

"An emergency."

"On a scale of one to ten."

"Eleven."

Simon knew it. "On my way."

It is my pleasure to offer my sincerest thanks to the following:

Peter Caprez, general manager of the JW Marriott Hotel Bangkok, as well as his incomparable staff, who served as my gracious hosts for my extended stay in Thailand.

Liz Myers and John Trivers, who allowed me the use of their lovely ski lodge, where I shut myself up to finish this book in record time.

Dr. Jon Shafqat, who read this manuscript, as he has many others, and offered valuable insights and commentary.

Charles Winkler, a longtime guest of the Hôtel du Cap d'Antibes, who unlocked a few of the hotel's secrets for a nosy author.

Richard Pine, my literary agent and dear friend, as well as the entire team at InkWell Management, including Michael Carlisle, Kim Witherspoon, Eliza Rothstein, and Claire Friedman. Words can't express my gratitude for all you do on my behalf: creatively, professionally, and personally.

Howard Sanders at Anonymous Content.

Amy Powell, Jon Liebman, and Marc Evans at Brillstein Entertainment.

Laura Kohani, for being at my side during good times and bad, and always brightening my day.

And finally, to my daughters, Noelle and Katja, to whom this book is dedicated, and who have both in recent years become my biggest supporters. I grow prouder of you every day.

About the Author

Christopher Reich is the *New York Times* bestselling author of *The Take, Numbered Account, Rules of Deception, Rules of Vengeance, Rules of Betrayal,* and many other thrillers. His novel *The Patriots Club* won the International Thriller Writers Award for Best Novel in 2006. He lives in Encinitas, California.

MULHOLLAND BOOKS

You won't be able to put down these Mulholland books.

KILLING EVE: DIE FOR ME *by Luke Jennings*

LONE JACK TRAIL *by Owen Laukkanen*

THE LESS DEAD *by Denise Mina*

WONDERLAND *by Zoje Stage*

MORE BETTER DEALS *by Joe R. Lansdale*

AFTERLAND *by Lauren Beukes*

THE PALACE *by Christopher Reich*

Visit mulhollandbooks.com for
your daily suspense fix.